I0599901

The Queen

THE ELITUS SAGA

by
S.H. Reynolds

Published by

Onyx & Amethyst LLC
ESTD 2025

To my Mini-Me & Forever Bestie, Rhiannon;
Your Kingdom is what you make of it.
Don't let anyone tell you, you can't do something.
Take risks, but also be smart. Be unapologetically you.
And at the end of the day, know you are loved, you have support,
and we are proud of who you are, and who you will be.

ONE

Bastian

Mental God. X Factor. Whatever nickname, I tune it out. People love labels—it makes them think they've got you figured out.

Elitus loves labels most of all. "Peacekeepers." "Wights." Sounds cleaner than contract operatives. But that's what we are.

Elitus, the group that handles us, is also the same group that created us. Us being myself, my friends, my siblings. We are genetically engineered, the product of Agent X serum. Agent X was meant for soldiers, but in vitro use created Wights — rare, not different, just superhuman.

I lean back in the chair, my desk a mess of papers and protein bar wrappers. I toss aside the docket I'm perusing. It's the dissection of an experiment from twenty-five-plus years ago. Something that didn't work out the way Elitus wanted with the Gamma group. But it was a crucial piece of evidence that helped Dr. Clarke determine how to make X work. It's the linchpin that led them down the path to in vitro success.

It was only a couple of short years after that piece of info that the first Generation was born. Gen One, who graduated a year ago from Elitus Academy, made up the first round. Since then, they've gotten better at creating Wights. Just not better at controlling what powers they were born with.

You see, like any successful scientist, Elitus uses labels to define the results of their experiments. They break us into Tiers and power Levels. All to add to their study and continued focus on making the perfect soldier. Us.

I pour myself another drink and pace the room. It's been far too quiet of late, dorms aren't as hopping as before. Probably because of a certain Spectrum who has toted the Elitus line and been the perfect soldier. I miss Mason; I miss the way she made everything more interesting. Not only her sarcastic nature that meshes so well with mine, but the way she can walk into a room and know who needs her attention, who is having issues, or who needs an ass-kicking.

Looking out the window of my first-floor room, I have a clear shot of the back area. Outside, the campus balcony is quiet tonight; the moonlight highlights the lack of activity on the grounds. It makes it seem even more depressing. The sprawling landscape is nothing but open land behind the dorms, waiting for more housing to be added. If Elitus ever lets us get on with our lives, that is.

The bourbon burns sharp, it doesn't kill the headache, but it softens the edges. I'm not an alcoholic, but the liquor makes the noise in my skull more of a hum than a scream.

You see, I'm a Tier Two, a mental. Tier Twos are supposed to be defensive; that's the official line, anyway. Healers, empaths, the ones who keep things in control from the inside; the mental powerhouses.

And me? I'm an X-Two, well, not officially yet—but regardless, I'm not just this glorified peacekeeper with a talent for de-escalation. I have off-the-charts X powers. It means I exceed every pre-determined limit they had.

I can crush a person's mind before someone blinks. Shred memory. Induce hallucinations. Cut the spinal cord. Paralyze someone. Trigger aneurysms. Stop a heart; like flipping a switch. All without even having to touch someone. Silent but deadly from a distance.

I don't use half of what I'm capable of. It doesn't mean I haven't thought about it. Repeatedly.

Am I a psychopath? No.

Could I be? Without a doubt.

I am well beyond ready to graduate. Mason has been so damn busy training everyone else, and being McGuire's weapon, that we don't even party anymore.

So, I've taken up drinking in my room, hacking Elitus files, and stealing classified PPG data—not that it is even a challenge, honestly. Amateur hour. I grab the tablet, scrolling through the latest data I dug up.

Most of its garbage. Tactical deployments. Mission rotations. A few blacked-out documents where Wight identifiers were redacted. Nothing I didn't already suspect. But it still pisses me off.

I have been digging into Latents. They were original X experiments. They were the first group to receive the serum, or the original version of it. Called Latent because power never emerged, or so it was believed.

Now, Elitus is focused on their children. The sad part is, their parents never stood a chance.

I've spent the last week combing through the original trial data. Alpha, Beta, Delta, Gamma, and Epsilon, I swipe through the results. Of the thirty-plus candidates in each group, most ended up as psych cases. Addicts. Suicidal wrecks. Some snapped at their handlers; others turned the violence inward. Not because X failed, but because Elitus did.

It wasn't the serum that caused it. I'd bet anything they themselves had latent abilities, signatures buried too deep to control and too strong to ignore. X amplified that, and with no bonds, and no controls, it consumed them from the inside out. No focus. No channel. No shields. Just destruction.

And now, Elitus wants to manufacture adult super-soldiers again. It looks like they've found some progress, so that's what they are focusing on. Trying to create something to enhance Latent abilities. Fucking Fantastic.

We're supposed to be Elitus' crown jewel—next-gen, engineered, elite. And they still treat us like kids who should sit quietly and behave. Even the Gen Ones—Wyatt, Kyle, Alex, Kate—should have the clout to push back by now. But they haven't, not really.

For me, I rot if I don't move. Routine chokes me. The longer I sit still, the louder everything gets.

I toss my tablet onto the desk. Do we need more backup on missions? Sure. Is another Gen that will take years to get ready the answer? Probably not.

But that doesn't mean that the Latent project is the answer either. But if what I am reading is true, then this could be a new avenue. Especially given that there are several candidates who already have military backgrounds. Already a step ahead of the game.

I should be focused on how to help them. How to improve it. When they did this previously, they didn't have Tier Twos — individuals who can scan, heal and read into someone's mental state. Now, if they incorporated us, then the results might be different. But Elitus will never give up control, nor allow us any say. They would have to admit that maybe we can be more than weapons.

The sad part is, even if I wanted to solve it. No one would listen to me. I wouldn't even have time to present anything.

So, I'll do what I do best; put something together and then influence someone to bring it to the table. Or possibly pass it to Dr. Miller. He'll give it to Clarke and Ross without wrapping it in bullshit. If I handed it over, I'd end up lecturing them. Like an arrogant prick. Which, yeah, I probably am. Doesn't mean I'm incorrect.

I take a moment to eat something, and my eyes drift upward toward the top floor.

That's where the Gen One singles are—Kyle, Wyatt, Alex and Her Royal Pain-in-My-Ass, Kate Ames.

Kate doesn't do "normal." Elegant, chin high, she struts around in four-inch heels like she owns the place. And somehow, that attitude worked out for her. Makes her stand out; she's the Queen of this kingdom.

Kate's already done with the Academy. She is a year older than me, a High One—elemental specialty. She never scraped X level, but she still demands combat status like she's the second coming of Mason.

And of course, Elitus gives it to her. They keep her on smaller ops; safer ones with limited exposure. Still, she acts as if she is frontline material.

Kate is good, don't get me wrong, but her in combat, high risk. That should be a no-go, but you try telling her that. She'd ice you with a look and keep walking.

She's precision and posture, fire and frost, pretending she's as lethal as the rest of us. And maybe she is, in her own way. Controlled. Calculated. Even when she's wrong, she looks like she's right.

She was working earlier in the common area with her buddy and our resident genius, Wyatt. Those two are attached at the hip 99% of the time. And unlike my interaction with Kate, Wyatt gets her laughter and attention without fighting for it.

Every time Kate steps into the room, the air shifts between us. My bonds pull. My focus shatters; shields bend slightly. It's not the way she looks; she's gorgeous; it's the way she owns the space, and me with it, that drives me insane.

She draws me to her, without even trying. The pull between us, the connection. It shouldn't be there. I already suspect what is causing it, but I will be damned if I let any type of fate or predetermined cosmic connection dictate my future. So I avoid it, push it down and instead, focus on what I can control. Namely, our interactions. Verbal sparring is our favorite pastime.

Kate's the only one who can match me word for word. I swear she lives for the arguments as much as I do. It's a game neither of us admits we're playing. Despite that, I look for her in every damn room.

It's only gotten worse since Mason has turned into the super-weapon McGuire always wanted her to be. Mason's focus and interactions used to keep me entertained, distracted from Queenie. Now, I find my eyes drifting to her whenever she is in the room. My attention is splintered between whatever lesson and Kate.

It's not Mason's fault, I need to deal with this myself, but for Mason, something shifted, changed to make her go from my badass partner and fellow X-Two to this by-the-book workaholic who specializes in following the Elitus line.

But there is no stopping her. Granted, she is more normal with me than the other Xs, but still. It's not the same; I miss my friend, my partner. I miss some level of entertainment.

Trying to avoid those thoughts, I know I need to find something to do. Heading through the common area, I note it's quiet yet again. No Queen or any of the regular crew. Frustrated, I feel out mentally to anyone in the dorm. My shields brushing against others, trying to feel out who's around, someone that can make me stop thinking for a bit. None of my regular crew — Kyle, Max, or even the girls — are here.

Aggravated, I decide to text my regular combat partner, and best friend, Kyle Ross. Kyle is an X-Three, a Gen One, like Kate. If Kate's the Queen, then Kyle is the King. He is the powerhouse, and the strongest mission operative we have. Well, besides Mason, that is.

I take a seat on a stool in the common area, phone in hand, fingers typing before I can second guess myself.

> *Where are you?*

> *Home. Why?*

> *Bored as hell. Need to get off base. Or do something. Any ideas?*

> *Should've gone home like your mom wanted.*

> *Re and the THREE would make me want to shoot myself. Besides, she would've roped you into staying after dinner as well. And that means you wouldn't have been able to go kiss McGuire's ass. So what do you say, you in or not?*

> *Whatever Bastard. I am almost done; let me finish up here. Anyone else coming?*

> *You, me, whoever wants to. Max maybe?*

Yeah, he texted earlier. We'll meet you out front in fifteen.

Good. Bring cash. I'm not paying for your shit again.

You still owe me from me for saving your ass last time, asshole.

He still won't pay. Kyle's a walking tab of IOUs.

Off base is a privilege. They make us fight for it, especially the girls. That's why Mason and Charley used to always be ready to burn the place down, because someone who never saw the battlefield wrote the rules; and still thinks this is the 1950s, where women must be safe, protected at home.

For us combat guys, off base means a few hours to drink, hit the clubs, just breathe.

If Elitus let us live real lives on campus, maybe we wouldn't need to get wasted to feel sane. I drain the last of my drink and grab my jacket.

Tonight, someone else can deal with the noise in my head. Just for a little while.

Kate

"Are you sure you want to do this?" Ryker asks for what feels like the hundredth time. I check my weapons, ensure everything is in order. I try to ignore him, but Ryker's tone is laced with that frustrating older-brother energy, even though he's two and a half years younger than me. Little Big Brother—towering, annoyingly insightful, and perpetually worried I'm going to get myself killed.

I shoot him a look that should be enough. "Yes, it's fine."

He opens his mouth again, but Charley walks in and saves us both. The redheaded combat enabled One is a siren, and could set the world on fire if she wanted to. She gives Ryker a sexy smile, which he returns to her.

She has been training a lot, even with me. Mostly because I think she is bored. Mason has been the perfect robot, and although she is taking tons of missions on, she still leaves some for us. Mason has been patient and working with everyone more. Being the trainer and the weapon.

And with Mason focused, that means the dorms have been quiet. Our dorms house over forty-plus Wights when at max capacity. For now, it's combat and High-Tier wights.

The dorms fell off without the constant hum of socializing that used to take place regularly. She and the other party girls usually provide the soundtrack to the dorm with laughter, low bass music, and the scent of liquor and poor decisions.

The halls feel more like a tomb. Dimmed energy, empty halls—everything is still. Even though I don't drink or party, her presence is a cooling balm on overheated skin. We are all wired most of the time, Mason more than the rest, but when she throws a party or is social, it makes the entire dorm feel different. The rules in place and controls aren't so overwhelming. That we are college kids, as opposed to weapons in training. Even when she's not trying to lead, people gravitate toward Mason.

We've never been close, but I respect her. I think she respects me too, in her own way. We interact little, but in holding our ground in a male-dominated system, we're on the same side. Mason doesn't back down, and neither do I. That's what makes it work. Plus, she is one of the few I can depend on when I need something done or a level head in the room.

The war room buzzes with tension, the sound of muted chatter, keyboards, and papers setting the stage for the review of the mission. On the monitor is the breakdown, including the details of the four of us on assignment. Highlighting our strengths, but also our weaknesses. It's all so clinical, as if we are weapons instead of people.

"Damn. Looks like the whole brass showed up to watch us screw up," Charley mutters next to me. I guess neither of us is used to this level of attention. I note not only is the military arm of Elitus; McGuire, Thompson, and Moore are here. But also Calvin James, our trainer, and my mother.

"Dr. Ames," I hear one tech speak with her. "Did you want to pull up any additional data?"

"No, I'm just here to observe," she comments. Yeah, right. She is as far from the military side as she can be, head of the medical division, Katherine Ames is still my mother, and she still thinks I'm going to break. Jasper, my other little big brother, is also here, it seems. At least he is working, the healing Tier Two today.

Roarke is the last to enter, with Siobhan beside him. Roarke's movements are smooth, quiet, and measured—controlled violence in tactical gear and weapons. His six-foot frame overshadows the pretty, dark-haired Siobhan. She is outfitted much as I am, with compact black combat gear, and a small weapon load. But her posture screams Tier Two: calm on the outside, but deadly on the inside.

Roarke does a quick scan of the room, nods once. He is always calm, always composed. Charley and I are joining him and Siobhan on tonight's mission.

Someone makes a joke about Roarke lucking out—leading a squad of women.

"You jealous?" he asks without even turning, his smirk the only giveaway. I roll my eyes. Typical.

The mission briefing is straightforward. Roarke and Charley will take the lead on offense. Charley's a Firestarter—no subtlety, just pure combustion. She and I have been training together for weeks, syncing our power for better range and timing. She taught me how to push my control further, how to keep up with someone like her.

Siobhan's Tier Two support—quick, mentally lethal, with a low spectrum of ability on Ones and Threes. She's one of Bastian's best Twos. She'll act as our shield if things go sideways. Roarke, as usual, carries enough weapons for three people. He's a High Three, similar to Mason and Riddick. With lethal precision and a calm exterior, he is the one who balances out any team he is on.

They call him the Peacemaker, but that's not softness; it's discipline. I've seen him end a fight in three moves, never raising his voice once. Even his silence is calculated. He breaks tension in teams with humor and reasoning. For Roarke, he fights because he must, not because he wants to.

Me? I'm here to prove I belong. I have been taking on more, showing them I can operate without being boxed in by protocol or outdated expectations; and I've done well. As a Gen One, I am the default leader, although I will defer to Roarke.

No one says it out loud, but I can feel it—like I'm just starting to matter. Even Bastian Monroe, my constant verbal sparring partner and pain in the ass Two trainer, stopped questioning my placement last week. Which must mean something.

We deploy under cover of darkness. Every step practiced.

Roarke teleports us to the designated location.

My skin prickles as Charley flares, the heat radiating through my gear, sparking adrenaline into my bloodstream. The air shifts in front of her as she torches the outer perimeter, the scent of scorched metal and lumber sharp in my nose. I stay close, feeding off her rhythm, extending her arc with my power, allowing us to get wider and further. We've drilled this exact sequence a dozen times. It should be routine.

But it's not. Coral comes into view, and my breath seizes. She's unchanged; sleek, calculating, in black gear that looks like it was custom-forged for a villainess. She tilts her head slightly, just enough to let me know.

They've been waiting.

We lock eyes across the clearing. She was born with power and privilege, no reason to hide it. She is the PPG's only X-level Wight; a master of Ones, and someone not to be messed with.

We're both Gen One, but her father defected during the Dmitri split when we were toddlers. He took her, and she grew up in a vastly different system; one that taught her she was better, that let her do whatever she wanted and allowed her to grow into her full power potential without a conscience.

The clearing between us is at a standstill, the crackling of fire, deep smell of charred ground, creating a haze between us. But it doesn't stop the reality of the situation. Stepping up next to her is Ophelia, Charley's counter power. Ophelia Bishop, although not as strong as a full water generator like Jared, can wield Ice. Which, in situations like this, allows for two High Powered Ones.

The sounds of boots and ammo loading, makes me suck in a deep breath. They have an army as well.

Charley is prepared to take them on, but she glances at me. She is always strong, confident, but even I can see the apprehension in her eyes.

This was supposed to be the moment I proved them wrong. Instead, it's going to be a failure regardless of the intel; I already know. Coral alone is a challenge. With Ophelia and a full squad? We wouldn't stand a chance. Even with Siobhan dropping a shield cover over us, it's not a good situation.

Roarke makes the call to retreat. I hate it, but I don't even protest.

But Roarke is right. He doesn't even blink before he reaches out and ports us mid-step, pulling us straight to the war room in a blast of power.

I hate this kind of failure — not screwing up, not learning the hard way—but real failure. Useless. Undone. Sent in blind and yanked out before we could even leave a mark.

McGuire said it was a soft hit. If it were a real strike, Mason, Kyle or Riddick would've been there. Not us. But that didn't stop them from throwing us under the bus.

We make it back to base in one piece, but the debrief is brutal. Roarke doesn't yell; he never does. Just paces the length of the room, jaw tight, eyes flickering from screen to screen like he's replaying every move we made and cataloging the ones we missed. He's already building a case to take to Kyle or Riddick next time. I hope he does.

I say little. I'm too pissed, too tired. My body still feels the echo of the port in my bones. The displacement of energy. The ghost-like sensation of being snapped out of existence and reassembled too fast somewhere else.

Afterward, I head back to the dorms, hoping to dodge everyone, but my brothers are already in the main common room, waiting for me.

The common room in our dorm this late at night is dim, but I can't miss them. Their energy precedes them. And it's not happy.

Ryker pushes off the wall the second I walk in. Jasper narrows his eyes, reading me like I'm a lab result. Both say nothing for a second too long. They are both Tier Twos; there is no point in bullshitting. They'd feel the lie before I said it.

"I'm fine," I say before either of them can speak.

"Really?" Jasper crosses his arms. "Because you don't look fine."

"We heard the debrief was a mess," Ryker adds.

"It wasn't our fault." I keep my voice steady. "The intel was incorrect. We were outmatched. Roarke called it."

They exchange a look. I know that look. It's the same one they've had since I first pushed for combat status. The same one my father wears every time he watches me suit up.

Disapproval masked as concern. Or maybe it's the other way around.

"You could've been killed," Jasper says.

"So could any of us," I snap.

"Exactly," Ryker mutters. They don't say it out loud, but it's always there. They want me in a lab. At a desk. Somewhere safe. Somewhere less... bloody.

But I've worked too hard, fought too long, forced my way into rooms no one ever wanted me in, just to be told to step back now.

I may not be Mason or Charley, but I've earned this.

Even if it scares the hell out of my family.

Even if I'll never be the strongest in the room.

Even if I'll always be the one they question—still proving myself every damn time.

I belong here.

Bastian

The second Kyle and I get back, I know something's off.

The dorm feels too charged, like the air's holding its breath. Energy clings to the walls, sharp and silent, and it sets me on edge. I clock Jasper and Ryker pacing as we enter the common room. The Ames twins have low voices but seem to be caught up in a full-blown argument.

Kate's not here, but I can feel her. That strange, distant hum that always lingers toward me when she's just left a room. Feels like her energy's holding on, waiting for me.

I head their way, already bracing for whatever storm this is. "What happened?"

"Charley, Siobhan, Kate and Roarke's mission was a failure," Jasper says. "Supposed to be low combat. Routine sweep."

I still, my stomach twists. "Supposed to be?" I grab a glass and pour a drink.

"Intel was shit," Ryker says, furious now. "PPG hit. Full force. Coral showed up with Ophelia and backup. Roarke had to abort."

The words hang in the air like smoke. My chest tightens, and my breath stalls. I don't even realize I've stopped moving until Jasper speaks.

"They're fine, but the debrief was a mess," Jasper says quickly, like it'll stop me from unraveling. "They are back at the dorm. No injuries." As the Tier Two assigned to the mission, he's giving his normal update. But it's got more heat than normal. Ryker and Jasper are both protective of Kate. They try to be her shield against anything or anyone who may wish her harm.

But as much as they wish to protect her, they can't. Kate was out there, unprepared, under-informed, and two seconds away from getting caught in a crossfire with a fucking X-One.

Siobhan may be one of my best combat Twos, but she is no match for that lineup. My grip tightens around the glass in my hand. I don't even notice the crack until I hear it—soft, sharp, traitorous. A slow trickle as bourbon seeps through my fingers.

"Fuck," I mutter, and set it down before I shatter it completely.

I say nothing else; I can't, or else I will lose it. So, I just walk away.

Half a bottle of bourbon later, I'm in my room. Lights off. Door locked.

The punching bag in the corner and I are old friends. I don't think; I just hit. But my mind still wanders. To the danger, the risk. I hate that we must be out there. It's dangerous, and we have no say in it. Elitus dictates everything in our lives. We have no real control other than what they give us.

My mind is on a never-ending loop.

What if Kate hadn't made it back?

If Coral had decided tonight was the night to send a message?

If Roarke hadn't been there?

My knuckles split by the third round; It doesn't stop me. I need the pain and alcohol to drown out the noise in my head. It's the only way to keep my urges under control.

Control. I know I need control. I focus, breathe, and push the power down, adding layers to my shields, thick sheets of mental blankets that keep in the urges that are begging to be let out. Until I can feel more like myself, less like a psycho.

My father used to call me a hothead. Says I take after my mom—Nikki Monroe, the original wildfire. Wild, reckless, untamable.

Now my baby sister Ariel's showing signs of the same temper. It should probably terrify him. If it doesn't yet, it will.

I stop, take a deep breath. Thankfully, I need little sleep because of my powers, but I need the noise to stop. Somehow. Deciding to switch tactics, I hit the shower.

The steam fills the room — a thick layer of smoke. The water hits like fire against my skin. I tilt my head back and let it burn. If it hurts enough, the noise might shut up.

When I finally level out enough, I do what I shouldn't.

I reach my mind toward Kate. She's asleep, but her mind is restless. She is always thinking too far ahead, too worried about everything being perfect; she wouldn't know what to do if things weren't exactly the way she wanted, needed them to be.

Kate has a relentless drive for perfection that won't let her breathe.

Elitus' Golden Girl. The Queen.

She looks the part: tall, blonde, poised like her nickname suggests. She is always in power suits and those sky-high red-bottom heels that click across the marble floors like a warning shot. The woman people stand straighter around without even realizing it.

If I didn't know Alex was completely obsessed with Andy, they'd be the perfect Elitus poster couple. The First and the Queen. Polished, powerful and controlled.

And me? I'm a mental misfit wrapped in a warning label.

But tonight?

Tonight, I want to tear the world apart at the thought of her bleeding out in a PPG ambush. My fists clench; my jaw is tight. This kind of rage isn't helpful. It's dangerous. Especially for me.

And that's not good. Because my focus shouldn't be on a Gen One, it should be on the entire group. On the threat, not of a potential revenge plot if something happened to one Wight.

So, instead, I sink into the mattress, lights still off, eyes locked on the ceiling like it might hold answers I don't want. I need to get my mind back in order. Calm down and focus on other things, so I do what I do when nothing else works.

I count. Multiplication tables. Prime numbers. Fibonacci sequences. Anything to force my brain into submission. But it's not working.

My mind drifts back to mission issues. The intel is getting worse. Teams mismatched. McGuire's either incompetent or intentionally playing us, and no one's doing shit about it. Not the Elitus, Alex, or even Kyle. Mason may be their perfect weapon, but they still keep many Wights in rotation.

And now they're throwing Kate into the cross-hairs.

She is good. But she's not like Mason or Charley. She doesn't hunt; she protects. She belongs in the field; she's earned that. Doesn't mean I have to like it.

If they get her killed chasing politics or someone else's mistake... I don't know what I'll do, but it won't be clean.

I press the heel of my hand to my eyes and count again.

Fours. Eights. Sixteens.

Control the numbers. Control my mind.

I try not to care. But I fail miserably.

Two

Bastian

Two days. That's all it takes for them to throw Kate back on the board like she didn't nearly get killed by a goddamn X-One. As if her name's just any combatant to shuffle, not a person who shouldn't be out there.

Like the failed mission wasn't a walking red flag from the second they handed it to Roarke, to co-lead with her. Without Kyle, Riddick, or Mason on it.

And now Kate's name is back on the next mission. And of course, I can't keep my damn mouth shut.

I catch her just outside the logistics wing, where she's preparing to head to the war room. She looks ready for combat, not an Elitus meeting or strategy session. Fitted combat vest, load-out tight to her frame, her blonde hair twisted up so clean, not a hair out of place. Elitus perfect.

She is taller than most, almost eye level with me when she is wearing those ice picks, but today, it's the standard issue combat boots. Out here, it's sharp lines and controlled movement. Combat Kate. The one that's just as hard to ignore.

I lean against the wall, arms crossed, watching her. She doesn't see me at first.

"You're not going on this mission."

She looks up, startled—but only for a second. Then, her posture shifts. Straightens. Sharpens.

Her eyes, a mossy green, are already blazing, locked onto mine with a force that could bring a lesser man to his knees.

She plants her hands on her hips. A power stance—defensive and daring. Here we go.

"You're joking, right?" She says, voice crisp. "Since when do you have any say in my missions?"

"Since I started giving a damn whether you come back in one piece."

"Last time I checked, you weren't in charge of me."

"I don't need to be in charge of you to know when you're making a stupid fucking decision."

I know this isn't the way to get through to her. It never works. But this is how we communicate. Words like weapons. Stares like fire. She argues with me like it's foreplay, and I give it right back because it's the only language we speak fluently. If sparring is the only way she touches me, then I'll bleed from every word. She lights me up without trying, and I fucking hate how much I want more.

I see it; her jaw tightens, and her hands twitch at her sides, like she is going to slap me or cause a hole to open in the floor and swallow me whole. Honestly, I wouldn't be surprised if she chose both.

For a heartbeat, I think she's going to snipe back at me. But not today. Today, she exhales sharply and controlled, her nostrils flaring. Tempering herself, I hate it.

"You think I can't handle myself?" She asks, low and dangerous.

"No," I say, and I mean it. She is more than capable. "I think you're stubborn as hell. And I think you're so determined to prove you belong that you'll walk straight into a situation you shouldn't."

I see it in the flicker in her gaze. Just a slight pause, a flicker of uncertainty, and then it disappears. Buried under her armor.

"I don't need to prove anything to you," she snaps.

"It's not about me." I push off the wall, closing the distance. I bring myself right up to her. Close enough to breathe her in, wildflowers and earth.

That's what she smells like. Not perfume. Not something curated. Something raw, elemental; Kate.

She tilts her chin up, challenging me with every inch she doesn't have. Four inches shorter, but she looks down on me like she's already won. God, it gets under my skin. "It's about knowing when to walk away. And this? This is a bad fucking call."

She doesn't back down, nor move back. She never does, always letting me know she is my equal. "You don't get to make that call," she says.

"And you don't get to pretend you're invincible."

"I don't need to be Mason," Kate says. "I'm me. And that's enough." And she's right on both counts.

I know it; she knows it. That's not the point.

The point is, I don't want to lose her in a blaze of glory she never should've been part of.

"I'm just saying," I murmur, voice low, heat rising between us, "maybe this isn't the best idea."

"Noted," she says, clipped. Then softer—deadly calm— "Now get out of my way."

I don't, not right away. Not until I see it again; that flash of something buried deep behind her moss-green eyes.

It's not just frustration, not just defiance. It's something else. Something just as dangerous as whatever the hell this thing is between us.

I step aside. She may win this battle, but I'm not done. Not by a long shot. Whatever this is between us, it's not over. Not until I figure out whether it'll burn us both to ash, or save us from everything else.

Kate

I walk back into the dorms. Eyes follow-Ryker's, Jasper's. Maybe even Bastian's. But I don't look. I don't slow.

Instead, I head straight to my room without a word.

The debrief will call it a success. I was an asset. My timing flawless, my control airtight. But it feels like a failure.

I did my job, but success feels like a failure. Because nothing about tonight felt like a victory. This wasn't the mission you trained for. The mission wasn't about skill, precision, execution, or teamwork. It wasn't even about proving I belonged there.

It was a side I rarely get to see; innocents caught in the crossfire, people we could've saved, but we're told not to. They weren't part of the mission.

Orders. Always the fucking orders. Even if I don't agree with them.

I shut the door and lock it behind me, keeping the world out. I lean back against the door, sliding down. Knees up, I put my head against them. Trying to get my composure back.

My anxiety creeps in, hidden but relentless. My skin flushes, my thoughts won't still; twisting inside my head, my mind racing. And what bothers me the most is not the fear of the mission, but the anger I feel about the situation and the utter lack of control I feel with these missions.

I want to scream. To throw something. To hit someone. But there's no outlet-only fury. Fury at the system. At McGuire. At Elitus. At whoever decided some lives just don't matter.

And underneath it, buried so deep, is doubt. No matter how strong I get, I don't get a say. Not on the missions. Not in whom we save. Not in whom we leave behind. And if I can't stomach it, if I can't do the job, then what am I?

After my shower, I brush out my hair, a soothing repetitive motion that I use to calm my nerves. It's not working. I sit on the edge of the bed and press my hands into my eyes, willing the memories away. I will not cry; I will not break. Instead, I focus on my breathing, trying to calm my mind and my anger. But my thoughts drift back to the mission, to the orders. It wasn't a strategy, it wasn't combat. It was cruelty disguised as orders, and we followed them.

What am I really? The golden girl, the rule follower, Elitus' perfect Queen? But if I'm still powerless, still told to obey while lives bleed out, what's left? Without a mission, without a goal, without perfection to chase.

And then, I hear his voice.

"So damn determined to prove yourself that you'll walk straight into a situation you shouldn't."

The words hit harder now. No, he doesn't get to be right about me.

Because if he's right—if I let this control me—then I don't belong here.

And if I don't belong in this world, then what's left? What am I without a mission?

Without a goal to chase or perfection to achieve?

I don't know. And not knowing might be what breaks me.

THREE

Kate

I smile at Andy as she heads to the pool with her sisters. She was a lifesaver these last couple of days helping me put the party together. We rarely do something this grand for birthdays, but I felt like we needed it.

It has been so dreary around here. I hate it. I petitioned Elitus for a Gen Four birthday celebration. Their birthdays spread across almost two months, but July's heat made a pool party perfect.

Red, White, and Blue everything. Even the food choices coordinate with the theme. No alcohol allowed, or at least not out in the public eye. This event is open to all Generations, which is a first as well.

The dorms' Olympic-size pool is usually packed, but this year, like everything else, is tame. I stand off to the side with the Gen Three females, bottle of water in hand, double-checking everything.

People are everywhere. Smiling, laughing. It's loud, but so needed. Even Mason came, bringing her youngest sister, Kennedy.

I watch Kennedy, at five years old, play. She is with some of the other younger Gen Six children of Elitus. At four and five years old, they're a much smaller cluster group, and the last Elitus ever created.

I make my way around, checking in with everyone I see. Although many are in the pool, some of my peers chat and watch instead. The non-combat girls, the ones who don't live in the dorms, are standing together. Nala, the ringleader of their little clique, grabs my attention, and chatters on about something or another, more to make herself appear important than having anything useful to contribute. I eventually excuse myself. That girl never stops talking. Her twin, Reese, escapes with me to join as I make my final loop around the general area. I stop inside the kitchen to check on the food and the catering team.

Joanne, Alex's mom, and our head meal planner helped with the menu. Summer BBQ themed. It smells outstanding, although with my white one-piece, I don't know if I can eat any of it, too afraid I will get something on me. I'll have to sneak some for later.

"You went all out for this," Reese notes as we head back out onto the back deck. "I think everyone is enjoying themselves."

"That's the goal," I tell her with a smile. "Do you want to take a seat under the umbrella?" Reese is quiet but beautiful, a petite brunette with soft brown eyes and an even softer voice. She doesn't have to be loud to be powerful, though. Reese is a mental healer by nature. She is Bastian's strongest Tier Two healer, skilled and unafraid of work. Today, though, she looks different. She isn't in combat, she has a fit body, which today is sporting a blue and white tankini, with a long flowy skirt. It makes her look feminine and much older than her nineteen-year-old self.

Reese is in Gen Three, like my brothers, Siobhan, Mason, and Charley.

Max, is Mason and Riddick's brother. He and Wyatt make their way to us. I note that Max's eyes are aimed on Reese. I am pretty sure he has a crush on her, since he hasn't taken his eyes off her since we headed outside.

Reese is oblivious, or she is ignoring it, maybe a little of both. They join us, Wyatt bringing some lemonade for us, and Max bringing the cake.

"You outdid yourself," Wyatt says, squeezing my hand while he sets the drink down.

"No such thing," I tell him. Wyatt is usually my date for any major event.

Wyatt and I are close. Best friends since birth, pretty much. Wyatt is a powerhouse. He is a Tier One like me, but X level. Although Wyatt refuses to do combat. Instead, he is the Teacher. He works relentlessly to ensure all the other Gens are up to speed. Academically, as well as with Tier One powers. He has been a main part of the Academy's success of late. Especially with reformatting what we teach to Gen Fives.

Reese takes small bites of her cake while Max updates her on presents for his three Gen Four siblings. The interesting part about Max's Gen Four siblings. He's not a full-blooded sibling to any of them.

Robert Clarke, who is his father, raised him. He grew up in the interesting but crazy Clarke-James family. Nine kids, two sets of parents, and lots of power. Their family tree is complicated; half siblings, cousins, science experiments, and scandals.

"Is RJ coming into the dorms soon?" I ask. RJ and Mya are the only two combat Gen Fours, but Mya is the only one in the dorms.

"No, probably not. He enjoys staying at home with the 'rents still. Unlike Aimee," he says as his gaze moves to the blonde bombshell in a revealing hot pink bikini. At seventeen, she is a force of her own. Also not allowed in the dorms, because she isn't a combatant. It doesn't mean she doesn't push to be allowed every chance she gets. "He said he hopes they get something other than dorms going, but if he goes full combat in the new year, he will consider it. Better for teams that way."

RJ, much like Max and Wyatt, doesn't want to be in combat. But their powers dictate it. For that matter, there are very few who enjoy being combat-enabled. But unfortunately, with the premier powers they possess, they must fulfill the role.

Trying not to sink back into that thought process, I watch as Kyle and Bastian head over to join us, along with Ariel, Bastian's younger sister, and Rina. Both are high-scoring Tier Twos, although only eleven, they outpace several Twos that are ten years older than them.

With them added to our little table, it gets loud. I don't mind. They are both so animated; they fill us in on all the gossip from the younger groups and their plans for the fall semester. Both girls want to go into combat, but their fathers and brothers are keeping them out of it for now.

Bastian

I join the Queen and her minions on the back deck. Ariel and Rina both want to sit, and seeing as though it's hotter than shit, I aspire to be at least under the canopy. I carry Ri's plate, along with mine. She is teetering on some high-heeled sandals that my mother allowed her to wear for some dumbass reason. Setting her plate down, she conveniently left a seat between Kate and herself. She thinks she's being slick; she's not.

I sit and push my shades on top of my head. My hair is freshly cut in a long fade. I lean back as I pop a grape into my mouth. My plate is overflowing because I didn't want to have to get up again. I spent all morning working with Mason, since she refused to miss any training time, but also knew everyone would be pissed if she didn't show up, namely her three birthday siblings: Aimee, RJ, and Mya.

I watch Kate. She has a half-eaten piece of cake in front of her, and an empty glass of lemonade, but not much else. I don't think I saw her eating earlier.

I drink my lemonade, which may or may not contain vodka.

Rina and Ariel dive right into their stories, and it's amusing to watch them. They both like the attention, and those of us at this table don't mind entertaining them. None of us wants to swim, and since we can't party like we usually do, I'll enjoy the stories and people watching.

I glance over to check on my brothers, who are screwing around in the pool with other Gen Four guys. The Monroe Three never let up on acting like idiots when together. When my gaze lands back on the table, I note Kate watching me.

"Yes, Queenie?" I murmur.

"Surprised you're up here, and not basking in feminine attention down there," she retorts.

"Nah, I'd rather be the center of your world today," I say just to get a rise out of her. She shakes her head, trying to hide her smile. Then she picks up my fork and takes a bite of my pasta salad. I watch her. I push the plate towards her. She looks at it, then at me, with a questioning glance.

"I got it so I could sit here longer," I mutter. She smiles a small smile. It's not much, but from Kate it means more. She picks around the plate, but sticks to the healthier stuff. Except for the pulled pork, which she is overly cautious about eating.

I can't say I blame her. Her bathing suit is all white. It's a one-piece but low cut to showcase enough cleavage to make my mouth water, and she is only wearing a short little see-through skirt, which also showcases her long ass legs that always draw my eye, especially when she is in strappy high-heeled sandals, like she is today.

When she has consumed more food than I thought she would, she pushes my plate back and grabs my drink. Taking a sip, I watch her. "Holy shit," she breathes. Giving me the evil eye.

"You okay, Queenie?" I smile at her, and Kyle chuckles across from us, passing her a water bottle.

"Was there any lemonade in that?" She asks me.

"Just a splash," I tell her. Taking my glass back, I pick up my fork and finish the plate. Most of the table watched our interaction and were waiting for the fireworks. It's nice that occasionally she lets her guard down, and in those rare moments, I can't find it in me to start an argument. Instead, I just enjoy her presence. It calms the storm in my head and helps my body relax.

More than any drink or fight can.

Too bad she is so far out of my league and only sees me as Kyle's annoying sidekick. Even if dating weren't forbidden, she would never drop her standards to be with me. She is the Queen, Elitus' darling daughter. And untouchable.

FOUR

Bastian

I'm irritable; I have been for weeks now. This time of year, after practice and training, we have bonfires or just hang out, swim in the pool, or just lounge.

Aside from the Gen Four birthday party last month, it's been extremely dull.

I spend way more time than I want to in training. Whether working in labs or the arena. Most of my Tier Two students in Gens Two and Three don't need me.

Siobhan is the strongest Gen Three combat Two, except for Mason. She has been at least somewhat entertaining. I've been able to work more with her on her combat skills since she has had to do more missions than anyone likes. Especially her half-brothers. Jared, Riddick, and Max, never mind her dad, our head of lab security, Flynn, want her at home safe and sound. Unfortunately, it's not possible. And even if it was, Siobhan, like the other combat females, will never sit back. They like it in trenches, want to be treated equally.

Today, though, it's Gen Fours on my plate. Mason usually takes them, but she is busy working on Tier Ones with Riddick. I find the Fours working on some lessons Calvin has designed. I interrupt and give them a chance to battle with me.

Mental combat with the Fours should be the highlight of my day, but they treat it like a chore. Their shields are sloppy, and their reactions lag. They just turned seventeen, and although they are way past the age of hitting dorms and doing full combat, the majority avoid it by choice. They stay home, staying out of combat trials. Most of them, honestly, will never be useful in the field. They can be defensive and have a few offensive abilities, but they aren't able to hit a high enough level to become the weapons that McGuire wants.

It's not a terrible thing. But it certainly makes it hard. They have no actual future, or at least none they can see. Which I know frustrates many.

The only two true combat Gen Fours are Mason's siblings. Mya and RJ. Both are trending Spectrum. RJ is strongest in Tier Ones, Mya in Threes.

RJ's off on a baby mission with Kyle, which leaves me with Mya today. Normally, I'd be thrilled—she's sharp, unrelenting, and a lot like her sister. Not nearly as skilled yet, but a challenge. Especially when she is focused.

Today, she's off. She's usually a little more open, more friendly. It's like she's running with a cloak of armor around herself and hoping no one notices.

Except I notice.

"You good?" I ask as we cycle through another round of drills. She's quick to react, just a fraction ahead of my projection—but not as fast as she can be.

"I'm fine."

What do they say about women who say they are fine...

"You seem off, is all..."

She shrugs, rolling her shoulders like she's trying to shed the weight of my question. She gives me a look that says *Drop it*.

She resets her stance, her movements precise, as we move into drills that use both her Twos and her Threes. I use Twos only to trip her up. She's doing well.

What we are doing is difficult, even for seasoned Wights. But Mya is well ahead of her peers and those in the other Gens. As one of the few Gen Fours who are gearing up to join combat, she has gotten a decent handle on this.

It should be impressive. But I can't stop watching her face. She's working from muscle memory and force of habit. Her mind's somewhere else.

"Roarke has been working with you on this?" I ask, nodding toward her technique. Its textbook Peacemaker—fluid pressure without flash, clean restraint over brute force. Roarke is a High Three. Who acts as a primary shield to Mason on missions. He has also taken Mya on as a private student for the last year or so. I don't know if it was Mason's doing or Alex's. Either way, he helped her get combat-ready. She is trending toward being in full combat in a few short months. No restrictions.

I watch her now, though she doesn't answer. Instead, she drives forward, knocking me back a step with a projected pulse, combining a mental shove with her physical one.

"Yeah," she says finally. "He has."

Then she leaves her side completely open. I react blindly, sweeping in low with a projected hit—easy, just enough to test her guard. But she doesn't defend.

She doesn't move.

The hit lands clean across her ribs, and she goes down hard.

"Shit—Mya!" I'm already dropping beside her, reaching to check the impact zone. It should've been nothing; she should've blocked me. Hell, she should've countered me.

But hearing Roarke's name distracted her. She grits her teeth, brushing off my hand like she's pissed at herself. "I'm fine."

"You didn't even throw up a shield."

"I said I'm fine." I hate that word from her.

Her jaw's tight, her expression closed off. She shifts her weight like she's going to stand, but I can see the wince before she even moves.

My hands move instinctively, blooming as I call on my power, focused and fine-tuned for healing.

"Hold still," I mutter, placing my palm just beneath her ribcage. "You cracked something."

"It's fine."

"If you say that word one more time..." I sigh.

That gets me a flicker of something in her eyes. Annoyance, maybe. Or guilt. It could be both.

I keep the healing slow but focus internally, scanning. It's not just the cracked rib. I can feel bruising across her shoulders, a strain in her lower back, micro-tears in her left bicep. All minor, all manageable, that will heal on their own or with a little focus from her. But they add up. She's pushing herself too hard.

I've seen Mason and Charley go down harder than that. But Mya, she doesn't bounce back. She internalizes it, carries it like it's her penance for being born. I know she has issues with self-esteem and her own perception of herself.

Her primary power that surfaced first, well that caused issues. Then, of course, there is the fact that her mother was Naomi Korsonov-Dividian, sister to Dmitri, the head of the PPG. Her dad, Dr. Clarke, makes her related to the strongest bloodline on campus.

She was created in vitro after Naomi's husband Conrad left, taking her twin sons, Mya's older brothers, with him.

They are also the head goons at the PPG; Gen Ones, Nikolai and Alexi. They are usually the ones who show up when we hit PPG targets. I know she fears seeing them on the field, although she would never admit it.

"Thanks," she mutters once I finish. Her voice is low, subdued.

"You've been training like this every day?"

"More or less."

"Roarke keeping pace?"

The way her body stiffens says more than words ever could. I don't push, but I clock it. Store it. Something's off between them.

They've been close; training constantly, pushing each other harder than anyone else would dare. And Roarke's good for her. He tempers her recklessness, grounds her. But lately?

She's been quieter. Edgier. Withdrawn, like she's trying to armor herself from something that already got in.

"I'm not stupid," I say, standing and offering her a hand. "You're not sleeping. You've got half a dozen fresh injuries every time I see you. And your shields are too clean—like you're hiding something behind them."

She doesn't take the hand.

Just stands on her own, brushing off the dust and dirt from her clothes, like it gives her back a small measure of control.

"I'm handling it."

"Mya."

Her name comes out low. A warning. A question.

But she won't look at me.

"Drop it, Bastian."

And that's the end. For now.

I let her go, watching her walk off the mats with her shoulders drawn tight and her head high, like she can keep everything from unraveling if she just keeps moving.

But I know that look. I've worn that look. Her sister wears that look too often.

And whatever's going on with her has Roarke written all over it.

Whatever made Mya shut down like this—it's not over. Not even close.

Kate

Roarke's already at the table when I walk into the strategy room, the screen in front of him flickering between Gen Four activity logs and updated combat readiness reports.

He doesn't look up when I enter. Just taps something on the screen and mutters a barely audible, "Hey."

That's not like him. Roarke Parrish is usually easygoing. He brings comic relief to a stressful situation, but in a controlled and responsible manner, and is always laser-focused on the objective.

He's always level-headed and focused, especially when it involves his family. He takes on more missions than needed to keep his twin, Andy, out of combat as much as possible. He takes an active role in helping shape the program and training for the younger Gens, which two of his sisters are in.

I settle across from him, placing my tablet on the desk and scanning the data we're supposed to be reviewing together.

"You're distracted," I say after a moment, because I don't believe in wasting time.

Roarke scrubs a hand through his hair and leans back in his chair. "Long week."

"Join the club."

His eyes flick to mine—dark, tired, and too damn guarded.

We're supposed to be completing next month's Gen Four advancement structure—who's eligible for combat prep, who still needs more Tier Two training, who's screwing up their evaluations on purpose just to get out of any type of combat. They just turned seventeen, so they just finished up the new trials. We are reassessing training assignments, tier compatibility for upcoming SIM rotations.

Delilah's name is near the top of the list for Tier Two. A mental handler. She is showing top results in persuasion and illusions. Successful tools for stealth work.

"She's ready," I say, tapping her profile. "Delilah's Tier Two focus is clean, her SIM response time is fast, and she's managing pressure well. If you're worried about her, don't be."

"I'm not."

His answer is too quick. Flat. I pause, watching him.

"She's your sister, Roarke. It's okay to care."

"I said I'm not worried," he repeats, but there's something about the way his jaw tenses that tells me he's lying through his teeth.

I flip the file closed and lean forward slightly. "Fine. If not Delilah, then what?"

He doesn't answer right away. Just stares at the wall like it offended him. "If you don't want to work with me on this or want another partner, I can make it happen," he looks up at me. Shaking his head, he sighs.

"Sorry, Kate, it's not you. It's me. Let's just get this done." I am not convinced; he reached across and patted my hand. "I swear it's not you; we are good. I've just got a lot going on," he tells me.

We work through the other Gen Fours, including most of the Tier Ones and Twos. When we hit the Threes, that's when I see him tense up. Especially when I pull up Mya's profile.

"She's made significant progress," I say carefully. "Her control's better. She's not overreaching like she used to. She's smart enough to learn from her mistakes."

"I know."

"She and RJ are close to full combat clearance."

"I'm aware."

Something sharp curls in my chest. He used to light up talking about her. Mya, who worked harder than anyone because she knew her name meant more, felt more pressure, had more eyes on her.

And Roarke believed in her when no one else did. He advocated for her in every meeting. Pushed for her to get more advanced SIMs, called her his strongest student.

Now, he won't even say her name.

"You two haven't been training lately," I say, watching his reaction.

His shoulders go rigid. Just for a second. But I catch it. "Been busy," he mutters.

Busy. Right. I narrow my eyes slightly. "You've been avoiding her." His silence is the only answer I need. "What happened?"

"Nothing."

"That's not true."

Roarke finally looks at me then, and for a heartbeat, I see something flicker across his face—pain, regret, guilt. Something twisted and hard doesn't belong to someone like him.

"She's not ready," he says, low and clipped.

"She is."

He leans forward suddenly, elbows on the table, hands clasped like he's trying to keep himself from flying apart.

"Mya doesn't think about consequences."

"She does. She just doesn't think the way you do."

Roarke shakes his head, eyes dark. "She's going to get herself killed." There's too much weight behind the words. It's not hypothetical. It's personal. "I can't be her shield."

Not stubborn, not angry, but broken.

I don't push further. Not today. But I file it. I don't know what happened, but whatever it is, he is torn up over it.

Whatever happened between Roarke and Mya—whatever snapped that bond—is still bleeding beneath the surface. And if she's half as shut down as he is, then this isn't just a falling out.

It's a fracture. One that could get worse if someone doesn't pull them back from the edge.

And knowing them? They'll both just pretend nothing's wrong until it's too late.

FIVE

Kate

I hit the training area in search of Wyatt. My best friend is usually working on himself in the late afternoon. He has been busy, between teaching our younger Gens and working to help revamp the training protocols.

But today, I know he was headed for the Tier Two sessions this afternoon. I was almost certain that Bastian was supposed to be running SIMs and drills.

They rarely tangle when there is no reason for Wyatt to engage with Tier Two combat SIMs.

When I step inside, I catch on immediately. It's a Combat Two SIM in progress. I scan the crowd, cataloging who is here. It's mostly Gen Fours, but Roarke and a few other combats are present.

Bastian's leaning against the wall in the back corner, arms crossed like this whole thing is a joke he's being forced to endure.

I don't see Wyatt right away, but then I catch him in a quiet conversation with Calvin and the techs. I take the long route over.

"Come to see your boy get crushed?" Bastian asks me as I stop beside him. I side-eye him.

"You're too damn cocky sometimes, you know that, right?"

He smirks. "Yes."

"Are you training them today or just observing?"

"I was going to watch. But hey, I guess I can do something to impress you."

"Please don't strain yourself."

He laughs as he heads over.

They huddle, he and Wyatt, with muted discussions on what to work on, what to show. This training room is for covert ops simulations—strategy, stealth, responses under pressure. Bastian flicks a look my way and flashes that signature shithead grin.

"Is this the part where you show us why you are a God?" I ask.

"Nah," he tells me. "I'm not a God. But if you want to get on your knees for me..."

Snickers ripple through the crowd. This asshole. "Actually," I reply, "I'd much rather knee you in the balls."

Wyatt suppresses a laugh beside him. Bastian just grins wider.

Calvin's team takes over. Explaining the simulation, laying out the objectives.

I can feel Bastian powering up. He's stretching lazily—mentally, of course. I can feel his Tier Two signature reaching out, probing the edges of every mind in the room like he's bored and looking for something to break.

He flicks his gaze at me. "Try not to fry anyone's prefrontal cortex today," I mutter, taking a seat in the front row beside Siobhan. I cross my legs, causing my tight suit skirt to ride up, and I catch his eyes dropping to my legs. It's time for me to smirk at him.

"Where's the fun in that? When I'm done wiping the floor with Wyatt's brain matter, I can give you some time," he tells me.

"No thanks, I'm good."

He gives me that smug, slow smile that usually makes people back off.

"Admit it. You miss me when I'm not arguing with you."

"I sleep better when you're quiet."

"Funny. I sleep better when I'm thinking about you."

The Gen Fours collectively try to figure out if that was flirtation or a threat.

Honestly, I'm not sure Bastian knows.

I roll my eyes and motion to Wyatt; his jaw is tight. He did not like that either.

Bastian

Wyatt's pissed. Between him and her two brothers, she hides. I've barely been able to get a rise out of her lately.

He might be the only other X in this class, but he's also her best friend. Her human shield, her diplomatic, impenetrable, sweater-vest wearing wall.

I know how Wyatt works. He's an X-One, with decent Tier Two capabilities. But he's not combat. Defensive only. The Teacher.

He stands with arms folded, watching the SIM layout like it's a case study. Not a hair out of place. He's cool under pressure, that's for sure. Meanwhile, I've been holding myself back all morning.

There were at least half a dozen times I could've tripped someone up or just been a pain and created unnecessary drama.

"So," I say, cracking my knuckles as I step into the zone, "you gonna play this by-the-book, or are we making it interesting?"

Wyatt doesn't even look up. "Do you ever play by-the-book?"

"Not unless I wrote it."

His eyes stay locked on the screen, but there is a flicker; he glances at Kate.

She's watching. Focused, but I can feel her. She's nervous.

"Did I bother you with my comments?" I ask, fishing.

"No. Does it bother you that no matter how hard you try, she will never be within your reach?"

Fuck this guy. I may laugh, but I am plotting how I am going to make him regret that one. I can feel Kate tense up even more.

"You know," Wyatt adds, "for someone who pretends not to care, you get twitchy anytime her name comes up."

There it is. "Must be hard," he continues, tone casual as if he's talking about the weather, "seeing someone who's... well, completely unimpressed by the whole Bastian Monroe routine."

I roll my shoulders, keeping my face blank even as heat flares in my chest.

"She's not unimpressed," I say. "She's just in denial. Happens to the best of them."

He raises an eyebrow. "Is that what helps you sleep at night?"

"No, that would be alcohol and mission recaps. But thanks for the concern."

The corner of his mouth lifts—half amusement, half threat. "I get it," he says. "She's sharp. Unattainable. Completely allergic to chaos. The exact girl who makes guys like you lose sleep."

"Guys like me?"

"You know—dangerous. Obsessive. Pathologically reckless."

"I'm not reckless."

"You're emotionally volatile."

"Says the guy who's been attached to Kate Ames since birth."

Wyatt's expression doesn't shift. But the temperature in the room drops about five degrees.

"You sound jealous," he says, his voice lower now. More precise. "She's not a game piece. Not someone to play with. You forget that again, we'll have a real problem."

A beat of silence passes. Because beneath the jokes and the posturing, he's right.

And I hate it.

Wyatt nods to the techs, and the SIM starts. Wyatt's moves are clean, efficient, and with no wasted steps.

I sync our shields, keeping pace mentally, while pushing forward. Mapping terrain and targeting threats.

I expect him to push back after all the bravado.

But he doesn't. He matches my rhythm; follows my guidance, not resisting, just collaborating. He's good. Great.

So, I push, a jolt to his shields. Just a hit, nothing serious; enough to see if he flinches.

He doesn't even blink. His shields are solid, locked in. I push again, harder. Still nothing.

I can feel it now. He's been practicing. Training for this, training to protect someone. My jaw tightens because I only need one guess as to whom.

He catches it, of course.

"You know," he says mildly as we pivot around toward the lead target, "you're the strongest Tier Two we've got. You've got more potential than just defense and mental battle. You can protect and fight."

"Thanks?"

"But until you figure out what to fight for... It's useless."

He doesn't wait for a reply. He hits me back, sending me back a step.

What the hell? My eyes flick to Kate. She looks like she wasn't expecting that. And from the way she is watching us now, she knows this isn't just training.

It's personal.

Kate

I watch them battle. Their banter, or whatever bullshit they have going on. I am going to give Wyatt an earful for baiting him. I don't know what the hell Bastian's issue is. I know he has been all over the place since his favorite playmate has become the ultimate weapon for Elitus. He's been drinking more than normal, and frankly, he looks bored out of his mind most of the time.

I haven't sparred with him as much as normal in the last several months. Now that I have graduated, I have less time in classrooms and less time to interact. He's not wrong. I miss the mental chess we would play. But what I don't miss, how he affects me well after we are done arguing. When the adrenaline recedes and I pick apart every comment he made, every retort I gave him.

I watch them battle both mentally and fight together and against each other throughout the simulation.

Wyatt thrives on this. He is a One by definition, but I know he has been working on Twos. I am fairly sure that over the last couple of weeks, he's worked with Mason more than normal.

Bastian thrives on battle as well; this is his forte. But for entirely different reasons.

I lean forward, elbows on my knees, hands intertwined, watching the way they move—two entirely different philosophies wrapped in the same lethal battle. I don't know what I am feeling, but it's a mix of nerves and unease.

Wyatt is all battle planning, calculating risk and reward. He is the teacher here as well, controlled and effective. He doesn't just command the battlefield—he orchestrates it. Like a game of chess. Wyatt doesn't do combat missions, even though McGuire pushes. What he does is lead the masses here, ensuring everyone is ready. He is the Teacher of everything.

Bastian, however. He is a warning label: beautiful, dangerous, and chaotic.

He moves fast and hits harder—not with fists, but with psychic force. I feel it from up here: the way his energy ripples through the terrain like a long black train of a tornado. He doesn't just read enemy moves; he controls them. He makes his opponent question everything; he makes their moves for them, and he is ready for what they plan to do. Pushes them off balance. Not only controlling their bodies and minds but also making them question everything. Without touching them.

They're both teachers in their own way.

But they both affect me differently.

Wyatt is my rock. He's been my best friend since we were toddlers. He's my sound-board, my partner in planning, the one person I trust to call me out without tearing me down. We don't have to explain things to each other—we just know.

And Bastian is a thorn in my side. The sarcastic, infuriating, reckless force of nature who seems to exist to challenge me. Which keeps me on my toes, but also, although I never will admit it, keeps me entertained. He keeps things interesting.

And more than that, he is also the reason half of these kids are even combat ready. A different teacher.

Every Gen Two. Every Gen Three. Almost every Gen Four.

Shielding? He taught them.

Mental combat? That's him too.

Healing, integration, tactical pushes under Tier stress? All Bastian Monroe.

And he never asks for credit. He never wants the spotlight. He just shows up and does the job. Leaves behind a battlefield full of stronger, smarter Wights.

I've watched him pour hours into trainees who never thanked him. Sit with wounded wights after medical cleared them, guiding them through the mental aftermath of a failed mission or training. I've seen him take mental hits for others, be a shield, and heal them physically as well as mentally.

He pretends it is nothing. But I know better. Bastian cares deeply, relentlessly, about what's right.

About the Wights under his watch, about protecting them from the twisted politics that run this place. He despises Elitus and just about everything it stands for. But he still fights and does missions. Not because it's our job, but he's out there to protect the rest. His friends, his family.

He just hides his true self behind smirks and jabs and that insufferable attitude.

Lately, he's been worse. More jabs, more provocation, more tension. I know he's daring me to bite back. I think he misses me.

And maybe I miss him too, but I'll never admit it. Afraid that if I do, then that leads to other thoughts about him. How he fits into my world. How I fit into his.

He's not Wyatt. He's not Alex. He's not Kyle, Roarke or Riddick. He's his own equation—a variable, like his beloved math equations. Only one I haven't figured out yet.

But I know this much: he's dangerous.

Not just in the field but in the way he gets under my skin and stays there.

His warning label flashes at me daily. I know the potential damage he can do to my head and my heart.

I watch as they finish up the last part of the SIM. As a unit, taking out the targets with precision and little exertion. They are on the same mental plane, which allows them to be efficient.

Bastian nods without a word; they sync together to hit the last target in perfect tandem. Brutally efficient.

The SIM ends.

Wyatt looks up at me first and gives a nod—cool and collected. He knows I will give him grief later.

Bastian doesn't look at me, not right away. Then, slowly, as if he knows I'm watching—he turns and winks.

I roll my eyes, but before he turns away, I see something else in his gaze. Something that doesn't belong there. Something I am sure I am imagining.

SIX

Bastian

Mason has spent the entire summer revamping everything; rewriting drills and training, ripping apart mission protocols, reworking SIM lab code. You name it. She's nonstop; McGuire's favorite new weapon.

She doesn't slow down. Doesn't blink. Breathes only when it's aligned with her next move.

It's Tier Threes today, so her younger siblings, RJ and Mya, are down with her in the training arena along with Kyle, as I observe from the tower.

I haven't brought up Mya's mess with Mason. I've kept tabs, but Mason's avoiding me. She knows exactly how I feel about the shift in her. And I am not the only one who isn't happy with what is going on.

Max and Alex have tried to get Mason to slow down, but no one is getting through. We are approaching the Gen Two graduation at a fast clip, and if she doesn't slow down, I don't know what else there will be for her to do.

She's been the teacher in sessions; Gen Threes and Fours hanging on her every word. And when they mess up, she doesn't yell. She's not even raising her voice; she's patient, calm, giving them something she never got: room to believe they are good enough.

After all, she was always pushed harder than everyone else.

Diamonds are made under pressure.

And that's what she is now, this brilliant, unique stone. That is worth more than all the other gemstones lying around.

"You're worried about her, too, huh?" Siobhan says as she steps up beside me. We are both in the tower, watching, in case of any medical needs.

"She is getting worse, not better," I mutter.

Siobhan sighs. "I know why she is doing it, doesn't make it right. But I get it. We won't change her mind, you know that?"

"So, what do we do? Just watch?"

"Support her the only way we know how." Siobhan's eyes are on me. "You control the chessboard like you always do."

She's right. When I can, I influence mentally, of course. The doctors in Elitus don't even know it when I make a slight change. I can't change everything, but I can glean what is what. I don't do it as much anymore, no need. But with her, and what she is trying to do. I need to make sure she has the support, but also the backup she needs.

After all, the whole reason she was under house arrest to begin with was because McGuire thought she could handle his nasty side missions solo. And they were nasty.

When Mason was on her sabbatical, I went through what I could hack on those side missions, strikes, espionage, and black ops. There was no oversight, no backup for her, just solo. And that's not okay.

I haven't seen any more missions of that nature running, or at least if they are running, they aren't being run by Mason or any of the main combat lineups. But knowing McGuire, it's the calm before the storm.

I side-eye Siobhan; she has been taking more combat missions herself, much to her family's dismay. She and Mason share Max as siblings. Part of the crazy extended family created by Dmitri when he raped three women on campus.

Max is known as the Quiet One, the nice guy, but to those who know him well, he's also confident, sarcastic, and strong. A Spectrum High One, dependable and protective, not only to his sisters but to anyone he cares about. Including Mya, who joins us in the tower.

Mason is still down there working with Kyle. Mya's face says exactly how much she hates it. Siobhan hands her water. They are not only friends but also roommates and cousins.

The fact is, we're still missing Mason, even when she's right there, center stage.

Because the real Mason, the one who fought like hell and grinned while doing it? That Mason is gone.

A training like this would usually be bouts of sarcasm between her and Kyle, with both of them screwing around after the trainees left. But that's not what we have now.

What's left is a mission-enabled robot.

"You know why she's doing it, right?" Mya asks.

"Yeah."

She exhales, frustrated. "Because if she's strong enough, no one else gets hurt," Mya says. "She thinks that'll be enough. That she'll be enough."

I swallow hard. Because I know that lie. I've lived it too.

We all have at one point. "RJ said she's been hitting the SIM lab at 0400," Mya adds. "Every day. She hasn't missed it. She's even been pulling the Tier Ones in to reset their shielding drills and maneuvers."

Siobhan adds, "She got into it with Riddick again last night. Tore his new curriculum apart."

Mya blinks. "Seriously?"

"He let her," Siobhan retorts.

"She's that good now?" Mya asks.

"She's that committed now," I correct. In the back of my mind, I know Riddick is a big reason she is the way she is. He has always been hard on her, and between Kyle and him, they have pushed her to where she doesn't see any other way to protect the rest.

We fall silent again. Down below, Mason hammers Kyle across the arena. He lets her do it. He looks beat. She doesn't even look tired.

Just... detached.

I watch Mason finish up; Kyle tries to joke with her. But she isn't biting. She is just reviewing the notes with the lab team. I see the look on Kyle's face from here. He's concerned, more than he would ever admit. Something we are all feeling.

Mason isn't listening to anyone.

She's not checking whether we're watching.

She doesn't care.

And that's what scares me the most.

Kate

Mason's name has been circling in my head since lunch. My mother sees the shift in her too, from rebel to soldier, almost overnight.

My mom knows that Mason and I, although quite different, are friends. She is someone I have depended on over the years when I need something done and the others are slacking. She has always been serious and dedicated to what the group needs. Regardless of how it affects her. Which I think is a big part of what is going on now.

I decide I have to try my luck at making an impact with Mason. Maybe I can get through. Even for a little while, to get her to slow down. Take a deep breath.

I find her in the gym. She's the only one here and clearly has been at it for a while. I watch her working through some moves, lithe and smooth in her form. I envy her. She is a force all her own. I've seen her take out guys twice her size. And that's without her power.

I lean against the wall, observing her. We don't work together often. My powers are elemental ones, and so far below hers. She mastered what I had to work for before she was even in the dorms. She notices me but finishes her round of exercises and moves.

"Hey," she says, stopping to wipe sweat off her brow, and drink water.

"Do you plan on taking a break soon?"

"Depends," she says, tossing the now empty water bottle.

She moves over to the locker room. I join her, my heels clicking on the tile. She jumps into the shower bay, and finishes up quickly, changing into a new set of leggings and a crop top. Her toned stomach is on display. She isn't trying to draw attention; it's just her. She no longer seems to care if the guys look.

"What did you need, Kate?"

"Dinner." She looks up, curious. We've never hung out, not like this, but there's a mutual respect between us. We work well together. Always have.

"Off campus or on?" I smile. Yeah, right, even with her being a powerhouse, if we left without a male escort. Too many people would lose their damn minds. "Thought so," she mutters.

We head to the cafeteria, but it's not a normal lunchroom. The chef responsible for our crafted meals is Mason's surrogate mother, Joanne, who makes sure we have plenty to choose from.

It's empty by the time we get there. A few stragglers from Tier Two finishing late rounds, but otherwise, quiet.

We grab trays. I grab a salad, a protein and coffee. Mason, she piles it on there. She has enough food to feed a small army, but she will eat it. We head for the back corner booth, where the cool kids usually are.

We slide into the booth. In everything, including eating, she is precise and focused; Mason is painstakingly methodical.

"You going to eat? Or watch me the whole time?" She asks.

"I figured we could work and eat?" Pulling up the info on my tablet, we spend most of the meal talking about plans for Gen Five.

She's a good person to go over this with; she is one of their primary trainers. Earlier, I watched her with them, guiding them through shielding drills.

She was effortless, answering their questions about combat without breaking focus. They just turned eleven this summer, and some are stronger than others. Normally, at ten, those wanting to go to combat would be allowed in the dorms. But this hasn't happened.

I know the delay is because there isn't room right now. But I think part of it is because the two strongest ones in that Generation are both female combat Twos. And they are the younger sisters of Bastian and Riddick; Ariel and Sabrina. They are Charley and Mason reincarnated. Wild, strong, and determined.

We touch upon the end of summer plans, if there is any vacation time. She passes on it but says others may need this downtime at the Palace.

We work; I finished up a while ago, but she is still eating. I refill my coffee and come back with a new dessert for her, knowing she has a major sweet tooth.

"You going to lecture me now?" she asks between bites of her new chocolate cake. "This is the part where you say I'm over-training, right?"

"Would it do any good?" I ask her.

"Nope," she says, smiling.

We move on to other topics: Gen Two graduation, details about dorm needs. She makes a great sounding board, and it's nice knowing that with anything I need help with, she will just get it done. That's how she is. She used to hate politics, probably still does, but if it's meant to help, she will do it.

We don't make small talk, don't gossip. Just work. But it's easy with her. I forget sometimes how much she pays attention to everything. Although focused on the combat side, she also keeps up with the politics, social and science part of it.

Before I know it, it's way past the time for me to head back. Never mind her; I know she is up before everyone else every day. We get up, tossing trays. I grab some tea to go, having already had too much caffeine. She snags a cookie and water.

"What's your next assignment?" She asks while we walk across the quad. The late August air is muggy, but not unbearable.

I hesitate. Just a beat. "Data Recon."

Her brows lift. "Real recon or Elitus recon'?"

I frown; she knows which kind. The kind I hate.

I want to ask her how she compartmentalizes it — the missions that go wrong, the mayhem, the dead. How she closes her eyes and still sleeps.

My last mission still lingers. The nightmares haven't stopped. I hate them. But I won't back out of combat. I've fought too hard to be seen as equal; to be combat enabled.

"You good?" She asks, picking up my thoughts.

I want to say something, but I don't know how. She eyes me with understanding. And for the first time, I realize it bothers her, too. Maybe that's why she is like this now? Is she preventing anyone else from having to deal with it? If so, that's a dangerous game. She can't save everyone.

"Are you?" I ask. She says nothing. I can feel the weight in her lack of answer, but no matter what, her dedication is a choice on her part, and she knows what she is doing.

"Thanks for tonight. I appreciate it."

"It was good, a change of pace. Plus, I know everyone else probably leaves you to deal with it," she smiles.

"Yep, Katie-Did it." I smirk, that dumbass phrase that never goes away. Don't worry about it, Katie Did It. That's how it's been since we started training. And I did it. A lot. Doesn't mean I aspired to be the only one. Mason laughs. As we enter the dorms, it's quiet. No one in the main area, no parties.

"They miss you," I say, nodding to the empty common room, once full of life, now silent and cold. A year ago, it would overflow with people, chatting, drinking, just being fun, young and carefree. Or as much as they could be in Elitus' world.

"No one is stopping them from being social," she tells me.

"No, but you set the tone. If you're dedicated, they feel like they need to be. I'm not saying it's your fault, but they don't know what to do." It flipped overnight for many of them. It's been months, but still. We just stand in the doorway. She looks a little lost, a little sad. She shakes her head, trying to clear it.

"Well, it's been fun, Ames," she says as she heads up the stairs ahead of me. I stand longer, looking over the area.

The artificial bar in the back, couches worn in from lots of social activities, a huge TV, usually playing some sporting event, but now it's black.

The quiet in here, it feels all wrong.

I was never a partier, but I did like the social aspect. The interaction. I knew many needed it. Otherwise, what were we?

Weapons. Soldiers. That's what we were made to be.

But with what future? To have our lives controlled by Elitus forever.

Our only purpose, mission-enabled, enhanced human weapons, or would we someday be free to make choices?

Without rules and restrictions.

To live.

SEVEN

Bastian

I'm bored, the kind that gets me into trouble. The kind I can't outrun or dull with alcohol or math.

No one hangs out anymore in the common area. Mason has set the tone for dedication, and no one wants to disrupt it. And I fucking hate it.

Just work. And more work. And what's worse? She's not the only one. All the girls have been acting that way. My regular crew of party girls—Mason, Charley, Andy and Mya. The untouchable ones.

But the feeling, the crawling under my skin—it's more than just the silence in the dorms; it's like something is brewing. Summer is nearly over, and the back deck with the firepit hasn't been used once.

I have had it. I guess I am ready to cause my own brand of drama.

So, I head to the back patio and start the pit, rearranging the chairs. I path Kyle and Max. Before long, it's not just us, Riddick, Roarke, Alex and the guys join. We just bullshit.

Someone brings out a cooler with beer. The fire crackles in front of us, but the air around us feels easier, calmer. Even Wyatt and Bailey join in. Charley comes through with her sisters, Marty and Paige.

Charley has been struggling more than most; Charley doesn't beg, she doesn't ask for anything. She just makes it happen. But she used her best-friend status to get Mason to bend, having her do a movie night on Fridays with all the girls. It's not much, but it's a start.

Mya and Siobhan come through as well, just for a small check-in, probably because they are both becoming just as dedicated as Mason.

Even Siobhan has been pushing her Twos and Threes, she's driving towards more missions. I'm not sure why. I know it drives all her brothers, including little Finley, and her dad, Flynn, our head of lab security, insane.

It isn't long until I feel Mason's energy the second she comes in. She beelines straight to her room. Doesn't even look our way. And just like that, I want to hit something. Anything.

Riddick and Kyle exchange a look. Fucking hell. None of us knows how to stop this.

I followed Siobhan's suggestion, and I tried to make minor adjustments. Push into some openings with Thompson and McGuire. A small nudge here and there, a redirect, a gentle push in a direction, to keep things going but not allowing for too much risk.

Nothing major. Nothing outside a normal deviation.

But it's enough to keep things running smoothly and reduce unnecessary risk. But I can't make a dent with Mason. Can't get her to stop, to take a break, to breathe.

But it's not just Mason. It's Kate as well. She has been distant, focused; leveraging Mason as well. Taking advantage of Mason's focus to get some help on things. I know Kate takes a lot on herself, but I just don't have the patience to deal with Elitus' bullshit. Never mind, Kate is way too controlling to let a loose cannon like me in.

We've both been too busy, too focused on everything except each other. I am getting ready to graduate and helping my peer Gen Twos get ready to level and finish up their trials.

Despite that, we haven't argued in weeks. I tried teasing her the other day in a session. She gave me that look, cool and unreadable, and then went right back to talking to Wyatt. We still spat back and forth occasionally, but now it feels more forced.

I don't get the energy I used to. She has no choice but to counter my point. Not that she wants to.

Before, I thought she enjoyed arguing. Now I feel like I am a chore for her, and I fucking hate it.

She is just stressed. Buried in planning Gen Two graduation and after party. With significantly more graduating, they are doing some social, something grand, I am sure.

As a Gen Two, I know many want it. But I also know it's overkill. Shit, most of them wouldn't have even made it through without me busting their heads mentally every day for the last couple of years. But still. The Elitus showcase, or whatever graduation is. It's just slapping a label on something. And I still hate labels.

I can't sleep. Even having a good night, the first one in a while. My mind still runs non-stop. Between Mason and Kate. Never mind the rest of the issues. I reach out mentally. Mason is up. No surprise there. But I don't want to get even more pissed off.

I feel out. I know I shouldn't. It's invading her privacy, but I can't stop myself. When I seek Kate's mental signature, I don't like what I feel. She is sleeping, but it's not peaceful. Fuck.

I send a small nudge, gentle. Just enough to push her out of whatever is haunting her sleep. Ease her out of REM without waking her. Just enough to let her breathe.

I hate that she is still having issues. She will never admit it, but she doesn't agree with the Elitus' combat bullshit. Kate won't back down, not even if it kills her, just to be seen as equal. Another goddamn label Elitus has her chasing.

EIGHT

Bastian

I'm sitting with Riddick when Mason comes through the cafeteria. She has a determined look on her face, and a file in her hands. Riddick and I exchange a glance. This can't be good.

Slapping it on the table, she grabs my dessert and takes a bite. Another bad sign.

Riddick grabs it first and opens it. His eyes scan it, then flick to her, and passes it to me. It's a data dump from a PPG server. I don't know how Mason got it, but it has data that Elitus will want if she didn't get it from them.

"Someone sent it to my personal, non-Elitus account. It was encrypted." Riddick tenses at her comment.

"Someone inside PPG sent it?"

"Looks that way. I don't think Elitus has this."

The documents—its birth records, power readings, details from doctors, labs, all about what PPG is calling Project Vanguard. Children of Wights, Agent X 2.0 in essence. Two Wight parents, or Latent and Wight according to some data.

"If this is real, X doesn't carry on, or at least not immediately," I tell her.

"Maybe it'll be latent," Riddick mutters.

"I doubt it. Coral carries the purple, like we do. Shit, Mason's eyes were ultraviolet until she was two," I say, smiling at her. "I would bet that his experiment for Coral wasn't a working mix. Does he have any X's in Latents?"

"I haven't scrubbed through all of it, but other than Coral and Tara, they appear to be the only ones named. The rest of the maternal candidates are numbered. Not sure what that means exactly. But I don't like it." I can guess what that means. Means they are vessels, incubators. The mothers don't matter. Only the results.

"Are you taking it to your father?" Riddick asks her. "Or McGuire?"

That's why she is here. Maybe she isn't McGuire's robot after all. She is including us in this.

"Let's go through it first before we give it to them." I tell both. "I don't need them going all gung-ho and starting their own subset. As it is, I am certain the Latent bullshit has been their primary focus; this will only add to it."

It isn't discussed, but all my data suggest they are. I haven't dug as much as I have wanted to, because I don't want to know.

Mason flips through and grabs out a sheet, which details what appears to be a Latent and a mother on X. Based upon their initial tests, although the child isn't born yet, the reading from the mother is high. The father, a Latent, who appears... Shit.

"X-One, X-Two?" I ask. "And we haven't seen them?"

"Maybe that's his hidden weapon?" Mason mutters. "I don't know, but I don't like it. And what I like even less is the number of trials they have going on with this. He's not only building an army; now he's birthing one."

"But why you?" Riddick asks. "It was on purpose, I am sure, but for what purpose?"

"I don't know," she says, but she's lying.

"Mason, what have you seen?" I ask her. Similar to Riddick and Kyle, Mason gets visions. She avoids them. She usually can control keeping them out, but major ones she can't avoid. It bleeds through. Her subconscious is warning her.

"That this, Vanguard. It's a turning point for PPG. If he can figure out the right combination, we're screwed."

Riddick isn't happy, but he also doesn't sugarcoat it, "and if you bring that to Elitus, they line up new mommies immediately." Riddick and Mason are both tense regarding that topic. I hate this kind of shit.

"Well, that's one way to get them to drop the dating ban," Mason mutters. It brings a little brevity to the conversation. "I don't know. I hate secrets, but I also hate the idea of what this will all mean, what this will change."

"Let me do some digging," Riddick mutters. "Have you traced it?"

"Not yet. I literally just got it an hour ago." And she sought us out immediately. "I was going to tap Kyle to assist, but..."

"But he's in McGuire's pocket." I finish for her. He may be one of my best friends, but sometimes he plays both sides of the table. Better odds for him. I know it's strategic, but still.

"I am the first one to argue with Kyle over some things, but this needs to be dealt with. Kyle can probably do some digging on his own side, see what Elitus may know," Riddick points out. The frown on Mason's face tells me she isn't sure he won't go to McGuire with it.

"Give him a chance," I tell her. Her eyes lock with mine. What I see in them. It's a mix of fear, trepidation, sadness and confusion. Riddick is watching all this unfold, but the longer she takes to respond, the more agitated he is getting.

The two are also on a never-ending roller coaster. He is her hardest trainer, a big reason she has become a robot. He is also her biggest advocate behind the scenes. Although he would never admit it, he has some powerful feelings for her.

Alex is aware, as are her other brothers. Mason has been the center for so many of us. Her bonds, her power. It pulls even if we don't want it to. I wasn't kidding about her having the purple for the first two years of her life. She has been my constant partner for as long as I can remember.

But for Mason and me, it was always more flirting, teasing, really. Sure, we used to joke around, with innuendos and mental sparring, but it's all play.

However, for Riddick, he pursues nothing because he doesn't want it to be a fling. Similar to Alex, he isn't willing to risk the Elitus' repercussions for breaking the rules. He doesn't want to hide, and right now with the way she has been, he isn't getting through her armor.

"I will bring it to him if you want," I tell her, trying to make it easier for her. She doesn't avoid things, but she and Kyle—that's a sticky subject; neither of them discuss it.

If I feel pulled to her, for Kyle, it's horrendous. Tier Threes pull the hardest. It's an undeniable connection, the power, and for two X-Threes, it's got to be brutal to avoid.

"No," she says. "Do you know where he is?" Riddick stands tossing our trash. It's a group field trip.

Finding Kyle heading out of a training room, he sees us approaching. He pivots and opens up a lab room for us. He knows if all three of us are here for him, it's a mission, or bad news.

"What's up?" He asks, Riddick whips out the file and hands it to him. He opens it immediately. "Where did you get this?"

I can feel Mason tense beside me. We both know from his tone that this isn't news to him.

"Does it matter?" Riddick asks. "Clearly, this did not shock you."

"No. But the only ones who even know about this are my father and yours," he says to Mason. "And that's all hearsay at best. They know about the births, Coral's and Tara's. And that it has been in the works. But not a full data set and details." He reads through it. Mason hasn't moved; she's still processing it all. When Kyle closes the file, he looks to Mason first. A sad smile on his face.

"I am assuming you read the details of Coral's pregnancy."

"Yes," she says. I snatch it back. I didn't read about that, but more just about the children/infants themselves. Skimming it, I don't like what I see. Although she hides it well, I feel tension from Mason. When pregnant, Wights are unstable. Power fluctuations, unable to control and shield, hormonal surges, and overall unable to defend.

"Fucking hell," I pass what I am reading to Riddick, who in a rare moment, reaches over and squeezes Mason's hand. She is spiraling. But what is more concerning is what this means for her, and any future she may want. She's already target number one for Dmitri. If she ever settles down, finds someone, and decides she wants to be a mother, then she will be at risk, and Dmitri would storm the gates for her.

Shaking her head, she smiles softly at Riddick. She holds his hand a tad longer than normal, a silent thank you, which is also rare. Their roller coaster never ends.

"My father is aware?" She asks. "Yet the rest of Elitus isn't?" Kyle frowns.

"Elitus doesn't know. Probably for the same reason you brought it to us, and not them. But they had nothing concrete," he nods to the file Riddick still has in his grasp. "That's concrete. So again, where did you get it?"

"Someone emailed it to me," Mason tells him. "I tried to trace it, but it came from a burner, fully encrypted. Whether it came from inside PPG doesn't matter. It's only a matter of time before Elitus knows about it. Who knows, maybe someone sent it to them too."

"Doubtful." I add.

"It's a warning," Kyle tells us.

"Do you want to take it to your father?" I ask her. "If he already has some knowledge of it..."

"The rumor has been out there, why she was not out on missions recently, why Tara was absent. So, I'm sure Elitus is aware, or McGuire is trying to gather the data. I would like to bring it to Ames. We need to avoid anyone getting pregnant." Mason pauses, the weight of the situation in all our minds.

"Awareness won't be enough. Protection won't be enough. Not if Vanguard is real."

Kate

Mom called and asked me to come home for dinner tonight. I don't mind, especially since I know my dad was off today, which means he's cooking, or grilling anyway. My parents are opposites in so many ways, but they just work. My mother has always been super dedicated to science and Elitus. She joined right out of college and was with them almost from the beginning.

My father was a star athlete in college, a football player for a D1 school. He had a promising career, possibly even going pro. But he met my mom, and their connection was instant. Before long, he changed his ways, at least in the partying part. Before the end of his junior year, he had switched majors to kinesiology and changed his future career plans.

Rumor has it my grandfather, his dad was pissed. Ran his home like a drill sergeant, and made sure Dad was dedicated to his physical fitness and always had to be the best. I've never met them. They passed when I was little, but my dad had a falling out with them over it. He told me once that he would always support me regardless of what choices I made. And he always has. He hates my being in combat, but he won't stop me.

Dad also hates all the bullshit from McGuire, as he points out to my mother often. He has made it his mission to make digs at McGuire whenever he can, even to his face. My dad is no slouch. He is the physical education coordinator and also works hand in hand with Calvin on the physical regiment for Wights. He designed the program that gets us ready to actually fight. He also keeps a second home at the gym. His best students, who are just as dedicated to gym days as he is, include his proteges Alex, Riddick, and Roarke. My dad's favorite pastime? Boxing and MMA. And he takes on Wights, regularly. Marty called him a DILF once, and I threatened to kill her if I heard that term again.

But my mom, she's always been smitten. She may keep secrets, but when she comes home, she drops the Elitus title, no work talk at home. That has been her steady rule. At least outside of her home office.

Finding my dad in the backyard when I enter, I notice it is indeed grill time.

"Hey beautiful," he says, kissing my cheek as I check out what's for dinner. "Mom will be home shortly. I have wine chilling in the fridge for you."

"Did I ever tell you that you're my favorite?" He smirks as I head into the kitchen. Noting a salad already made, some sides in the oven, and my wine chilling. I grab a glass, corkscrew and a fresh beer for him and head out.

On the back patio of our parent's house, it's all open fields. We are next door to Mason's mom and dad. In between The Clarkes and James. It was always fun because they used our backyard as a gateway to the two, since they were all raised together. Before long, my mom comes out with her own glass and pours herself some wine, kissing my dad and squeezing my shoulder as she sits across from me.

"Do you want to eat out here?" I ask them.

"If you'd like. Probably 10 minutes for the steak," Dad tells us.

"How was work?"

"Good," she says, but her tone doesn't express that. I hate seeing her tense, but I know it happens. Since she won't talk about it, we don't push.

After a delicious meal and lots of laughs, I join my mom in her office. She rarely approaches me about work, but I can tell that her request was more than just missing me at the dinner table. Seated across from her, I take a moment to appreciate the room. The walls of her office are painted a light mauve gray, with gleaming oak bookcases that even have a fancy little ladder. Her desk is a huge oak monstrosity that is always covered with papers, texts, journals and more.

On her desk though, there are always family pictures. The most recent one from my graduation last year of all of us, smiling, happy. She has a couple of us much younger. Back when Ryker and Jasper were little pipsqueaks driving me crazy and not trying to tell me what to do.

I pick one up; this one is of my parents. From the early days, before I was born. They look beautiful together, all blond and carefree. My father isn't looking at the camera; he's looking at her, and the longing on his face, the utter dedication. It makes me sigh. That's the fairy-tale shot right there. It's why I think I won't settle for anything but that in my life. I've seen the love, dedication, and respect the two of them carry for each other, and I want that. I need that in any future person in my life.

After rummaging through her bag, my mom comes around with a small item in her hand. She sits down next to me and places it on the edge of her desk. It's a small packet of pills. 28 of them. I look at it, then at her.

I blink at the pills. My mom's never brought this up before. "You're putting me on birth control?" The dating ban has made it so I can't approach any techs about it, and my mother would want to know why or who I needed it for.

"Yes," she says quietly, but sure of what she is saying. She doesn't seem happy about it. "I can't tell you much. Most of Elitus doesn't even know, but I got some information today that has me alarmed. And until I can get it out there, I want you safe."

"Safe? Mom, I am not hooking up with anyone."

"Not yet," she tells me. "But it won't be long until someone breaks the rules on campus, or maybe you meet someone, and you experiment. Regardless, I don't want you to be pregnant. Not until you are sure that's what you want, and you know the risks."

Risks? What the hell. "Mom?" She shakes her head.

"Pregnant wights are unstable, power and shield wise. And for you, with your empathy already an issue, I know you have become good at shielding Kate, but this is such an unknown, and until I have my own data sets, I just want you to be careful, and if this is all I can do to protect you right now, I will."

"Is someone pregnant?"

"Not in Elitus, or not that I know of."

It clicks. Holy Shit. It's a rumor, but no proof. The rumor mill says that the PPG has been experimenting. Namely, that Coral, their only X, was expecting or had a baby. With Nikolai. And her sister, Tara, and possibly some others. Dmitri has moved on from trying to amp up soldiers and now is just creating them.

"If Elitus doesn't know, or doesn't have this data, where did you get it?" She is quiet. There are only two people that I know who make it their mission to break into Elitus data files and know what's going on; Bastian and Mason. And both hate secrets. So, whatever they've found, if they took it to my mother only, that's a problem. "Just you?"

"No, Robert and Ross are aware. They had an inkling, but nowhere near the detail of the data I saw today. Kate, you can't say anything. We have a couple of days to figure it out before I bring it to Elitus, and even after that, I don't know if it'll get brought out to the Wights. But if you know of your friends who are breaking the rules, then please discreetly let me know. It's always better to be safe than sorry." I nod because what am I supposed to say to that? I don't know of anyone who is having sex—well, not female wights anyway. But then again, outside the combat wights, and those that are top trainers, high powers, I interact little with them. "I will set it up, so I can get these to you in ninety day prescription, but keep them in your room. When you get your next period—"

"I'm aware of how they work, Mom," I tell her. "I looked it up just as a precaution. But trust me, I have no one in my sights right now, but yes, I will start taking them. Thank you."

"You are welcome, Kate, no matter what, your safety matters to me. I know it may not seem like it, since I too often have to quote the Elitus lines. But I would never put you at risk. And I am always trying to do what's best for all Wights, not just my children," with a squeeze of my hand, she stands. Her office faces James' side, and I see Jonah out mowing the lawn. It's weird how we can be so different, and yet so normal too.

"I'm going to say goodbye to Dad and then head back to the dorms. I have some stuff to finish up, including graduation plans for Gen Two." Hugging her, she follows me out as I say my goodbyes.

Back at the dorms, my eyes keep drifting back to the pack of pills next to my bed. What it represents. I really wish I had whatever data she got to make her want me to go on birth control. She said Coral was unstable, but what does that mean? I hate the unknown, and I hate the lack of control. She wouldn't share the info, and odds are, knowing Elitus, they won't either. They'll underhand it or something along those lines.

Fed up with being aggravated, I seek the one person who hates secrets, and if she isn't already, she needs to be aware.

Descending to the female floor, I knock lightly on Mason's door. She answers, her hair wet from the shower. She looks at me questioningly. Seeking her out in the dorms, gets her on edge. Then she glances at what's in my hand and opens her door wide.

"So, you are aware?" I ask. She looks at me. Debating how much to tell me. I understand that a little, but she doesn't enjoy keeping secrets, so why is she keeping this one?

"Because if all of Elitus knows, then we become vessels instead of weapons." We take a seat on her couch, but I ponder what she just insinuated. No, they wouldn't. Who am I kidding? McGuire would in a heartbeat. But our parents? "What did your mom tell you?"

"Not much, just that I am at risk, pregnant. She mentioned briefly, didn't confirm, and basically just said to tell her if I suspect anyone is at risk, i.e. hooking up. She said that they haven't brought it to Elitus yet, and that they will decide who needs to know."

"Which will be none of us," Mason mutters. "I was the one who brought it to your mom. So, I know what's in the files. Kate, why come to me?"

"For answers, I was hedging my bets that either you or Bastian figured it out. But also because if you aren't aware, you need to be. If I am at risk, as a mostly sidelined combat female, you, Charley, mainline defenders. You need to know."

"I already took care of Charley and Mya, don't worry. They don't know why, but still. Your mom agreed to figure out a way for the rest, even if they don't tell them the real reason," she looks away from me. Lost in her own head, whatever is in those files is messing with her. I reach across and grasp her hand. She gives me a sad smile.

"Our parents, as much as they may push us, and allowed all the training, my mother would never allow us to be used for that purpose."

"Isn't that what she was? My mother, all of them. We had parents on Elitus, but how many trial moms left after they had their babies? Just handed them over? How many parents don't even know what their children are?" I can't help but think about that. It's not discussed. Most who are in the program live at home. But there are several who have been raised without biological parents. Raised in almost a foster-type of situation. They were loved, and all had the same opportunities as other wights, but still.

"It won't be the same," I tell her. "Mason, I don't know about your mom, but my mom wanted this. She wanted a child. If I were latent, or not powerful, she would love me just the same. Using X was different. Now granted, if we were born with defects, and all the trials stopped, things would have been different. Yes. But she still would love me. As would Maria, I am sure."

"I don't know. I guess it's my own issues, never mind the risk. Kate, those files, if what's in there is true. Pregnant, unstable power, huge swings in power levels, shields are all over. Dropping and raising up, with no stable control over them. Heavy Two support was needed for Coral. Tara was similar. They have data on latent pairings, etc. They were lab rats, numbers, not names. And the children? The ones that don't appear as powerful. Defective." Her voice gets rougher, the agitation bleeding through her words. Her entire demeanor is adjusting to what she is feeling. I can feel the anger, but what lies underneath, the genuine problem. The fear.

"It's all new data, right?" I try to hedge. "A couple of samples doesn't make it fact; we can speculate all we want. Mason, unless things have changed that I am not aware of, you and I are both a while off from even considering motherhood. And knowing our parents, they are going to examine the crap out of whatever info you gave them. Will they want to test it out? Sure. But unless they plan on dropping the dating ban sometime soon, then they would pollute the genetic pool they have worked so hard to perfect," we both smile at that one. "Besides, we can't do anything about it. Other than taking these pills, and giving Elitus time, and the PPG time to get more data. Maybe they can counteract it. Maybe some type of bond or enhancement of hormones can offset any instability."

"I know. And no, nothing has changed. I am still dedicated to McGuire, with no plans to have any children. But someday," she says wistfully. She has an enormous family that spreads across Elitus. She grew up in a loud, loving household. I am not surprised that she has thought about having children. Then again, she has been nothing but a weapon for such a long while.

"Is there anything I can do to help?" I ask her. She shakes her head, standing.

"No, not really. Do you want access? I can get it for you."

"Will it help me understand anything or just freak me out more?"

"It'll probably piss you off," she tells me, and I smile. "Up to you."

"I'm good for now, but if you think I need more info later, please."

"You know I wouldn't put you at risk," she whispers.

"I know that, Mase," I say, touching her arm lightly. Her power radiates up my arm. She is always a live wire. "Thank you for bringing it to my mother and trying to help everyone. We don't deserve your loyalty and devotion."

"Yes, you do," She smiles softly. Mason has never had it easy. I was always fair to her, but many were not. She was pushed harder than anyone else. Granted, she was the strongest, and everyone knew it, but still. Her power and her dedication to her fellow wights, is what make her the leader that she is. She puts everyone above herself. "I mean it; let me know if you need help with anything." I head toward her door.

"Kate," I turn back to look at her. "Thank you for looking out for me. You didn't have to tell me or come to me. But you chose to. It may have been to get the scoop, but the other part, the part that makes you who you are, cares just as much as I do. Otherwise, you wouldn't go to such lengths for the balls and events."

"That's all trivial, just optics."

"No, it's not. Maybe on the surface, but the time you put in, the dedication. It's appreciated, sometimes to the point I think you need to make some of these other idiots do it, so they understand. But I know you take on a lot to make our lives a little more normal. And I appreciate it."

I am speechless. What she is saying, it's not necessarily news to me. But to have her admit it. It means more than I can even explain. I nod my head and open her door.

"Get some sleep." We both smile at each other as I shut the door behind me. I stand for a minute, trying to get my bearings. Her words follow me out the door, heavier than the pills in my hand.

NINE

Kate

Elitus didn't admit that there were pregnant Wights at PPG. Instead, they dragged in all combat females and pushed birth control—sold as a 'health option'.

The rumor mill lit up, especially once Coral and Tara were confirmed to be mommies. It didn't take long for people to speculate about the dating ban.

McGuire shut it down fast; dating was still off-limits.

Wights, as mission-operatives need to be focused. Relationships, especially romantic ones, create additional drama and distractions.

I am all for being focused, but miserable; that wasn't what I wanted. And right about now, that's how I feel.

Wyatt and I are in the corner of my office. Or this closet-size room that I commandeered for myself. The AC is running nonstop, trying to combat the heat and humidity which hasn't stopped. Indian summer my ass. Wyatt is lounging in the chair across from me, half paying attention.

He's my best friend, but I am not blind. Wyatt is different. He looks so well put together, so confident. Smart, too smart, but he has the sexy/cool professor look. Although he refuses to do combat and missions, he is still a powerhouse in Ones.

He looks relaxed. Sleeves rolled up to show lean forearms, hair longer than usual. He hits the gym with my dad daily. Me? I avoid it except for cardio.

He's reading some business newspapers and ignoring what I asked him to do here.

"Wyatt" he doesn't look until I flick a pen at him.

I arch a brow at him. "Are you going to help me? Or are you just here to avoid work?"

"I thought this was work?"

"For me, maybe." He sighs, finally sitting up to take some papers. I smile. "Dinner or ball?" I ask regarding the finalization of Gen Two graduation events.

"Dinner," he blurts.

"Really?" I ask. Wyatt has been my date for all the balls since forever.

"Yes, because I know you. You'll over-plan it, perfect every detail. Gen Two won't even care. It'll be a production that will take up way too much of your time, and thus mine. Besides, they'd rather have a party."

"A dorm party or social event?"

He gives me a look. "Bastian will want a party."

I groan. Of course, he would bring him up. "Since when do I care what Bastian wants?"

"You've been avoiding him," he tells me. Thank you, Captain Obvious.

"So?"

"Look," he says in a rare serious tone. "You don't have to admit anything, Kate. But at least admit he's more than a pain in your ass." I give him a look, my Frosted Queen look. Wyatt shakes his head, amused and bewildered.

"Fine," I say. "I'll admit he is the reason we have so many successful trainees lately. He and Mason both. But it doesn't mean the self-proclaimed Mental God is anything more to me than a strong combat partner."

"Uh-huh," Wyatt mutters, already smug. I glare at him, but my stomach betrays me with a knot I can't explain. Damn Bastian.

Bastian

"Are you trying to piss me off?" Mason mutters as she shoots me a glare.

I smile, not even trying to pretend I am innocent. I am on the bench to the side, arms stretched across the backrest. Chilling.

"No, I am just done with this day already," I tell her. She sighs, we have been working with these kids, Gen Fours and Fives, for like three hours now.

"I would've invited Siobhan if I'd known it would just be me working..." she mutters. Who is she kidding? She's still a machine and doesn't need me.

Nine months ago, she wouldn't have even been involved in this training. Would've left it up to Jasper or Reese. Now, she makes it her personal mission to work with every one of them. I get it; she is making an impact, but still. I get up and call a kid over. Most of the ones here are all minor players, without a lot of power. But they still need defenses, and even if they are never in combat, Elitus will find some way to incorporate them in labs or on the campus.

Normally, Ryker, Jasper, Nala, and Reese handle this. But they're at some training enhancement briefing, and Calvin dumped the lesson on us.

Correction: her.

She wrote it. Asked for help, and I just... showed up.

With a smirk and zero intent to contribute.

When the last of them clears out, Mason strides back over, flicking her wrist to summon some water bottles. She tosses one to me without asking, the cap already unscrewed.

"Cheers," I say, clinking mine against hers.

She finally exhales, pulling her braid over one shoulder. She's still wound tight—too tight—but there's a shift when it's just us. Her posture softens.

"You want to play?" I ask, draining half the bottle and tossing it aside as I stand.

She raises an eyebrow, unimpressed.

"Get your mind out of the gutter," I grin, stretching my arms overhead. "Combat SIM. Unless you're scared, I might win this time."

"Oh please," she says, already stripping down into a sports bra and leggings. I admire the view. I'm not blind. But Mason and me. We work. We are partners, and although we have lots of innuendo and flirting, neither of us is serious. After all, the two of us together would cause heads to turn. Never mind; it's a dangerous combination.

"Load up the SIM for us," I tell the techs.

Mason loosens up, eyeing me. Already planning how to attack. I smirk; she doesn't intimidate me.

The SIM boots up, and we are in a different scenario. Looks like the techs want to challenge us. Or challenge me. This will require some focus. Although an X-Two, I have no real power abilities outside of mental warfare.

"You want full shielding?"

"You need it?" She counters with an eyebrow raised. I laugh.

"Nope." I don't wait; I lash out hard. She is ready, though.

We have done so many missions together over the years; we know each other's moves. But Mason, she's been working harder, and I am certain she's got some new tricks she hasn't shared.

I feel her brush up against my shields. It's different from what I usually get from her. She is testing me.

"Don't hold back," I tell her.

She smirks, the spark in her eyes lighting up. "I wouldn't want to make this easy for you," I laugh. And we tangle. Hard and fast—we push power at each other, trying to cripple the other. She comes at me physically too, not with power, but good old-fashioned fighting moves.

She feints left; I dodge right. We are playing more than anything else. The SIM fades into the background noise. What matters is the way we move together again—the light in her eyes tells me she's missed this, even if she'll never admit it.

When we are done, both of us spent, she summons more water. We sit on the bench, side by side.

"You missed this," she mumbles.

"Yeah," I admit, no smirk this time. "I missed you like this," I look at her. It's been a long time since I have felt this. "I missed Us."

She nods. And then reality comes back in, heavier than the sweat clinging to us. She may have been a little more herself since she received the file on Vanguard and the PPG children. She may be McGuire's best weapon, but her head isn't in it as much as it used to be. Especially given the amount of BS she has been taking from Kyle, Mya, and Riddick. They have been working hard to break through her outer shell and get her back to us.

As much as I enjoyed today—the sparring, the glimpses of old Mason back—I know this won't last. I can already feel her pulling up her shield cover. Her blanket of armor, she wraps around herself. But right now, we're synced. And if that's the best I can get. I'll take it.

TEN

Bastian

With graduation looming, I feel it under my skin.

That itch; the one that tells me no matter how much I resist, everything is about to shift.

Not just the usual post-graduation realignment. But Everything. The way we operate, the way we train, the way we move in formation. The way we lead.

I've been the unofficial trainer for years now—teaching shields, layering, tactical breakpoints, and pulling kids back from mental collapses they didn't see coming. But now?

Now it's going to be official: the medallion, the title, the weight of it, and the expectation that comes with being an X-Two and holding the system in place.

Kyle and I have been working late hours on restructuring the combat rotations. Adjustments to response teams, reinforcing Tier assignments, attempting to streamline our emergency command.

Once the medallions are placed, there'll be three Xs on the combat roster: Kyle's X-Three, my X-Two, and Riddick's X-One Spectrum.

Three of us expected to carry the next generation forward while Elitus smiles and pretends they saw it coming. But the truth? It's Mason who leads.

She's still a year and a half out from graduation, but none of that matters. She's already surpassed most of us—strategically, mentally, physically. Focused in a way that's almost clinical now. All mission and structure, no hesitation.

She's out-pacing the rest of us, and it's not even a close competition.

We wrap for the day, Kyle and I slipping out of the labs, exhaustion nipping at the backs of our necks, both of us too tired to pretend we're not running on fumes.

We make it three feet before Andy's voice calls out behind us. "Hey!"

She jogs to catch up, waving with more energy than she should legally have after a twelve-hour day. "Got a second?"

I glance at Kyle. He shrugs. "Sure," I say, distracted. "What's up?"

Truth is, I've been checked out for hours; half my brain stuck running diagnostics on Mya's latest shield form, the other half caught in a loop about Kate's avoidance and Mason's continued success as Elitus' premier weapon.

She may have lightened up some, but she's still a damn robot.

A hyper-functional, mission-obsessed, emotionally unavailable robot. Mya's words, not mine, though I'm not disagreeing.

Mya's been struggling more than she'll admit; Siobhan has been heavy-duty training. Roarke is still a mess, avoiding everyone now. And Kate is so focused on planning graduation, you'd think the President was attending.

"What do you say?" Andy asks again, bright and expectant.

I blink. Shit, I missed that one completely.

Kyle is already smirking, that infuriating look that says, you're not getting out of this.

He smiles at her and gives what we just agreed to a go. "Of course. But you'll have to loop in Roarke."

Andy beams and bounces off like she just won the lottery.

I turn to Kyle. "What the hell did we just agree to?"

"Chaperoning," he says, far too amused. "Andy and Mason want escorts for an off-campus shopping trip. Graduation outfits."

I blink. "Shopping?"

"Mason's idea."

And suddenly, I'm listening again. If it gets her off campus—even for a few hours—fine. I'll carry her bags, be her mental shield, and hopefully get her to relax, eat an actual meal, and maybe be the old Mason.

In class, I reach out to her mentally. We are always available to each other.

So, where to this weekend?

Italy. With you and Kyle on board, we can go broader. Might have to deal with the time zone issues, though. You game?

Absolutely. Did you read what I sent you?

I shift in my seat, half-smiling. I might be shamelessly flirting. This line we toe—it's a game. One neither of us fully commits to, but neither of us walks away from either.

Push. Pull. Tease. Repeat. It keeps her connected to me sometimes in the only way I can anymore. I know she's just a distraction to me. Other times, I wonder if she's the only person in this place who truly understands me.

Yes, you pervert. I did. I'm surprised you have that kind of material, Bastian. Far too mature for your age bracket. It said PG-13 on the cover.

Did it give you any ideas?

Not as many as the porn I sent you this morning.

I blink, my eyebrows raising.

What the fuck? Across the room, she doesn't even look at me. Just smirks.

I check my inbox. Nothing. I shoot her a look; she winks.

Then she turns back to the instructor like she's been paying attention to the Civil War lecture the whole time. I wait until Kate makes one of her overly polished points—something about Union supply lines and sociopolitical impact—just so I can argue with her on principle.

If I can't get Kate's attention in the old-fashioned way, I'll piss her off instead.

At least then, she'll look at me, talk to me.

The weekend comes fast, and the shopping trip abroad. Although I'm not sure if this is a shopping trip or a double date.

Kyle's pretending it's casual, but I know better. He's not slick, no matter how much swagger he piles on. Mason's ignoring him as usual.

Years ago, those two were two peas in a pod; very much like how Roarke and Mya were. But something happened right about the time missions started up. They grew apart. Not to the point of pain like Mya, but to it being obvious things shifted. I know it was Kyle's doing. He would never talk about it. But Mason hasn't forgotten or forgiven him for stepping away.

Kyle isn't even bothering to get her attention today; instead, it's all aimed at Andy. Can't say I blame him. Andy is beautiful, and she likes attention, even though she is half in love with a different Gen One. And Kyle likes the chase, especially if they are off-limits.

Mason, though—she's a different game altogether.

For the last week or so, she's been very attentive toward me; working more, more mental play. I don't waste the opportunity.

Andy and Kyle go off for some cappuccino. Mason and I stop for gelato; she's relaxed, talking, laughing. It is outstanding to watch the real her; not McGuire's soldier, not the one who tries to handle everything, not the robot Riddick has allowed her to become.

The one I miss; my friend, my Two partner.

"You want to tell me why you invited me?"

"Andy invited you actually, not me," she says, smirking. "Bastian, you think I don't want you here?"

I laugh, "I think you've been playing with me more than usual."

I brush my fingers along her arm slowly, seductively. "Since when don't you like to play?" She asks with an arched eyebrow. Damn her.

She knows exactly what she is doing. This fun side makes me miss her so goddamn much. I hate the thought that when we head back, she may turn right back into an unfeeling machine that I no longer recognize as my friend.

Mason and my relationship has always been complicated. She was the first one I could connect to mentally. Ever since we were young. Her mom would let me spend time with her at the daycare. We connected then, and it only grew with time. She is the only one who gets the drama that floats around inside a Two's head. She is the one who taught me as much as I taught her. The two of us designed half of what we teach. More her, than me, I just took what she knew and implemented. Tier Two training, mental shields, combat maneuvers. It's all hers. I enhance it and add my twist, weaponized it. But Mason, she is the brains behind it.

I question nothing she gives me. She has never been mistaken.

She offers me a lick from her spoon. I don't pass on it, and she watches me. She's playing with fire, and she doesn't care.

But Mason and I, we aren't a couple. Too much power between us, too much alike. But on the outside, we look good together. And the connection between us, the power we create, could light a city on fire.

All tension, passion and determination.

It might help that X-Twos are rumored to be the best kind of lover. We can do seduction like no one else. Mental powers extend well beyond just reading someone's mind. Pushing their limits, impacting hormones, wants, needs. To prove my point, I flex a bit. In the right mental direction, a pulse of power meant to provoke a reaction. She blocks me easily, immediately. Practiced and precise.

"Bastian, don't play like that..." She chides, licking her spoon in a slow, tantalizing way. "You know you'll lose."

"Yes, you and your damn armor. Making me feel like an amateur lately."

"Hmmm," she says. A flicker of interest in her eyes.

"I enjoy playing Mase, especially with you. After all, there is no one left to challenge me."

She smiles and gets up to toss her empty cup. "Time to head back," she says, extending a hand to me. I don't miss the look she gives me, one full of friendship, and connection. One I've missed so damn bad.

I certainly don't want to miss the opportunity.

Back at the dorms, the night hasn't ended. For once, she is being social. Andy and Kyle are on the back deck with us. The air feels tight, though, like something is brewing.

I watch Kyle and Andy. Mason is watching as well. I know what this is; it's a distraction for both of them. It's a game Kyle should know better than to play.

It's reckless. But I am happy Mason is still here.

I had a good time today, Bastian.

I did too. Your dress looked good on the hanger—but even better on you.

You're such a cad. Want to grab a drink?

Minus them? Absolutely.

We head inside, and she's flirting back without hesitation. It's a break. A moment; a pause from the war zone of duty and leadership.

To others, we look like a couple. And even if I wanted to, even if she wanted me like that, I wouldn't go there. Because crossing that line with Mason? That's not just messing around. That's serious. We may care, we may flirt, but going there, it won't happen.

She's got armor on the outside, but it's protecting her core. I would ruin her without even trying.

Then, as if someone else is trying to ruin everything, Alex walks in. Checking on Mason, but his expression is tight. He was concerned but knew she had escorts. He is doing his usual big-brother routine.

However, when he does his normal room sweep, he glances toward the balcony. The moment he spots Andy with Kyle outside, well, that's the end of a good night.

Before any of us can react, he storms outside and punches Kyle. A hit meant to knock his head off.

Andy hollers at him, Kyle is arguing. Mason tries to intervene. Alex goes to connect again, out of control completely. But this time, Mason steps in between the two Gen Ones.

Fucking hell.

The blow clips her side, sending her staggering back, bleeding.

It's like everything stops for a second. Then it is chaos.

I lunge forward just as Roarke arrives. We work on her, healing, our energy pushing in.

Andy's yelling. Kyle's fuming. And Alex?

Alex looks like he just had an out-of-body experience.

Mason's already trying to wave me off. But more people are pouring outside to see the commotion. This is the most action we have had in forever. I hate the spectacle.

"Bailey, get me out of here," she mutters, trying to sit up. Speaking to Reese's brother. Her voice is rough. Controlled. She wants him to take her to Reese rather than the infirmary. Trying to avoid reports and to protect Alex, Bailey scoops her up; she doesn't protest. She'll be fine; she always is.

But I hate this. I hate that she got hurt.

I hate it happened in my presence.

And I hate that she's the one asking me to take care of Kyle.

Kyle's unraveling fast. I need to get his shit cleared, or else this will escalate quickly.

Kyle's pacing, spitting fire. He isn't even mad at Alex about the punch; he's more pissed about Mason getting caught in the middle. I know him. He's worried about Mason and feels like he caused her to get hurt.

Which is totally ridiculous. Kyle's a shitty Two, so I can read him. He isn't even thinking about Andy. He's mad about Mason's attention toward me today. If I didn't have this drama going on, I'd laugh.

He's still pacing; Alex is a mess. Andy had already left to follow Bailey to check on Mason. It's getting a little more controlled, then Riddick hits the back patio.

He doesn't hesitate; he bypasses Alex and heads straight to Kyle—and clocks him.

Harder than Alex just did.

"You fucking need to learn when to leave well enough alone, Ross."

Kyle stumbles, blood on his lip, eyes blazing. "*Me?* Fuck you, Riddick. I'm not the one who just gutted my sister."

Kyle ports out. Good.

Now I can unleash on this asshat who made Mason into the robot she is.

I spent all day trying to bring her back. Trying to give her space to breathe, to be back to normal. Have fun Mason, come back and stay.

And the principal person who pushed her into that military-grade machine thinks he can play big brother now? Fuck that. I step forward, my jaw clenched, my voice low and sharp. "You know what, Riddick? For a guy who thinks he knows everything, you're dumb as shit." He eyes me. "Maybe if you weren't such a dick to Mason all the time, she wouldn't need all that armor. Do you think pushing her is helping? You're turning her into a fucking robot. You want to protect her? Try listening instead of treating her like she's a goddamn soldier first and a person second."

Silence is its own weapon. But he knows I'm right. He won't admit it; or if he can, he doesn't know how to get her to back down. What might have started as something small has morphed into a transplant from friend to commander.

We all hate it.

He shakes his head and storms off. I hit the bar, grab a bottle and head to my room. I check in with Bailey and then wait for Mason to return. And wait for the inevitable fallout.

Kate

My night had been peaceful, quiet even. A rarity for me. I can focus on smaller things. I read a little for fun even, a special treat, but with the graduation planning done, I gave myself a day before I started working on the ball.

But then I felt it. Not just felt it but heard it. An impact, a scream, yells out back. What the hell?

I move quickly off my bed, change out of PJs and into something presentable, and head down. I am never casual outside my room or my parents' house. It's my version of armor.

By the time I made it down to the common area, I had missed most of the major drama. But that doesn't mean I don't understand the issue.

Siobhan fills me in. "Alex lost it." She summarizes Kyle flirting, hands on Andy, being his normal tomcat self. Then Alex saw it, and he lost his ever-loving mind. Alex has had feelings for Andy for years, but Elitus has always banned relationships. Alex, like me, will never step out of line. We are Elitus' perfect children.

Kyle isn't interested in Andy. He flirts as if it is a power all its own. He smiles at all the girls, giving that panty-melting grin, dimples and all. But he is also McGuire's favorite son. A kiss-ass, who plays the politics game better than anyone. The perfect Wight; McGuire's favorite weapon before Mason took his title.

If he put the moves on Andy, then he stepped over a line in full view of the dorms. That makes it a big problem. Elitus will react.

But that's not what makes me worry. It's what else happened.

Mason stepped in between a battling Kyle and Alex. Alex, who is a living weapon, whose skin can turn to metal, including a blade. He was so out of control; he was fully armored and weaponized, prepared to cut into Kyle, literally. Only it wasn't Kyle he hurt. It was Mason.

"She was with them all day," Siobhan says casually. That gets my attention. Then Charley's voice slides in, "Her and Bastian. Bastian looked super pissed. Guess that ruined their date."

I freeze. My mind blanks, Bastian, on a date, with Mason. Now I feel like I'm the one who got skewered.

I should've seen all the signs. After all, they look good together. She matches him in power, and both are dangerously beautiful.

I work to get myself under control before my mind can wander anymore. I try to hide away the hurt, not let it show. Keep it together.

"They went shopping," Charley tells me. She looks concerned about Mason, about Alex, and about her brother Kyle. About what will happen when Elitus finds out, because they always do.

Not just about Kyle and Andy, and Kyle making a move.

But because of Alex's reaction.

This is exactly why Elitus banned relationships. They drilled into our heads that love, connections, relationships only complicate things. That we are soldiers, a team, a unit. But that's it.

No romantic entanglements. Or anything that could make us question our loyalty to Elitus and the mission.

Relationships, intimacy, would be a distraction, a weakness, causing us to lose focus.

And unfortunately, Alex proved them right tonight. His feelings for Andy overrode his control and judgment.

I take a deep breath; part of me believes their logic. I like rules and structure; I understand all about distractions and focus. But I also yearn for more; a connection. Something to make all this worthwhile, a future outside of missions and lab work.

I have to be more than Elitus' social planner, the Gen One Queen.

If this is all I have to look forward to out of life, then am I living?

Or am I just a robot too?

ELEVEN

Kate

The morning kicks off as it normally does for me. Some quick workout using my walking pad while I catch up on emails, then some yoga, shower, perfect outfit, down to matching jewelry and bag.

Then I head to my office. Where I plan a day of meetings and follow-up. All structured. All routine. My mid-morning coffee update with McGuire's admin, along with a quick pop into my mother's office. By lunchtime, I had done most of what I needed to do.

Gen Two graduation is fast approaching as fall encroaches outside. But before long, my phone goes off. A text from Alex, asking me to report to the Elitus chambers.

That makes me pause. We are on opposite committees. He's deep in contracts and mission details. He never asks me to help with work-related topics. I rarely come to Elitus meetings unless it's related to a function I am coordinating.

I can't help but let my anxiety spike.

When I walk into the room, it is obvious something is up.

Gen One Wights are all present—Alex, Wyatt, and Kyle. And all the Elitus are there as well. Guess they found out about the night before.

Wyatt's the first to reach me, gently touching my wrist, reassuring me. A silent acknowledgment, anchoring me. Letting me know everything is okay.

Then Alex talks, and everything shifts.

A change; our world is adapting. Elitus is giving us some control; they are allowing us to make some decisions about our future. And it takes every ounce of my willpower not to cry.

Not because of the work that'll come with it; but the relief.

That someone is finally making them see we need more purpose, more interaction than just being weapons and mission operatives, lab rats.

I don't know how he got it done, and I don't really care either.

Alex breaks it down. What Elitus wants, actual integration; Elitus representation, and a plan for future generations. Not just assets or soldiers; but leaders. A true future.

I look around. Some of Elitus looks relieved; McGuire doesn't look happy, but he also isn't protesting.

And like that, I shift gears. I put aside all the thoughts running in my head, and go straight into what my brothers still call, Katie-Did mode. The strategical genius. The leader and dictator, organized with a tablet, binder and an agenda.

Before we even break off, I am envisioning what this will look like. The oversight, the committees, the rules. It isn't long until we are in our own conference area, and the invisible power I have—that of being the maniac organizer—comes out. Of course, my three Gen One peers let me do it.

And for once, this is something I am even more passionate about. This isn't a fun gala or event. This is something that has the potential to change everything for everyone.

Four hours later, I've built the framework. Not because it's complicated, but because I'm the only one doing the actual work.

Wyatt and Kyle summoned a chessboard a while ago. They are completely useless; Alex at least pretends to be helpful. He's pacing, trying to look invested, but I can tell—he's tired. This wasn't easy for him. He moved mountains to make this happen, and now that the dust has settled, he's not sure what to do next.

Fine. That's what I'm here for. "So, it looks like we can organize four primary groups—one for general housing and residential, one for social and community events, one for academics, and one for training." I tell them. "Yes?" I press.

They all nod in agreement. I shake my head at them. "Great. I'll oversee everything, but I need each of you to lead a section. Alex, I'll be nice and take social events one. Obviously, Wyatt gets academics, and Kyle takes training—which leaves you with residential."

"We can call a meeting tomorrow," I let them know.

"Tonight."

"Tonight?" I check my watch.

"Tonight," Alex repeats. "I'm not waiting. We can at least introduce the idea and give everyone advance notice. Then you can figure out how people will apply to or join committees. It also gives them time to think about it. I know it adds more to Gen Two's plate with graduation coming, but at least it gives them options."

He's right. Damn him.

This is a chance for the Gen Twos to step into something more than just a title. Something tangible. A future. With graduation around the corner, we can offer them more than medals and missions.

We can give them a future.

"I don't care either way," Kyle says, stretching. "I just want to ensure we get a say in who joins these committees. I'm not letting some idiot redesign training if they're not combat-enabled."

"I've got some ideas," Alex tells him. "I'll work it out with Calvin and a few others."

"Okay, well—since you want it tonight, you can coordinate that," I tell them, standing. "I need to change. I guess we'll hold it in the auditorium?" Alex grabs his phone, sending out details to someone to coordinate. I let him and Kyle know they can update Elitus, and step away from the table, tension finally bleeding from my spine. My mind is still moving, but there's a sliver of something else beneath the efficiency.

Relief.

This is real.

This is happening.

We're not just weapons anymore, mission-enabled soldiers, but people. People who can have a future: connections, a life.

This is ours.

It makes me feel something I didn't expect.

Hope.

Not something they told me to feel, not a vision that Elitus has conjured up; but a chance to be real. To build something, to make an impact, to show that we are not just weapons. That all the time we have spent hasn't been for nothing.

This is our chance to build something: a legacy for future generations.

There's still a lot of work to do. But for once, I don't mind the thought of Katie-Did. I want to do this to make my mark. And even if I must drag them all with me through the planning, I will. There is no going back. It's time for it all to change.

Bastian

When Alex tells me to get everyone to the auditorium, I already know it's something big.

This is it. Finally, Elitus is changing. I know what's coming. They are lifting the ban.

I am sure after last night they know it's inevitable. We are human after all, hormonal creatures, enhanced through X. What did they think would happen?

But I know this won't be easy. There will be controls and rules that go with whatever changes are happening. But whatever that means, I'm all for it.

I know McGuire. He won't give up power or control; that means there will be some backhanded shit that I will have to watch for.

And Alex? Whatever he negotiated for this, it has got to have some major backing. I send a path through the dorms, nudging anyone still dragging their feet. Pushing some into action, suggestions, alerting them of my presence, and how with one sharp push they need to get moving.

Within minutes, the auditorium is full. It's full of energy, everyone on edge. We haven't done this before. Not like this; this is new.

I can feel the room and all the different vibes—anticipation, anxiety, curiosity, suspicion, and buried beneath is Hope.

When Elitus calls a meeting, it's usually bad news. But this time it isn't Elitus. It's Alex, our default leader. Robert's son, The First Wight.

When he walks in minutes later, hand-in-hand with Andy. I laugh. He just shocked the shit out of most of them. A wave of disbelief, followed by a spike in nerves. The air shifts; it moves on its own. Others are looking at each other, trying to figure out the catch.

Many would have heard about last night, but to see this. Some glance at Kyle, who isn't showcasing anything. He's locked down.

The front row that I am sitting in is all combat enabled. Every one of us, the leaders in our fields and on missions. Alex pulls Andy down the aisle. She is nervous, but Alex, he isn't. He has a purpose in his step. He is ready for this.

He is making a statement with this scene. To push the envelope a little more, he takes it one step further. Before he can leave Andy with us in the combat row, he pulls her around and kisses her.

Not some innocent peck. A full-out, unapologetic, screw-your-rules kind of kiss. Meant to show passion and heat; it works. Before long, there are cheers and smiles all around.

It sends a wave through the room, louder than any comment could've. Andy is bright red by the time they separate. And for a beat there is a pause, Alex checking with her. Making sure she is good before he leaves her to climb the stage. Andy takes a seat between her twin and Mason.

I look down the row, checking in with everyone. Because right now. It's a shift. Not subtle; an earth-shattering, bone-deep change happening. Not just for us in combat, but for all.

It is the realization that we can be us. Human, just slightly enhanced. At this moment, this change means more than any medallion, title, or label does.

It means we can feel. We can interact. We can be free.

And with it, with this feeling of freedom; is the undercurrent of hope that is swelling amongst the crowd.

I catch Kyle's eye as he sits on stage, checking his reaction to all this. He smirks at me. That shithead.

I knew it was odd for him to flirt so hard with Andy, to make a move. But he pushed this. Pushed Alex, knew what would happen. I'm sure he didn't count on Mason being caught in the middle, which explains his going off the rails last night. He uses his visions to put options in front of people. It's still about choice, but he certainly makes moves to get what he wants. What we need. I can't fault him, though.

It's well overdue.

And whether Alex did it for love, pride or just to prove a point. It doesn't matter. Because it worked. And it's time to see what we are capable of.

"We've asked you all here for some excellent news. Elitus, after much deliberation—and some pressure from myself and others—has finally agreed it's time to plan for a future beyond just missions and science." Alex takes a moment to pause, letting it sink in. "Starting this week, we'll be forming committees in a variety of focus areas. Kate will walk through the process shortly. Also, Elitus is opening applications for six Wight members to join the Elitus board."

Board seats? Really. Wow, figurehead or real. That'll be the key. The next generation stepping into genuine power—not just mission-enabled assets, but actual leaders. Helping to run things, shape policy and rules.

Kyle steps forward next. "The details of the selection process will be released soon. It's open to all Gen Ones, Twos, and Threes." He pauses. "Kate will break down the committee groups and high-level goals. We wanted everyone here in case there were questions."

After all, Kate thrives on control and order. She'll run this with color-coded files, a project management binder, and precise weekly recaps and meetings.

But that's the thing about Kate. She makes it work.

Kyle adds, "We specifically asked Elitus not to attend. This is about building a more cohesive unit—our unit."

And then Kate steps up, PowerPoint already queued up. Someone passes out some summary papers as our phones go off with links to digital files. She's like a magician with this stuff.

I watch her; she is in her element. She's practically glowing. Poised as Elitus' perfect daughter, the Queen. Commanding the stage in a way that makes everyone listen, even when she is talking about boring shit.

Every Slide. Every Bullet point. All detailed, crisp, organized, and planned.

Her committees, her systems. Her interactions, expectations, and timelines. It is over before it starts. But she outlines it. Clear, structured, and perfect; just like Kate.

Four primary groups, each led by a Gen One.

Clear focus with guidelines for each, but more than that, it is an opportunity for everyone to have a say.

Everyone is locked in, interested, invested. And that's what this is all about.

I watch how the various generations react.

Gen Twos, the non-combat ones, look extremely interested. Many of them have been questioning what lies ahead for them.

Gen Threes, even the weaker combat ones, want a say so badly, but played second fiddle for so long to the older Gens.

Then there are the Fours. Most of them non-combat, including my triplet brothers. Lost, but now maybe they can be found.

Gen Five — it's exciting. I can already feel it. They are so young, but many of them have seen what mission-enabled and combat training looks like. They don't like it. This will give them a chance for more, even if they aren't on Elitus; most of them are our younger siblings, our friend's siblings.

The older Gens will build a better future for them without a doubt.

Alex steps forward again. "In case you missed the memo earlier," he says, a flicker of amusement in his voice, "Elitus has agreed to remove the ban on dating and social interactions."

A little brevity to lighten the load. It's all-around laughter, cheers, smiles.

"But—not without limits. This includes off-campus events and more freedom in coming and going. But all of it comes with guidelines we will help define."

Kate nods once beside him. "We'll send out a full packet with expectations and committee access. If you have questions, come to me."

She'll take the brunt of it, manage the fallout. She always does.

Mason pings me with a private path.

Orgy in the dorms tonight. You in?

She's joking. Probably.

She also lets me know she has secured alcohol for a party.

Knowing her, it's an open house for Gen Fours—meaning it'll probably be more semi-chaotic hangout than an actual orgy. Then again, we haven't partied in a long-ass time. I am sure it'll be crazy. And I can't fucking wait.

TWELVE

Kate

I am prepared to do my thing. With a fresh outfit and coffee. I sit on stage next to Kyle, waiting for Alex. When he comes in, I see he forgot to mention something. He's with Andy, together, hands intertwined, not hiding.

Andy looks like she wants to disappear, her nerves all over. She rarely minds attention, but she's half a bottle deep by then, usually.

This is different.

Alex, with the look on his face. He's determined. And now it all clicks into place. This was more than Elitus allowing us some control, allowing off-campus events. It was lifting the dating ban, allowing for relationships. I don't mean to, but my eyes flick to Bastian, who is watching Alex and Andy. I look away quickly.

Alex brings her to the seat between Mason and Roarke; but he doesn't let her sit. Instead, he kisses her. No hesitation, no permission needed. It's a fairy-tale kiss, all passion and promise.

I guess that sure sets the stage for what's coming. Smirking at us all, Alex kicks it off, Kyle follows up, then I lay it all out. Phones ping like a symphony across the room. My Gen Four sidekicks pass out the summaries and details. It's all organized and controlled, just the way I like it. I see them react; I see the realization.

What I like the most? I see them light up. They want this.

The eager look in their eyes, at not only at the changes but at the chance. Their future is not set.

Before long, we break, ready to get to it. The dorms will be chaos, I am sure. I don't drink, but I'm sure I should stop by for at least a glass of wine. I watch as our friends interact; Bastian is talking with Siobhan and Kyle. Watching him, something twists inside me. I think back to that kiss.

Alex was unapologetic about it; he didn't care. He was making a statement, a stand, declaring Andy as his. Whether it was to shove it in Kyle's face, or to make it clear she is off limits to everyone. It's the statement I long for; how he shows he is all in.

The twist in my gut tightens a little more. Now the rules have changed, and I wonder what that means for me.

Our birthdays are coming soon, although legal adults for years. Now, with all this freedom, all these changes? It leaves me feeling eager but also nervous.

Alex has always been the default leader; not afraid to stand up for what is needed, what others need.

He has been all about Andy forever; it seems. Although he kept back, didn't break the rules, he still barely looked in anyone else's direction, and he hasn't been off campus like the rest of the guys in a long time.

But that's the difference between us.

He could always seek freedom while still staying within the lines. Andy is perfect for him. She will challenge him, but she also levels him out. Grounds him. They orbit each other and provide balance.

Now that they are together. They will be even more in sync.

And me? I am still standing on the sidelines. Controlled, precise, polished, and alone.

I've spent my entire life trying to be perfect. The perfect daughter, the perfect wight. Focused on everything else, every I dotted, every T crossed. I am all about efficiency, discipline and order. Making sure I stood out to Elitus. That I was someone they could trust and depend upon. Someone who couldn't be replaced.

But at what cost? Now, what do I do? Without some rules, with more freedom? It is good for us, but it makes me uneasy. I like routine and control.

I'm not stupid; I know there will be fallout. This won't be easy. And I already know I'll be the one stuck dealing with the mess.

It'll keep me busy. Too busy to care that I am alone, to care that as the relationships form, I may be left behind. But that's okay.

Because after all, that's what I do. I organize, I direct, I fix it. I make sure it is good for everyone else to enjoy. While I sit on the sidelines watching.

The dorms are packed tonight; I watch, sipping something Wyatt handed me. Too sweet, not wine, but enough. I watch the energy shift, the change. Gen Four is here, including Aimee, who is having a grand time. I catch my brother Ryker in the corner with Lissa. They are talking, but the way they are leaning into each other.

Wow, I didn't realize. I'm so lost in my drama; did I miss this? They look good together. Mom will love her for him.

Before I can move on, I spy Mason, who climbs up on the bar top. Bottle in hand.

"Alright, assholes, listen up!" she calls, lifting her drink high. "Tonight, we celebrate! He may be modest," Mason continues, raising her glass, "but we have Alex to thank for finally growing a pair and standing up for all of us. With that being said," she adds, louder now, "congratulations to *Alex and Andy*—the first official in-house couple." Cheers and a round of applause break out. "Remember what I said. Behave. Control yourselves. And keep it in check. Gen Four, if you mess this up, it'll be your last time here. So, with that being said... To our future!"

I laugh, the sound catching me off guard. It feels good, too good. We all toast, and the energy shifts. Becoming lighter, easier.

I spot Bastian ducking out with Kyle toward the back patio. Beer pong, as usual. I try not to watch him, but I can't help myself.

"You okay?" Wyatt asks.

"I think so," I reply. "But it's a lot. All good though."

He holds up a glass of wine, way more my speed. We clink and toast. "To our future," he tells me.

"Let's try not to burn the world down," I tell him with a smile.

He throws an arm over my shoulder and leads me to the back corner. Where we sit, with a bottle of wine and people watch. It's louder than I like, but the mood, the feeling; it's worth it.

Tonight, we turned a corner. And I am proud of where we have been and where we are going.

Headed to bed, I'm more tipsy than usual. And when I hit my floor, I'm overwhelmed. Alex and Andy are down the hall. I can feel them. I try to block it out, but it's too hard. My elemental powers also blend into empathy. I feed off energy, and the energy in that room...

Shit. It's a blessing and a curse right now.

They are happy. They are connected, sharing something that is special; that's the vibe slamming into me. It makes me ache all over, not just in my body but in my heart and my mind.

It's not just them though; I can feel it.

Heading to my room quickly, I try to escape. Closing my door quietly, I sink down on my bed, my chest heavy with too many things I can't name.

I helped make this happen, helped build this moment.

And yet, it hurts. I want what others seem to be finding so easily.

I strip, hit the shower, letting the hot water distract me. It's all I can do.

Because no matter what I want. The fairy tale I've been dreaming about all my life; the happy couple vibes, like Alex and Andy have. It may not be in the cards for me.

I pretend to be polished and perfect, but I'm not.

I am a fake.

A cool polished exterior, but inside I am a mess. An emotional mess. Who uses shields, control, and perfection as cover.

Because that's what everyone expects from Elitus' Queen.

Perfection.

Bastian

As usual, Kyle and I are killing it at beer Pong. We let the Gen Four think they stand a chance; they fail miserably, of course. Even Riddick and Max take us on and lose. Then it's Mason and Charley.

Those two are our only actual competition, but Charley is a sore loser, so sometimes I think Kyle loses on purpose for her. Which is the total opposite of what Kyle normally does, since he is almost as bad as she is at losing.

Tonight, we have more of an audience than normal. Nala and her gaggle of non-combat Gen Three friends are here. They are all minor players, some healers, barely mid-level mostly. Some minor One and Three powers that don't even warrant any type of consideration for combat nor defense. They are used in the labs and in secondary work. None of them are called up unless there is an emergency. But they are all annoying as hell, half in the bag, and Kyle, being the flirt that he is, keeps playing into their attention. Gen Three and Four guys are also out here, mostly because of the girls that are here.

Mason and Charley, keep up with us. Charley gets aggravated as her brother keeps baiting her. It's amusing to watch, but more than that, I am watching Mason. She is letting loose for once, but I can also feel her shields fluctuating. Riddick comes out, after having taken a break inside, and gives her a look. She nods and then lets up the shielding. It doesn't take a rocket scientist to figure out what they are shielding down. Especially since Alex and Andy disappeared recently.

Mason may be the stronger shield, but that's her brother, Riddick is a much better choice for that kind of shielding. Chuckling, I raise my glass to Riddick. He merely nods; he will handle tonight. But we need to get some kind of plan in place for the long term for these couples. Shitty shielding will basically broadcast whatever is going on. And since most have very little experience, Mason's joke about an orgy isn't that far off.

"Kyle," Charley taunts as she gets her and Mason down to one cup. We have two left, and they both landed theirs, so odds are we lost. "You promised a rematch, shot for shot earlier, no rules." I swing my head towards Kyle. That's always a bad idea. Especially if it's a rematch. Riddick and Mason are not the ones to out-drink. I know my limits. I like to stay steadily intoxicated, not drunk and disorderly. Enough to blur out the noise, not puke my guts out or make a fool of myself.

"Are you playing?" Kyle asks her.

"Sure," Charley says. Mason laughs; we all know Charley can not handle her liquor to excess. She is a fruity-drink kind of girl; straight hard liquor of any type is not her friend.

"Okay, if you win, I'll even let you pick the liquor," Kyle tells her. She smirks and tosses her ball. Landing it easily.

"Tequila it is!" She yells. We all roll our eyes.

"You're an idiot," Mason tells her.

"Nah, it's Kyle's least favorite, so that means better odds for you," she tells her bestie. Laughing, they head inside, and line up at the bar.

"Is this open to anyone?" Riddick's younger brother Zack asks.

"If you want," Riddick laughs. "But be warned, even Jared won't play with Mason and me when we are doing shots." Zack nods his head but clearly isn't deterred.

"You playing?" I ask Roarke, who has the bottle out and is lining up shots.

"No," his eyes are still locked on De and her crowd of Gen Fours still playing cards. Mya is reigning supreme at that table. They all appear to be having a fun time, with my three idiot brothers flirting with them all. "But I will judge who needs to get cut off," Roarke mutters.

Aimee glides up next to her sister. Mason rolls her eyes. "Aimee, you will not last 5 shots."

"So? I am going back to jail tomorrow!" She shouts. Clearly already half drunk. Most of us just laugh. They miss out on a lot of this, so it's good to see them having a fun time. But there are plenty of non-drunk Gen Threes and Fours here too, simply happy to be hanging out.

"What's the damage?" Riddick asks. Referring to whatever the heavyweights will go for.

"Besides bragging rights?" Mason asks.

"What good is that?" Kyle asks. "I don't know, let's say winner vs. 2nd place for champion teams in Spring." Ouch, that would be tough.

Each spring we have a tournament of champions; it's like something out of the 80s gladiator show. Various training and simulations, weapons, and overall combat maneuvers. We usually split into teams by tiers. But last year, Mason was on her hiatus from training when we held it. So, she missed out.

She was pissed, especially since that meant Kyle kept his reign on the title of Champion.

This year, she is going to smoke all of us. It's not only about power; it's also about physical aspects and being overall well-rounded. So, besides her smaller stature, she's fast, which makes her a tough opponent. The Gauntlet, which is usually the last event, has no power. It's literally a take on Ultimate Ninja Warrior, only it's got a lot of simulation components, which makes it unpredictable, and impossible to fully train for.

"In additional to tier teams?" I ask.

"We have never done mixed teams," Charley points out. "And you guys always make the Spectrums pick and limit them. If we do mixed teams, then we should make a rule right now to allow full powers."

"You trying to kill someone?" Wyatt asks, joining us. I should avoid it, but I don't. I check to see if she is still here. Kate and Wyatt are usually attached at the hip, and I saw her here earlier, longer than she usually stays for these things. Feeling out, because I am a glutton for punishment, I feel her heading upstairs. Ignoring the disappointment, I focus on the conversation, which has turned into a debate on what would be fair.

"Compromise," I tell them. "We can do mixed teams, but we can also do individual competition, which we haven't done in years. That way when Mason smokes us, we can at least win something." Mason smiles at me. Kyle scoffs, clearly unable to give up his title.

"Sounds good to me," Mason says with a wink at me. Riddick laughs. Kyle looks between the two of them.

"Fine, but we do dodgeball-style team picking, one then the other."

"Yes!" Aimee exclaims. "And each team needs to have at least one from each Gen, including Five."

"A maximum of ten per team," Riddick points out. "And let's make it interesting — four teams total. First through fourth." Roarke laughs.

"You should be glad that he's giving you a chance, Kyle," I point out. He flips me off.

"Okay, let's do this. Anyone who bows out before ten has 6am trainings with me next week," Mason tells them. "So, decide now."

"Ten isn't a problem," De says. Earning a glare from her brother. Mya has joined us as well at the bar. It seems like most of the siblings in Four are here for this.

"You puke in the bathroom, you're cleaning it," Roarke tells his little sister. She just smiles and raises her glass.

"Alright, let's do this!" Aimee, clearly intent on puking herself, says. Mya shakes her head at them. She isn't joining since she seems to be the responsible one tonight.

Shots one through four go down smoothly for most. By five, I see some of the younger ones regretting their life choices. Tequila is not my favorite, but I'll take it over vodka or rum. Six and seven, some decide training with Mason is better than alcohol poisoning.

Aimee seems like she is going to fall off the stool, so when she goes to grab her next shot, RJ grabs her hand. "You're done," he tells her.

She looks to Mason and then Mya for saving; they both shake their heads. "You guys suck!" she slurs as RJ takes her arm and helps her down. De reaches out for RJ too. He nods to Roarke. Mya helps them, along with Hope and Siobhan, who were smart enough not to start this game.

Zack doesn't seem that fazed. Two of my three dipshit brothers were smart enough not to start. Can't say the same for Ty.

I clink shot glasses with him, and down number eight, and subsequently number nine. He blinks at me. "You're an idiot," I tell him. He nods his head and does his tenth. Then walks away, well stumbles away.

"At least he got out of training," Wyatt points out. I laugh; there is that. Eleven, Twelve and Thirteen. Roarke is on bottle three now. Mason has her lime pile growing. She hates tequila, but she is so damn competitive, she won't bend. I'm okay, but I no longer enjoy it.

Mason, Riddick, and Kyle are all barely phased by it. Charley is struggling, as suspected. But now that Riddick said one through four, she is more determined to outlast everyone other than those three. I figure I'll make everyone's life easier.

"Charley, if you are number Four then you can't be on Mason's team, and you'll most definitely lose at the tournament."

"Fucking hell," Roarke mutters. Charley turns her shot glass upside down on that comment. Mason and I exchange smirks. Just to piss them off, I should let Max, who is the only one that still stands a chance of beating me, win fourth spot. But I don't have it in me. Once we hit twenty, it's literally those three, Max, and me. Mason isn't happy with tequila. Kyle isn't handling it either.

"Roarke," Mason says. "Do we have to stick with this?"

"Yep." He tells her. I expect her to grimace, but she smiles at me. Aw Fuck. Before I turn my glass over, she does to hers.

"FUCK!" all of us exclaim simultaneously. That means that we have to keep going to see who picks first. She set us up.

"Have a good night, boys," she says, laughing. Charley is steamed up, since she bowed out for nothing. Odds are she and Mason won't be on the same team now. But I can't fault Mason for playing an excellent strategy. Not only that, but she would have a tough time picking people since she hates hurting anyone's feelings.

Roarke lines up three more for each of us. I frown at the sucker.

"Who's holding Alex's shields?" I ask Riddick. Mason could now that she bowed out, but not a good idea.

"Jasper took over a while ago," he tells me. "He is shielding down the whole damn dorm it seems tonight," Riddick says with a head nod to a couple of people pairing off, some I already saw sneak away. Hopefully, it won't create drama tomorrow, but no doubt the dorm will not stay calm and collected. Relationships are always messy.

Max throws back his three and smirks at Kyle. Kyle does his three, but even I can tell, he isn't burning it off. He lost that ability a while ago. The three of us are far superior in twos and can burn pretty easily. He's dead in the water. And he knows it. By about twenty-seven, Kyle frowns at all of us, but Max, the good guy that he is, turns his glass upside down.

"You owe me," he tells Kyle, as he taps his brother on his shoulder and heads over to where some other non-combat Gen Twos are seated. The night is wearing down, so soon we will all head to bed.

Riddick has downed his shot; Kyle is looking at his. I should feel bad, but he started this bullshit. He could've passed on it. Just like last time, he bit off more than he could chew. Although he will never admit it. He doesn't stand a chance against Riddick. I could, but I would have to burn more than I want to. He nods at me, flips his glass. And then I take my shot and flip mine. Riddick smirks, downs one more for good measure. Roarke gets us both water to hydrate. It's a relief to look forward to tomorrow and the future.

THIRTEEN

Kate

The Elitus board selections were predictable, but we still had to endure the hellish process.

Alex Clarke. Kyle Ross. Wyatt August. Max Mason Clarke. Reese Miller. And of course, I joined the board.

Lately, I have been buried in committee drama. We all have a lot of work to do. But it seems my workload is more than others, as usual.

Things are changing. The lifting of the dating ban has opened the door; flirting, dating, and relationships. Everyday interactions take on more meaning. It's everywhere.

The dorms haven't calmed down in the last couple of weeks.

If anything, it has gotten worse. I know my mom and Dr. Miller reiterated their speeches on hormones. And had another birds and bees lesson, with more focus on safe sex, and options available to all.

Love is in the air, and raw sexual energy is in the dorms.

My powers have always made me more susceptible to emotions, and the hormone fluctuations have only added to it, along with power surges and general shitty shielding from many. It has made it impossible to ignore. I have no choice but to seek out Mason, because I sure as hell am not going to Bastian for help.

I find her in the infirmary working with some fellow Gen Twos who are finishing up their trials for graduation. Observing for a bit, taking it all in. She has become a better teacher during the last several months while she has become Elitus' best weapon.

I note in the way some more timid Gen Twos are interacting with her. They used to fear her—not because she would harm them, but the sheer power she radiated. But now, with all the lessons she has done, all the dedication she has shown, her working with everyone, giving everyone time if they ask for it. It has made her approachable. Made her real to them, not just the ultimate Elitus weapon, but a fellow wight, a resource, maybe even an ally.

When she dismisses them for the day, she nods towards the attached office, where I know she is probably going for a snack. Her power burn is immense; thus, she has snacks and goodies stored everywhere. I have noted over the years that someone is always bringing something in and giving it to her if she has been in back-to-back trainings. Her siblings, her girlfriends, even her combat team keep her stocked.

Sure enough, she offers me some trail mix, but I decline. She mixes a protein shake while I take a seat. This is a community space for Wights when working on classwork, or lab techs who are dissecting someone's trial information. It's barren—a desk, some chairs. Sterile beige walls, a single window overlooking the infirmary area.

"To what do I owe the pleasure?" Mason says with a smile. Knowing her, she already knows what I am here for.

"I need some more... advanced shielding lessons."

"Shielding won't help you," I suck in a breath. "Even if you shield and they shield, their emotional waves will break through. But," she says with a dramatic pause. "I think we can work on something for you. I helped Reese, who had some similar issues when this all started." She pauses, looking at me, dissecting me. "Why did you wait so long to come to me, Kate? It's been over a month."

"I was hoping it would get better with time," I whisper. "But it's getting worse."

"I bet," she sighs and takes a seat next to me, not behind the desk. "Listen, I won't be able to make it completely disappear, but it'll definitely quiet everything. It will be trial and error for you. It won't be easy, but I can get you there. But I won't lie to you, blocking at the level you may need may make you vulnerable." I look at Mason, and my anxiety spikes. Feeling my reaction, she reaches over and drops some shielding over me. "You'll block out emotions, intentions, energies; but you'll also miss threats. Use it in the dorms, you'll be fine."

That doesn't put me more at ease, it's going to be a choice between shielding or control. Being vulnerable is something I am not okay with, but unless I plan on moving home, then I have to do something.

"I'm working on some things, or at least I submitted some trainings to Elitus, but as usual they ignore them," she says with a half grin/half grimace. "If you talk to your mom, maybe she can help push it through. I know you aren't the only one with issues, but your elemental connections make it even worse for you."

"I can certainly try," I tell her. It would be nice if something could get worked out, or something adjusted. I know the residential committee is working on some plans for long-term couples, anyway. But hook-ups are still happening, and will happen. Thankfully, most of the smarter Wights are staying away from random hook-ups. At least on base anyway. I know some others still go off-base. I grimace at that thought. I have never gone off base without Wyatt or one of my brothers. Not only because Elitus demanded it, but because I didn't feel the need. The public is even worse for me to deal with from an emotional standpoint. So, I avoid it.

"You ready?" Mason asks. I nod, although I don't know if I'll use it. I'm thankful for something, anything to make it a little easier to handle.

Bastian

I head to the war room, although not going out tonight. I'm on primary for healing, with some trainees. This is the part I like; I can keep a pulse on missions and teach something useful. Showcase that there is more to combat than just hitting targets.

Mason's out on a mission with Riddick. Simple recon, so there isn't much to do. But I don't mind. It gives me some control over the situation. With all the changes, I have had little of that. It's chaotic; dorms are an emotional mess; social/emotional overlap is happening everywhere. People are unfocused in training, some more than others. But simultaneously there have been some positive wins.

One win? Robot Mason has been absent. Or at least she has been more like the old Fun Mason. She has still been getting random messages from PPG. The latest one was confirmation of the birth of Tara's son. Along with more info on the children of Vanguard. More detailed breakdowns of the treatment and testing of the Wights while pregnant. It is important to get the info, but every time I see it, it affects Mason. Makes her a little more focused, less fun. But that's usually our sign, her combat team, to distract her. Focus on the good, not worrying about something we can't control.

My trainees today are a troublesome twosome; Ariel and Sabrina. Both are here for observation. They are learning how to handle healing in combat cases, what protocols we use, what is too much, or not enough with mental and healing powers. Field medical triage and lab/infirmary needs.

They're here to shadow me. Both of them are powerful, and it won't be long before they want to move beyond healing, and into combat training. Learning how to be offensive and defensive.

But I demanded they learn this first. This is stuff no one ever taught us. Mason and I had to figure out how to do all this for ourselves. The information, procedures, and methods that we have used to give purpose to Twos outside of being mental weapons. We've worked hard to create the program, and it's crucial they know how to heal, how to help.

Before they learn how to kill.

"Pay attention to the signals. Don't just listen to what they tell you. Scan," I point to the tablet. "The mission details are only part of it. Some will hide injuries. Some will demand attention first, but you must decide. Focus on what you can fix. And know what they can fix themselves. It's important to know the combatant's baseline when you are on this side." I pull up the lab docs and showcase both Mason and Riddick on screen. The war room is composed of several monitors, which project both mission details and information about the basics of each combatant assigned. It also, for some missions, has camera feeds.

But I don't need to look at the information. I know all the primary combat team specs from memory.

"Riddick is her shield, so usually he's going to have more physical injuries, same with Roarke. They both stand in front of her. Doesn't mean she lets them. She will take a bullet for either of them. And she will internalize it. So, she doesn't distract them. Know them, watch them in the arena, watch how they work."

"How set are the teams?" Rina asks.

"Some are more common than others. It depends on the mission and level of complexity. Or who they are likely to come up against. Intel is important, but we work to ensure the team is balanced. Riddick and Mason are the most versatile Spectrums. If Kyle's out, he gets a strong Two with him, same for Charley. They are weak Twos, but powerful. Typically, if it's high combat, It'll be me." Ariel looks at me. I see the wheels turning. She knows that if she wants to be a Combat Two, she needs to get stronger physically, but that's her goal. I see it in her eyes, the same look I had. And I fucking hate it.

They nod and ask more questions. They remind me of myself, eager to learn, to make an impact. Ariel is focused. She is controlled and precise, but Sabrina is looser. She is chaotic but also dedicated. A natural, like her brother. They balance each other, and their third amigo, Finley, Siobhan's younger brother, is the only other Gen Five Two who might make combat. But he needs to get stronger first. When his growth spurt hits, we will see where he ends up.

The key to being a Two is that it's an imperfect balance. Between life and death. The more power you have, the harder it is to control. The more you are viewed as a weapon. A bad guy disguised as a good guy.

I've always felt like the Tier Twos are my responsibility, but with these two, Ariel and Sabrina, I feel it more than ever. It's personal. Between Riddick and me, we both know what's coming for them.

Because as much as we want to shield them away and protect them from it. They won't let us. But I will be damn sure when they step out into the world, that they are prepared for what's coming.

Mason and Riddick return just after eleven with no injuries. Other than Mason bitching. "I swear to God," she says, dropping her debrief on the closest tech. "You are the most overbearing handler. I was fine. I blinked, and you were on my ass."

"You blink too much," he comments, off-loading his weapons. Riddick is armed more than normal. Probably because Roarke wasn't on this one. He doesn't need the weapons, but he takes them when he is with her, always cautious, protective. Sabrina is laughing at her brother's reaction, as they both just watch the two interact.

Mason rolls her eyes at him. She looks good, not stressed. She's really just giving him a hard time more than anything, which is a change from what they were doing before. It's like whatever frost that had been between them has thawed.

Mason looks around and smiles at my sidekicks.

"My favorite Mini-Mes!" She says, heading over to them. She asks all about what they learned. Mason always gives them more time than any other trainees. Part of it is because they are our siblings; the other because she sees the potential in them. She wants them to have it all, and not struggle like she did for so many years.

She takes our sisters with her, probably getting fuel and going to spend some time reviewing everything that I have already taught them. I shake my head at that. I get it, though.

Female combatants are a minority. Female Two Combats, even more so.

And potential X-Two Females, in the same Generational class. It's unheard of.

It's a target painted bright red on their backs.

They will be more than assets; they will be weapons.

Riddick catches my eye as they walk out. He feels it too. What this all means for our sisters. "They're pushing too hard, too fast," I tell him.

"They are trying to outrun the leash before it strangles them," he comments.

Exactly. They know that the changes, a lot of them, are designed for non-combat options. Those two, they want it. Similar to how Mason, Charley, and Mya felt. They were all pushing for combat, when Elitus wanted to keep the girls out of it. Now that there are options, Sabrina and Ariel, both afraid the door will close to them, and they won't be allowed in.

Our sisters are leaps and bounds ahead of their peers. They are quick, fast learners and lethal. Both in Twos and in the physical aspect. Charley and Mason both have them in training with them; building them into defenders.

Sabrina is going to end up getting the height of her mom and siblings, probably reaching Kate's height. But Ariel, she's more petite. Built more compactly, she's a clone of Charley. Both in looks, style and attitude.

They're still young, both eleven, but before long. Puberty is going to come, and I am going to lose my goddamn mind.

That's the other unspoken problem with their going into combat. Entry into the dorms. Where all the bullshit we pulled with Mason will come back to haunt us.

Fuck, Alex should've killed me.

And Ariel and Sabrina are at the top of the Gen Five food chain. Shit, they are even outpacing Tier Twos in Gen Threes and Fours.

But the higher they climb levels; the more people take notice.

Elitus, lab techs, other Wights. But it's not just them; it's a known fact that Dmitri and PPG have spies. And they will certainly draw his attention: People fear what they can't control.

Riddick, Kyle, and I find them not long after. In a common area outside the labs. It's crowded. Smack dab in the middle is Mason. She has a pizza in front of her while she works with them. They are all spread out. Gen Fours and Fives. All listening to her every word.

Prior to her robot tenure, many feared her. Instead, while she became a robot, she also became their teacher. Their protector. It changes a lot of minds in the younger Gens.

I watch Ariel and Sabrina as they interact as well. Sharing some training points, teaching at eleven.

They are natural leaders, commanding the room and the masses.

Before long, we are noticed, and they make room for us. Mason smacks Riddick's hand as he grabs a slice, but it's all in good fun. I throw my arm over the back of the couch behind her. Riddick summons her some chocolate as payment for the pizza. She smiles at that one.

Before long it's twenty questions, and we are knee-deep in combat stories, and lessons. It's a break from what we usually discuss, but it's good.

Mason excuses herself to hit the bathroom. Instead of returning, I note her heading out the back door, wiggling her fingers at me. Slick as ever. Pulling strings to get us here. More mentoring and leading, helping us to build relationships with the younger ones.

FOURTEEN

Bastian

The sun sets earlier every day. The heat finally broke in late September, and now mid-October has brought the leaves turning and cooler air. I spend a few minutes outside the backdoors to the Auditorium. Wrapping my head around all the changes, and what I am stepping into officially today. The future gets a little clearer to see every day, but that doesn't mean it is getting easier to navigate.

Adjustments, not only with the committees and Elitus but also with interactions and relationships. The responsibilities and the shift in leadership. It's a lot to handle, and with it comes the mental load that I carry and try to work to ease for my peers. But today, I am going to take a little time to breathe, to let go. I don't often, but it's long overdue.

Today is graduation day. I've been at X-Level for years, so my trials were not much of anything. I stretch my neck. At my mother's insistence, I dressed up, but I can't wait to escape the shirt and tie for a t-shirt and jeans. I take one last deep breath of the crisp fall air and head back inside. I immediately spy that the auditorium is filling up. As usual, it's all done up in hues of purple, black and silver. Lights gleam off the stage; it's quite the spectacle, each year getting a little bigger as the class sizes increase.

The rows with the various Generations are filling up. For those of us in Gen Two, we will sit on stage to start and then, as we medal, join the rest down in the first and second rows.

Mason catches my eye; I already know what she's wearing. She bought it along with a handful of other dresses when we were in Italy a couple of months ago.

It feels like a freaking year ago with everything that has happened.

She should graduate too, but Elitus keeps pushing her off—stalling, delaying, pretending like they have a say in what she is.

She's stronger than I am most days. They won't admit it, but they know. We all do. Granted, she has her Ones and Threes to balance her out, but if it comes down to a fight? No one in this room stands a chance against her.

Everyone looks good, nerves are there, but that's to be expected. Gen One's on stage getting prepared for this. And because I have no control over my body, it seems, my eyes automatically gravitate to Kate.

She looks like a damn supermodel. Slim lines in a fitted light green dress, the kind that makes you look twice. The shade highlights her eyes; the hem draws my gaze down to her legs—long, toned, regal in those expensive-ass shoes. Kate, ever the perfectionist, wouldn't settle for anything less than flawless. Diamonds in her ears. Her smile is blinding.

She planned everything, the details of the ceremony, the dinner planned for afterwards. It's better than a ball. But I am itching to go to the after-party. No Gen Fours this time.

The shift in power is real today. I should feel proud. I earned this. We all did. I head up the steps and take my seat with my peers. Looking out at the audience, I spy my siblings, my triplet brothers, who are there with the rest of Gen Four. I know those idiots will cheer like I won the Superbowl when my name is called.

Dr. Ross starts the ceremony, moving through the names, each Gen Two graduate called up in order of age. Their names, generation, level, and tier. If they have a family member on the council, that family member presents their medal.

Neither Andy nor Roarke's parents are on Elitus, and they are up first, as the oldest.

My parents work in the labs, not on the council, so Dr. Ross will give me mine. I step forward when my name is called.

"Sebastian David Monroe. Gen Two. X-Two."

The room cheers; I hear my family. And like the spectacle that this is, I take a bow. I spy Mason, who just rolls her eyes, but she is smiling.

Because she knows. We are Elitus' least favorite children; but even with that, they can't deny our power levels.

The power of X.

Riddick goes last. He gets what he's been working toward: X-One Spectrum.

So now, with Kyle, Riddick, and me, there are three to lead an army.

Too bad we all know Mason is the one who leads us.

Because—ranks, medals, and ceremony aside—she's the one we follow. And we wouldn't have it any other way.

At the dorms, I'm outside with Kyle. Reigning over the beer pong table like it's our kingdom. It's stupid, but it's us. I missed it. The competitive side of Kyle comes out. But he is on edge.

Probably because he still has issues with Mason. Which escalated when she took a side detour with Riddick earlier and came back sporting a new piece of jewelry. A sparkling, X power-pulling magnet of a stone.

A purple diamond, at least a carat. Set in platinum. It's high-grade, expensive as hell; meant to channel and draw down power. One of that size is difficult to get, and Riddick gave it to her.

He's making quite a big statement with it. His intention is apparent.

I should care, but I don't. Mason and I? We're fun; we flirt, push each other's buttons. We don't play politics, and we sure as hell don't care about rules. We take risks, fight for what matters; we're partners, not lovers. That's why we work.

But Kyle. Seems like he isn't as far detached from her as he would like. He has always looked out for her but kept a distance. But this, now with the ban lifted. He seems to be torn between what he has done for the last several years and changing directions to throw his hat in the ring.

He'd better act fast if that's the case, because the smile Mason is sporting tells me she likes the attention she is getting from Riddick. Mason, the weapon is fading fast; Mason; the woman is coming out.

Speaking of the devil; Mason and her hellion partner head toward us, challenging us to a round. They don't like beer; mixed drinks are their game. While Charley mixes, Kyle and I both look at Mason, then the beacon on her wrist. She plays it off. But she doesn't miss the look or the tension. Roarke joins us to supervise, pulling up a stool.

"No cheating." Kyle cheats at everything.

He just laughs as Mason and Charley take aim. Charley might be best with fire, but she's also got a decent handle on air too. They shoot simultaneously, both shots landing. Their little cheering squad erupts. It's our whole combat crew and friend group out back. The other wights are inside.

Charley loves the attention and takes her own bow. Since they both scored, they go again. Cups drop from ten to eight to six. I can feel Kyle next to me. He hates losing more than anything, and since at the last party Charley took him down, he wants to win this time.

Mason catches his scowl, and instead of aiming for the cup, she nails him in the forehead instead.

"Don't be such a spoilsport" I just motion for the cup for her to drink. She toasts him as she does, with a look that is a mix of provocation and something else. She's playing with him.

Kyle and I even things up, then I miss—totally not on purpose—so Charley gets another shot.

Mason, being a smartass, doesn't even look. She just shoots. The crowd is hyped up now, bets placed.

They're down to two cups, one away from clinching it. Mason lands hers, leaving the last shot to Charley.

Charley's shot nicks the rim, spinning around the edge. Kyle seizes the opportunity, blowing it out.

"You'll pay for that," Charley mutters. We win.

With the game over, the party is in full swing. I let Kyle have his moment. I need to check on Mason. Tonight wasn't easy, and while she won't admit it, I know she needs to be here with us instead of handling everything on her own. Finally, leaving her armor behind.

I find her leaning against the railing, quiet but not withdrawn. When she sees me, she smiles. "Given up?" she teases.

"Not quite. Didn't want to ruin everyone's fun, Kyle went to play cards. You looked lonely."

She eyes me. "Lonely? No, just relaxing. It's been a hectic couple of months."

"You've been overdoing it."

She grins, leaning into me. "Yes, Dad."

I huff. Hell, she doesn't even mean to do it, but she still pulls at me. Her damn X-Level power makes me react regardless of whether I want it to.

She eyes my medal, running her finger over the X. "At least now you can shut Kyle up. You're on the same level."

"Level, yes. Shut him up? Doubtful anyone can do that."

We both laugh, and I grab her hand, leading her back inside. "Come on, you owe me a shot or two."

"For what?"

"For looking like that. It drives me to drink."

She laughs, looping her arm through mine, and we step back inside. Eyes flicker toward us. Kyle and Riddick are watching—neither of them looks thrilled. She smirks at them. Looks like old Mason is back.

She heads to the bar, grabbing a bottle of 151. Dangerous choice, but I'm not about to say no. She pours shots for everyone.

We toast, refill. Before long, it's casual and easy. Until it isn't.

The energy shifts, a pulse outside. Mason is moving, heading toward the yelling. Charley is shouting, blocking Mya from McGuire's spawn and his sidekicks.

I follow, the entire mood of the night snapping into something sharp, something tense. "What the hell is going on?" Mason demands.

Mya is a hot mess, all nerves and anxiety. Not like her.

Whatever these assholes did, it was enough to set Roarke off. He comes out of nowhere and clocks Connor.

Fucking hell. Everything explodes at once. Roarke doesn't just stop at one shot; he nails him again, eventually knocks his ass over the railing. He vaults and still goes after him.

We eventually get him off of Connor just in time for Alex and Andy to arrive. They take Mya out. She hates being the center of attention.

Riddick gets Connor out. He's alive, but Roarke is still hot.

Way too angry and out of control. Mason the handler, comes out. Taking over; trying to calm him down, but I already know this isn't over.

I go back inside. Not for long, though. Mason is not sober tonight, because as she goes to drag Roarke in, she loses her balance and winds up in Roarke's arms. The pulse of energy and spike of hormones—it's ridiculous. Every X-Level reacts.

Riddick yanks her back, which, of course, pisses her off.

"What the hell is wrong with you?" she snaps. "Jesus Christ! I think it's time for y'all to be cut off." She is scowling but then laughs. Fuck, if I hadn't missed this side of her so much, I would give her shit. Instead, we follow her in for a last shot before she heads up to bed.

After the party has died down, we are still on edge. We were drinking but burning off as we went, mostly because we wanted to monitor the situation. Especially after what went down between Mya and those dipshits.

A lot of changes have been happening. Faster than probably planned.

Never mind; old Mason is returning. And a side effect of her swings is that they cause all of us to react as well. Her highs and lows impact everyone, but those of us in combat, even more. She's our X. The center of all Tiers. The one that everything revolves around. She hates it, but she knows it's there.

Her power pulls us all in, makes us move with her. If she is level, we are. She keeps her shields up high to keep everything more stable. But when she lets go, even a bit, it has an impact.

It's not news to anyone. She has entire documents about it: studies, data sets. It's not something she can control; it's just a function of her and her X level.

That doesn't make it any easier for us.

Roarke downs another shot, shaking his head like he's trying to clear it. The alcohol dulls his aggression, which is good—he's been like a live wire lately.

Alex comes and updates us, then heads back up to Andy. Mya won't talk about what happened, and Charley is tight-lipped as well. Roarke is still agitated, but there is more to his reaction than their being idiots. It's one more thing I need to deal with.

But Roarke, being Roarke, distracts us from his problems, and stirs shit up.

His gaze flicks toward Riddick, amusement curling at the edges of his mouth as he tilts his glass. "Some piece of jewelry Mason's sporting."

The words hit the table like a challenge. Riddick's jaw tightens, but his voice is even. "It's a power amplifier." Although he is not wrong, we all know it means way more than that.

"So, you say," Kyle says. Agitation is clear. "I get your purpose, Riddick, but seriously. You should know better."

Tension sharpens in the air. Roarke is smirking. "What, Kyle?" Riddick's tone is clipped. "It is. She needs it. The boost—even if it's just surface-level."

Kyle doesn't reply immediately. His frown deepens, fingers tapping against the bottle he summoned. "What do you expect me to do? Sit back and watch you chase her?" Kyle's voice is cool, but there's heat under it. "Not happening."

"Since when are you afraid of a little competition?" Riddick counters.

Kyle walked away from her first. Even if he ever wanted another shot, he would have to work long and hard, and he is now realizing she will not wait.

I don't know, but the look in his eye. I know that look. It's a challenge. I just hope it's not just because someone else stole his toy.

He fucking knows better. Mason isn't a toy. She is our center. And as an X-Three, he can fuck up more than their relationship; he can set the entire structure sideways, fucking with her. And he knows it.

Roarke? He isn't serious about Mason at all. He just likes to start shit.

I stay quiet, watching, assessing the situation. To avoid any more tension, I get some cards. We deal. No one speaks. We just play.

The pile in the center grows—chips, money, bets stacking higher.

Then Roarke, still grinning like he's enjoying the whole damn thing, throws down his cards and leans back.

"I fold." He stands smirking at us. "She's all yours."

The words hang there; he's not wrong. Whether or not we meant to, this game isn't just about money and chips. But we all know what he means. And even if Mason isn't a prize, we are all placing bets, trying to get the best hand.

If she knew we were even sitting here like this—circling, unspoken rivalries simmering beneath the surface—she'd cut off our balls and hand them to Elitus in a gift-wrapped box.

We flip our cards.

Motherfucker.

Riddick has four queens.

FIFTEEN

Kate

Gen Two graduation was last week, and now the mission lineups are changing, leaders shifting. McGuire, as suspected, did not give up any control of missions, teams or assignments.

Related to combat, the only thing I can control is whether I am out on them. I don't get slated often unless I want to. Just to stay up to speed, I do, much to my father's dismay. Even if combat became voluntary, I have no intention of pulling myself out.

Relationships and never-ending emotions batter me in the dorms and in the labs. Couples and connections are growing in places they never could before. It's not a bad thing but distracting, so I can't prepare for it.

Emotions I'd rather not deal with are affecting me more than I want them to. It's creating a tough environment for me—one I can't escape.

Instead, I do what I do best. Throw myself into work. Control, structure. Organized. That's the only thing that makes sense to me.

It would be nice if occasionally I could catch a break. Not that I expect one.

Mason conveniently avoids all the committees. She claims it's so everyone else can have a say, but she knows damn well that if she joined, she'd be stuck coordinating, managing logistics, and dealing with diplomacy. And Mason hates dealing with people's bullshit.

So instead, I'm the one who is herding my three Gen One peers, making sure they follow through while leveraging whoever is on their committees to keep things moving.

Alex at least, will get some shit done. Wyatt as well.

But Kyle and his dipshit partner Bastian? They're going to be a pain in my ass. Deadlines mean nothing to them. They'll either push everything to the last minute or, worse, handle things in a way that causes more problems than they solve.

People signing up should be a positive thing—and it is, in theory. But years of being voiceless have turned into an avalanche of opinions. Some ideas are solid, others are ridiculous, and all of them require sorting, revising, and actual implementation.

My committee finally got the go-ahead for a night out. They've had some smaller adventures, shopping and movies. But Charley pushed for this—a club—and I let it happen. It's tonight, but I know I won't be going. Partying has never been my thing, and honestly, I'd rather spend the night at home with a book and a glass of wine than deal with the drama. It might be quiet for once.

I'm in the conference room, working with some of the Gen Fours on details of the upcoming Ball, when I get tapped to head to the auditorium.

Mason has something to show us this time. I sigh, rubbing my temples.

Heading down, I immediately notice the entire auditorium is packed. All of Elitus is here; that alone tells me this isn't just some half-baked theory Mason cooked up; this is something serious.

I slide into a seat next to Lissa, who leans over and fills me in. Mason's theory: shields can be broken.

I inhale slowly, letting that thought sit. No wonder she is being pulled in. Shields aren't just a combat tactic; they're the foundation for our defenses. One of the first things we learn to do.

If Mason is saying they can be broken, that changes everything.

I don't doubt her. I know Bastian or Mason could break them. But to suggest that we could all learn to do it. That shakes something, and I don't know if I can handle that thought.

I thrive on control. I like my shields in place, but if this is true. Then it is something I can't control, and no amount of training can fix that.

Mason walks in, and the room goes quiet. Not because she demands it, but because her presence alone shifts everything. Her power, even when not running high, causes reactions, bonds pulling, shields shifting. Every Wight in the room feels it.

Kyle trails her, moving in the lazy, confident way he always does. Elitus' lackey but also a strategic political plant. He knows how to ride the fine line of Elitus puppet and daredevil. He never steps away from a challenge, and for years has been right there with Mason at the front, leading. Kyle takes a seat while Mason joins Nick Thompson at the front.

Thompson opens with a few dry comments, but Mason's already impatient. She steps forward, and the room stills again. "I believe any Wight can path, shield, and self-heal. Pathing is a language; everyone can learn to at least read it, even if they can't speak it. Self-healing for all. We're already enhanced. Bonds help us regenerate faster. We've seen it. Felt it."

"When you exert too much power, your shields can falter. If you are shielding others, they drain. But once you can read a shield's structure, you can dismantle it."

She's not just speaking to the Tier Twos anymore. She's talking to all of us. And that's what scares me.

"No shield is impregnable. No ability unbreakable. Contrary to popular belief, we aren't almighty nor immortal. We have weaknesses. As they like to break us into 'tiers' and 'levels', it is common that we assume they cannot be combined. You don't have to be a spectrum to hone other abilities. You don't have to be a Two to have powerful shields. I," as she stresses that word, "believe that with the right amount of dedication all Wights can shield, path, and self-heal. Pathing is complex, and although most can read it, they can also communicate with it. They just need to learn the language. For self-healing, we already have increased strength, abilities and healing properties. For some, it may be possible to close wounds or other minor injuries. But we are here to talk about Shields."

The words strike harder than they should. Her tone isn't loud, but it cuts clean.

"Shields will make or break you. If you let your shields down, we all know we are vulnerable to attack, be it mental or physical. Emotional shields function the same way." She's pacing now, her movements fluid, deliberate.

I observe her. She's not just presenting data—she's delivering a sermon. Her gaze scans the room, sharp as glass, and none of us dare look away. "Think of it like building blocks." She goes over the whiteboard, drawing a diagram. "Each block is a different shape or color. However, everyone has the same basic blocks. Some of us have the basic set. Some went out and spent more money and got the cool ones. The colors may vary, and they also may change with moods, hormones, or actions. As you move the blocks around, you get different things. Sometimes you build a ranch; other times, a mansion. That's the basics."

"Now, everyone knows that blocks need a firm foundation. That's what we taught you. Same with shields, 'Do this to shield that.' Everyone was taught the same way, so the foundation is the same. You can use these foundations to build on. Hone taller buildings, create better shields. If you keep building and building, you get a tall tower. You can add in doors and windows, to show parts to others, while the foundation still stays. But all it takes is knocking out the foundation to have it crumble. We don't build houses out of clay anymore for a reason. We use bricks and steel. We use cement and other materials to hold it together."

Some get it quickly; others not so much. "Okay, enough with the blocks. Regardless of what you do, you are not invincible. All it takes is enough power and pressure, and your shields will crumble. The more power you spend, the harder it is to hold your own shields. You may require help. Once you learn how to read your own shields, you can identify another's."

"It's like signatures. Each one, although it looks the same, is unique. You can hide your signature, cloaking it. But it takes power. Everything does. For High Twos, as mental players, this will be easy. It will probably be easy for X's as well, since you should have stronger shields, thus better architects. The better your shields, the better you are at helping another."

"And breaking them?" McGuire asks.

"To break them is not so easy. Once you read them, you can push on them. A strong shield won't break easily. But it all depends on which block you are pushing on. Dependent upon the signature, and the ability, you can decipher which one will make it crumble. As your shield is pushed, it's natural to push back, or adjust. Once you see how they adjust, you can learn them and then be able to determine how best it is to knock it down."

"If it's a weaker opponent, and you are stronger mentally, with enough pressure you can bust right through. Like water at a weak dam, it doesn't stand a chance."

I inhale slowly. Around the room, I see it sinking in, eyes widening, some narrowing. Everyone calculating in their heads. If what she is saying is true. Then the defenses we all thought would keep us safe. They are flimsy, and with the right amount of pressure...

This isn't theory. It's a threat. And she knows it.

Mason continues, calm and clinical. For those who question it, she intends to prove her point. "You want to see?" she asks. "I need a volunteer."

Half laughing, many look around. She just smiles.

"Okay," Bastian says without hesitation, and my stomach drops. Either they planned this, or he's about to be humiliated.

And honestly? Part of me wants to see that. He's been grating lately. Arrogant. Too cocky for someone who hides behind sarcasm and smirks.

Mason doesn't hesitate. She powers up, and the second she does, the entire room reacts. The energy shifts, thickens, pressing against us like static in the air.

Bastian does too—instinctively reinforcing his shields, setting himself into a stance that says this is just a game. But Mason isn't playing.

She presses. At first, he barely reacts. Then his jaw tightens, his smirk fades.

She hits him, his head jerks up, the room goes dead silent, and Elitus is on their feet.

And then I see it—his eyes shift. Pure solid ultraviolet. I guess they didn't plan this. I'm stunned by the silence. I've never seen Bastian like this; no one has.

For a split second, the smartass is gone. What's left is something colder, sharper, powerful. The Mental God in the flesh.

This must be what they mean when they talk about the power of Twos. No jokes, no charm, just raw mental energy. But even with that, at his strongest. It's not enough, because Mason's levels are still climbing. She isn't even at max level yet.

She hits him again. He amps up, but not enough to counter her.

Then it happens. Her frown deepens. She finds the weak spot.

Then she *breaks him*.

Bastian drops. For a second, I forget to breathe. That's Bastian, our X-Two, and she leveled him like it was nothing, in less than five minutes.

Mason catches him before he hits the ground, her fingers gripping his torso, lowering him carefully. The auditorium erupts. Dr. Miller rushes forward, already calling for medical aid, but Mason, she's standing steady, her breathing controlled, eyes scanning the room—not for approval, but for reactions.

She already knew she could do it. She knew exactly how this would go.

Now, she must deal with what comes next.

And it doesn't stop with Bastian.

Mason is still powered up; it's obvious. With her energy on the surface, her eyes have an eerie violet glow. But just as the noise settles, another presence moves through the crowd: Riddick.

He doesn't speak at first, but the shift in Mason's expression is immediate. Her shoulders tense, her gaze sharpening in his direction.

Riddick steps forward, meeting her in the middle. Something in his stance is all wrong. He is challenging her, and that causes all the men in the room to react. Their levels are rising to defend.

Mason's jaw locks, her weight shifts slightly like she's preparing for something. "Don't." She tells him.

"Scared?" he asks, standing right up to her. Toe to Toe, towering over her. Even though he is almost a foot and a half taller, she can match him in power, and he knows it.

"Not really. I think they have seen enough today." He doesn't back down, just continues to push her shields. It looks like she wasn't the only one who knew this secret. Not playing games, she hits him back like she did Bastian, and the room electrifies once again. But before it can go any further, Kyle steps between them. His voice is low, calm, but what he says is enough to make Riddick reconsider. He frowns at Mason, something unspoken passing between them, then finally backs off. Only then does Mason face Elitus.

McGuire clears his throat, pulling the conversation back into control. "Can you do it to everyone?"

Mason nods, still tense. "Yes. The principle is the same. If I wanted to, I could erect a shield over everyone or just a small group. If that were my primary focus, I could probably hold it against a high-level onslaught." There's more discussion, but I am too focused on the room. Many are still in shock.

I am pulled out of it when Roarke, always thinking ahead, asks, "Can you teach us?"

She hesitates—just for a second—before saying, "Yes."

Robert Clarke, her father, steps forward. He places a hand on her arm, his expression unreadable.

Mason blinks, her shoulders drawing back slightly. She braces, waiting for dismissal, rejection, the usual brush-off.

"You'll start teaching them on Monday."

Instead, Elitus is listening to her. She nods. Another shift. Another change. And I think she's realizing this is only the beginning.

SIXTEEN

Bastian

My head is killing me.

The infirmary cleared me, but that doesn't mean I'm recovered. Mason did a number on me.

Kyle, of course, gave me shit the entire way back to the dorms because that's what he does.

"Dude, she wrecked you," he snickers. "Like the big blocks. Duplos." He's fucking hilarious.

I scowl, pushing the door open. He's not wrong, but I don't need it thrown in my face. Mason would've had him on the ground in two seconds if he had tried to step up.

I should stay in tonight, rest, and let my mind settle after what she did. But there's no way in hell I'm letting these girls go out without me.

The guys were supposed to hit a different bar than the ladies, but plans changed—now it's a full club night. Even the ones slated for missions have been let off the hook.

Elitus acts as if what she did today was a groundbreaking revelation. Pretty sure it was in some dossier she sent them months ago. Mason and I have worked on it over the years. But not like that. Not with that kind of precision. That kind of power. She has been working on that in secret, refining it. Pushing it further than even I knew was possible.

She dismantled me quickly, too quickly.

And if she can do it to me, then I should be able to do it to any X as well. Once I learn it, that is.

McGuire is going to take what she showed him today and capitalize on it the first chance he gets. I'd be an idiot not to be ready.

This is unknown territory. It changes the game.

After a shower and some food, I'm feeling human again.

I head downstairs, joining the rest of the group. Because Kyle is the designated driver for the guys, Roarke ended up getting grouped together with Mason and her crew.

Before I get in the SUV, I hear my name. I turn and fuck me; Mason is walking toward me, and I have to get myself under control. She looks good in a tight black dress, some knee-high 3" spiked heeled boots, and with her hair in a high ponytail. She looks dangerous, and she is. It's been a while since she has done herself up; she doesn't even realize the attention she is bound to get like this.

"You're going to kill me," I mutter.

Her brow furrows, guilt flickering behind her eyes. "No, I'm not. Are you okay? I'm sorry. Do you want me to help?" This woman. I laugh, grabbing her hand, calming her down before she spirals.

She doesn't need to feel guilty. She did exactly what she was supposed to do. We have done little besides work lately, especially with Riddick clarifying that he's playing for real. But that doesn't mean I won't take an opportunity when I see it. Get her attention for a little while.

"Baby, you already have," I smirk, squeezing her fingers. "Go back to your girls before I steal you for the night."

"Get in the fucking car, Bastard!" Kyle yells. Oops. He's mad.

I wink at Mason before sliding into the SUV.

The club is overflowing, with a line around the block. Luckily, Kyle knows the owner, so we can get in with ease. The girls pretend we aren't here, which is fine—that's the game. Doesn't mean we aren't watching. Or that others aren't watching them. Because they are.

Alex's focus is on Andy, and he doesn't seem to care about the rest of us other than Mason. It won't be long before they disappear completely. He looks good pussy-whipped.

I scan the room, picking up signals, reading the energy signs. The dorms have been a jumbled mess of hormones and feelings lately, ones I do my best to ignore or shield away from. While it could be worse, I can't say I love it.

It makes my own needs rise to the surface, and I haven't been out in a while to pick anyone up. Too busy, too focused on changes.

More and more of my Tier Two Wights are settling down, grounding themselves. This not only helps their focus but their power as well. I knew sex, whether with a commoner or a Wight, boosts power, but these couples; charting higher than before.

Including Kate's brother, Ryker, who is settling down with another Two of mine, Lissa. Both are good at healing. Ryker is combat-enabled, although he doesn't go out that much, but Lissa she's a healer through and through.

I'm happy for them. Ryker and I have a complicated relationship. Not because of anything between us directly, but because of Kate. He tries to play keeper, always running interference. And Kate—she lets him.

She hides behind him whenever she doesn't like what I have to say. And lately, that's been too often.

I lean back, swirling the ice in my drink, letting the night unfold around me. Tonight is about change. And I need to be ready for it, all of it.

Mason is enjoying herself, despite Alex hovering like a big brother. But when I see a douche cornering her, Kyle and I move simultaneously.

"Yes, you are," she says, trying to shake the handsy idiot off, but before it can escalate, Kyle and I intercept. Well, mostly Kyle. He's livid, and he isn't even drunk. Lately, anytime she is in any position or situation, he has been flaring up. Which means I have to cover his shit more.

"You got a fucking problem, assholes?" the drunk slurs at us, wobbling slightly. We just laugh at him. His loser friends attempt to pry him free from Kyle's crushing grip, but it's not working. Kyle isn't even looking at them—his focus is locked on the idiot in his hands.

"He's not worth your time, Kyle," Mason tries to defuse the situation, but when he turns to her, his eyes are lit up like a purple beacon.

He's pissed, and judging by his grip, he must have gleaned something from the guy's head that is making his territorial instincts flare up. I try to shield him.

Mason pushes some power at Kyle, trying to calm him as well, but it goes right through and shocks the moron in his grip instead. The guy twitches violently before collapsing, and Mason yanks her hand back, eyes widening.

I exhale sharply and drop to one knee, pressing my hand against the guy's chest, healing him. While I'm busy doing that, Mason makes her escape. She is pissed at herself.

Kyle shakes his head, trying to clear it, his fists clenching as he watches her leave. I glare at him. "Nice job."

He exhales sharply, rubbing the back of his neck before we both move, knowing damn well we can't let Mason wander off alone. Riddick wants to intervene, but Kyle cuts him off. He made this mess; he will fix it. Or I will more than likely.

Kyle and I plan, I can feel Mason, but she's blocking. Kyle is the one who forces the path open.

What do you think you're doing?

What do you care, Kyle? Go back and have fun. Please. I just want to go home.

"You're not taking a Lyft," I tell her when we find her. She doesn't look happy that we used her teachings to triangulate her signal.

Frowning, she shoves her phone into her bra. "Then you're both done for the night because you're taking me home. I can't stay like this. I'm bound to kill someone."

She's not wrong. She is too wired, her power crackling in the air around her.

We sit on either side of her. Kyle leans back, his arm across the bench behind her. I take her hand, pushing her levels down. It's easier than usual because I'm still exhausted. Power transfer for a Two isn't simple, but I learned it for her.

As soon as I take it in, I self-heal to neutralize the effects. Standard practice now. "All better," I say, releasing her fingers. "Let's go."

Mason looks at Kyle; his levels are back down as well. I notice the frown she is wearing. She says nothing, but I know his reactions lately have been bothering her.

She turns and studies me for a beat before shaking her head. "Bastian, I'm done in there."

"No, you're not," I counter, taking her hand again and pulling her up off the bench. "You owe me a dance for making me eat dirt earlier. Come on."

She rolls her eyes, but I don't release her hand and half-drag her back inside. Kyle follows.

By now, most of the Wights have regrouped, avoiding the commoner bullshit. Kyle peels off, knowing he's in the doghouse. Besides, I already told him I was going to get the goods from her regarding her kicking my ass today. She knows I want to know how she did it.

She doesn't hold back, but gives me a lesson, walking me through it. Although it's not overly complex, she knows she will have to take me on as a solo student as I try to learn this quickly.

After a while, I drag her out for the promised dance. Pulling her closer, feeling the shift between us; she takes a slow breath, her shields shifting slightly.

I can't help but grin. I still affect her, even when she tries to avoid it.

Her eyes flick up to mine, searching. I flip it on her, nudging at her shields, poking at her defenses. She smirks and gets that gleam in her eye. She grins at me, all knowing, "Want to go again?" she whispers against my ear.

Power surges. So do my hormones. It's instinct. She's playing with fire.

I tighten my hold around her waist, steering us toward a more open section of the bar, and finding a seat.

She orders water. I nudge the bartender to make sure we get a few shots instead. She eyes me but doesn't argue, taking the glass when it's set down and knocking it back with me.

"What are you doing, Sebastian?" she asks, watching me carefully.

I meet her gaze head-on. "I have no fucking idea."

She laughs and orders another. She's relaxing. That's the point. And I'm more than happy to have her attention, to let her have mine.

Since the one who usually holds mine has bailed as usual. Kate may chair the social committee, but she isn't social at all. She'd have to stoop to our level to fit in, and Queen Kate will never do that.

I down another shot, and before I can nudge Mason into something else, she beats me to it. She pivots in her seat and sends a pulse of energy up my arm.

I curse under my breath. She wants to work now. Damn her.

She lets me test some things out, raising our power levels as we go. Leading me through her shields, showing me the complexities of her structures—her so-called Lego castles.

Mason won't show me everything. But she shows me enough to make my mind spin. To make me want more. "You won't have those," she tells me, flicking one of the layered barriers into place. "They're One and Three's. I can teach you how to mimic them, though. How to fool someone. How to break them. You'll probably be the only one capable."

I raise an eyebrow. "Maybe Riddick?"

She shrugs. "Doubtful. He probably won't make it to X on Two."

I study the formation again, turning over what she's saying. "Make it to X? You make it sound like you can grow your level."

She doesn't answer directly, just gives a small, knowing smile. More theory. "You ready for more lessons?" she teases. "Elitus has me teaching soon enough."

I smirk, leaning in. "I like you as a teacher. You can discipline me after class."

Her eyes flash.

What are you trying to do, Bastian? You can't handle me.

You never know, Mason.

You wish.

She grins, then drags me back to the dance floor for the rest of the night.

After several hours, I'm over it. Most of us are. The night has been good, but even the best nights have a limit. When we head out, I grab Mason, maneuvering her toward our SUV. Not that she fights me. Alex isn't leaving Andy's side, so that leaves our group to handle her. Kyle and I guide her toward the SUV, where the others are waiting.

She slides into the front seat, stealing my seat, while I hit the captain's chairs in the back with Riddick, Wyatt, and Max.

"I say we get something to eat," Max comments lazily from the far back. "The girls are all babies. Mason can hang. Kyle, can you?"

Kyle flips him off in the rearview mirror, laughing as he veers toward town.

About twenty minutes out, we pull into a diner. This is going to be interesting.

Mason leads the way, stepping inside like she owns the place. The moment she slides into a booth, I drop in beside her. It doesn't go unnoticed.

I smirk at the small but noticeable power spikes behind me. Even now, everyone can feel her highs and lows. Mason pretends not to, thrumming with the salt on the table, moving the grains with her power.

The conversation turns to shielding. Her eyes flick toward Riddick. There's more to that look than she's saying. After she knocked me out cold, Riddick challenged her. And apparently, he knew more about this than even I did.

"Are you going to teach it?" Wyatt asks, leaning forward. Wyatt is the designated adult on this adventure, but he is also one of Kyle's oldest friends and a level head if anything goes wrong.

"Oh, she can teach you," I say, enjoying the way her power flashes slightly at the comment. She slaps my arm. More amusement than malice.

The food arrives, and we settle into bullshit and banter, the kind that makes everything else fade. It's easy like this; our crew. Mason relaxed, all of us together.

Mason excuses herself to the bathroom, and when she returns, something is different. She seems to be more shielded, composed, a little too put together. She has put back on some of her armor.

Maybe realizing we are out like this. Or not wanting to deal with Kyle, Riddick, and now apparently my advances.

I frown. Something's in her head now. And I want to set her mind at ease, I push a power, letting her know we are good.

She sits, pulling off her boots and leaning back. None of us are in a rush to leave. This is comfortable. We order coffee, round two of food. Chat, talk shop, make some more social plans. Wyatt updates us on other committees. It's a break from the reality of missions and training.

But good things never last in the Elitus World.

Mason jolts up suddenly, throwing open a path between all of us.

All our heads swivel to the door when we feel the pulse of power.

Fucking Hell.

Be normal. They won't engage us here. Let's see what they do.

She says this in our heads as the Dividian twins walk through the door. Alexi and Nikolai. Dmitri's top pair, and Riddick and Max's cousins.

Kyle's power flashes dangerously as Mason kicks him under the table. He's been off all night, and this is not the time for another outburst.

Across the room, they take a seat, ordering coffee, but watching us.

The tension shifts. Round two of our food arrives, we eat. They drink coffee.

Mason never skips dessert, so she orders it to go as she puts back on her boots. Deliberate, calculated.

She's waiting.

They're waiting.

Then she breaks the silence, opening the conversation, communicating with us mentally.

What's the plan? Kyle asks.

No plan. We leave. If they follow, we deal. They're fishing. If they were an actual threat, Coral would be with them. Mason reminds us.

I don't like this. Even if the others are back now, they must have known we were out. This much power in one place has to hit their radar. Riddick sends.

Because all your power spikes have helped, Mason chides. *Thus, my lessons on shielding will come into play. Pay the bill. Let's go.*

Mason stands first.

Both Alexi and Nikolai rise as she does.

We all power up simultaneously as a wave of tension rolls through the diner. Heads turn, and conversations still as we draw everyone's attention.

Mason mutters for us to chill, grabs my hand, and we head out. Kyle throws down cash for once and steps up to her other side. Riddick pulls up the rear as we hit the lot. Mason doesn't stop; she's hoping they'll just let it go. We are never that lucky.

It's not long before we feel it.

A pulse of energy slams through the air. Mason throws up a shield over our group instantly. It's instinctive in her. The shield is taking a lot of her power, but it's the best way to deal with them right now.

We all pivot, taking the standard position: protection detail.

Kyle moves in front of both Mason and me, bracing. Riddick steps to the side, giving him a clear pathway to the enemy, while Max guards our flank. And Wyatt, although not normally in combat, powers up to be defensive as needed, stepping to our other side.

Our power levels rise quickly, shields flickering into place.

Mason kills the noise of the car alarms that blare as the forces of our powers collide. The vibration—never mind the power pull going on—is immense. She isn't drunk anymore. None of us are. She burned off most of our alcohol for us. But that doesn't mean we are in an advantageous position.

Kyle is the only one sober from the start, but even he has been off balance tonight with all his hormonal surges. Her being threatened again has him back on edge. This is not the time to be dealing with some of PPG's top dogs.

"What do you want?" Kyle asks, voice sharp, unwavering as he addresses the other Gen Ones.

Nikolai smirks at us. "Just wanted to see what you were up to. Better keep her close, Kyle. She sure is tempting."

Kyle's response is immediate; he sends a small volley of power in warning. The burst of energy slams into them, knocking the Dividians back a step. Nikolai just laughs at him. "Temper, temper," he says. "Dmitri said you could come join us anytime, Mason. They're wasting your talent away. We would treasure them and you."

Mason scoffs, arms crossed. "I could say I'm flattered, but disgusted is more like it. Besides, I have more than enough here to keep me satisfied." Power pulses dangerously between all of us; too many unstable levels, too many hormones and energies mingling.

Nikolai frowns, but his interest in Mason is clear. Her beauty, her confidence, her power. She's their X as well, even if she refuses to acknowledge it. "Besides, Is Coral not enough anymore?"

Damn it, Mason. She's pushing them now. We all know the files claim Coral is Nikolai's mate, but I don't believe it. They share a child now. And much like we are with Mason, Coral is their top power. And that jab, it hits them. They react.

Kyle, sensing the shift, steps forward. "What do you want, Alexi? We both know you didn't come to fight; you'd lose rather quickly."

"Would we? Are you so sure?" Alexi tilts his head. "Look at you. You didn't even know we were here until we were practically on top of you. The others? They would've been toast. Don't be cocky—it'll be your downfall." He nods his head toward Mason. "We told you what we wanted already."

Max lunges forward, and Riddick steps forward to physically grab him. "Don't. He's testing you," Mason mutters to her brother.

"A test you've failed." Alexi says, looking at us, "When the time comes, she won't be able to save all of you."

He backs away, stepping toward their car, Nikolai right behind him.

"When you finally figure out that you're nothing more than a distraction, Mason," Alexi calls over his shoulder, "you know where to find us. Come play with the big boys."

They depart, and Mason's power levels surge, full X-range now.

We all feel it, the energy, the pulse in the air. It's like a pressure valve pressing down on us, needing to be released. "I need to go to the Boot," she says.

Kyle scoffs, his frustration spilling over. His eyes blazing. "To what, train?" He needs to get his act together quickly. "That won't solve anything," he hollers at her.

Fucking hell. I drop some shields on him, trying to contain the mess before it spirals even more. Mason turns sharply, eyes narrowed. "Train? No, to purge. But all of you should train." She exhales sharply, tempering herself just enough before delivering the blow. "He wasn't joking—you all failed badly. None of you cloaked, none of you shielded worth a damn. You were broadcasting your emotions and intentions like you had a mic hooked into your ass. If Coral had been with them, she would've roasted you. Wake up, Kyle."

"You think what I showed you this afternoon was child's play? It's not. You, more than any of them, need to work on it. You're a low Two at best. You can't always rely on Bastian to cover you."

Kyle's jaw clenches, but he doesn't argue. And neither do I, because she's right. Max tries to step in, but Mason stops him with a look.

"Don't." She's on the edge, not just from the fight but from what it means. "You all just put a massive target on our backs. Alexi and Nikolai aren't playing games at night like we are. This is real to them. Dmitri may be a pompous, psychotic, power-hungry prick, but at least he hasn't held them back. He's pushed them and let them develop into the powerhouses we're all supposed to be."

We all know she's right. Dmitri didn't chain them. He didn't balance their power with politics or class work, limit them or control them. He let them become what they were supposed to be: powerful weapons.

And us? We were held back. For safety, for control, for Elitus, to keep their illusion of power.

Mason is the closest we have to what we should be. She's not just ahead of us; she's well beyond us. And if Coral had been with them? We would've been dead.

I was useless. I wasn't equal to Mason. Not even close. For all my arrogance, for all my confidence I've built in my abilities, when it mattered, I wasn't enough.

I knew Mason was beyond me. I always knew that. But tonight made it clear just how far behind I am.

Earlier, she took me out like I was nothing.

And the Dividians? They didn't even see me as competition. I wasn't a threat; I was a liability.

The weight of that realization sinks into my chest like a lead weight.

I knew I had work to do, but this changes everything.

Elitus has spent years controlling how we train, how we develop. They've kept us just strong enough to be effective, but never strong enough to be uncontrollable. And it worked. Because when it counted, we weren't ready.

When the actual fight comes? We'll be slaughtered if we don't fix this.

I'm the one who's supposed to lead the Twos. To be the strongest among them. But I am not. My body is tight, anger and disappointment rising fast. I look at Mason. She feels it too.

She exhales one last breath and straightens. "Go home," she orders, her voice final. Then, without another word, she ports out.

Kyle lets out his frustration on a nearby tree; the crack of wood splitting echoes through the silence. Max turns to Riddick. "Take me to her."

Riddick doesn't move. "Leave her be."

Max's nostrils flare. Half-brothers or not, Mason always clouds their judgment of each other. "Leave her be? Fuck you, Riddick. Alone is not what she needs right now."

"He's right," Wyatt interjects. "She needs to let her power out. Any of us being there will only aggravate her more. Unless someone wants to tangle with her right now, which is ill-advised."

Max exhales sharply, his hands clenched into fists. But he knows, we all do.

Letting her burn it off is the only option.

Wyatt looks at Kyle. "Let's get back. Kyle, you need to call Elitus."

SEVENTEEN

Kate

The Elitus Chambers are in chaos this morning. I shouldn't be surprised, considering the bullshit that happened after the social event.

Aggravation simmers beneath my skin. This is exactly why Elitus bans these gatherings in the first place—too many spikes, too many unchecked emotions. And now, one incident, and they're already scrambling.

I don't care if they ban it again. What I do care about is all the work we put into making this happen not going to waste. The last thing I need is for the progress we fought for to be undone because people couldn't handle themselves.

Luckily, after a bit of arguing, the topic is tabled for later, meaning we can focus on more critical issues.

Or so I think. Not even an hour into the meeting, the back doors blow open with a force. The echo of the doors slamming against the wall ripples through the room, making all our heads turn, as silence engulfs us.

Mason. She moves like she's on a mission, a storm brewing, unstoppable.

"When?" she shouts. "When were you going to tell us the Latents are ready? Before or after you gave them my job?" I look at Elitus, and they don't seem surprised by her accusation.

The reports say they're nowhere near a working version. But Mason wouldn't make a scene unless she was sure.

McGuire demands to know who told her about the latent trials, about the program's supposed success in creating a new X. Mason laughs, "Your buddy Dmitri—when he and his goon squad cornered me in the quad last night."

The room erupts. With the doors wide open behind her, many Wights linger, crowding in the doorway, watching, and with Mason's revelation, I can see the shock and concern on many faces. Before long, her combat team is there—Roarke, Riddick, Bastian, all united behind her.

"What did he say?" Robert asks, getting down to check on his daughter. She looks at him with part disgust, part sadness.

"That you're making replacements."

Silence crashes over the room. They don't deny it, and that is confirmation enough.

They weren't going to tell us. Mason looks disappointed. I feel it too. But she keeps talking. "He wanted to extend his offer for me to join them personally. Too bad, I think I matter more here than there. They could've killed all of us last night, and there wouldn't have been a damn thing any of you could've done about it."

Mason looks around the room, making eye contact with each of her fellow Wights, me included.

Then she turns around and walks out.

Kyle goes after her immediately. But no one else moves.

She walks in here, tears the blindfold off, and leaves us to deal with the mess. And she's not wrong; that's what pisses me off. Not the secrets. Not the fact that we're years behind where we should be.

But the fact is that if Mason hadn't been the one to find out, we might never have known until they were already on base, replacing us.

For all the planning, for all the work we've put into structuring things, organizing training, trying to push for more resources, she's the only one who sees it for what it is.

Not a fight that's coming; a fight that's already here.

The reality of the risk and threat is taking over.

The Elitus chambers are tense, thick with unspoken frustration and rising agitation. The combat crew remains behind, grilling Elitus with questions. They aren't backing down this time. There's no point in pretending everything is fine—not after what just happened.

"What stage is it at?" Max asks.

"Live trials have already started," Robert admits.

Alex is tense. He, too, is frustrated with the situation, as we all are. "What does that mean exactly?"

"We've been conducting live testing of Latent X candidates at various degrees," his father explains. "Some are former soldiers from our first Alpha groups. Others are their children. So far, we've been able to identify key traits and variants that yield better results."

Kyle, returning from checking on Mason, isn't impressed. "And Dmitri? He has access. He walked onto our campus with an army last night, possibly using your serum on his soldiers."

McGuire cuts in before anyone can answer. "We can't track down every latent, Kyle. Do you know how many test subjects that would be?"

"How many do you have?" Alex probes.

"We have twenty-five participants in Trial Three, all exhibiting increased Tier Two abilities prior to the serum."

Roarke shakes his head, clearly frustrated. "Mason saw Dmitri's army, and they aren't just mental players. They were enhanced." Roarke comments, saying what we are all thinking. "Whether they are latent or created, either way, they are a threat."

Dr. Mason interjects, speaking for the first time today. "We have two working serums; Y is in live trials, Z is in development. We're taking a methodical approach; it's not meant to replace any of you—I'm sure that's what Dmitri implied, and what Mason thinks."

"But the goal," he continues, "is adding fighters, spreading resources, allowing those who wish to remain on base to do so. Y has shown progress. But Z... if successful, there's no going back."

Robert clarifies, "Y stabilizes and enhances latent traits, Z is... conversion-based. If it works, it wouldn't just enhance—it would create."

I've had enough. "Why weren't we informed?" I can't hide the accusation in my tone. And today, I don't want to.

Before anyone can answer, Bastian walks back in. He was out trying to calm the masses, ensuring everyone was okay. And based on his face, they aren't. "Because, as usual, Elitus loves its secrets."

McGuire sighs. He's a mix of frustration and uncharacteristic concern. "Mason's download isn't complete. He locked her down fully, but she wasn't wrong. They could've wiped us all out," Bastian points out, having gotten the download Kyle took off of Mason, since she was done with speaking to anyone, especially Elitus, today.

Roarke stiffens. "Do we have video?"

McGuire shakes his head. "No. It was blocked. Twenty-two minutes—completely blacked out. The guards weren't even aware that anything was happening. They have Tier Two talents, that's for sure."

"We need to set a time to meet and discuss," Alex suggests.

McGuire is quick to comment, "You have nothing to do with this. Your role, like all Wights, is a function of Elitus. I handle all security, missions and combat. No need for a meeting."

"So, you think," Riddick mutters.

"Let us discuss internally, then we can address everyone," Robert tries to get us back on track.

Bastian laughs dryly, shaking his head as he walks away. "So, you can make up some bullshit to tell us later? No thanks. Same shit, different day."

I watch him go; my heart in my throat. I mirror his frustration. His retreat hits harder than I want to admit. Because he's right. The rest of the combats are just as tense, ready to explode in their own ways.

I turn back to McGuire, my voice measured but sharp. "I hope you make the right decisions and consider the progress we've made in the last couple of weeks," I say, unable to stop myself from reminding them. "This type of secret sets everyone back. I don't care about adding more people; I care about our purpose. We need to be aware of changes that affect our future."

I glance at the door, which slams behind Bastian. My chest tightens.

I hate that he feels this way. That I feel this way. I steel myself, forcing my expression blank. "This is your chance to show us we are part of this. That we can evolve. This is a good thing, not another hidden secret." I squeeze Alex's arm as I leave, my steps quick and determined.

I find him outside, staring up at the sky, tension lining every part of him. He's in training gear still, black cargos, a tight t-shirt that showcases how hard he has been working on his physical game. His arms are crossed; his entire stance is rigid, vibrating with barely contained frustration. He knows I'm here, but won't meet my eyes.

I stop beside him, taking a deep breath, preparing. "You okay?"

He looks at me then, his eyes are sharp, the rim of purple around his chocolate irises wider than usual. He observes me the way he does when he's dissecting someone. Breaking them down piece by piece, analyzing their every move.

"Did you honestly think they would be more honest with you?" he asks, his voice rough and laced with irritation. He shakes his head, making me feel like an idiot. "The Wights on Elitus is just a show tactic to make you feel you have some control. Don't be fooled. McGuire and the rest will never give up real control. It's all need-to-know."

My jaw tightens. "It has gotten better," I argue. "I know they will never be fully transparent. But this? Latents? A fresh group to introduce? It's a different avenue." My voice drops, the weight of the situation settling in, frustration and disappointment rising to the surface. "I don't know," I murmur.

I feel it before I see it—his shield brushing against mine. A subconscious effort to comfort me. I shake my head, not letting myself lean in.

"You look good," I say instead. "Thought you'd still be in the infirmary."

He laughs. "You wish."

Then he holds out his hand, palm open, gesturing for me to join him as we head back to the dorms. His usual distraction tactic. I let him do it. Sometimes, verbal sparring is easier.

Even when we fight, even when we don't agree, even when he's infuriating.

I still trust him more than them.

Eighteen

Bastian

Elitus holds more meetings in secret. It's their favorite tactic: stall, spin it, and control the narrative. They schedule the conference for later in the week. Supposedly to inform us what is really going on. In the meantime, we are on lockdown.

Mason's in angry robot mode—pissed at Elitus, Robert, and us. Maybe not pissed, more disappointed. Which is worse. Either way, she's taking it out on all of us.

She's a maniac in the boot again, pushing herself and everyone else; especially in Twos, to get everyone back up to speed.

She doesn't wait to get started. Normally, Calvin builds a plan based on her teachings; but she bypasses that. Tactical maneuvers, mental battles, never mind full combat training with mental shield busting. For all tiers. It's brutal, unrelenting, and designed to push every mental and combat Wight, to see what we've got and whether we can handle it.

It's calculated.

Focused.

And she isn't slowing down.

I get it; I do. She would never admit it, but Dmitri, the PPG, being taken, is always under the surface as the perfect way to destroy us. To destroy her.

She is the strongest, the ultimate prize for him.

That has her back up, her armor on, and is the reason she is pushing so hard. Her plan is to get the main combatants up fast. We run all day and night, pushing to catch up. Even Kyle is working on it.

She incorporates many of us to assist. In getting the others up and running, especially the youngest ones. The fear is always that they will be turned.

PPG just walks right onto campus, and no one notices. What happens next time? She doesn't say it, but she knows if they did it once, they will do it again.

I know that was part of Dmitri's purpose. Make us question everything and everyone. Just when we were making improvements. Now we are back at square one. Questioning Elitus, questioning where we fit.

Kyle has been getting private lessons from Mason. He demanded it. He freaking needs it. But it puts them closer than they have been in a long time. Her playing around in his shields and his head. When two high Tier Threes sync up, it shifts things. But two X-Threes, it's a dangerous situation, because they both could cripple the entire system; they are two pillars holding up the rest of us.

But one side effect, whether good or bad; someone has dug out all Mason's lessons. Several years too late if you ask me. The training is piling up. Some are more focused than others, but it's a big learning curve.

Riddick and I both scale up quickly to help. Never mind; based on what's going on, the missions get reduced. Only Mason and Riddick get sent out now.

Unfortunately, Kate is in the mix, trying yet again to prove she belongs in combat, sitting in on every session. Here's the thing, Kate? She will never master this, at least not as an offensive ability. She's got too many emotional and elemental charges flying around to focus.

But she needs to defend. She can path, organize and control the room, but in combat and warfare. She will never be a killer.

But it doesn't stop me from watching; the way she doesn't limit herself, adapting every lesson, trying to twist it into something she can use.

I know I should focus on Mason, on how to assist more. But part of me, the part I hide most, is concerned just as much for Kate. Because Kate is Elitus' Golden Girl. She isn't nearly as protected as Mason is. She is out there; and wouldn't grabbing her make quite a statement?

Fucking Hell. I don't need this. Aggravated, done with the day, I head to the auditorium. It's time to hear the bullshit from Elitus. I don't trust any of them.

I show up at the conference early, slipping in the door just behind Mya. Seated in the front row are the usual suspects, the combat crew.

Mason sits front and center. She saves me a seat; that's us: Trouble 1 and 2. Back at it again, the rest eye us. They know that when we are united on something, and Elitus is involved, it could go sideways.

Mason is calm. Also, never a good sign.

She has some data she has been working on, courtesy of her latest data dump from her PPG admirer. That, along with the latest data I have regarding Latents, and the previous data reports. Shit, I worked on this a year ago. I passed it along. And it makes me wonder how much I gave them has helped them.

It's a thought, but one that doesn't hold much merit. Mason is looking into it. She tries to gather evidence. Tools. Things to hold Elitus' feet to the fire.

She's speaking with Riddick, who sits on my other side, but I lean into her space, smirking. "Don't share all my secrets, Clarke."

She doesn't even look at me. Just pushes my head back and keeps talking to Riddick. Mya slides into the seat on her other side, already in the loop. Whatever this meeting is about, we're not walking out of it the same.

I shift slightly in my seat, glancing at Riddick. "We ready to give them hell?"

His eyes stay fixed on the front. "Let's see what they give us first."

Fair enough. The weight in my chest tells me the truth; this meeting isn't about rules or classification. It's about the shift.

This is the one we've been waiting for. The one we've been building for years without knowing it.

Everything's about to change. And not just for Elitus.

For us.

For me.

Kate

Elitus sits on stage in the director's chairs, their postures composed but their eyes scanning the crowd. They're prepared for this. The lights showcase their united front to us, but they don't reduce the tension of the crowd.

I sit in the front row with my Gen One peers and combat-enabled friends, my back straight, my mind running through the outcomes of this meeting.

I listen to them, the summary. The official line.

They seem honest. Genuine, even. But Elitus is always careful with their words.

They hint at how the original variants caused complications—aggression, heightened hormones, enhanced physical abilities at the cost of control.

I glance toward Bastian and Mason. Neither of them looks surprised by this revelation, which means they already knew. Of course they did. They have their own sources, their own data sets.

What surprises me is how many kids there are, how far they've taken with this project. Farther than we were led to believe.

There's a secondary location. A trial group has already been selected. Long-term plans for integration.

How long has this been going on? My mind flickers back to Bastian's comment from the other night.

Are the Wights on Elitus just a distraction? A way to focus our attention while they worked on this latent project in secret. Never mind Vanguard—the name for the PPG kids, the second generation of Wights.

I shift in my seat, trying to push down the unease curling in my stomach.

"In the new year, we'll go live with this," my mother announces in a smooth tone. I exhale sharply. She knew. She and my dad had argued for years about the role she plays in all of this, the secrets she keeps. "We'll keep everyone updated," she continues. "By late Spring next year, we expect to integrate them into true power training. And that's where we'll ask for your support."

My fingers tighten around the armrest. Ask for our support? How generous of them. As if we've ever had an actual choice.

"We've also moved Gen Three's graduation up to the new year," Robert adds. "Many of you are beyond ready to test out. With that, we'll create another committee to help develop training, using Mason's previous dockets to build a plan for adult training. For Latents and more non-combat focus."

"Missions will continue. At the end of next week, those wishing to be combat-enabled will go through testing that Calvin developed based on Bastian and Mason's training regimen. If you pass, you're enabled. If not, you keep working." McGuire informs us. "This is not a replacement but an addition. These are trained individuals meant to strengthen our ability to run contracts. If Y and Z work as expected, they'll be fully immersed in the program. Even if it doesn't go as planned, they'll be integrated next year."

"This will give us more bodies, security, and options. But if you want to be enabled and clear all testing and requirements, you will be. What the mission lineup looks like, I don't know. But funding for this isn't cheap—so it's time to earn your paycheck."

"We'll allow for questions," Pepe says, opening the floor.

I look down the row. I already know who will go first. Rolling my eyes, I watch as Bastian stands. Of course, he'd go first; he always has something to say. "How many total Latents are you planning to incorporate next year?"

"Although not definite numbers, we have three groups of twenty-five selected. The first group is slated for the New Year. So ideally between fifty and one hundred." Holy crap. That's a lot of people being added to our infrastructure.

"And what is the long-term plan if Y doesn't work?" Roarke asks.

"We are moderately confident of the success of Y; however, each person selected would take a role in our community. As you know, we are looking to expand, not only in housing, but the labs, and the additional manpower can help. There are lots of roles on campus that can be filled," Dr. Miller points out.

"Where will they stay?" someone asks. "Because I don't see any new dorms being built. And Alex's residential plans include family homes & townhomes—not more barracks nor dorms."

Dr. Ross responds smoothly. "We have separate housing planned. The old lab next to the dorms is to be converted into three floors of rooms. We'll add a common area and a mess hall. We plan to break ground before Christmas."

Alex stands next, his expression unreadable. "And for those who don't want to go through enabling next week—is that an option?"

"Yes, it's not mandatory. But I suggest getting enabled if you can. Then, we can discuss mission loads. If only the two main primary teams enable, their workload will be brutal."

My fingers tighten around the armrest. Primary teams comprising Mason, Riddick, Roarke, Kyle, Bastian and the others, are already stretched thin.

Hearing this, every part of me screams to move. I'm not a spectator; never have been. Mason and Riddick are carrying too much; I won't let them break under the weight we all helped create. My mind is made up. I will enable. And if I must fight for my place, I will.

"What about training? If they are going live on Y, then who is teaching shielding?" Siobhan asks.

"We are working on that. We were hoping to have all this completed before we brought it to you, but we didn't want to delay bringing what we have currently forward," my mother says. She looks directly at me. "I know that this is a surprise for many. But I want all of you to know, we are learning just as you are. What the future entails, and how we can work together. I won't excuse the secrets," she side-eyes McGuire, and I can't help but smile. "But we will work together to make all of this work."

They drone on with more plans, but all I can think is this: secrets have ruled us long enough. Maybe finally they are ending.

NINETEEN

Kate

The next week passes in a blur of training and repetition. The pace is relentless, but I push forward, determined to clear combat—despite my father's disapproval. Exhaustion weighs heavily on those of us in combat, but we made it through.

I've mastered enough to clear the requirements with no issues. I'm not great, not yet, but I'm competent. I'll still need a Two with me, but that's normal for me, anyway.

Mason remains the steady teacher. Her patience is stretched thin by the sheer number of people here, half of whom will probably never reach the level they need.

Still, she keeps at it, her tone light, even teasing at times.

I also notice something else; Riddick and her.

They've always been close, but now? Watching their interactions, far more comfortable, playful even. They're still a force, but something has changed in their relationship.

Bastian is still there, but now she's the teacher, and he the student. The dynamic is shifting.

Mason walks in dressed up today. That's new; she looks good. Not in a suit like me, but in a skirt, high-heeled boots, hair down and loose for once. Just enough effort to be noticeable.

If I didn't know her better, I'd say she was trying to impress someone.

All the guys notice. I catch the way their eyes track her. I focus, trying to push the thought aside. It doesn't matter.

She starts, her tone commanding as always. "So, as I've mentioned before, you should never fully drop your guard. Once you master your shields, you can control whom you block and whom you allow a connection with."

"Some pulls are stronger than others. Sibling and familial bonds are easier to connect with. Some signatures have similar markers."

"Even though Max and Alex share no blood, they share me. With enough skill, they could use that connection to bridge the gap between them." She smiles at her brothers, who sit next to each other. "I haven't tested it, but I'd guess that if shields were completely dropped between two people, the connection would be like a live feed."

A murmur spreads through the group, people realizing this isn't your standard lesson. Everyone is sitting up a little straighter, paying attention.

"It's not a good thing in combat," Mason adds, her expression sharp. "You'd feel every hit twice as hard."

"When would you want that type of connection?" Reese inquires, curiosity laced in her tone. Reese is a strong Two healer, one of Bastian's best and most stable right hands.

Mason just smiles slyly, shaking her head. "I can think of a few situations," she teases, winking at Reese.

"So, in my professional opinion," Mason continues, some chuckle at that comment, "is that if a healer could enter someone's shield cover and drop it completely, they could investigate the issue internally. For Bastian, that would be critical in life-or-death situations. He'd need to do it to activate the X power. Same with some Tier Three abilities."

My mind races, trying to visualize how that could work. Could that connection be controlled? Could it be severed easily, or would it be permanent?

Wyatt, sitting beside me, raises a hand. "What about outer shields? Could you still shield others while maintaining that connection?"

Mason nods. "Yes. If I dropped my shields between Max and me, I could still build up my outer ones. A strong bond would form, locking us together like a power feed. It would strengthen us, but if the outer shield broke, we'd both be in danger. Not recommended. At least not yet."

I take a slow breath, my mind working through the possibilities, the risks. This is more than just shielding. This is rewiring how we understand our own abilities and shields.

The air in the room shifts, like static before a storm. My eyes flick between Mason and Bastian as her lesson pivots from strategy into something far more intimate, uncharted.

"The bonds," someone asks from across the room. "Are they permanent?"

Mason tilts her head, considering. "Yes, and no. Once you learn someone's full signature, they'll always be easier to pick out of the crowd. They'll always be closer to you in that way. But it's not permanent. You can shield yourself from that bond or connection. Like I said, I haven't tested it. It would make both parties vulnerable."

Vulnerable. That's what catches my attention. I understand shields. I understand power. But vulnerability, that's something else entirely.

"If it's a bond," Siobhan speaks up, "would you say it risks being addictive? Like power can be?"

Power-sharing is dangerous and difficult to regulate. I already struggle to separate emotions from my abilities. If I got pulled into someone's power structure, it'd consume me. Mason confirms my fears. "Yes. It's powerful to share at that level. It depends on the bond."

"If I dropped my shields with a low-level Wight, they'd go into overload. It would amp them up massively, but when the bond broke, they could experience withdrawal," the murmurs pick up around the room, at the thought of it. "Those of you who have reached X level before—you know what I mean. Power is like a high. It makes you jittery, unstable. You must burn it off, or it consumes you," Mason continues.

"The bond could be like that. Being bonded together in a shield cover isn't bad necessarily, but choosing who you bond with is the actual issue. You'd be giving them a part of yourself."

The gravity of it settles into my chest. I make the mistake of looking toward Bastian. With his jaw set, his eyes locked on Mason, it's almost as if I can feel his tension from here. I watch him consider something, then he asks, "Like between mated pairs?"

What the hell? Mason doesn't hesitate. "Yes."

"So, you believe the claims? About mates?" Andy asks, her voice carefully measured. Of all people, she'd know. It's obvious to everyone; Alex and she are already living proof.

Mason nods. "Yes. Elitus denies it, but I don't. It's an attraction, a connection. Like with family, but stronger. As you've learned about signatures, haven't you noticed common patterns based on tiers and levels? That's how they connect."

Many nod their heads in agreement; she has everyone's rapt attention now.

"All your life, you've flocked to those in the same tier. That's not a coincidence. It's the same principle. Not that mates have to be in the same tier," she adds, "but some kind of Agent X attraction may be at play. It doesn't mean you have to follow it or that it has to be mutual." I suck in a breath; I know exactly how that feels. "If two people were bonded, dropped shields, they'd become even closer, remarkably similar to any bond. Even if they were on opposite sides of the world, they'd feel the connection. They could find each other."

A shiver runs down my spine. The room is dead silent. Bastian doesn't look at me, but I can feel his energy shift, his shields probing out, testing. He's thinking about it. Just like I am.

"Could that bond be broken?" Bastian counters. His voice is calm, but there's something beneath it, something I don't like.

Mason exhales. "By you or me? Probably. The rest depends on the bond. If it's shielded, maybe not. It's all speculation. I don't know."

She pauses, then smirks. "Get me in the same room as Coral and Nikolai, and I'll give it a shot."

That gets the room going. A ripple of laughter, shock, and interest. The energy shifts again. "So, are we fated to have only one?" Charley asks, her tone half-serious, half-hopeful.

I can't help but smile. God, I hope not. Mason's lips twitch. "No. You can have many," she jokes with her bestie.

Charley huffs. "No, seriously."

Mason sighs, muttering under her breath, "Elitus is going to kick my ass for this."

I lean forward, resting my elbows on my knees. "Go ahead." I say, I'm invested now. "You already opened a can of worms. Might as well dump them all out."

Mason shrugs. "One mate for life? Maybe. It depends on Agent X. All of us are on the same Agent X, different enhancements, but the base. It's the same. Some are closer in structure. But other than that, I don't know. I'd say our options are limited. It doesn't mean everyone has a mate. It's like M&M's—you don't always get an even number, and some end up alone."

Laughter ripples again, but some people aren't amused. I watch Bastian; he's unreadable.

"If you have a mate," Mason continues, "then I'd expect you'd be drawn to them more than anyone else. But I don't know. We're hormone-based animals at our core. Agent X only amplifies that. Your hormones shift. You adjust. For many, you're pulled to someone based on your Tier, and more so to your X. The leader, the powerhouse. Your power is affected by his or hers. Even if you aren't mated, it doesn't mean you can't have a relationship."

"We're all connected more than commoners. The power itself is its own pull, its own connection. A lever. Shields pull us together, or they push us apart. It's up to us. Don't stress it—it's all theory, anyway. No proven results."

The chatter picks up again, with a hundred different conversations overlapping.

I glance toward Bastian. His jaw is tight, arms crossed; thinking; calculating.

I'm not sure this was Mason's intended lesson for the day, but it's the only thing anyone is going to talk about now.

Bastian

The conversation about bonds and mates doesn't die after class.

If anything, it spreads like wildfire. It's in the way people glance at each other now, second-guessing every pull, every flicker of energy or shift.

The air feels fresh, charged and uncertain.

And I hate it. Not because I don't believe in it, but because I do.

I've felt it. The tug that everyone talks about. That gravitation pull towards something, someone. The problem is, I don't want it.

I see it happening all around me. Alex and Andy — their bond is undeniable now. Their connection, the pull, it's been there forever, and they both just ignored it. Primarily because Elitus made them. But now I watch them. I can't help it. Whenever they are in the same room, they are never far apart. Alex reads her energy, her mood, from across the room. They move in sync. It's like a thread constantly pulling them back to each other, regardless of what is going on around them.

Then there's Lissa and Ryker. A perfect example of the mate bond in action. Theirs is solid, rooted. Unshakable. Sharing the same Tier, they were already connected. They complement each other's energies. Now, with the bond in place, she has a spark, a confidence she didn't have before, all because she has him by her side. And Ryker, her presence steadies him, how she gets him to relax, let go. Settles him in ways no number of shields or control could.

Me, I don't want to feel anything. I don't want to be tied to someone, forced into a connection I can't control. I have been fighting this very concept for so long. But now that it's out there, I can explore more. Probe the bonds, test them. I can figure out how to break it before it even begins.

The first thing I do is test the bonds that are already forming. I ask Alex about his connection with Andy, trying to figure out if it's a choice or just inevitable.

"It's not that simple," he tells me, shaking his head. "It's not just attraction; your energy shifts to match them. Like a lock falling into place and she was the only one with the right key."

I don't like that answer. I don't want to be locked into anything.

Then I go to the one person who might know how to break it. Mason.

"What happens if a bond is forced?" I ask her.

She raises an eyebrow. "You mean like an arranged-mate situation?"

"Yeah," I say, not bothering to correct her. She exhales, leaning back, thinking. Mason doesn't just give answers; she calculates them first. Identifies how much to say, what it will lead to. No one questions her answers, so she is cautious.

"I don't know," she admits. "I think if both parties resisted it hard enough, it wouldn't form fully. It might linger but not lock."

"So, it can be broken?"

She tilts her head, studying me. I feel the weight of her stare, like she's trying to piece something together. "I don't know if 'broken' is the right word," she finally says. "But maybe blocked. Or severed before it cements."

That's what I needed to hear. Because if it can be severed, then it can be avoided.

TWENTY

Kate

November was a blur, and Christmas is coming fast. Committees, ball planning, Elitus meetings, training — it's consuming my life.

I throw myself into the work, focusing on keeping busy. It's the easiest way to ignore the hearts, butterflies, and flowers all around me. Sappy couples have solidified since the change several months ago. I still train and help with Elitus academics, but most of my focus is on the New Year Ball and the Gen Three graduation. I don't run many missions, and normally I would complain, but lately I'm too busy to care.

So, when I get slated for a mission, I assume it's something simple, a routine assignment. But when I pull up the docket, my stomach tightens.

This isn't simple.

Ryker finds me almost immediately, a deep scowl on his face. "We rarely get sent out on the same mission," he states, his voice edged with irritation.

"That would be fine," I murmur, scanning the list again, "except Mason is the only genuine power on this team. No other X support. None of her usual combat partners either."

"I told McGuire this is a bad idea," Ryker says, jaw tightening.

"It'll be fine. It looks straightforward. Between you and Dean, we should be fine. It's mostly mental manipulation."

Ryker doesn't look convinced. No one likes Matt Dean. Not Ryker, not most of the combat teams, and not me. He's an ass-kisser, a politician disguised as a soldier. That and he's buddy-buddy with Adrian McGuire only makes things worse.

Honestly, I'm surprised he was even enabled. He and others like him. Their shields are weak; their skills are mediocre. They bring nothing valuable to the table.

At least I have a purpose outside of missions. They're just dead weight.

Later in the war room, the tension is thick. Uneasy faces. No surprise there. This lineup? We've never worked together.

I scan over the mission details, forcing myself to focus on the objective, not the team. Mason, at least, is calm. "It'll be fine," Mason says, steady as ever. We believe her because we have to.

At first, everything goes smoothly. Easy, even. Dean goes in for mental manipulation while Ryker and I hang back.

Dean emerges with our target, and I immediately know something's wrong. The guy turns on his own people, eyes wild, like a psychopath.

My stomach drops. This wasn't on the briefing, he has applied too much mental pressure, causing a break.

Dean has screwed up big time; this freaking jackass is going to get us killed. Everything unravels in an instant.

I drop my shielding, power rips out of me, my shields collapsing, leaving me raw and exposed as I push it outward, towards civilians, reducing as much collateral damage as possible.

It's the only choice I have. But it makes me vulnerable. Wide open. It triggers other issues as well; ones I don't have time to process. Not now anyway. Mason and Ryker are pinned down behind us. Dean is useless.

I have no choice but to act. I kill the target. Not part of the mission, nor the plan. But necessary.

Dean stares at me, wide-eyed. Like I'm the problem. I want to kill him next.

Before I can move, the pain explodes through my side.

Now, we have a fresh problem. I go for cover, pressing my hand to the wound, attempting self-healing. It's weak. I have little left. I'm already headed for burnout. My shields are already a mess after burning so much power in defense. Black spots appear in my vision, my body trembling from power and blood loss.

We need to get out. Now. I look to where Ryker and Mason are; they are struggling as well. Ryker has taken some damage, and Mason is taking on more than she is used to, with no true power weapon other than her. It's all falling on her and I hate it.

This is going south fast, and my anxiety spikes even higher. I can feel concern from Ryker as well. Then, like someone heard my plea, the cavalry arrives.

Well, Kyle does. Riding to the rescue, pulling us all out. Mission over.

Back at base, the labs are in chaos. I'm barely holding on, power-drained and bleeding. I drag myself onto a gurney, black spots dancing at the edges of my vision. Ryker drops next to me. He is injured himself, but he is too busy glaring at Dean to let the healers patch him up.

Mason looks like hell. But we're alive. Somehow.

Nala and Reese work on me, but then they're replaced. By Bastian.

He looks furious. His power and anger are palpable in the air, as he focuses on healing me. I blink up at him, my body too weak to fight him off. But I can tell by the look on his face what he is about to say, and I really don't want to hear it.

I already know I fucked up. And Bastian looks like he wants to kill me for it.

Bastian

I can't believe she's fucking hurt like this. If McGuire wants to play games with mission teams, he needs to know there will be repercussions.

I push more energy into Kate, forcing the healing to take faster, watching as the worst of her wounds knit themselves together. She murmurs something barely coherent. Her mind is fractured; her power flickers in and out.

I catch pieces of it. The guilt. She thinks failure is hers. Even though she was just doing her job.

I squeeze her hand, feeling the smallest response. She stirs, blinking up at me with those green eyes I see in my dreams, but she is too exhausted to hold any focus. It makes my chest tighten.

I nod at her, letting her know she'll be okay; that she is safe.

I drop extra shields on her, calming, grounding her. She needs to rest, not spiral. She shouldn't even have been out there. Kate doesn't belong in combat.

She's too damn valuable here at home, keeping things running.

She doesn't need to be on the front lines, bleeding out while I try to keep her alive. But she won't listen. She thinks she has something to prove. I swallow back the frustration, letting her fall asleep.

Then, I turn on Mason.

"What the hell happened?" I demand, stalking toward her. "How did this go sideways?"

Mason blinks at me, disbelieving. "Are you kidding me?" she snaps.

"Shield cover on ops prevents this!"

She shoots daggers at me. "And who taught you that, asshole?"

We don't have time to finish the fight because Elitus arrives. McGuire. Moore. Thompson. They look beyond pissed.

The mission was a disaster, and accusations fly. The debrief turns into a full-blown interrogation. Even though I'm furious with what happened, I know Mason isn't the one to blame.

Dean. That dumbass motherfucker. He and his clown crew are useless on a good day. And only get activated because McGuire's spawn is in their clique.

The second I get my hands on him; I'll make sure he never fucks up another mission again. I let out a slow breath, my rage barely contained. Mason zones out under the weight of it all, her shields fraying.

I nudge some stability into them, steadying her the way she always does for the rest of us. She finally lets me burn out her power. Pulling her down into exhaustion.

I should apologize later for lashing out when I knew damn well this wasn't her fault. But right now? I just want to burn something down.

Kyle takes Mason back to the dorms. She won't stay at the infirmary.

The room is tense, suffocating. The mission was a disaster, and we all know it.

McGuire and Thompson, however, have already decided who to blame.

Mason.

Because she was the lead. It's easier to throw her under the bus than to admit this team was a bad idea from the start. It's easier to ignore the fact that this should never have happened.

Calvin and Robert are already on the defensive, trying to back her up. But McGuire and Thompson? They aren't having it. They need a scapegoat.

Then they have the audacity—the absolute fucking balls—to suggest removing Mason from combat.

I nearly lose it; I healed Kate first, not Mason, Kate. That says enough. Both are important, but this mission put them both at risk. I will not let this slide.

Riddick and I buy time, stalling as long as we can, refusing to let them pin this on her. "You sent her out there to fail!" Riddick hollers, his rage unchecked. His father, although part of the mission decisions, has been quiet. Stephen knows this is going to cause changes. Nevermind, he'd have to be blind not to see what is going on.

Riddick is livid—more than usual. They've been getting closer. Not mates, but closer than friends. I can only imagine what this is doing to him. Because if I'm this pissed, he must be ready to fucking snap.

"She needs to lead no matter who she has with her," Thompson counters, voice cold, dismissive.

That's it. I've had enough. "You really think so?" I lash back, my voice razor-sharp. "I have Kate and Ryker's downloads. Dean went off-op. He's a wild card and unfit for action. None of them are. Kate shouldn't be out there either. She's far too valuable here."

"She doesn't want to be," Riddick adds, his voice low, threaded with violence. "This isn't Mason's fault. She won't take the blame this time."

"She didn't even defend herself," Thompson points out, leaning back in his chair like this is just another argument to win.

"Oh, and you would have believed her?" Kyle strides back in, fresh from taking Mason to the dorms. His eyes are sharp, ice cold. Something is brewing beneath the surface of his calm exterior. "Regardless," Kyle says, tone clipped, controlled, but dangerous, "Dean and the others need to be removed. I'd rather take on twice the mission load than deal with another disaster like tonight."

The room is silent. Because we all know he's right. Elitus wants to pretend that this was just an unfortunate mishap, a logistical error.

But we know better. This wasn't a mistake. It was a setup. One that almost got Kate and Mason killed.

We leave the meeting, the weight of the night clinging to my skin. The hallways are too bright, too clean, too quiet for what just went down. My pulse is still thrumming with rage, but I force my steps to steady.

Riddick mutters curses under his breath, jaw tight as we head to the dorms. Kyle's silence is worse—controlled, precise, a blade waiting to be drawn. Alex keeps pace on my other side, his power crackling just below the surface.

But it's Kate and Mason my thoughts circle back to. Both of them too pale, too drained, both of them damn near casualties of a setup we all saw coming.

I glance ahead as we approach the dorms, where Mason is out cold, and then I glance back to the infirmary, where Kate rests. That small flicker of her hand in mine won't leave me. It reminds me of why I can't let this slide.

Dean, McGuire, Thompson; someone thinks they can play games with us.

They're wrong.

TWENTY-ONE

Kate

Whatever happened after I passed out differs from what normally happens on a mission that fails that badly; because Mason is still enabled. And so aren't the rest of us. Well, maybe not Dean, thank heaven for minor miracles.

There's little debriefing. However, Elitus is shifting gears, pushing for full combat status, and fewer liabilities on missions.

I try not to wonder where that leaves me.

Frustrated, uneasy, and unsure of my future, I head to the main cafeteria, grabbing a salad while I skim through documents and complete last-minute approvals for the ball. I have a short meeting with Elitus and the residential committee in an hour, but I want to eat first, clear my head, and get some things off my plate.

I hate losing time, hate falling behind. This morning, I let myself rest; I had to. But the lost hours weigh on me, nagging at the back of my mind. My schedule is out of whack.

Halfway through jotting down notes on my phone, reviewing what I need to complete, the scrape of a chair snaps my attention upward.

Bastian. He leisurely drops down across from me completely uninvited. His presence makes me blink, surprised. He never ... approaches me.

I study him, trying to figure out his angle. Bastian does nothing without a reason. "Yes?" I ask, observing him.

"You good?" he asks, his tone casual, but I know what he means. He's asking about my mental state. He could cut through my shields easily if he wanted to, but he won't.

I exhale. "Yes. Thank you for yesterday."

He doesn't acknowledge it, just steals my bread from my side plate. I would never eat it anyway, but still. I watch him eat it like it's his right. He does things like that—crosses boundaries like they don't exist.

"You shouldn't have been out there." I glare at him, already bristling. "Not on that kind of op, anyway," he continues, his voice edged in frustration. "Not without more offense. Never mind that Dean should never be out again."

He's angry. Last night, he kept it in check, focusing only on healing me, shielding me, making sure I was safe. Now he's saying what he didn't then.

I bite my tongue, choosing not to remind him that he doesn't get to tell me what to do. "Don't worry," I murmur. "I'm sure I'll be disabled soon enough."

His hand covers mine; his grip on my hand is immediate. My breath catches. I look up and meet his gaze. Something in his eyes tells me last night scared him as much as it did me.

"If you want to be enabled, you will be," he says, his voice quieter now. "But that doesn't mean you have to do missions."

I search his face, waiting for the catch. There's always something with Bastian. A barb. A challenge. A reason.

But I find nothing.

I worry they won't even enable me, that I won't be given a choice. He must pick up on the apprehension because he sends a calming pulse through my shields.

I hate that it helps. More than that, I hate that his presence calms me at all. I give him a soft smile, letting some of the tension slip from my shoulders.

"I'll think about it," I say. Then, shifting topics, "Is Mason okay?"

"She's good," he replies, but his tone lacks its usual sharpness.

I know Ryker is still pissed, but if anything, he is more bothered by how the situation affected Lissa. She's a mess with all his pain and mental load. Their connection magnified it, and as someone not used to combat, nor that level of stress, she was having a hard time dealing. She is better now, but it is one more reason mission teams need to be more carefully selected.

I push the rest of my salad toward Bastian. He doesn't hesitate, finishing it quickly.

"Dean's off assignments," I tell him, sharing intel from my last meeting. "Several others are being pulled too. They're out of the dorms until we can screen for combat next year. We're restructuring the team lineups, better groupings and smoother operations."

"Good," he comments. Then we talk, not argue. It's weird. He shares his thoughts on what that means for missions and rotations. Everything in the future, including training and combat trials.

When we leave the cafeteria, he walks me to my meeting. We didn't argue once; we just stated our different viewpoints calmly.

No sharp barbs, no jabs, no short, backhanded comments meant to dig deep.

And that is odd; it makes me put my back up.

I am not used to stability from him.

And I don't know if I like it or if it terrifies me.

I sit at the dorm bar with Wyatt, sipping my wine and watching the party unfold. Since hearing about Dean and his band of misfits getting yeeted out of the combat dorms, Mason declared a celebration was necessary. I laughed, but I didn't argue. No shots for me. Just wine.

The atmosphere is lively, almost electric. People are more relaxed, like a weight has been lifted now that the deadweight has been cleared out. I swirl the wine in my glass, half-listening to Wyatt as he comments on the music choice, an eclectic mix of rap, hip hop and rock all courtesy of Mason, when Riddick walks in, brows raised as he surveys the scene.

"Did I miss the memo?"

"Nope," I say smoothly, taking another sip. "Mason said something about celebrating assholes getting tossed out. Can't say I blame her."

Kyle and Alex saddle up on his other side, dropping a file in front of Riddick. He flips it open, scanning the contents, his expression shifting.

"Room reassignments?"

"Yeah," Alex confirms, not looking thrilled.

"Andy moves in with you. Why do you look unhappy?" Riddick asks, eyeing him suspiciously.

"You won't be happy either when you check out page three."

Riddick flips through, and his entire body tenses. I already know what names he's looking at.

"Abso-fucking-lutely not."

Sabrina. Ariel. Aimee. De.

"Aimee is going into combat?" Riddick asks, voice tight, as he slams it down on the bar top.

"I guess," Alex mutters, as Bailey comes through with Max, joining the card game currently in progress.

"They still have to pass trials first," Kyle points out, but it does nothing to lessen the frustration simmering around Riddick.

"That won't help me with Rina. Goddamn it."

Before I can comment, Bastian walks in, flashing his usual cocky grin at Mason.

I grind my teeth. He doesn't know yet. I could have told him earlier, but we were having a rare moment, and I didn't want to ruin that. But now? Now he's smirking, flirting with Charley and Mason, and it's irritating.

"What about the other Gen Fours?" Riddick asks, flipping through the folder, his fingers clenching slightly.

"Looks like they're opening it up. If they enable, they can petition, but these are the top contenders," Alex explains. "Zack passed on it—wants to help set up non-combat dorms. RJ approached me about assisting, since combatants should have a choice once we get more housing open."

"Sounds like the combat dorms might turn into party central again," Wyatt quips.

Bastian slides into the open seat beside me, grabs my wine, and takes a sip.

I shift in my chair, smirking as I watch him. "Bastian, how do you feel about party central in the dorms again?"

"Fine by me," he says easily. "Although, I'd switch it up to actual alcohol, not your wine."

I snatch my glass back, spinning it slightly before licking the rim where he drank from. His eyes flare purple.

Wyatt slides him a drink, and I drop the bomb.

"I wonder how you'll feel in January when Ariel moves in."

His glass pauses at his lips. "Excuse me?"

I push the folder toward him. "No. Fucking. Way."

His power spikes hard, rolling through the room. His shields counter his reaction, but not quick enough. Everyone can feel the slight vibration of his shields adjusting; it catches Mason's attention immediately, as she moves toward us, unfazed.

"You see this?" Bastian demands.

Mason grabs the file, flipping through it. Unlike Riddick and Bastian, she doesn't explode; she smiles, "It's about damn time."

Riddick looks ready to break something. "Whatever, Riddick," Mason waves him off. "You can't keep her locked up forever. We entered the dorm at ten. They're eleven. They're stronger than almost everyone except me and you, Bastian. It's time for them to master it."

"Take some lessons from Alex and Max," Mason adds with a laugh, snagging the shot Wyatt slides her way. "Just go with it."

"Aimee is on there," Riddick growls.

"So?" Charley chimes in, appearing behind Mason, arms crossed with a knowing smirk. "If Aimee makes it to combat—and we all know she might power-wise—she still must be combat-enabled. Honestly, I doubt she'll go through with it. But she wants to get out of the house. Let her. Once Alex gets the other dorms going, she can transfer," Charley shrugs.

"The other dorms are secondary to latent housing," Wyatt notes, ever the realist.

"That's fine," Mason says. "Regardless, it is what it is. We're not here to be downers—we're here to have a good time." She drags Riddick away into the party, effectively cutting off his protests.

Bastian, however, is still stewing. His tension is palpable, the sharp edge of his energy crackling around us.

Wyatt refills my glass, and I watch Bastian nurse his whiskey. I almost feel bad for him. Almost.

Ariel is just like him. Wild. Reckless. Out of control. Her and Rina? Absolute chaos. And now, with the dorms open and dating no longer off-limits?

I touch his hand lightly, feeling the charge of his power immediately. It surges, familiar yet unsettling. I shield myself before he can glean too much from me. "She'll be fine," I whisper.

His gaze snaps to mine. "You know no one will let anything happen to any of them," I continue. "Besides, you'll be able to shield her for a while at least."

He exhales, tension still coiled tight. "I know," he mutters. "Doesn't mean it makes me happy."

Downing his drink, his eyes flick to my half-empty glass. "You sticking for cards?" he asks.

I give him a look. Like hell. He just laughs, grabbing the bottle before heading off toward the game.

I catch myself watching him walk away. I can't help but notice the way he moves; the extra time he's been training with my dad is clear. Making his body more of a weapon than he already is, gearing up for whatever is coming in the new year. It looks good on him.

I spin back around only to find Wyatt watching me, amusement clear in his face. I roll my eyes. He just chuckles and distracts me from my X-Two problem.

Bastian

The party is still going, but the energy has shifted. Most of the chaos has faded into the background. It's just the core group left, the main combat squad. Well, the guys and Mason, anyway.

I lean back in my chair, surveying the room. "I don't know if this party is lame or if we're just old now."

Mason laughs. "I'm not even twenty-one yet!"

"We've been drinking for six-plus years, babe," Riddick comments, taking a sip of his drink. I note the way Kyle doesn't miss the endearment.

Mason rolls her eyes. "Whatever." She downs another drink, then leans forward, her expression shifting. That's never a good sign. "I have a question," she starts. "Ever think about launching our own mission?"

Kyle's eyes narrow. "Where are you going with this?"

Mason taps a finger against her glass, considering. "Talked to my dad today," Dad, not Robert. "He needs more intel on Dmitri's soldiers, what they're using, results, weaknesses. Apparently, McGuire can't get anything solid."

I raise an eyebrow. "Are you suggesting we hit a PPG lab?"

"Either that... or capture one of their latents for experimental purposes." She's dead serious.

Roarke exhales, shaking his head. "That's a line we can't uncross, Mase."

Her frustration spikes through the room like a live wire. "Are we at war or not?" She grips her glass tighter, jaw tense. "Dmitri came here. He made a blatant threat. That should be enough for us to ensure we're prepared. We run scared all the time, and I'm sick of it. We need to go on the offensive before it's too late."

Kyle sets his drink down, his expression unreadable. "Do you want to involve Elitus or McGuire?"

"If McGuire could get something going, he would have by now." Mason waves him off. "Honestly, we don't need him. We have our own access. I'm not saying we do it, but we must consider it."

Riddick folds his arms over his chest, leaning back. "What's your dad looking for? What's missing?"

Mason sighs. "He says the odds of Latent X, Y, Z working are good. Really good. Maybe too good. He's worried that if it keeps manifesting, there could be side effects—maybe even death."

I scoff, shaking my head. "Bet they aren't bringing that to the table."

"Of course not. And look, I don't want to be replaced, but we need to be prepared, and more protection can't hurt. I think it's worth looking into. Never mind the additional data I want on Vanguard," Mason says regarding the children at PPG.

Roarke leans forward, fingers tapping against the tabletop as he thinks, the Peacemaker working through it, helping to solidify a plan. "Riddick and I will work logistics. Kyle can get us McGuire's data. We'll start piecing something together." He holds up a hand before Mason can thank him. "No promises."

Mason grins anyway. "Thank you."

Roarke studies her for a beat, then asks, "What else did your dad say?"

"That I'm awesome," she quips, smirking. Kyle groans, flicking a playing card at her. She laughs before adding, "No, he just said you all defended me, which I appreciate. I know I was a bitchy hardass for a while, so thanks for waiting me out."

I shrug. "As long as you don't turn into Robot Mason again, I'm all good."

She rolls her eyes, but we all know what I mean. Things are shifting. The war is coming, whether or not Elitus wants to admit it.

We bullshit some more, the easy camaraderie of the night gradually shifting, a muted tension settling beneath the surface. Riddick steps away to take a call, nothing unusual—but when he returns. I know immediately that something is wrong.

"What?" Mason demands, sharp as a blade. Riddick doesn't respond, just gestures for a private audience. Mason shakes her head. "No, I don't fucking care. Where is she?"

His jaw tightens. "Seems like McGuire's 'secret missions' didn't stop. He just found someone else to run them."

Silence, for half a second. "I'm going to fucking kill him," she says. Then Mason is gone in a flash of energy, porting out before any of us can react.

Fucking hell, McGuire. I can already take two guesses who he tapped for this bullshit. And neither is going to end well. We follow fast, materializing in McGuire's office just as Mason's rage crashes into the room like a goddamn storm.

"You asshole!" she snarls, charging straight for him.

Before she can even reach him, Roarke is already there—slamming McGuire into the wall so hard the drywall cracks.

Shit, for the Peacemaker, that's a hell of a reaction.

Mason doesn't even get the chance to hit McGuire before Kyle, Riddick, and I intervene, barely prying Roarke off. He's immovable, rage vibrating through him in thick, lethal waves.

I nudge him mentally, sending a sharp push. *Enough.* He releases McGuire, but not willingly.

"You sent her out there solo, with no fucking backup! What the hell is wrong with you?" Roarke snarls.

McGuire isn't even fazed, after nearly getting his skull caved in.

"You honestly thought the missions would stop?" he spits at Mason.

Her entire body is deathly still. "So, you go to my younger sister?" She asks, voice quiet but laced with venom. "Is she the only one, or did you tap RJ too?"

The room drops several degrees. Mason at full X-level isn't something anyone wants to deal with.

I don't have time to process the implications before Roarke breaks free of our grip, lunging again. This time, Mason stops him.

Not physically. She just moves in front of him, locking eyes, freezing him in place with her power.

"Did you do this?" she demands.

"Of course not," Roarke mutters. "I don't want her out there at all."

Mason's gaze narrows. "You had her pulled."

"She's enabled."

"Now. But before? You pushed her off." Her tone is pure disgust.

Roarke's jaw clenches. "She shouldn't be out there."

"Why? Because she's a whore?"

You can hear a pin drop. Roarke flinches as if she actually hit him.

What the hell? That isn't a casual accusation. Mason wouldn't have said it if she hadn't meant it.

"That's what you called her, right?" Kyle and I exchange glances. This is bad. But it is giving some explanation of the Mya/Roarke situation.

Mason is already dangerously close to losing it, and now she's turning that rage fully on Roarke. "It's complicated," Roarke grits out.

"It's not complicated," Mason snaps. "You hurt her. And I am so goddamn mad at you."

McGuire, the smug bastard, just watches. Enjoying the chaos he created.

Before she can unload on him, the door slams open. Stephen and Ace stride in, assessing the situation in an instant.

"Goddamn it, Teddy," Stephen growls, already piecing together the mess.

"These need to go," McGuire says, brushing himself off like he wasn't just slammed into a wall. "You know this, Stephen."

Stephen barely looks at him. He's looking at us. At Mason. At Roarke. On the fine line, chaos is riding in this room.

"This should have come to the Elitus table!" I snap, my temper fracturing completely.

McGuire doesn't even blink. "This would never fly. It's under the radar and black," he shoots back. "Are you volunteering to run them?" He gestures to all of us.

Before any of us can respond, Mya ports in. She looks relatively unharmed, but the tension in her stance is obvious. She doesn't even look at us, just hands off her debrief to the techs.

Mason stalks toward her. "Why? You know you don't have to do this."

Mya just lifts her chin, giving Mason a knowing look. Too knowing. "And who do you think he would go to next?" she counters. "He needs a certain skill set, Mase."

Mason's expression hardens. "So, you took the bullet for RJ."

Mya doesn't deny it. "As would you." Mason's power pulses outward.

"Fuck that," Roarke snaps. Riddick steps in, a hand on Roarke's shoulder, forcing him to back down.

"Mya, side missions are done. Effective immediately," Riddick tells her. He turns on McGuire. "You can have black missions," he growls. "But they need to be controlled. No more solo bullshit."

McGuire tilts his head, feigning interest. "What are you suggesting?"

"A different committee," Mason interjects smoothly. "With some other concessions."

McGuire laughs. "You don't dictate how things go."

Mason just smiles. That smile she gives before she goes in for the final blow. "Don't worry, I'm heading to my father and Pepe after this," she says lightly. "Trust me—you're grounded, asshole."

McGuire opens his mouth to argue, but she's already gone, porting out with Mya in tow. He exhales sharply, turning his attention to Riddick.

"Don't even think about it," Riddick warns. His voice is icy. "We'll meet tomorrow and figure out what the fuck we're doing here. But goddamn it, McGuire, it was one thing to use Mason. Now Mya? You fucking took advantage of her need to prove herself. Of her loyalty to us, over her brothers. You saw an opportunity and pounced."

McGuire shrugs as if it doesn't matter. "She wanted this," he says simply. Riddick's hands curl into fists.

"Did she?" I ask, but McGuire doesn't answer.

Kyle pulls us all back. "Let's go."

The anger is thick between us as we enter the dorms. We all know the truth. McGuire isn't stopping. He's just getting better at hiding it.

And I don't think this was even the worst of it.

TWENTY-TWO

Kate

I'm stuck in another exhausting Elitus meeting, barely absorbing the discussion. The air in the chambers is tight with tension.

McGuire's been running side missions behind Elitus' back again, and this time even his usual allies look pissed.

Mom reminds me often that not everything is as it seems. There are things Elitus does, things we all do, that aren't broadcasted for everyone to see, but still need to happen. I know that. I know that our funding and the missions we take are murky at best. Whenever the government is involved, there are always scales to be balanced.

But sending people out without proper intel? Without backup? Risking them as if they are disposable. That's a whole different level of recklessness.

I push my irritation aside and focus on the committee work, reviewing last details and sign offs, when the back doors open and everything shifts.

The door clangs against the wall, and the air in the room gets even tighter.

Bastian leads the charge, with Riddick, Mason, Mya, Charley, and Roarke flanking him. Their footsteps echo across the tile. They walk in like they own the place.

McGuire barely masks his irritation. "This is a closed meeting," Thompson snaps.

"Not anymore," Bastian fires back, striding forward with a cocky smirk that sets my nerves on edge.

He drops a thick document on the table in front of my mother, while Mason and Mya make similar moves along the table.

I watch my mom. She picks it up, reads it carefully, her expression unreadable, but her lips twitch. I know that look. She likes what she sees.

Without a word, she passes it down the table. I get up, moving closer as Alex scans the pages he's looking at.

McGuire's face contorts with fury. He doesn't even finish reading before he stands, his chair falling back as he slams the papers down.

"What the hell is this?" he demands, fists clenched and pressed against the table.

I glance at the contract—then freeze. My breath hitches; it's a petition, a union contract. A fucking power shift.

Bastian grins. "It's your pink slip. We as a collective unit have decided you will no longer run us."

McGuire's color deepens as he stands to his full height. But his expression only hardens.

"It's a petition," Bastian continues, voice dripping with satisfaction. "Signed by all Wights, but the six here. Within it, we lay out the terms of our contract for services. You will no longer have free rein over us. All decisions go through the six of us."

Silence.

"No fucking way," McGuire snaps, his voice sharp enough to cut steel. "You think you can just waltz in here and dictate how we do our jobs? You've seriously overstepped."

I scan the table. Disbelief. Shock. Some intrigue. I can't believe they're doing this. And they didn't even tell us first.

Only six of us weren't aware they were even meeting. Kyle is eyeing Bastian hard.

"Actually, we can," Riddick says smoothly, arms crossed over his chest. "Either you accept the terms, or we walk," he adds. "And by walk, I mean we don't train. We don't run missions. We do nothing until you agree."

McGuire rounds on him, his fury palpable. "I don't need you," he spits.

Stephen steps in, clearly about to defend his son, but Mason cuts him off.

"You may not need him," she says, voice cool and controlled. "But you sure as shit can't function without me." She lets the words settle, unshaken by McGuire's glare. "Don't doubt that we mean business. What are you so afraid of?" she presses. "If you read the fine print," she continues, "you'll see there's even room for missions of a different... color. Otherwise, you're out of options. For all missions."

McGuire's nostrils flare.

"We'll let you discuss," Bastian adds. "The highlighted points are open for negotiation. We'll await your reply."

And just like that, they turn and leave.

I don't wait. I shove back my chair and follow them, catching up before they get too far.

Bastian

We walk out of that goddamn meeting, leaving Elitus in chaos behind us. The contract is a direct shot across the bow, a warning that we're not just weapons to be deployed whenever McGuire sees fit any longer.

But Kate, I knew she wouldn't let this slide. Her footsteps are quick behind me, her heels clicking across the marble, her determination just as sharp as her damn tongue.

"Wait," she calls, her voice echoing off the pristine walls, as she catches up. Before I can react, her fingers curl around my bicep, stopping me in my tracks.

With her hand on me, her touch is like a live wire straight to my core. I grit my teeth, not turning, not reacting. But she doesn't let go.

"Bastian, think about this," her voice is low, urgent—not quite pleading, but close. Kate doesn't plead. She negotiates. "Do you really want to make an enemy of McGuire? He'll find every reason to fight this."

I shake her off, rougher than I need to be. I need distance. Now.

"Wake the hell up, Kate." I snap, finally facing her. "He's never been on your side. He's out for himself, and damn everyone else."

Her eyes flash, but she doesn't back down. Kate never backs down. I can't stop though; I have had it. "I get you want to manage every situation and avoid conflict, but there's no way around this." She frowns; lips press together like she's swallowing a dozen arguments. Which only pisses me off more.

"Elitus will never be what it once was," I press, stepping closer, voice rough. "There's too much at play now. What happens the next time McGuire wants a side deal done?"

She drops my arm but doesn't step back. She needs to hear this; someone needs to get through to her.

"What happens the next time he wants something done off the books?" I push, tone hard. Her shoulders are rigid, but I keep going. "He doesn't look at us as people, Kate. He never has and never will."

Her breath hitches, eyes narrow, but I go for the kill anyway. "Shit, he doesn't even look at his son that way." The words hang between us, thick and weighted. But the last blow—I don't know why the hell I say it, but I do, knowing damn well what will happen. "It's time to show where your loyalties lie."

She finally cracks. Her power surges outward, hot and sharp, slamming into my senses like a wave of static. And then she shoves me.

Not just a push, but a full pulse of energy, crashing into me like a shockwave. My boots skid against the tile, forcing me to lock down my muscles before I lose more ground. She's angry. Maybe she'll finally stop pretending everything is fixable. That she can control every outcome.

"Loyalty?" she hisses. Her eyes glow with unchecked fury, and for half a second, I feel it.

All of it. Her frustration. Her hurt. Her anger at me. And something else buried underneath. Something she's just as unwilling to name as I am.

"How dare you, you arrogant ass." She steps closer, power-licking against my skin like heat off an open flame. "My loyalty has always been to my family. You think I'm happy about any of this? Fuck you, Bastian."

The words hit harder than I expected. She shoves me again, this time with nothing but her bare hands. "You do not know how I feel or what I want," she growls. I watch her, taking her in. She's furious.

But there's hurt woven into it, a crack in her armor. "I'll be loyal," she says, voice tight, but her hands tremble slightly. "But maybe you should rethink what this is really about." My stomach twists. "This isn't just about busting McGuire's balls." She keeps going, relentless. "This isn't just about besting Kyle."

My jaw tightens. "This is a lifetime commitment to your peers." She lets the words sink in, lets them hit. "Think long and hard before you make a promise you can't live up to."

She pivots, stalking away. The sound of her heels clicking against the floor echoes in my head long after she is gone.

I stand there, my fists clenched, my pulse hammering.

She's right. I know she's right. And that only pisses me off more.

I can't do this with her; I can't keep fighting her, wanting her, needing her to push me just enough that I feel something but not enough that it ruins me. My head and heart are at fucking war every day.

My temper rises fast, blinding me to anything but the knot in my chest. I lash out, fist driving into the wall beside me.

Plaster cracks beneath my knuckles, leaving a deep, jagged hole. I don't even feel the pain. I just feel her words sinking into me, lodging deep like a blade. "That fucking woman," I mutter, shaking out my hand before stalking off.

Behind me, laughter erupts. Mason. Charley. Riddick.

"That went well," Mason comments dryly.

"Better than expected," Charley snickers.

I flip them off over my shoulder.

Assholes.

TWENTY-THREE

Kate

I stride back into the chambers; I can't even think straight. How fucking dare he say that to me! I do everything for the Wights. I sacrifice my wants and needs far too often to keep things running smoothly. And he dares to question me?

When I return to the table, McGuire is still arguing—but losing.

Wyatt hands me a cup of tea, his expression knowing, as Reese offers a small, sad smile.

I exhale slowly, gripping the cup. Guess this changes things.

After gossip spread about Elitus bending to the will of the so-called POWER COUN-CIL—what a dumbass name—they headed off-site to celebrate. Off-campus events are still a go for some, it seems.

I know Bastian is at the center, reveling in his victory over McGuire and Elitus in the most predictable way possible. Probably hooking up with some random commoner, the way I hear he always does after a big win.

That thought alone twists in my gut like a blade.

Why does it bother me? I already know how he operates. I know the type of girl he goes for—casual, uncomplicated, fun. And I am none of those things.

I force my attention back to my work, focusing on committee planning with a few of the Wights. Paige, David, and Siobhan have been helpful, not just in finalizing the New Year training plans but also in distracting me.

It helps. For a while. But the reprieve doesn't last long. Before midnight, they return.

And the moment I see Bastian, my temper spikes so fast it's a miracle I don't launch something at him.

He's plastered. Collar loose, shirt wrinkled, his smirk lazy with the satisfaction that makes my blood boil. And right there, smudged against the fabric of his collar—lipstick.

It shouldn't bother me. Because no matter how many times I tell myself it doesn't matter, it does.

He has never looked at me the way I want him to. Never lets himself want me the way I've secretly, shamefully wanted him. And maybe that's why I'm so furious right now.

"What?" I snap, stepping into his space. "How was it? Celebrating your big victory? Whoring it up?"

His smirk widens. He's just drunk enough to be dangerous.

"What's wrong, Katie-Did?" he taunts, slurring that stupid childhood nickname. "Jealous?"

I inhale sharply, reining myself in before I do something reckless. "You're drunk," I bite out, turning away before I hit him.

"And you're a pent-up little girl hiding behind designer suits and your brothers." I stop. My stomach twists, his words cutting in ways I refuse to acknowledge. Because maybe he's right. Maybe that's how he sees me: cold, rigid, controlled, untouchable.

That deep, aching need to be wanted, to be seen, to be something other than just capable coils inside me, bitter and unwanted.

He doesn't wait for me to respond, though. He keeps going. And that I can't tolerate. I follow him down the hall, my temper rising just as fast as my power.

Bastian

I make it to my room, attempting to slam the door behind me, too drunk, too wired, too fucking fed up to deal with anything else tonight. Especially not her.

But I'm not alone. Because Kate's on my heels, too fast for me to shut her out. I try to push the door shut, but she shoves back, hard.

Her power is amped up, making it impossible for me to stop her.

"You fucking prick!" she spits, storming in. "How dare you say that to me?"

I don't even have to ask what she's talking about. I already know. "You, who hides behind your damn shields all day long," she seethes, stepping closer, her energy crackling around her like a live wire. "Letting no one in. Always acting like the tough guy. You may be an X, but you don't fool me."

I try to breathe past the burn in my chest, but the alcohol makes it worse. I'm too raw. Too fucking tired of fighting this. So instead, I lash out.

"Fuck you, Kate. Leave."

I yank the door open, gesturing for her to get the hell out.

She doesn't move. Instead, she slams it shut again.

My blood boils. I whip around, jaw clenching so tight it aches.

She tries to pry into my shields, but I don't let that shit slide.

Even drunk, she doesn't stand a chance against me.

I slam back at her, pushing her out and shattering her outer defenses like glass. Her breath hitches, but instead of backing down, she does something completely fucking insane.

She drops all of them. Every shield. Leaving herself completely open.

Then she moves—fast as hell, using a burst of her energy to shove me against the door and kiss me.

Goddamn. She tastes fucking perfect.

I react, my hands latching onto her hips, pulling her against me.

It's fire and tension and everything I've been holding back for too damn long.

But she's not the only one with strength. I move, switching our positions, so it's her against the wall, taking my time with her mouth, her neck.

I force myself to pull back, panting, my hands still tight on her waist.

She's drunk with power. I'm drunk on actual alcohol.

"We are not doing this," I tell her, my voice rough. Kate tilts her head, eyes gleaming, challenging.

With a wicked smirk, she kicks my legs out from under me. I hit the ground like a sack of bricks. Before I can recover, she's on me, straddling my hips, pressing me down. Her skirt rides high, and I catch a perfect view of her toned thighs, the glint in her eyes. She knows exactly what she's doing.

I don't have time to breathe before she's kissing me again.

Her hands drag up my chest, her lips on mine, soft and urgent, sending my head into chaos.

Fuck.

This is not what I need right now.

This is not how I want this to happen. But my body? It doesn't give a damn.

She's everywhere—her scent, her warmth, her fucking mouth, claiming me like I'm hers to take.

And part of me wants her to.

Badly.

But I can't.

Not when she is angry, and I am plastered. I growl, gripping her hips and flipping her, pinning her beneath me, arms locked above her head.

"Kate, you are not ready for what I will give you," I say through gritted teeth.

Her chest rises and falls rapidly, power still buzzing beneath her skin. "This isn't some business deal, or some fucking assignment," I warn. I pull back, forcing myself to let her go. I slide to the side next to her.

She looks at me, her eyes flashing with something I can't quite place.

And then I feel it. Rejection. A sharp, visceral pain I wasn't expecting from her.

Shit. She doesn't even try to hide it. With her shields still blown apart, I feel everything.

And it wrecks me.

But she recovers fast, slamming her emotions into a tight, impenetrable box, slipping on that perfect, untouchable mask.

Her voice is cool. Controlled. "Unlike you, Sebastian," she says evenly, "I know what I want."

The way she says my name hits like a goddamn knife. She stands, fixing her skirt, smoothing herself out like this never happened.

"Not to worry," she adds, tone polished, detached. "I'm now well aware of what you think of me." She turns, striding toward the door, her heels clicking in time with my pulse. "Sorry to have ruined your night."

Then she's gone. I sit there, still on the goddamn floor, breathing like I just went ten rounds in a fight that I lost.

Because I did. I lost everything in that moment.

And it's entirely my fault.

Fuck.

I shove a hand through my hair, trying to pull myself together. I can't let it end like this. I get up fast, heading after her before she disappears completely.

When I reach the parking lot, she's already yanking open her car door. "Kate, wait," I snap, reaching for her arm.

She doesn't stop. I slam the door shut instead, pinning her between my body and the car. "Wait. Talk to me."

She spins to me, and fuck—she's crying. Tears brimmed in those sharp green eyes.

I did that. I send her a calming pulse instinctively, trying to steady her, but she shoves it back at me.

"Don't," she says sharply. Her voice shakes just enough to gut me. "I don't need your pity."

She swipes at her face, anger overtaking the sadness. "You made it very clear." Her throat bobs as she stares at me, her breath unsteady. "Don't worry, I won't make that mistake twice."

She tries to move past me, but I block her. "Don't tell me how I feel, what I think," I bite out. "You came out of nowhere tonight and threw yourself at me. You know damn well I've been drinking, and my brain is fuzzed."

Her eyes flash. "Think? Think long and hard! Think forever for all I care!" Her voice rises. "I don't care, Bastian. You had your chance. You blew it."

I barely process what's happening before I get punched in the ribs. I spin to defend. But then Ryker nails me in the face.

"Ryker, no!" she yells, but fuck, I deserve it.

Riddick appears, separating us before this gets worse. Mason moves in, taking Kate home in a port.

I stand there, feeling the weight of my worst mistake.

I let her go, and I don't know if I'll ever get her back.

Kate

Mason ports me straight to my room, and I don't even have the strength to protest. I'm grateful I don't have to face my mother. Grateful I don't have to endure the look of concern and quiet judgment, the kind that says, *I warned you about him.*

Because the truth is? I knew better. And I did it anyway.

I collapse onto my bed, my body folding in on itself like a crumpled piece of paper.

The tears come hard and fast, wrecking me from the inside out. My shields are gone, shattered into nothing, leaving me raw and vulnerable in a way I haven't been in years.

I can still feel him. Not physically, but in my core.

I let my guard down, letting him in.

And Bastian Monroe, of all people, knows exactly what that means.

I dropped every single shield in front of him tonight. There's no taking it back.

"Do you want to talk about it?" Mason's voice is soft but steady.

I try to smile, but it's weak. Pathetic. "There's nothing to talk about." My voice cracks, barely holding together. I wipe at my face as if erasing the tears could somehow erase what I just did. "I was mistaken. I should've known better."

Mason doesn't move, doesn't push, just watches as I curl into myself.

"He's been getting under my skin for weeks—more than usual." I let out a bitter laugh, the weight of it crushing me. "I don't know. Watching everyone else pair off must have made my wires cross."

The words taste bitter in my mouth. This is a pathetic excuse for my actions.

I stand, needing to change. Get out of this outfit. Burn this skirt. I need to peel off these stupid clothes, wipe away the scent of him still lingering on my skin.

"Kate." Mason's voice is gentle, too gentle. "Is he your mate?"

The words hit me like a gut punch.

I can't look at her. I won't. Because if I do? If I meet her eyes, I'll break even more.

She doesn't push, just stands and pulls me into a hug. It's warm and grounding, but it also makes the tears worse.

We've always been friends, but we're different. Mason is so goddamn smart. A hero. She cares about everyone's well-being, even when people talk shit about her for it.

I wish I could be like her, but I'm not.

Deep down, I hate that.

"I can't be like Nala," I whisper, my voice breaking. Speaking of the way she chases Kyle when he isn't all that interested in her. "I won't settle."

Mason doesn't speak, just holds on. "If he's not all the way in, I don't want him at all." My voice hardens, but it's a false conviction, a shield I barely have the strength to keep up.

That's when the realization slams into me like a wrecking ball.

I don't have a shield anymore. Not against him. Bastian knows everything I feel. And what's worse, he didn't want it. He saw all of me laid bare, and he still pushed me away.

There's a beat of silence, and then I let it out, the ugly truth that's been festering inside me for too long. "Some days? I hate you, you know."

Mason stills. I exhale shakily, my hands trembling as I try to explain. "They all would die to be with you." My throat tightens. "Even my brothers."

Mason shifts slightly, but I keep going, the words tumbling out like a confession I can't stop. "When I see you with him, I want to scream." I don't have to say who. "I may not have much Two abilities, but I learned a long time ago how to shield myself really well." My lips curve into a humorless smile. "I had to."

Mason lets out a small breath, like she's putting together something she should've realized a long time ago. "How long have you known?" she asks softly.

I laugh, but it's hollow. "Forever, it seems." I wipe my face, trying to erase the damage, but it's pointless. "And it just makes me so mad."

I shake my head, hating how raw I feel. "I like the fairy tale, Mase. I want the goddamn fairy tale." My voice drops, barely above a whisper. "When I'm near him, I just go crazy. I can't help but fight with him." I swallow hard. "And now? I don't know what I'll do."

Mason lets out a short laugh. "Want some advice?"

I sniffle, still trying to pull myself together. "Not really."

She ignores me. "Make him suffer." I blink. Mason grins, but there's something knowing in her expression. "He needs a reality check," she continues. "And I hate to break it to you, but when he decides he's ready for you?" She shrugs as if it's inevitable. "You're done for."

"That's not—"

"There's something about a High Two that can't compare," Mason interrupts, her smirk widening. She leans in slightly. "Ask Lissa—she'll tell you."

I roll my eyes, but it's weak. Mason's voice softens. "Go after what's in your heart, Kate. If you don't lay it all out there, you'll always come up short."

I wish it were that simple. I feel like I already did. But I didn't stick around to hear his excuses. Too scared of him voicing his rejection, too scared to realize I will never get the fairy tale dream I've always wanted.

Now I have to move on. I need to get my suit of armor back on. I need to bury this. I can't afford to be exposed again. It's what I must do, even if it makes me miserable.

Bastian

I drop into a chair, popping the top of a beer, holding it to my cheek, letting the cold bite against my face where Ryker's fist landed.

My jaw aches, my ribs throb, and my head is pounding, but none of it is worse than the fucking mess in my head.

I don't even bother healing myself. I deserve it. What the hell did I just do? I'm a goddamn idiot.

No—worse. I took the person who's always been a constant, the one who's challenged me, fought me, and pushed me, and broke her.

I saw it, felt it.

When she dropped her shields, when she let me see everything—her feelings, her want, the depth of it wrecked me.

Instead of doing what I've wanted to do for years, instead of taking what was right in front of me, I shoved her away.

Like a fucking coward.

Because I'm an asshole.

Because I'm scared shitless.

Because if I let her have all of me, there's no going back.

And I know damn well I'm not who she needs. I'm not polished or proper. I'm a mix of chaos and clutter.

I am completely the opposite of Kate. A rule breaker, never a follower, always questioning the whys of everything. I don't mind combat; I thrive on the power, the abilities I have. I know it is dangerous; I choose to temper it with shields.

I will always be front and center on any battlefield. So, the risk to anyone with me is substantial; they are a target.

Even if she wanted to be with me, she shouldn't. She's too important, not only to her family and friends but to Elitus. She keeps everyone in line and keeps it moving. And she should never take that kind of risk on a guy like me.

I take a long pull from my beer; the bitterness does nothing to drown out my thoughts.

After Jasper and Ryker finished ripping into each other, they both turned on me. I get it. I fucked up.

Ryker wanted to throw another punch, and if I had any ounce of self-respect, I would've let him. But I grabbed my beer and took a seat, tuning them all out, trying to rationalize the goddamn train wreck I created.

But what's worse is figuring out how the hell I fix it. If it can even be fixed. Kate will not make it easy.

I know her. She'll rebuild those walls, reinforce her shields, throw herself into work and avoid me like I'm a fucking plague.

I dig my fingers into my hair, elbows braced on my knees, trying to sort through this disaster I can't outrun.

I just keep seeing the way she looked at me when I pushed her away. That moment—her heart in her goddamn eyes, laid bare for me to take.

I should beat my own head in.

Mason comes through not much later, dropping into the seat beside me like she already knows what's coming. Lissa shoves a new ice pack and another beer at me. Leaving us be.

I take it without a word. Mason eyes my drink, unimpressed.

"Oh, yeah, that'll help," she muses, leaning back and folding her arms over her chest. I don't bite. I don't have the energy.

Instead, I ask the only thing that fucking matters. "Is she okay?"

Because I am sure as hell not. Mason studies me, her sharp gaze cutting through every defense I have left.

Which isn't much.

"She'll be fine." I scowl. That's a lie. She won't be fine. I fucking felt her break.

Mason nudges my shields, and for once, I don't push her out. Maybe because I need someone to tell me what the hell to do. Maybe because I don't know how to fix this on my own.

She laughs at me. A low, knowing laugh that makes my chest tighten.

"Oh, Bastian," she says, shaking her head. "You're an idiot, and in over your head." I exhale slowly, tilting my head back. "Where's Ryker?" Mason asks.

I shrug. "Icing his hand, probably," I mutter.

She tilts her head. "And Jasper?"

"Bitched Ryker out about minding his own business," I sigh. "Riddick took a fist to the face prying Ryker off me." Mason grins, shifting in her seat. "You should go kiss it and make it better." She smirks, nudging my bruised ribs. "Sorry I ruined your night," I tell her.

"You didn't," Mason pushes herself to her feet, eyeing me the way someone might watch a car crash they can't look away from.

She's not wrong. She's rarely wrong. "You should give up, you know?" she says, tilting her head.

I look at her, tired and done, because I already know where this is going. Mason grins, always enjoying being two steps ahead.

"Instead of fighting so hard to suppress your feelings," she continues, "you should put that effort into winning her over." My chest clenches. "She's more than you could ever want," she adds, her voice softer. "And probably better than you deserve."

I close my eyes, the weight of those words settling heavy.

Because she's right. But it doesn't matter, because I've already fucked this up beyond belief.

Mason leans down, pressing a quick, teasing kiss to my temple. "Too bad, too. I was thinking of giving you a shot."

I let out a rough laugh, shoving her away. "In your dreams, babe."

Mason smirks and walks off, and this time, I really look at her.

Not in the way I have before. Not as a distraction.

Not as the person who was my power equal, my partner, the one always calling me out, always played the same reckless game I did.

No.

I look at her because she was never the one I was supposed to be chasing.

She was never the one who made me want to be better, never the one who pulled me back from my worst moments, made me crazy, or made me need.

I think that's what's really fucking with me.

Because if I ever had a shot with Kate, if I ever had a real goddamn chance, I might have just lost it.

For good.

Twenty-Four

Bastian

By morning, I know I have to do something. I am not the type to sit around and let shit fester. If there is a fight, I fight. If there is a problem, I fix it.

And this? This is a goddamn disaster.

Kate never came back to the dorms last night, not that I expected her to.

Still, it drives me insane knowing she's out there, pissed off, hurt and that I am the reason.

I haul ass over to Dr. Ames' house, praying to a higher power that Coach Nate isn't home. Although I can take a hit, I'm really not in the mood to get my ass kicked before breakfast.

I ring the doorbell, preparing for a battle.

I should've known I'd have to get past her guard dogs first. Ryker answers the door. His expression is a mirror of the pure disgust I feel for myself. All I can do is brace for whatever he's going to throw at me.

"Your face looks better," he says flatly, blocking me from entering.

"Yeah. Mason healed it last night."

His eyes narrow. "Shame."

I grit my teeth. "Kate home?"

"She's busy," he says, blocking the doorway. Right. That's not a no. But not a yes either.

Lissa appears behind him, placing a calm hand on his arm. He turns towards her, his entire body softening at her touch, and I have to look away. Not because I begrudge them any happiness, but because of my desire for the same thing.

And the only person with whom I could ever have that, won't even look at me.

Ryker turns back to me, his gaze hardening once again. "Bastian, I'm not Roarke." His voice is sharp, cutting. "You hurt her again, and I don't care if you're my X. I'll end you."

I nod once, because I fucking deserve it. Ryker finally steps aside, leaving the door open behind him so I can enter. He hollers up the stairs, calling her name, leaving me standing in the doorway.

The moment I hear her footsteps descending, my gut clenches. And then, she appears. My shields nearly slip just from the sheer impact of her.

She's still in her pajamas, a tank top and ridiculously tiny shorts that leave too much of her legs exposed.

Her long, toned, infuriatingly perfect legs.

Her hair is loose, down, and slightly mussed, like she just rolled out of bed. It takes everything in me not to imagine what she'd look like waking up tangled in my sheets.

She looks so different from how she normally does.

No sleek designer suit, no sharp heels, no pristine perfection that makes her seem untouchable.

She looks relaxed, comfortable, real.

And I hate it. I hate how goddamn beautiful she is. I hate how much I want her. I wish I could go back 12 hours and react differently; not fuck this up.

"Sebastian," her voice is pure ice, cool and impersonal. The formality of it cuts deeper than I expect.

"Kate," I say carefully. "I wanted to apologize for last night."

Her expression doesn't change, but I catch the way her hand tightens on the banister. She just tilts her head slightly, assessing me as if I'm some insignificant thing she has no time for.

"No need." Her lips curve into a smile so sharp it could slice through my ribs. "What's done is done. Don't worry, I've already moved on."

She shields herself before I can even try to press past her defenses.

Not just with her own power. But with her brothers covering her as well. I'm not here to start another war. Not today anyway.

I force my breath out. "Kate, I want to talk to you."

Her smile doesn't waver. "Talk?" she echoes. And I know before she even says it, I'm fucked.

"No, I don't think so." Her voice is light, almost playful, except there's nothing playful about this.

"You had your chance to talk. To do anything you wanted, really." She leans in slightly, her voice dropping into something softer, deadlier. "You blew it."

I tense, "Kate—"

She lifts a hand, cutting me off. "I'm done talking, Sebastian." Her smile widens, cruel and deliberate, but her eyes still showcase some of the sadness I put there, and it makes me hate myself even more. "Or doing just about anything with you."

That? That hits like a fucking bullet to the chest.

She steps around me, fully intent on leaving me in the doorway like I'm nothing. Instinct kicks in.

I reach for her arm, but she yanks it back like I have a communicable disease. And maybe I do. Maybe I am a fucking disease to her.

A mistake she doesn't intend to make twice.

"Now, if you'll excuse me," she says smoothly, not meeting my eyes. "I need to get ready. I have plans."

The insinuation is clear as day. It's not work. It's not anything to do with me. That pisses me off more than it should.

My temper snaps, but before I can say anything, she pivots, her ass taunting me as she heads back up the stairs.

And I stand there, my heart pounding, my head a mess. And for the first time in my life, I feel completely and utterly powerless.

TWENTY-FIVE

Kate

I spend the next several days attempting to avoid Bastian Monroe like my life depended on it.

We still have Mason's lessons, our training sessions, briefings, every unavoidable moment where we must exist in the same damn space. He's worse than usual. An asshole every time we cross paths.

Arguing just to argue. He'll take the stupidest side just to drive me insane. I swear if I say the sky is blue, he'll swear it's green.

I shouldn't care. I shouldn't want him to fight for me, not with me.

But a part of me—the stupid, delusional, desperate part of me—thought that maybe he would. Maybe when I pushed him away, when I told him I was done. That maybe that would make him, I don't know, do something.

I told Mason I want the fairy tale; I still do.

But this isn't a fairy tale. And although I wish things were different, I don't think they are ever going to be.

Leaving the last class, Andy races to catch up with me. Now that she is with Alex, we talk more, especially about committee business. "I meant to talk to you the other day, but you were out of class, so fast..." Andy says as I slow down for her. Although I'm in four-inch heels and she is in sneakers, I shorten my stride, so we walk together.

"Sorry, I've been focused. How are you?"

"Good, Alex and I are excited for the ball this year," she says with a smile. I bet now that the dating ban is lifted, they can be together without hiding. "Listen, it's none of my business, but if you needed someone to talk to," she says quietly, "I'm not the best at talking, but I am good at listening, and I kind of know what you are going through."

"Thank you, Andy," I say, putting a hand on her arm. "But I am fine. I'm not sure what you heard, but it was a mistake on my part. We are back to arguing; it's all good."

Andy dealt with her own drama with Alex. Her relationship with Alex is the reason the ban was lifted. The difference though is Alex wanted Andy as much as she wanted him. That is not the case for me. "Well, my offer still stands," Andy says, letting it drop, even though I'm fairly sure she sees right through me.

"Thanks, so did you go dress shopping yet?" I say distracting her from my drama. We walk and talk as we head over toward the labs and offices through the covered walkway. It's nice to hear her excitement; she is blissfully happy, and she and Alex make a beautiful couple. They are the first Wight couple, which is only fitting with Alex being the oldest.

I know he has been balancing a lot and working hard to get a new housing community up and running. It is much needed, especially with couples like Alex and Andy, who I am sure will be engaged before long. We're growing beyond dorms and our parents' houses. If Elitus expects us to be on campus long term, then there need to be more solutions. We have plenty of land. Right now, it's about prioritizing.

I can't help but wonder if there are other mate options. With the expansion and adding of Latents in the back of my mind, I can't help but think if the serums work to grow powers, creating new Wights, then it would stand to reason that with their powers come potential bonds, including mate bonds. When Andy and I part, we make plans to have dinner soon.

I am home for dinner with my parents when Jasper brings in Hannah. It's interesting to watch them together. They do not have a mate bond, but they are dating. They fit. Both quiet Tier Twos in the Gen Three class. Both healers by nature.

When my mother mentions at dinner that I'll be accompanying Mason to the Palace to help her recharge and organize the Power Council, I almost choke on my wine. "The Palace?" I repeat, blinking.

"It makes the most sense," she says calmly, cutting her steak. "You'll be able to coordinate logistics for the Power Council while Mason recharges. Wyatt will join you of course, and Riddick, Jared, and Charley as well."

Lovely. Like a romantic getaway.

The Palace is our fortified play place. We don't go often, but it's the one place we can actually relax—an estate tucked away from prying eyes, stress, and, for once, missions.

And, more importantly for this trip, no Bastian.

Arriving the next day, the warm air and ocean breeze do wonders to take the edge off. Wyatt and I help Mason and Charley go over key pieces of the Power Council meetings, and before long, it feels like we can finally relax.

I'm not staring at a stack of files, not worrying about Elitus, McGuire, Bastian. I can just breathe.

The girls decide to head off to the beach, leaving Wyatt and me to a chess match. He's staring after Mason when she leaves, though. I study him carefully. "You okay?"

His jaw tightens. "Yes," he mutters. Then, after a pause, "I don't want her to get hurt."

It doesn't take a genius to figure out who he's talking about. Mason and Riddick. Their budding relationship, whatever the hell it is, has been brewing for a while. I shake my head. "It'll be fine."

Because it will be. Mason and Riddick both know what they're doing. They don't play games. They don't tiptoe around their feelings or run from them.

Unlike some people.

Wyatt turns his sharp gaze on me; we haven't talked about it—about Bastian, about what happened.

I don't want to. Because what is there to say? I made a mistake. I knew I was making it when I did it.

Now I must live with it.

Wyatt knows me too well. He leans back, studying me. "Kate." I ignore him. "You know it won't go away," he says smoothly, making his next move.

I slam my piece down, not even thinking about it. "So?" I snap. "Doesn't mean I have to do anything about it either."

Wyatt sighs. "Kate—"

I stand up, done with this game, chess, Bastian, all of it. Instead, I decide a walk on the beach isn't such a bad idea. Anything to clear my head, to make me stop feeling.

We walk and stumble upon Riddick and Mason talking, but it looks more intimate than I have seen them be out in public. They don't have a care in the world. I turn to Wyatt, raising a brow. He's got a frown on his face; I know he wants to talk to Mason, at least to make sure she is okay with this.

Wyatt and she have always been close from a friendship/academic standpoint, although part of me wondered if Wyatt didn't wish for more.

"Go ahead. I'll deal with it," I tell him.

I grab Riddick and drag him away. If Wyatt wants to have whatever kind of talk with Mason, he can have it. Not that I think it'll change anything, but more to set his mind at ease.

Riddick and I walk for a while. He's smart, practical, and, more importantly, he doesn't bring up Bastian.

For that alone, I am grateful.

Before long, we leave whatever weird date vibe is happening between him and Mason, and Wyatt and I head into town.

I need a distraction. Something to scrub the last few weeks out of my brain. "Jazz club?" Wyatt suggests, already knowing the answer.

"Perfect."

Dinner, wine, my best friend. That should cure everything.

Should. But somehow, I already know it won't.

Bastian

The Palace trip means one thing: Kate's gone.

For a few days, at least. It shouldn't make a difference. I should be relieved. A break from all the tension, the bullshit, the constant need to be in control of my own reactions whenever she is near me.

But I feel like I've been pacing in my own fucking head since she left. Not that I'm going to admit it. Not to anyone. Especially not Kyle.

But he's been watching me like he knows something, like he can see right through the carefully constructed wall of fuck-off energy I've been exuding.

We're at the training grounds, sparring for no real reason other than burning off steam.

The hits are harder than usual. They are more controlled, but still violent in their intention. We're both wound too fucking tight.

Kyle doesn't hold back, and neither do I.

Eventually, though, the bastard takes a cheap shot to get me down. I hit the mat, knocking the breath out of me. Kyle grins. "Sloppy."

I roll my shoulders, pushing up to my elbows. "Eat shit, Ross."

Kyle just smirks, like he's been waiting for an opening. "So," he says, too casually. I don't like this already.

"What?" I grunt, wiping my face with the back of my hand.

"How's life without Queen Kate breathing down your neck?"

I still, it's barely noticeable, but Kyle catches it. Fucking hell. He's pushing. Deliberately.

Because that's what Kyle does—he needles until you react. I force a smirk, settling back onto my heels as I pull off my gloves. "Better."

Kyle snorts, shaking his head at me. "Sure."

I grab a towel and lean against the ropes. "What? You think I'm losing sleep over her?" I scoff. "Trust me, I'm fine."

Kyle tilts his head, considering me. "You say that a lot."

I toss the towel at his head. He catches it with ease. "You should just fix whatever it is."

I exhale sharply, already done with this conversation. "Not my problem to fix," I mutter.

Kyle laughs outright. "That's rich. You two are so goddamn stubborn, it's painful."

I roll my shoulders, not in the mood for this shit. "Maybe. But at least I don't have a crisis brewing like you do."

Kyle's eyes narrow slightly, his body growing tense. "The fuck is that supposed to mean?"

I grin slowly, knowing exactly where to hit. "You know what it means."

Kyle's jaw tenses. I don't have to spell it out. Nala. His current distraction. His easy outlet. She's not stupid; she knows what they are.

He isn't a liar, but he knows this is a slow burn to nowhere.

Kyle glares, wiping his face with the towel, buying time. "You know nothing," he mutters.

I just laugh, shaking my head. "Nah," I say, voice casual. "I know exactly what's happening." Kyle tenses further. "Nala is easy," I continue. "She's comfortable. Safe."

Kyle's fingers flex around the towel. "You care about her," I add, shrugging. "But we both know you don't love her."

His eyes flash with warning, but I don't back down. "You're just replacing what you've suppressed for years."

Kyle scoffs, but it's a little too forced. "You're full of shit."

"Am I?" I push off the ropes, tossing my gloves onto the bench. "You're never going to love her the way she wants you to. You know it. I know it." Kyle doesn't answer. Because he knows I'm right.

Because we both know who his first choice is—who it always was, if he had ever let it happen. But he doesn't.

He doesn't talk about it, but I know him. Something spooked him away from Mason. Something that keeps him at a distance, but he hates it. So instead, he goes with someone simple, but it won't last.

Kyle exhales, shaking his head. "You're an asshole."

I grin, my cocky facade on the surface. "And you're avoiding reality."

He tosses the towel aside and grabs his water. I let the silence sit for a second before pushing further. "You worried?" I ask, watching him.

He takes a sip before answering. "Not yet."

But he will be. Because when it finally crashes, when he has to make a choice, I know exactly what he'll do.

And Nala won't be the one standing beside him in the end.

I grab my water bottle and head toward the doors. Kyle calls after me. "You're one to talk, Monroe."

I keep walking, raising my bottle in a mock salute.

"Yeah, well—at least I'm not lying to myself."

And with that, I leave him to wrestle with his own fucking mess. Because I already have enough of my own.

TWENTY-SIX

Bastian

It's been a couple of days since Kate returned, and it's been difficult, to put it mildly. I can't wait to leave tomorrow for my turn at the Palace. Alex is there now with Andy, Siobhan, Roarke, David, Marty, and Paige. Although Alex is in charge, I would bet he's holed up in a cabana with his mate. And David and Paige will be MIA as well. Lucky bastards.

That means poor Roarke is entertaining the other two. He's used to all that feminine energy. Maybe someone will straighten him out with whatever bullshit is still going on with Mya. God knows Marty is almost as crazy as her younger sister Charley, but maybe that's what he needs. An escape.

When we get there, I know I should've stayed at home.

I don't really know what the hell I'm doing here, but Mason made sure my name was on the list. Like she always does.

I want to know who picked these damn groupings. Max, Kyle, Mya, Nala, Reese and I work on some of the finer points of what the interactions should be for Power Council and Elitus. We are only here for a couple of days, so we tried to get all the work out of the way first.

Nala has nothing useful to add, since she isn't on either Elitus or the Council, nor is she on any committees. Honestly, I do not know what she does with her time, other than follow Kyle around like a puppy.

On the surface, it looks like Nala's got her claws deep in Kyle. But it's surface level. Kyle plays the part, don't get me wrong, but it's an act on his part.

He doesn't talk about it, doesn't explain it, doesn't justify it.

Which means he knows exactly what the fuck he's doing.

That's what makes Kyle dangerous; he doesn't make spur-of-the-moment choices. Every move, every decision, and every deal he makes is calculated.

Kyle Ross doesn't play games unless he's already predicted how they'll end. I watch him now, leaned back in one of the lounge chairs, Nala draped over him like a goddamn accessory.

She's acting too, playing her role perfectly: flirty, touchy, just the right amount of sultry to keep his attention.

He lets her do it, doesn't pull away, but also doesn't push forward. Nala is easy. She isn't a risk. And the most important part is, she isn't Mason.

Kyle has had visions for years now. His are snapshots of the future. He never talks about them outright, but I know how calculated his choices are. He uses them more than Riddick or Mason.

He uses it to make changes; gearing up for war, deciding, shoring up defense. Wheeling and dealing with McGuire, which pisses many off. But I know why he does it. He's trying to keep everyone safe. His sisters. Mason.

Kyle's never been one to outright admit what Mason means to him, but I don't need his visions to tell me what's obvious. He's avoiding Mason because he has already seen something.

Something that makes him think he can't be with her.

And that's why he is with Nala. She is a distraction, a replacement, a way to keep his focus somewhere else.

But it's not what he really wants. Because Nala isn't enough for him. Even if he wants her to be.

He knows it. I know it. Shit, Mason probably knows it too. But no one is saying a damn word.

I grab a beer from the cooler and take a seat beside Kyle. He doesn't look over, just takes a sip of his drink. His eyes are across the patio, where Nala and Reese are talking with Max. Nala is overly bubbly and fake as hell. But at least she let go of Kyle for a bit.

"You enjoying yourself?" I ask dryly. Kyle smirks, finally glancing over.

"Like you wouldn't believe."

I take a long drink, letting the moment stretch. After letting him sit in it, I go in for the kill. "So, what are you avoiding?"

Kyle tenses, his grip tightens just slighting on his glass. "What the fuck are you talking about?" Got him.

"You tell me," I say, stretching my legs out. We may be friends, but with that comes no bullshit between us. "Because the last time I checked, you weren't one to waste your time on things that don't matter," I nod my head to Nala. "And she doesn't matter, not really."

Kyle takes another sip. Not answering, but that is answer enough.

"She's easy, isn't she?" I probe. "Comfortable, safe, and an excellent distraction for you," I see his jaw clench. "But she's not Mason, is she?" He finishes his drink in one gulp, cracking his neck. He hates that I am right. "What have you seen, Kyle?"

Kyle finally looks at me, really looks at me. And I see it. The weight of whatever it is, sits heavy on him. Whatever vision or snapshot he had, it has fucked him up.

Maybe he saw her choosing Riddick. Maybe he saw himself choosing someone else. Or maybe he saw something that he refuses to let happen and is doing everything he can to prevent it.

He doesn't answer my question; instead, he exhales, his voice lower now, more serious. "What do you want, Bastian?"

I scoff, "You mean besides figuring out why you're playing house with a woman you don't give a shit about?"

Kyle shakes his head, his eyes sharp. "No. I mean with Kate."

My stomach tightens. I should've seen that coming. Kyle and I have known each other too damn long for him not to flip this back on me.

I glance toward the water, knowing I can't lie to him. But I can avoid the truth. "It doesn't matter, does it?"

Kyle observes me. "You really think that?"

I don't answer. I don't know anymore. Kate made her feelings clear. And instead of fighting for her, I pushed her further away. Instead of fixing it, I made it worse.

Kyle sighs, rubbing his temple. "You're both idiots."

"Takes one to know one," Kyle smirks at that. We both fall into silence, drinking, thinking, avoiding.

Later, we leave Kyle and Nala behind—mostly because we're all sick of her hanging off him like a goddamn leech.

Even her twin looks annoyed, and Reese is the nicest person I know.

It's awkward as hell, but not my problem. I gave him my opinion. It's not my problem to fix. If Kyle wants to pretend everything is fine, that's on him. But he must see that it's grating on everyone around him.

In town, we look for something to do. Reese wants to see a museum. No thanks to that one. Lucky for her, Max is a sucker, and Mya knows exactly how to play her cards.

She subtly nudges her brother toward Reese, and before Max even realizes he's been maneuvered, he agrees to take her. Reese and Max are good together. She's my backup Two, the one who helps me keep everyone else in check.

She deserves someone solid. Someone who won't treat her like an obligation or a game. Max is the Quiet one, but lethal when he wants to be.

Kyle, Max and I are good friends, and have always worked together well. He cares more than most, even if he doesn't always show it. Mya watches as they disappear into the museum entrance, shaking her head slightly. Then she turns to me. "You think Max will grow a pair?" she asks, blunt as ever.

I bark out a laugh. Mya never minces words. She has finally got herself back to somewhat normal. Mason won't talk about it, but I know she has been working with her. Roarke, I think, is a lost cause at this point. He's still a hard-ass, avoiding Mya.

"They'll go at their own pace," I say, shoving my hands in my pockets. "Unlike some of these other hookups, they actually make sense." I shoot her a look. "Besides, I'd much rather be doing something else."

She grins. "Then let's do something else."

We end up at a local arcade. It's a perfect distraction. Noisy, crowded but fun, no thoughts about work.

We're supposed to be working on some briefing materials, but surprise, surprise, Kate and Mason already did all the heavy lifting. Two control freaks and perfectionists. I skimmed it earlier. It's solid.

"You going to talk about what's up with you and our resident Peacemaker?" I finally ask while we eat.

Mya doesn't miss a beat. "No." She pops a fry into her mouth, chewing slowly. "He needs to change his damn name if he keeps hitting people."

I snort. "Yes, but the people all have a theme." She arches a brow. "They all wronged you."

Her lips twitch, but she doesn't confirm or deny. I've been drawing some conclusions lately, and she knows it. "It's fine," she says eventually. "Whatever his deal is, it's his deal. He's made it clear he hates me."

I lean back in my chair, studying her. "He doesn't hate you."

She scoffs, rolling her eyes. "Oh yeah? He sure as hell acts like it."

I shrug. "Maybe he just likes to push."

She gives me a look, smirks, and laughs. "Are we talking about Roarke or you?" I don't flinch, but it's a near thing. "I heard all about you and Kate," she adds smoothly. "And the blowout after I went to bed, post-Power Council celebration."

I don't know what to say about that. Everyone knows. But Mya doesn't pull punches. She's blunt, honest, and usually a fairly good sounding board. She may be reckless and a wild card in the field, but in our group of friends, she always listens and gives honest feedback. Kinda like Roarke does, now that I think about it. "It's complicated."

Mya grins, "Can't be that complicated. You went off base, like you and every other stupid male always does and it bothered her. Maybe because she has feelings, and instead of admitting how you feel, you fucked it up. Sound about right?"

I laugh, "Yep." She laughs, shaking her head at me. "Well, if Roarke ever earns your forgiveness, then maybe you can tell me what to do to fix it then."

Her entire demeanor shifts. She glares at me, eyes dark with an edge of something else, hurt, maybe. "What makes you think he's the one who screwed up?"

I mull that thought over. I just assumed. But then again, Mya is usually logical and doesn't hold grudges. Roarke, however, has a long memory, and if she did something, I can see him reacting. But to hold a grudge this long, to cut her out when they were so close? I sigh.

"You want to talk about?" She glares at me. Guess that's a no.

"You want to talk about Kate?" She counters.

"Touché."

I don't push further, nor does she. But I know one thing for sure, whatever the hell is going on between her and Roarke?

It's not a simple fix, and far from over.

Kate

I spent the evening at the dorms, going over committee notes, trying to distract myself with anything that might keep my mind busy.

It doesn't work; all I can think about is him.

I have too much going on to waste time thinking about him.

New Year Ball planning, committee schedules, Power Council coordination. Everything that matters. And yet...

The frustration lingers. I was the one who pushed him away. I was the one who told him I was done. So why the hell am I still so angry?

Maybe because I expected more from him or maybe because, despite everything, some delusional part of me thought he'd fight for me. Thought he'd give a shit. And unfortunately, I have too much damn pride to take it back. I won't beg for his attention.

So instead, we argue. He has been more unbearable than ever. Petty. Snide. Taking every opportunity to get under my skin like he's making a sport of it. And what's worse? He's acting as if he doesn't care. Which maybe is the point. Maybe he doesn't. But I hate that part.

Because I still do. I care. And that's the part that makes me feel like an idiot.

I give up on work eventually, tossing my notes aside.

The common area is quiet tonight. Most people are out or in their rooms, which makes it easier to breathe. I had dinner with Alex and Andy, which was a change. We talked about work, but more than anything I observed them interacting as a couple. It was so easy for them; they were in sync. And maybe that's why I can't get him out of my head.

I pour myself a glass of wine, needing something to take the edge off.

I close my eyes and take a moment to enjoy the silence.

At least until Roarke shows up. I glance up as he enters, his usual controlled presence frayed. He looks exhausted. Not physically, but mentally. And that's rare for him. He has always been unshakable. The calm in the storm. He grabs a drink without acknowledging me, but I can tell he knows I'm watching him. He always knows.

We both drink in silence for a bit, both in our own heads. I take a sip of my wine, then decide to just say it. "You want to talk about it?"

Roarke doesn't even glance at me. "No."

I lean back, swirling my glass. "You all set for Christmas?" That at least puts a small smile on his face.

"I guess. I let my sister's order whatever they wanted this year, so I think it'll be good. Are you?"

"Luckily, everyone in my family is easy to shop for. But it's weird shopping for Lissa and Hannah," I murmur. He shares a sad smile with me.

"They both seem happy," he remarks.

"Yea." I sigh. I can't help it. Trying not to dwell on anything, we chat about our time at the palace. Roarke updates me on plans, including his concerns over De entering the dorms. I get it, but we both talk logistics. There will be some room swapping in the new year and adjustments.

"So what do you really think about the Power Council?" Roarke asks. I look at him. And try to shield my thoughts.

"I think it's ambitious." I take a sip, trying to think of the right words. "It is needed given what continues to happen with McGuire. I just don't know how this will work exactly. Hopefully, it is smooth."

"Are you going to be able to handle us in the Elitus chambers?" I give him a look. And he smirks. Typical Roarke, stirring up shit.

"If you're asking about Bastian and me, then yes. We will be fine. Professional as ever. I've learned how to ignore insignificant things." He laughs at me. But I know he knows I am full of shit.

Figuring two can play this game, I smile at him. "You know, you sure seem to be in a lot of fights lately."

His jaw tightens. He takes a slow sip of his drink, not answering right away.

"Strange pattern too—all the people you go after seem to have wronged Mya."

That gets a reaction. That's what I thought. "So?" he mutters.

I raise an eyebrow. "So... seems a little personal."

He scoffs, shaking his head. "It's not."

I set my glass down. "Rumor has it you had her sidelined, keeping her off missions. To protect her."

"I look out for my team."

"Sure. That's why you and Mya aren't speaking, right? Because you're such a wonderful team."

Mya, for all her recklessness, all her smartass comebacks and sharp edges, has been acting differently for a while now. She is quiet, almost as if she feels guilty.

And Roarke? If I didn't know any better, I would say he's punishing her for it. Not openly. Not cruelly. But with distance.

He used to be her biggest defender, her advocate, her trainer. Now he is a stranger to her. "You're an idiot."

Roarke exhales sharply, finally looking at me. "And you're one to talk?"

I flinch before I can stop myself. Yes. I deserve that.

We sit in silence for a long moment after that. And for once, neither of us knows what to say.

When I head up to bed, I can't sleep. Instead, I think about the couples. Not just the mated ones, but the others making it work. Jasper is building something with Hannah, not mated, but dating. They are making a go of it. And then there is Mason and Riddick.

The way they just went for it. No mate bond, no excuses; they just chose each other. And maybe that's all it really is—a choice.

Maybe it doesn't matter if Bastian and I are supposed to be something. I don't know if I even believe in fate, so maybe he isn't supposed to be anything to me at all. Maybe I just need to move forward. Give up hope for us.

Wyatt will always be my best friend, my constant.

But we both know there's nothing more there. We don't talk about his sex life, but I know his preferences. I know what he looks for when he goes out with Kyle. And I am the opposite of that.

I just wish I had an option, someone who just fits. Maybe I'll find that in the new year. Maybe I won't. Either way, I'm done waiting for someone who doesn't want me.

TWENTY-SEVEN

Bastian

Christmas is always loud, chaotic, and ridiculous. And I wouldn't trade it for the world. My parents are both insane, but then again, the apple doesn't fall far from the tree. Nikki and David Monroe are a fucking force. Wild, fiery, reckless when they want to be, but unwavering in their love.

They never lose their passion; the spark between them never dulls.

After all these years, they still bicker like newlyweds, still look at each other like they're the only two people in the room.

And that's what I want. Not just someone to be with. Someone to match me, who can fight with me, push me, burn bright beside me, and never dim.

I shove the thought aside, because now isn't the time to think about that shit. Now is the time for Monroe Family Game Night. And my triplet brothers are already in full campaign mode.

The Monroe Three—Trevor, Travis and Tyler. Identical as hell in looks, but not in power.

They don't even need to speak half the time; they just know what the others are thinking, moving like some telepathic hive mind of chaos.

They team up against me immediately, which is standard.

Claiming it's because I'm the oldest, but they just like to gang up on me because I'm the most fun to take down.

They don't succeed. But they try. Every year.

Dad leans back on the couch; arm draped over Mom's shoulder as they watch us battle it out over Monopoly. Mom is sipping coffee, shaking her head at the absolute disaster unfolding on the board.

"You're all terrible."

"Not our fault Bastian's a capitalist," Ty mutters, eyeing my expanding empire.

Travis grins, tossing in, "Ariel should be playing. She'd have burned this whole thing down by now."

They're not wrong. My baby sister, who is not a baby anymore, is across the room, curled up on the other couch, soaking in the unwavering attention of the extended family.

She is, as usual, the center of attention. And I am, as usual, watching her like a fucking hawk. I don't trust anyone around her.

She's young, reckless, and way too much like Mom, and she's not moving into the combat dorms until I'm sure she's ready. "Stop glaring at her. She's not doing anything."

I narrow my eyes. "Yet."

Tyler laughs. "She's literally drinking cocoa and talking to Aunt Sarah."

I cross my arms. "She's plotting something. I can feel it."

Trevor snorts, not bothering to argue.

Travis raises an eyebrow. "You realize that treating her like a hostage is just going to make her fight harder, right?"

Yes. I do. That's what scares me. Because Ariel is too much like me. And I know exactly what I was like when people tried to hold me back.

"Bastian's just mad she's growing up," Dad's voice drawls from across the room, full of amusement.

I glare at him. "You should be concerned too."

Mom just laughs, reaching over to squeeze Dad's hand. "She's fine. She's smart, and she knows what she wants. Sound familiar?"

Unfortunately, yes. Dad smirks, eyes flicking toward me.

"So do you. Just a shame you keep running from it."

I don't bite. Not this time. Mom leans her head against Dad's shoulder, and I swear to God they still look like they're twenty years old and head over heels for each other.

It's disgusting. And I want it. I just don't know if I can have it.

The game drags on, and I win—like I always do. The Monroe Three are conniving bastards, but I'm better. I'll always come out ahead. I wish it applied to everything else in my life.

But in the end, it's just a board game. Real life?

That's a whole different battlefield. And I'm still figuring out how to play.

Our extended family clears out early—a compromise since they aren't Elitus. It's always a fine line to walk, trying to let them in just enough without compromising them. They get to be normal. We don't.

For a while, though, the house is calm and comfortable. Board games, shit-talking, and Ariel being the absolute menace she was born to be.

Hot cocoa all around, including Ariel stealing my marshmallows, it's nice to have a break. Ariel updating us on all the antics from Gen Five, a lighter load than the one I have been carrying for the last couple weeks.

But I should've known. Good things don't last at Elitus. The moment breaks when Kyle fucking Ross ports in, looking all business, dressed like he hasn't even entertained the concept of relaxation in a decade.

Fucking hell.

He doesn't even bother with pleasantries, just throws a file at me. "Get dressed. You're up."

I don't move. Just stare at him, then at the file now resting on my lap. Kyle crosses his arms, giving me his usual impatient stare.

"Are you planning on reading it through osmosis?" I sigh, flipping it open, scanning the contents quickly. Another mission. No break.

I snap it shut, shaking my head. "This can't wait a few more hours?"

Kyle's expression doesn't change. "If you'd rather take it up with McGuire, be my guest."

I grit my teeth. I hate him because he's right; this shit never stops. If I don't do it, someone else will. And I'd rather it be me.

I push off the couch, standing. Mom watches me, her arms folded, lips press into a thin line. I know she hates this. Hates that we're out there. That her children, her baby girl, are part of this world. I lean down, kiss her on the cheek, trying to reassure her. Trying to ease the ever-present worry. It doesn't work. It never does.

But she doesn't object, doesn't stop me. Mom is a feminist to her core. Right up there with Mason's mom, Maria, and Riddick's mom, Sarah. She doesn't believe in holding anyone back. Which means, no matter how much I begged her to keep Ariel at home, it will not happen. She loves us fiercely, but she won't clip our wings.

That's what terrifies me the most. Ariel is going to run headfirst into this war, whether I want her to or not. I can't stop her; I know that. All I can do is make damn sure she survives it.

We head into the war room, and I immediately clock Mya getting outfitted like she's gearing up for World War III. I raise a brow, watching as she straps another knife to her thigh, checks the clip on her sidearm, and readjusts the weight of a compact rifle against her shoulder.

She looks focused, calm, and completely unfazed.

The only person not unfazed?

Roarke.

That bastard looks like he's seconds away from snapping. His jaw is so tight it might shatter, his hands clenched into fists at his sides. Mya doesn't acknowledge him. Not directly, anyway. But I can see the tension in her shoulders, the way she's evading his gaze.

These two are almost as bad as Kate and me. Almost.

I shake my head, stepping up beside Mya as she finishes checking her gear. "Planning to fight an army solo, or are we invited to the party?" I ask dryly.

Mya smirks, tossing me a small blade. "Figured I'd at least give you a shot at keeping up." I twirl it between my fingers, assessing the balance.

"Cute." Kyle steps up beside us, his expression unreadable, but his energy sharp. "Stay light on this one," he says, not looking at either of us.

I arch a brow. "Is that an order, Boss?"

Kyle finally meets my gaze. "It's a warning."

Mya and I exchange glances. Because we both know what that means. Kyle doesn't give warnings unless there is something he has already calculated, something he has already seen. We're being set up. Or at the very least, this isn't what it seems.

We finish up the briefing, Mason and Kyle both taking the lead, while we review the basics and the entry points.

The mission is split. Kyle, Mya and I will branch off, handling secondary objectives. Mason, Roarke and Riddick will gather data and samples, along with handling security and transport.

It goes smoothly, too smoothly. Which makes me uneasy. It's almost like we're being led down a path, being played.

We move down the hall, slight static in the comms, but they aren't needed. We keep our mental comms open. The cams on our gear showcase back to the war room what is happening.

Kyle isn't saying much, but he is watching. Our footsteps echo off the sterile walls. Mya moves in sync with me, covering my blind spots, working with the effortless coordination that makes our team one of the best for this type of op.

For all the times we bicker and give each other hell, when it comes down to it? We operate like a damn machine. I signal to Kyle that we're pulling back. He relays the message that they're right behind us.

This is part of the job. It's done. But I have a feeling we just kicked off something we can't take back.

When Mason lands back at base, she's not alone. She's got a prisoner.

The guy doesn't look right. His skin is too pale; his eyes are vacant, unfocused, like he's caught somewhere between awareness and a drug-induced haze. It's as if he is under a trance. I take a quick read of him, pushing him a little mentally—not enough to damage, just enough to see if there's anything left of him under whatever the hell they pumped into his system.

His mind isn't blank, but it's fractured, unstable, and most definitely altered. It's not just from some basic narcotics or combat stimulants. This is something else, something worse.

Mason's jaw is tight as she watches McGuire step forward, already planning. None of us like this. What it could mean. What this prisoner is going to tell us about the power McGuire has been gathering.

But we got what Mason wanted. What Elitus might need to push the Latent program forward. The additional data on Vanguard is for Mason. But at what cost? Going after the PPG, on their own base. That looks an awful lot like aggression.

And if it backfires? It won't be a war in the shadows anymore.

This feels like a declaration of war. And I don't think any of us are ready for what comes next.

Kate

The time between Christmas and New Year's is usually quiet and mission-free. But supposedly, it didn't happen. A mission ran, with no casualties, but that's not what has me on edge. It's that we launched a mission onto PPG territory. An off-site facility, which houses their own Latents, granted it was successful. But what worries me is the message it sends to Dmitri and the PPG.

I thought the whole point of the Power Council was to avoid this. But maybe not. I guess it's not about the type of missions, but who is on them.

Sitting in the lounge area, I note it's not as calm as it should be. I see Max come in and beeline to the bar, grabbing a beer. He is scowling. Usually the Quiet One, calm, controlled. He has a temper, don't get me wrong; he wouldn't be Maria's son if he didn't, but he hides it. I make my way over to him to have a conversation. See if I can help at all.

"You okay?" I ask him, sitting down next to him.

"No," he tells me. "I hate biology." He mutters. I blink. This is about his parentage. Max, like Riddick, Jared, and Siobhan, are all Dmitri's children.

"What happened?"

"Dmitri was lying in wait for Riddick and Mason when they were shopping."

"Are they okay?"

"No threat, really, just Dmitri making it clear he still wants Mason. And now, apparently, my brother as well. He wants to build an army, with them leading."

My nerves and anxiety spike. Dmitri would like nothing more than to add two X-level Wights to his army. He is already a threat; with them, he would be unstoppable. But it'll never happen. Riddick hates him and everything he stands for. And Mason, she hates him even worse. She knows she's his number one target. I think that is the reason she pushed herself so hard this past year; to be ready for him. To defend all of us against him and his brand of evil.

Mya comes through and joins us. She has her own issues with biology. She and Max are biological cousins, though raised siblings.

"You hear?" Mya asks. Max nods. "It's fine. Mason is more worried about Riddick than herself," Mya muses. "I just hate that she can't even go out to the mall. Online shopping sucks," Mya tries to break the tension. I bubble up a small laugh; she merely smirks at me.

"It'll be okay," I try to reassure them both, putting my hand on Max's. He looks at me with a soft, sad smile.

"It has to be," he murmurs. Clearly done with that discussion, he changes the subject. "Is the ball ready?"

"Yes, are you taking Reese?" I ask Max. He says nothing, nor looks my way. "You asked her, right?"

"You are a dumbass," Mya says. "Max."

"I haven't asked her, no. But I know she is going."

"And Bailey is going with his mate, and Nala is going with Kyle, and whatever bullshit situation she thinks she has with him," Mya mutters.

"Are you saying I should ask her?"

"Yes, you dipshit," Mya snaps. "You better make it special for her and stop being such a dumbass." He laughs at her. Nodding to us both, he heads off.

"Is he going to ask her?" I inquire.

"He better," she says to me. She gets two glasses and opens a bottle of wine. "You have a date?" I look at her. Is she serious?

"Wyatt," I tell her. She tries to hide her grin in her wineglass.

"You?" I ask. She looks up, but her expression; it's a mixture of sadness and despair. I hate that look. "Mya, do you want to talk about it?"

"Nothing to talk about," she says. Downing her glass and refilling it. "Besides, RJ has promised to entertain Aimee and me. Aimee, of course, shopped for our outfits." She chatters about other things. Before long, some others join us at the bar, including Bailey and Wyatt. We talk about the ball. Some people throw out suggestions on how to celebrate the Gen Three graduations that will happen in the New Year. It's a change of pace. And it helps to distract me, at least for a little while.

Bastian

The strategy room is quieter than usual, with just the low hum of terminals and distant chatter as people wrap up assignments.

Most of the others clear out, but I stick around because I know Mason will find me. And sure enough, she does. She moves like she's carrying the weight of the world on her shoulders, which, if we're being honest, she kind of is.

I lean back in my chair, arms crossed as she drops into the seat across from me. She looks like hell. Tired, worn thin, but still standing. It's a familiar look. I see it in the mirror.

"You look like shit, babe." Mason shoots me a flat look.

"Thanks, sweetheart. That's exactly what I needed."

I smirk but don't push. She exhales, rubbing her temples. "Dmitri."

I nod. I already heard, "You and Riddick ran into him off-base?"

"He was waiting. Not for Riddick, though."

I already know the answer, but I ask anyway. "For you?"

Mason's jaw tightens. "Always."

I watch her, letting the silence settle between us. She's got Riddick now. They are steady, unwavering. But there are things she won't talk to him about. She can't.

Not because she doesn't trust him, but because his protective nature will override any rational discussion. She needs a soundboard. Someone who is objective and will look at facts, not just emotion. And that someone is me.

"He thinks he can turn me," she says.

"He's delusional."

She snorts. "Agreed. But he's not stupid."

"No." I lean forward, elbows resting on my knees. "He's playing the long game. He will wait for the right opportunity."

"And he's watching Riddick now, too." That gets my attention. I sit up straighter. "He wants him as an heir, someone to hand his kingdom over to."

Max is the oldest, but Riddick is the strongest of them, the most logical choice. Dmitri knows Max is too by-the-book, too integrated into Elitus.

But Riddick has always had that edge. The Dark One. Not afraid to push boundaries, to do what is needed, not always what is right. He isn't afraid to take a stand, push, and use lethal measures to ensure those he cares about are safe. He's fiercely protective of everyone he cares about, and his hatred for Dmitri, what happened with his mother, sometimes blurs the lines.

And now that he's with Mason? That's a power combination Dmitri would kill for. They are the ultimate power couple.

"I know what he is doing," she says. "He thinks that if he can't have me, he can plant a seed of doubt in Riddick. Make him question whether he is on the right side of this."

"That won't work, you know that."

"I know," she says. She is contemplating trying to plot it out. But the problem: Dmitri is dedicated, focused, and obsessed. And once he has eyes on something he wants, he will do whatever it takes to get it.

The question is, what does he want? Mason. Riddick. Or Both.

He won't think twice about taking something to make them come over to his side.

Never mind that we just launched a mission on his territory. So, he can retaliate. He wouldn't be able to get Mason. But another Elitus prize? Like, say, the perfect Elitus daughter. Fucking Hell.

Kate isn't out of this equation. She's on Elitus. A Gen One. The oldest female in our ranks. Mason may be The Weapon, but Kate is the Queen. That makes her a target alone.

Dmitri doesn't see women as equals. He sees them as disposable. Vessels.

He wouldn't think twice about grabbing Kate, especially if it would get under Elitus' skin.

Even if Kate and I are in this cold war of avoidance and petty fights, even if we may never have what I want, the idea of her in their clutches.

I wouldn't just burn the world down for her; I would destroy every single person responsible. Give them as much pain as possible and then turn their brains to mush.

Mason must sense my shift in energy, because she pauses, studying me. "You're thinking about something."

I should tell her. But I know I don't need to. She has told me on more than one occasion I am an idiot.

But I don't know how to fix it. I am still the asshole, still pushing. Because Kate, she's got her armor on. And even though I want to go to her; I don't.

My ego and stupidity are in the way.

But I still do what I can to protect her. At least now, with the Power Council, I have some control myself to make sure she is safe. Changing the security on campus to make everyone safer. If that's all I can do right now; I'll take it.

Mason sighs, leaning back in her chair, getting me back from the edge.

"We have to keep moving forward: push the Latent project, strengthen our teams, keep eyes everywhere. We can adjust," she tells me.

"That's a lot of effort for a guy who 'doesn't concern you.'" She huffs out a tired laugh.

"I never said he doesn't concern me. I just said he doesn't stand a chance."

Mason reads my expression and sighs. "I know what you're thinking, and you're right. This isn't over."

"Not even close."

She runs a hand down her face. "I just don't know what his next move is."

That makes two of us. Mason exhales heavily, looking at me for a long moment. "You worried about your girl?"

I scowl immediately. "She's not my girl."

Mason smirks, crossing her arms. "Could've fooled me."

Twenty-Eight

Kate

The pressure I feel to make sure the winter ball is perfect is immense. It is the first proper celebration since everything started changing. I've spent weeks preparing, months planning, and the last seventy-two hours fine-tuning every detail.

With the ban lifting, mated couples emerging, the Power Council, and the shift in control, Elitus finally allowed us to have a say. Plus, it's New Year's Eve. We must celebrate.

It's a night where people can breathe, forget about training schedules, missions, and impending war. Where they can just be themselves.

Even if my love life is a complete and utter disaster, at least I can live vicariously through everyone else. There are so many new relationships forming, bonds strengthening, connections deepening. It's what I wanted. What I worked for.

And yet...

I can't shake the feeling that it's all slipping through my fingers, that while everyone is finding their place. I'm standing still. Like I am watching the world move around me, untouchable, unable to make a change.

I shove that thought down, focusing on what is important. What's in front of me. Seating arrangements, flowers, guest lists, table arrangements—ensuring perfection over the only things I can control.

Bastian

Mason and I don't need words to communicate. We never really have. We work in sync; it's instinct, years of practice, and we're efficient.

Our current project is dismantling and rebuilding Elitus, specifically mission plans and teams. Combat-enabling requirements, training requirements and regimens. All from the comfort of her and Charley's living room.

The place is surprisingly homey, considering the two most dangerous women on campus live here. Mason is on the floor, her laptop open, notes scattered around her. She leans up against Riddick's legs, while he is stretched out on the couch, one arm draped lazily over the back, but his other hand absentmindedly running through Mason's hair as she types. She is focused, but you can almost feel the connection between them. It's interesting to watch; they are natural. Casual, comfortable. Together.

I have to look away. Not because I don't want that for her, but because it's too hard to watch. I sit back in my seat across from them, kick my feet up on the coffee table, and open a new stack of files.

We've been at this for hours—rewriting policy, adjusting protocols, preparing for whatever McGuire is about to pull. Charley comes in, looking way too energized for this late at night, carrying two cans of energy drinks.

She tosses one to Mason, then takes a seat on the arm of the couch, next to Riddick. "So, are we still calling this 'Power Council,' or can we upgrade to something less obnoxious?" she asks.

Mason smirks but doesn't look up from her screen. "It's growing on me."

Charley rolls her eyes, then focuses on the plans. "Okay, where are we?"

"Defense enhancements," I tell her, gesturing to my notes. "McGuire's black ops programs are still a wildcard, so we need to track movement without him realizing we're watching."

Charley hums, scanning over the notes. "We need a separate surveillance team—off-radar, answerable only to us. Not Elitus. Not McGuire." Charley is a strategist. You'd never know it, but she thinks like a military general, especially with defense, battle maneuvers. She is crazy about history, and she has worked hard to build defenses for us. She is all over this, although she is usually a lazy student.

Mason nods, adjusting some notes. "We also need more shield training. If they're breaking through at the levels we're seeing, our mental defenses are weak."

Riddick snorts, lifting an eyebrow at her. "You're just realizing this now?"

"Shut up and read, Riddick," she mutters. Charley grins, flipping through the combat assessments. "We can fine-tune this with Kyle. He's got the best read on enhancements and combat simulations."

I grimace. "He's also McGuire's favorite business partner."

"Which is why we use him," Mason says simply. "He gets information, and he plays the long game. He won't screw us over."

I don't argue; she's right. I grab my phone and shoot Kyle a message.

Come to Mason's. We need to go over combat updates.

Less than fifteen minutes later, he ports in, looking freshly showered, dressed in his usual casual-but-deadly look.

His gaze sweeps the room, the files, the chaos, before landing on Mason's setup. Or, more accurately, the way Mason is leaning against Riddick, his fingers still running through her hair.

Kyle's jaw tightens. I can tell he wants to say something, but reads the room, and just looks at me. I pass him some papers; he flips through them quickly.

"You need better tiered training," he says. "We're still grouping people wrong. There's too much focus on general levels and not enough specialization. If someone's going to combat, they need to be trained in all tiers—shielding, defense, offense, enhancement. No more single-focus training."

Mason nods. "That's exactly what I've been saying. We implement this after the New Year."

Kyle exhales, flipping to another page. "We also need a new combat group. The ones we pulled last week were barely capable."

"We already flagged them for removal," Charley says. "Next batch is up for assessment soon."

He glances at me. "And you? What's your angle?"

I shrug, leaning back. "Making sure McGuire doesn't fuck us over the first chance he gets."

Kyle smirks. "Ambitious."

"Necessary," Mason corrects.

Kyle's gaze flickers over the documents one last time, his jaw tight as he exhales sharply.

"Fine," he mutters, clearly not happy but not fighting it either. "I'll help with McGuire. But I'm not taking on anything else. My focus is keeping our defenses up and making sure we don't get wiped out the second Dmitri retaliates."

Mason nods. Her expression is neutral, but I catch the way her fingers tighten slightly on the edge of her laptop. Guilt. She won't say anything, won't acknowledge it, but I know she feels it.

Kyle was her first crush, her three-battle partner. But he doesn't even look at her when he ports out, leaving behind a quiet tension.

Riddick looks satisfied, leaning back on the couch like that was the exact outcome he expected.

I watch Mason carefully, noting the way she doesn't immediately move on, like she's still processing something. Something I know she won't talk about.

Not to me, anyway. She has never come right out and said it, but I know whatever went down between her and Kyle years ago shook her. He took a big step back, never explained himself.

She took it personally. She was too young to handle the whiplash of being someone's entire world, then suddenly pushed aside.

I watch her, frowning down at her papers; then I feel it as she pulls her blanket of armor back in place, buries herself in the files, and shifts the conversation forward.

"We need to complete the schedule for next month's trainings," Riddick hums in agreement, but he's barely paying attention now, eyes flicking to the basketball game playing on the TV.

He throws in a comment here and there, adding to the conversation when needed, but mostly, he's just there. Present. Supporting Mason.

Not trying to fix everything for her, not trying to protect her from herself. Just exists in her space, letting her be exactly who she is.

I watch them, and it hits me. They're making this work. No mate bond, no cosmic, predetermined pull. Just them, building a partnership through trust and effort, not instinct.

And for the first time in weeks, maybe months, I feel like maybe if they can do it, then maybe it's possible to be happy.

Maybe I don't need a bond to make it work. Maybe there is someone out there for me other than Kate. I don't need the universe forcing us together. If I just...

No.

The thought dies before it can even fully form, because I know better.

I had a chance. I had her in my arms. And I fucked it up.

She was right there, giving me everything, and I pushed her away.

So, I will sit here like an idiot, watching Mason and Riddick prove what I want is possible, but not for me.

This is my punishment for my stupidity. Proof that I don't deserve her.

Twenty-Nine

Kate

The ball is exactly as I envisioned it.

Months of planning, weeks of stress, and countless hours of fine-tuning, every detail, all of it—culminated in this one perfect night.

The music hums softly under the laughter, the chatter, the sheer energy radiating from the room.

People are happy and carefree. For once, they're not soldiers, nor weapons. But they get to be young, vibrant, and most importantly, alive.

The couples are everywhere; some newly official, others now allowed to be out in the open. Some make it work despite a cosmic connection. All of them enjoying this night.

It's a sight I wouldn't have believed a year ago could happen. And I am happy for them.

But it also makes my situation ache just a little more. My fairy tale will never happen. I am resigned to that fact now, and I promise myself in the new year. I will move on.

But as I remind myself of this, I catch sight of him.

And God help me, he looks edible. He has spent way more time in the gym, working with Riddick and Roarke. His tux, a new one at that, fits him as if it was molded to his body. No bowtie, his collar is undone, and his hair is a tad too long.

I can't help watching him, even though I shouldn't. One last time. That's what I tell myself.

He sticks to the edges for a lot of the night, but before long all the single ladies drag him onto the dance floor, including his sister and her hellion partner.

Bastian appears to be making it his personal mission to entertain all the younger girls. Gens Three, Fours, and Fives all seem to be enjoying themselves. His triplet brothers are out there too. It's fun to see, a distraction from all the couples around.

He takes his turn, dancing slowly with all of them. He winds up back with Ariel every other one, though. Probably to keep the rest away. She may be eleven, but she is beautiful, wild, and reckless. Just like her brother.

I make my way around, thanking everyone for their comments about how wonderful tonight is. It took a lot of work, but I don't do it for the praise. I do it because we deserve this; we earned it.

I try to avoid Bastian, but my eyes keep gravitating there. What bothers me the most is that he hasn't looked at me, not once.

I know in the New Year, I will have to work to shore up my shields, find some other distraction. With the Power Council officially integrated into the Elitus world, Bastian and I will have to work together more often. And that means we cannot fight constantly. Even though that is our favorite pastime.

Elitus isn't like a classroom. It's all business, no nonsense. If we make it personal, then we will be removed. I have worked too hard to get where I am to let a little headache get in the way. I am better than this; I must be.

With a sigh, I finish my glass of champagne, grabbing another off the tray of the passing server. I try to tune it all out. Wyatt, as usual, is providing a distraction, or trying to anyway.

He is sharing stories about his brothers, his mother and her never-ending drama. Normally, I would be more engaged. But tonight, something feels off. Heavy. More than just my drama, and before I know it, I see the tension, and the reason for it.

A disturbance in the air, a mood shift, that affects everyone. I see the commotion on the other side of the room, my eyes narrowing immediately.

Matt Dean, one of Adrian's lackey's has gotten Mason to dance with him, and it looks like it is going south rather quickly.

"Seriously?" I mutter, setting my glass down with a little more force than necessary. Wyatt follows my gaze, brows raising. "Of all the dumbasses in the room, of course it's him."

We both watch the disaster unfold. What the hell is he thinking? Anyone with half a brain cell knows better than to approach her now.

Especially with Riddick in the room, and they clearly being together. Their entrance tonight turned heads and made a very big statement: she is off the market.

Wyatt smirks. "This is going to end badly."

"Obviously."

Sure enough, Riddick rides to the rescue. Whatever bullshit Matt just said must have been stupid, because Riddick doesn't even hesitate before clocking him.

Matt staggers, blood spurting from his busted nose, looking outraged but not nearly as upset as he should be. His pathetic little crew is there as well. Adrian, Connor, Everett and Jaden. Nothing but Bad Apples. That's what Charley calls them.

Adrian is McGuire's spawn, and a slimy little snake. He looks almost happy about the incident. Connor and Everett play it off, helping Dean out, but they are just polished turds.

Jaden has always been a pain in my ass. A Tier One, but not nearly as talented as he thinks. He's a magnet, but what I hate about him is that he cheats, doesn't care about the rules, and has been a thorn in my side for years.

They drag Dean out, their little squad forming a protective shield, probably whispering some pathetic plan to "get even." I watch Mason, who doesn't look all that upset. She's grinning up at Riddick, clearly amused.

They look good together, mesh well, are connected, and have a partnership, even without a mate connection. And I must admit, that gives me a little hope.

Because I want that, I need that. Someone to balance me out. And since it appears I'll never get there with the hotheaded X-Two, then I will have to figure out how to get there with someone else.

Although I have never explored it, a commoner isn't outside the realm. We have plenty of office workers and lab employees on campus, others who know what we are, that we interact with, that aren't a security risk. Many are close to my age as well. It's a possibility.

But it tastes sour. It's not how it should have been.

Wyatt nudges me, sensing my shift in mood. "Alright, what's going on in that head of yours?"

I shake my head. "Nothing. Just appreciating the sheer stupidity of the men in this room, and men in general."

He laughs, clinking his glass against mine. "Well, at least that's a constant."

I force a small smile, but my gaze flickers toward the dance floor, toward where Bastian was earlier.

Because as much as I don't want to care? I still do.

The ball is winding down, but the energy in the room is still high. The afterparty is set, and I can tell the alcohol is already flowing. Some have left for a more private New Year's celebration.

Another slow song starts up, and my eyes immediately seek him out.

My breath stills, because he isn't dancing with his sister, or one of the younger girls. He's traded up for Charley, who looks like sex on a stick.

She is a flame; her dress fits every curve she has. Charley is wild, confident, and effortlessly bold. In a way, I wish I could only be. Not only in life, but on the battlefield. She carries the same energy through everyday life.

They make sense. Both are passionate, reckless, and constantly pushing boundaries. They love fighting, combat, and challenges. And right now? He's smirking down at her, his cocky grin in place, as he twirls her around the floor. Her head is thrown back, laughing at some smart-ass comment I am sure he has made.

I hate it. Hate watching it. I hate that I care. But more than all of that, I wish more than anything I could hate him.

But I don't. And I know I never will. I have spent weeks trying to master all of Mason's shielding techniques. Training myself in how to lock down these emotions, to block the pull that has me always seeking him out—but it's not working.

And with the amount of champagne I've had...

It's coming forward. Everything I have suppressed for the last month, even longer if I am going to be honest. My whole damn life, it feels like.

I down the rest of my glass, Wyatt eyeing me like I am a bomb about to explode. He's right, because I feel like I am.

I scan the room, forcing my focus elsewhere. Ryker and Lissa are dancing, completely wrapped up in each other, lost in their own little world. Jasper and Hannah look good together. They all look so happy, so effortless.

Why can't I have that? Why does it feel that no matter what I do, no matter how hard I try, I will always watch from the sidelines?

Why does it feel like I will never have something, someone that's just mine?

My eyes drift back their way, of their own accord. Like I can't control my eyes any more than my mind. And I can't stop the tightness in my chest. The ache is all-consuming. The song slows again, the atmosphere shifting, thickening. And instead of leaving, instead of letting it go, I decide.

Another stupid fucking decision, but hopefully the last one, because it's now or never. Following Mason's advice, I give it one last chance, one last shot at the fairy tale.

He sees me coming, and his violet-rimmed eyes flicker to mine. His usual smirk he wears is on his lips as he passes off Charley to another and pulls me close.

I can feel the shift between us. He knows why I am here, yet he still pushes me anyway. "What are you doing?" I ask, my voice as calm as I can manage with my nerves a hot mess inside me.

"Trying to enjoy myself," he answers smoothly, moving us across the floor in the practiced way that he is so damn good at.

His grip on me is loose, teasing, his confidence annoying. His smirk lets me know I will not like what comes out of his mouth next.

"Are you jealous again, Katie-did?"

That damn nickname. It makes me give him a sad smile. This is a game to him, always a game. He never takes me seriously, not in the way I need him to. I realize I've been wasting my time hoping for something, anything.

Stupidly believing he will be the knight in shining armor in this stupid fairy tale that I think I deserve, that I want.

But it'll never happen.

Maybe THIS is fate. Tonight is supposed to be about a new year and new beginnings. This is what I need—the final nail in the coffin of any hope for us.

I tighten my grip on his hand, nails pressing into his palm, just enough to make him feel it. Because I am done. Because no matter how much I wished, I hoped, I prayed for more with him. I realize I will never win.

"Jealous?" I scoff, shaking my head. Stepping a little closer, close enough that I can feel his breath against my neck. Close enough to whisper in his ear, to make him think I am still in this.

And then I rip away, pushing him back. Shaking my head at him, hiding the pain, the heartache, the only way I know how. To pretend.

"Oh, Bastian, if you only knew," I smile. His grip on his façade falters, just a fraction, like he wasn't expecting me to push him away. He thought I would let him toy with me more. Maybe he thought I liked this game.

"I'm just disappointed, that's all." I watch him, watching for any sign. But he has those damn shields up to me. I just shake my head, turn and walk away.

The moment I turn my back, I feel it. His power flaring up. That sharp pulse that cuts through the room. A reaction. Something I am sure he doesn't even mean to do.

But I no longer care. My head is a mess; my heart is in pieces. I know I am spiraling, but I don't know what else to do. Because I just can't do this anymore.

Be the one chasing, begging for some sliver of attention, real attention.

Not just an argument or cold indifference.

I scan the room, looking for an outlet for all this that is bubbling up inside me. Someone else. Someone who can make me forget, even if it's just for a little bit.

My gaze lands on Roarke across the room. He is already watching me. Eyes drifting back and forth between me and where I left Bastian.

His eyes are sharp, assessing, like he knows what I am about to do. Even though I am not entirely sure of it myself.

I stride towards him, and when I reach him, I don't hesitate; I don't give him, or myself, a chance to second-guess. I simply smile, grab his hand, and lead him outside to the back balcony.

We slip into the night, cool air against my heated skin. It's a wake-up call, but I don't care. I want to burn, burn this whole damn event to the ground.

I want for once to let loose, to be reckless. Be wild, free, let the control slip. Let someone else pick up the pieces of whatever disaster is going on; to feel alive.

"You really want to do this?" Roarke asks as he accompanies me to the balcony that overlooks the campus grounds. Hills, trees, and a view that goes on for miles. It's peaceful, even though the storm inside is not.

Roarke isn't mocking me or pushing me away. But he is cautious, caring, the Peacemaker, like he always tries to be.

He is asking, trying to give me an out. Putting this on pause before I take it further, going down a path we both know leads to disaster.

I should take it, turn around and go back inside. Put on my cool demeanor and present the calm, collected, perfect Kate.

But I can't. Not tonight, not now. I need to get lost in something, someone, anyone, really. Roarke reads my face, his eyes assessing. I'm not hiding, but he knows I am hurting. He nods, understanding. And I murmur, "Yes."

I don't give him time to think about what I am planning; I shift beside him. Momentarily surprising him as I maneuver him, putting his back to the railing, me up close to his front. I burrow into him, and he lets me. Holding me.

I sigh, fighting to keep the tears inside. To keep myself together. And in his warm presence, I can.

"Are you okay?" he asks. "Kate," his voice is softer, his concern clear. But I don't want his concern, his pity, his understanding. I want someone to make me forget. Someone to hold on to. Someone who can take the burden of all this.

He lets me hold on, and I slide my hands up his chest, feeling the warmth of his body. I feel his pulse. Steady. Capable. Calm.

I nuzzle into the curve of his neck, resting my head on his shoulder. He's a solid presence. That calms something, even if he doesn't mean to.

He mutters something under his breath, an inaudible murmur. I feel his hands ghost over my hips, not pulling me closer, but not pushing me away, either.

Because he knows. He knows I'm not serious. That this is not about him, but if this is what I need, what will help me rebuild some of my walls, ease whatever is going on; he will let me do it, because that's who he is. I take a deep breath, trying to relax.

But then I feel Bastian. The sharp, unmistakable spike of power behind us. It coils tight and volatile, pressing against the air, like a storm rolling in fast.

He taps on my shoulder. I ignore it, ignore him.

Instead, I press a light kiss along Roarke's jaw.

I feel Roarke tense beneath me. But he doesn't push me away, doesn't move. He just waits, letting me decide what to do.

Because Roarke gets it. He knows it's a game, a war of stubborn morons. He knows that Bastian and I fight for no reason other than that neither of us knows how to communicate in any other way.

Bastian taps my shoulder again, this time more incessantly. I finally turn, looking at him, but not stepping away from Roarke.

"Can I help you?" I ask with as much confidence and bravado as I can muster. And when I look into his eyes. For the first time, I see it. The fire. The fury. The absolute destruction that is written on his face at seeing me in another man's arms.

"Choose. Now." Bastian's voice is low, dangerous, a warning. It's a command and a challenge wrapped up in one. "If you continue this game, there will never be an us. I have waited too long for you, Kate. You told me you were done, but I don't think you are. And neither am I. It's now or never. You've had your fun; you've kept your distance. But I am done playing games. I am done waiting. You want to play with Roarke, hide behind him. Then do it. But if you want me, you better tell me now."

I blink at him like an idiot. My mind trying to comprehend what he had just said to me, what he had just asked of me. I feel off balance, the mixture of champagne and adrenaline making my brain stutter to get online. To get with it. To respond.

All I know is this moment; it's slipping through my fingers. And I can't seem to grab hold of it.

I watch as Bastian shakes his head, his jaw tightening, power spiking higher. He closes himself off, taking my silence as an answer.

A No.

And then, like I did to him mere minutes ago, he turns and walks away from me.

My heart kick-starts. My brain comes online. Panic slamming through my system. He is almost at the door when I finally find my voice.

"Sebastian!" He turns back, eyes burning into me. Waiting. And I swallow, hands shaking.

I take a small step away from Roarke. I don't hesitate this time; I gather my courage and take the last leap I can. "You." My voice is quiet. But I know he hears me. "It has always been you."

He doesn't hesitate, not for a single second. Without breaking stride, he heads straight for me. Roarke moves aside, stepping way out of the way, as Bastian closes the distance.

Then he is on me. His hands grip my waist, his body crowding mine. His mouth crashes against mine with an intensity that steals my breath. The passion and power between us flare to life.

I moan, my arms wrapping around him, pulling him closer. I feel desperate. A raw need. While the rest of the world fades away, even for a moment.

The noise, the people, the tension all disappear.

There's only him. Bastian. His touch, his heat. The way he holds me tight, like I am precious, and he won't let me go.

Then, of course, our bubble bursts, as the peanut gallery ruins it.

Cheering.

Fucking Cheering.

I break away, just long enough to glare at the small crowd of onlookers. I know my face must be burning. Bastian mutters a low curse, pulling me back into his arms, his forehead resting against mine.

"I wish I could fucking port," he growls. I let out a shaky laugh. Still breathless from all of this. Instead of answering, I just burrow my head into the curve of his neck and hold on. I let him wrap me up tighter, and get lost in that familiar, intoxicating scent of him.

Bastian

I don't know if I have ever felt this way before. A sense of relief so sharp that it allows me to breathe for the first time. Like something inside me has been coiled so tight for so long, and now, with Kate in my arms, it's finally unraveling.

My grip tightens as I pull her flush against me. Fingers trailing up and down her spine, trying to ease her tension, and the emotions I put there tonight. By being a complete fucking idiot and almost losing her for the second time.

The reality of the moment, and how we got here. It's a lot, and I'll dissect it all later, much later.

For now, I am thankful she's here, in my arms. That she is real, that she chose me. I don't think I realized how badly I needed to hear those words until she said them.

You, it has always been you.

Everything aligned; we had to take the long way to get here. But now we are here; she is in my arms, and I'm never letting her go.

I spent years fighting against this. Pushing her away, arguing to argue, was a defense mechanism. Watching from a distance, convincing myself that she would never want me the way I wanted her.

But now I can finally stop running. Stop pushing her away. Just be together. I can already feel the tension evaporating, the connection between us settling. The calm between us I have been missing for what seems like forever.

I press a slow, lingering kiss to her temple. She's shaking slightly, but I know it's not fear. It's from everything crashing down, adrenaline and years' worth of tension. All the fights, miscommunications, the sheer fucking weight of the drama that has been between us for so long, finally breaking.

I cup the back of her head; she shifts and pulls back slightly, looking me in the eyes. Her eyes are wide, green and endless, searching mine like she is still trying to put all this together, if this is real, how we got here.

I smirk, brush my thumb along her cheek, watching her lean into my touch. So subtle, she doesn't even realize she is doing it.

"I was starting to think I'd never get you to say it," I murmur. She rolls her eyes, but she has a slight tremble. Her armor is shattered right now; the unspoken vulnerability she is letting me see.

It fucking kills me, because I never want her to doubt this. Doubt us. I never want her to think I am not all in.

I kiss her again, slowly, deeply, taking my time with her. She melts into me, her arms moving up to pull me closer, wrapped around my neck. Her fingers are playing with my hair. Slightly tugging.

And fuck, if that doesn't send a pulse straight to my groin. I moan into her mouth and get lost in her. Because if I thought I needed her before; nothing compares to what I feel right now. Knowing that she is mine.

Kate

Most of our audience filters back inside. The show is over, apparently. But on the edge of the balcony, I catch another moment unfolding. Mya and Roarke.

Their body language is tense, their voices low but heated. Another fight, or maybe something more. My stomach twists with guilt. "Damn," I murmur. Bastian just presses a soft kiss to my temple, his fingers brushing over my spine.

"They need to resolve their shit too," he tells me. But his focus stays on me; his hands stay on me. I take a deep breath, seeing Mason and Riddick watching it unfold as well, and it won't be long until Mason has had enough.

I turn my eyes back to Bastian, who is watching me. I don't miss the way his eyes roam over my face; we say more with our eyes than we do with our words in that moment. He makes me forget where we are when he looks at me dead-on like this.

His hands reach up, cupping my face, his thumbs brushing over my cheeks, my lips. And when he closes the distance between us again, his lips find mine. I don't hold back, don't look back, just let myself fall.

THIRTY

Bastian

Just for once, I would like a break. One fucking night. Without a mission, without bullshit, power plays, or a war creeping into every goddamn part of my life. But no.

Because of course, the second I finally get my hands on the one thing I have wanted more than anything; Kate in my arms, the universe gives me a big fuck you.

I'm already moving Kate and I toward Mason, ready to drag her off Roarke, since she looks about two seconds away from breaking him in half. When I feel it.

The air shifts; the energy in our area gets thick, suffocating. Something dark is crawling over us.

Every head snaps towards the hill, and there they are.

A full goddamn PPG battalion.

And who is with them? None other than the Bad Apple Idiots.

Traitors. All of them. McGuire's spawn: Adrian, with Connor, Everett, Jaden, and that sleaze Matt Dean.

I should be shocked. But I am not, because I put nothing past them. They have always been a problem, one I should've taken care of years ago.

I feel the tension spike, a ripple of power. I barely notice Kyle stepping up beside us. He must have felt it as well.

He doesn't say a word at first; just takes it in, same as we do.

How bad is this? How much damage are we about to suffer? This is an outright declaration of war. How many of us will be standing when this is over?

And then, the reality of it all slams into me. Before tonight, before I finally had Kate in my arms; I wouldn't have thought twice about this battle. About giving as good as I got. I'd be happy to battle it out.

But now I am afraid.

Not of them, never them.

Not the fight. But of losing her, the risk to her.

Of what could happen if I'm not fast enough, strong enough, good enough to keep her safe.

Because now it's all shifted, she is the single most important thing in my life. And I will be damned if I let anyone take her from me.

The tension on the balcony is thick. Heavy enough that it coils around my ribs, pressing tight. This isn't just a standoff. It's not posturing either. They brought the fight here. To Us.

Again.

"Are we supposed to say goodbye?" Kyle comments. His arms are crossed as he continues to assess, just like I am, plotting scenarios.

I shift my focus, counting heads, tagging signatures, scanning for anything that doesn't fit. Nikolai. Alexi. Ophelia.

No Coral, nor Tara.

Mason and I both lock in together, extending our senses, searching for an opening. A way to disable them before this turns into an all-out war.

But something is off. Wrong. I can't place it, but this isn't what it seems.

"It's a diversion," Mya whispers. Everyone looks at her. Then, Mason reacts.

"We're compromised," she says, and before we even know it, it's a blur of movement, mental commands and control.

You see, we all follow Mason for a reason. She has zero hesitation, no wasted motion. She doesn't just give orders; she controls the entire chessboard.

Her power pulses outward, hitting every Wight in range, forcing them into action. Defensive, offensive. She lays out the plan, assigns the roles. And we all listen.

I feel her link in with me, to Kyle, Roarke, Riddick, Mya, into everyone she needs to be in sync with. There is no panic, no doubt. Just calm resolve and absolute focus. Just precision.

Mason isn't just stronger than any of us. She isn't just the most powerful Wight on the planet. She is smarter, faster, always three steps ahead.

This is why she leads.

Kyle moves in front of Mason and me. Riddick and Roarke slide into position, Mya as well. I notice Kate shift slightly to the front, and I make a note to kick her ass later.

Elitus and many other combatants are now out. I glance towards the doors. McGuire doesn't even react.

No flicker of emotion, almost as if he knew this was coming. He has been waiting for it. Mason notices as well. Just one more thing to file away.

Mason is scanning. Her gaze sharpens, power surging. And before anyone can question it, she is gone, porting out with Riddick right behind her.

Because wherever the real fight is, it's not here. That sets my teeth on edge. This wasn't an attack; it was a message.

They are still playing games, still pushing us. Testing us, and for the second time tonight, the cold realization of the situation settles deep inside.

They don't care how many times we win; they are just waiting for the one time we don't.

Riddick returns fast, moving like the dark shadow he is. A silent executioner. He doesn't come back empty-handed. He drops two lifeless bodies in front of Nikolai and Alexi. The weight of them hitting the ground with a sickening thud.

The air tightens, a realization of their failed mission.

Nikolai merely raises an eyebrow, completely unfazed by the corpses at his feet. Beside him, Alexi shakes his head, sighing dramatically. "I sure wish you would join us," his voice is smooth, but coiled with a sharp edge to it.

His gaze locks on Mason, who is now back with Riddick firmly at her side.

She doesn't respond, doesn't even acknowledge it.

Which only seems to amuse them more.

Both Dividians let their gaze slide along all of us. Smirking. And then, like knowing exactly what button to push, Alexi takes a long, lingering look at Mason. "When you get bored with Riddick, let me know."

The temperature around us drops, and the power surges. Mason's own power wraps around Riddick's power spike as he locks his jaw. Trying to get himself under control.

But I am done at this point. Something inside me snaps; I am moving forward, my shields already flaring out, every ounce of my power licking across the lawn, ready to end this, right here and now.

But before I can reach them, the air bends. A distortion of energy, a signal of a port signature. Kevin Bishop. PPG's only Wight-class porter arrives, but this time he isn't alone.

He materializes alongside two other soldiers. I try to read them but can't break the shield cover. It's stronger than a normal mental block, too strong.

It looks like the PPG has upgraded. This isn't just a game to them anymore. They aren't just grabbing scraps and experimenting with whatever rejects they can find. They are building an army.

And they have some high Threes. What worries me more is that they must have some high Twos as well, based upon the shield cover. Ones capable of moving, shielding, and strategizing at levels that put me on edge.

Kevin doesn't even look at us, just puts a hand on Alexi and Nikolai, and ports out. A steady stream, with their soldiers taking out the rest.

Gone in a single seamless port. Just like that—no words, no threats.

Because they don't need to say anything, the message they just sent is clear enough.

The PPG is watching, and they just got on campus again. The threat is genuine, and it's at our door. If we don't adjust soon, it may be too late for any of us next time.

That's something I won't tolerate. I just got what I have wanted, and I am not about to let anything or anyone take that from me.

Kate

My mind is a storm that I can't seem to quiet down. The weight of the night presses down. It feels suffocating, and I just want it to end.

The threats, the tension, the way we're always bracing for another hit.

I want to breathe, to focus on the things that should matter. I want to work, build, and plan for the future. Not sit here, debrief and plan for another battle in the war I never asked to be a part of.

I sit in the conference room, surrounded by the main combat crew. Kyle, Bastian, Mason, Riddick, Mya, Roarke. I realize more than ever that there is a line between us. And I will never be on the same side of it.

The combat elite, the ones who never hesitate. The ones who don't think twice about what comes next, because they are built for this.

And me? I have been pretending to be combat-ready. Demanding to be part of this war. Thinking that I can keep up. Though tonight highlighted the difference between us.

The way I will never be like them. That I may, in fact, be a liability.

Bastian sits beside me, coiled tight, his posture rigid. His fingers tapping a slow rhythm against the table. I can feel his anger and frustration simmering.

Mason is worse. She isn't just angry. She is furious. Like a loaded spring, coiled and ready to snap. She doesn't speak, doesn't move. Riddick watches her closely, ready for the fallout. Kyle is monitoring the entire room, as if he's calculating next steps, while trying to deal with the fallout on campus.

Mya sits stiffly across from me. Her shoulders squared, expression blank. And Roarke. He won't even look at her.

The guilt eats at my insides, swirling inside me. I hate that I may have added to their drama with my own stupidity.

I already apologized to Roarke. He just gave me a sad smile, the kind that makes my chest ache. I have worn that look myself too many times. I hate that I hurt him, hurt Mya. I want to fix it—no; I need to fix it.

Because whatever is going on between them. It's much worse than the drama Bastian and I created with our idiocrasy. It's like a deep wound that is still oozing months later. Not just anger and pride getting in the way; something that if it doesn't get fixed soon, will surely kill them both.

While we still wait for Elitus, Mason finally speaks up, voice cold, sharp. "So, what is the plan?"

Mason and Riddick take a moment and update us. Lay it out.

PPG wasn't just here for a show of force; they were after something—information. Data on the latent experiments and Elitus research. This isn't just recruitment anymore. It's theft; espionage, war.

Besides me, Bastian is a live wire, his power crackling below the surface. We haven't talked. We haven't had a chance, but I want to help him. Calm him. I reach out, just a simple touch, trying to get him to relax. It's instant. He takes a deep breath and lowers his levels. I flick a gaze in his direction. He is still focused on the conversation, but he has now taken my hand in his and has placed it on his thigh under the table. Anchoring me.

Bastian

When Elitus finally drags their asses in, Mason snaps.

"This," she announces before McGuire can even start, "is why I don't oppose the Latents."

She doesn't even sound mad. No, Mason is calm, sharp and utterly dangerous. Which means she is beyond words pissed.

"Nice to see you finally coming around," Thompson quips. I can't help but roll my eyes. This isn't the time for his bullshit.

The air is too tight; there are too many people. Too many egos and not nearly enough answers.

"How about we talk about the elephant in the room?" I finally say, my voice cutting through the tension. McGuire shifts his gaze towards me. I feel Kate's hand in mine, grounding me. It's the one thing that has kept me from losing my damn mind tonight, from flipping this freaking table over.

But it won't deter me. I keep my focus on McGuire. "Adrian turning is an issue." I say it like it is. "How much does he actually know, McGuire?"

McGuire doesn't flinch, doesn't show a damn emotion.

"Any info he has is minimal," he states smoothly. "Aside from any inner workings, which are being locked down."

It's bullshit. He knows more than that. If he is underestimating that, then we are all freaking screwed.

"And the latent program?" Mason asks. Her eyes are sharp, voice cutting. She isn't questioning him; she is cornering him. "I find it coincidental that the latent data is what they were after."

"Quid pro quo," Mya murmurs. We all look at her, but her gaze is on her father. "We took his info, which honestly wasn't very hard to get at," she leans back. "He probably hoped we would get it, knowing Elitus would make enhancements. Letting us do the work for him."

Mason's expression doesn't change, but I know she is contemplating it. "If that's the case," Mason says. "He didn't get what he wanted."

Dr. Ross clears his throat, stepping up to the table. "Progress has been good, but we are still way off from perfecting it. Especially Z."

"What we took from them; it answered a lot of questions and identified some unacceptable results. Gave us some parameters to work with."

"PPG doesn't really care about the long-term effects for most of its soldiers. Or Wights for that matter," Kate's mother points out. Dr. Ames' voice is steady. But I feel the weight behind it; she is angry too.

"There are some key individuals—though not named—that we can identify based on power alone." Her eyes flick toward Mason, Kyle, Riddick, and me. I know exactly what that means. Some of us? We're valuable. But others. They are expendable.

I clench my jaw, already knowing where this is going. "It means no offense, McGuire, but Adrian and those idiots just became guinea pigs."

McGuire frowns, looking like he just sucked on a lemon. I almost smirk. But none of this is funny. He flicks his gaze toward Mason, and I feel the shift in the air. And he knows it too. Adrian isn't the real threat. This is about Mason.

"He made his choice," McGuire says stiffly. "I doubt he was coerced."

Riddick snorts, "He was probably given the same promises Dmitri made to Mason, only Adrian is dumb enough to believe him." Riddick's voice is sharp, edged with something deeper. Something I don't like.

"We can tighten everything up," Riddick continues. "But I'd suggest you make a plan for this latent project."

Mason exhales, shoulders going rigid. "And probably cancel any major events," she mutters. The air gets sucked out of the room. Riddick and I both pivot to her. Locking in instantly. She is suggesting pushing her graduation, and that of Gen Three's. There is no way that is happening.

"Mason," her father interjects. She lifts her chin.

"I'm not saying don't finish our testing or have us graduate," she says. "But a ceremony? Fancy dinner? It should get pushed off. Draws too much attention, and since half the time Dmitri seems focused on me," she trails off. I hate this fucking asshole. "Well, it's a target I don't want over my head."

I speak up before this goes further. "We can still do a ceremony," I nod to Riddick. "Just skip dinner. I'm sure a dorm party can happen." Because there is no way I am letting McGuire turn this into another sacrifice play for her.

Riddick shifts and looks at his father. "And moving the newer combats into the dorms?"

Stephen observes him, then sighs. "I know you hate it, Riddick, but they are ready to move forward," he says, speaking of both our sisters, who are supposed to be moving into the dorms next week. His voice softens, almost as if he is trying to convince himself as well. "Trust me, I hate it as well."

Mason and Mya exchange a look; Robert does as well.

"Payback's a bitch," Roarke mutters. I feel his smirk before I see it. "I've had to worry about Andy for years, and I can only imagine how it has been for Max and Alex, with these two daredevils out there," Mason smirks at that one. "It'll be fine," he continues. "Besides, I heard they are moving in next to Charley and Mason, great role models."

Everyone laughs. Well, everyone except Stephen, Riddick and me.

Thirty-One

Kate

Being dismissed, I exhale slowly, grounding myself. I check in with my mom, needing to hear from her directly; she assures me they have security on lockdown, that she and Dad are fine, my siblings are safe.

It should be enough; it should calm me. But it doesn't, because I want more. I need to know everything. Information is control, and I refuse to stay in the dark.

Before I can press for details, I feel a strong hand wrap around mine. Bastian pulls me away, effortlessly redirecting my focus. I glare at him, but he doesn't care. He never cares when it comes to doing his job. And right now, his job is me.

I don't fight him this time, there would be no point. His grip is steady, grounding, unyielding. Not a touch, just a reminder. That I am not alone, that he has me.

We hit the dorms, even though they should be quiet by now. It's not; there is energy in the air, whispers about what happened, what's coming next.

Bastian releases my hand, but only so he can take control of the main area. Control the room, check in. He moves with purpose, shielding those who need it. Sending out calming vibes to others. Quieting the unease that is rippling through the dorms.

He doesn't just talk; he absorbs their worry, their fears, their uncertainty.

Roarke may be the Peacemaker, but Bastian, he's the Protector.

I should be scared. Should feel nervous, overwhelmed, anxious. But I don't. Because for the first time in too long, I feel alive. I don't just want to survive, but I want to live.

Bastian turns back to me, eyes sharp, unreadable, squeezing my hand. But his voice is firm when he says, "Go to bed."

"I'm not—"

He cuts me off with a look, the kind that allows for no argument. The kind that says he won't let me fight him on this one. So, I decide to pick my battles.

Rather than argue, I'll head upstairs, but before I do, he pulls me into him. Kissing me senseless yet again. It's what I needed, but based on the way he doesn't want to release me, he needed it too. When I go to step back again, the need is in his eyes. It's a mirror of mine, and I take a deep breath. I head upstairs, stripping off the weight of the day. I take a long shower, letting the steam burn away everything. The tension, frustration, exhaustion.

The shower doesn't clear everything, though. I wonder whether he will come to me. I want him to, but Bastian is stubborn, and so am I.

Before I lose my nerve, I decide to take the choice away from him.

I grab some files, slip down the backstairs, heart hammering in my chest. And then without hesitation, I open his door. And step inside.

Bastian

The dorms are a ball of tension, everyone on edge; the unease is palpable in the air. I do what I can. Reassure, calm, keep everyone from losing their shit.

You can feel the tension. It's the unknown and the betrayal mixing. The fear, not just PPG on base, not just the threat they pose. It's a fact that now some of our own voluntarily joined them.

That's what has everyone rattled.

By the time I finally escape and make it to my room, I feel like a truck has hit me. I just want to shut down and close my eyes. But I know I need to see Kate, want to see her, even if it's just to check on her.

However, I need a shower first. I told her to go to bed hours ago; she looked dead on her feet. If there was ever a night when I needed her just to listen to me; it was this one, and thankfully she did.

I open my door, exhaling as I step inside. Only to pause. She's here. Waiting for me. I should've known.

Closing my eyes, I shake my head, only half pissed. "I told you to go to bed."

She comes to me in jeans and a T-shirt, her hair pulled back into a low ponytail, her face a little pale from exhaustion. She looks as tired as I feel.

"Haven't you learned anything?" her voice is soft, teasing. "I always do the opposite of what you tell me."

Before I can respond with a retort, she's pulling me forward by my shirt and has her lips on mine. Aggressive, demanding, and hot as hell.

That's one way to wake me the fuck up.

My arms wrap around her instinctively, pulling her flush against me, melting away the weight of the day. She loses herself in the kiss and allows me to take back some control, maneuvering her around like I need to anchor myself to her.

Kate's not a small girl. She is one of the tallest here, at 5'10" without her heels. But when she is in my arms like this, my need to protect her jumps out. She meshes her tongue with mine, taking everything I give her, pushing back enough to drive me insane.

Our hormones surge; my power flares. I try to get it under control. Wrap my shields around the two of us. But before I can do that, she breaks the kiss, pulling me into the living area before I can even think.

Then, like she owns the damn place, me included, she pushes me down onto the couch.

That's when I notice the stack of files on my coffee table. She has been working. I don't even know why I am surprised. She never stops, never slows down, never lets herself breathe. Even now.

I am going to have to do something about that.

She disappears into my kitchenette, rummaging around. A second later, she emerges, carrying food. She hands me a plate, but I don't even glance at it. I put it to the side, and instead, I grab her wrist, tugging her right back into my lap.

"You're avoiding me, Queenie," she glares at me.

"I brought you food, asshole." Her comment has no bite to it. I smile.

Without giving her a chance to reply, I use my other hand to maneuver her and kiss the shit out of her.

Everything I haven't said, haven't done, haven't been able to express since the moment I let her walk away—I pour into this. The frustration, the tension, the fucking need that she wakes up in me every goddamn day.

She adjusts her position, straddling me on the couch, meeting me with the same level of need. Her hands grip my shoulders, my head, nails scraping against my scalp. My hands grip her hips as she grinds down over me. Her body and her mind reaching out for me, trying to ground herself in something.

I feel it then, the shift. The wetness on her cheeks, her tears.

My chest is heaving, but I pause. For the first time since I started this, I really look at her. She has already released her shields again to me. No defenses, no hiding. Just Kate.

Her eyes are glassy, her breathing shaky, her body trembling in my arms. The adrenaline, the night, everything that has been going on forever, it seems.

And I know, I know it in my gut.

She has been carrying too much. She's been hiding, but not just from me. From everything. She is breaking on the inside, running ragged. And I want to kick myself for not seeing it sooner.

I press my forehead against hers, taking a slow, measured breath. Then, I do the only thing I know how to do. I send her a pulse of energy, wrapping it around her like a mental shield. I take away the weight of the pressure, the pain, the self-doubt. Even the fear.

She shudders, her body relaxing against mine. And just for a moment, we breathe together.

"Are you okay?" I murmur against her temple.

She nods and moves back, but her hands rest on my chest. Her fingers curl into my shirt, gripping it like she's scared to let go.

"You need to stop trying to handle everything yourself, Kate," I whisper.

She lets out a soft laugh, shaking her head. "I don't know how."

I sigh, tightening my arms around her. "Then let me help."

She doesn't respond, but the way she leans into me tells me enough.

Her eyes are still glassy, emotions crashing through her in waves. She's exhausted, soft, pliant, her usual sharp edges smoothed by the night.

Her cheeks flushed, her hair a mess from my hands, and her lips.

Fuck.

Her lips are swollen from my kiss, parted slightly, still trembling. She looks shaken, vulnerable, in a way I rarely get to see.

Because The Queen doesn't break, she doesn't bend. She doesn't let people in. Right now, though, she is completely, utterly mine.

"I will protect you, Kate." My voice is low, rougher than I intend it to be. I tighten my grip on her, as if that alone will make it true. "They will never get to you."

She swallows hard; her gaze locked on mine. I see it then.

The fear she doesn't want to acknowledge, the way the night rattled her more than she will ever admit. She always puts on a good show, always in control.

Her lips quiver, and I curse under my breath. Fucking hell, she already has me wrapped around her damn finger. In less than a few hours, I'm totally wrecked.

Who am I kidding? She's had me since birth.

I let out a slow breath, trying to ground myself, trying to rein in my need for her. I brush my fingers along her jaw, tracing the curve of her cheek, committing every inch of her to memory.

Then, because I've never been afraid to be blunt and speak the truth, I smile softly before pressing the lightest kiss against her lips. "I love you."

Her breath catches.

"Oh, Sebastian." She latches onto me, her arms winding around my neck, her body pressed so tightly against mine, I swear I can feel her heartbeat syncing with mine. Her shields are completely down, so I feel it all. All of her, raw, unfiltered, undeniable.

I try to reel it in, slow us down. Keep it under control, but she won't let me. She doesn't even try. The need coming from her overwhelms me.

"I love you so much," she whispers, her voice a plea, a promise, a surrender. Her lips graze my neck, breath warm, needy. "I need you. Please."

I'm done. Fucking done.

Lifting her effortlessly, she gasps, legs instinctively wrapping around my waist. Her nails dig into my shoulder, my grip tightens on her thighs, her back, her everything.

I walk her to my bed, my breath ragged, my pulse a fucking drumbeat in my ears.

I lay her down, hovering over her, taking in the moment, the weight of it. The permanence. Laying her down, I force myself to go slowly. To savor this. Because I know exactly what this moment means.

She has never done this before, and I don't want her to be nervous or scared. I want her relaxed, needy, and completely fucking mine.

So, I take my time. I let my hands explore; my fingers trace the curves I've spent years pretending I didn't notice.

I look at her, take a good long look. Her flushed cheeks, parted lips, the way her chest rises and falls. She is perfect. I push a pulse of energy into her, watching as her back arches, her body responding immediately. I grin, wicked and dark, loving the way her eyes go hazy. She is going to learn tonight what a Two can really do.

Before I can flip us, before I can tease her more, she sits up, reaches down, and...

Holy. Fuck.

Pulls off her shirt. No bra. A low, guttural moan rips from my throat. I can't hold it back. I don't want to. Then she smirks, fucking smirks.

Pushing me back, she straddles me again like she's been doing this for years. My hands find her hips. I rise, my lips at her neck, my tongue tracing the pulse point there.

She shudders, her fingers dragging through my hair, her nails scraping lightly down my back, up my shirt, her hands on my back, hot and hungry.

I need her naked. Now.

I shift, rolling her beneath me, sliding my hands down her body, pressing my mouth to every inch of her I can reach. She whimpers, her hips lifting into me.

I take my time, peeling her jeans down her long legs, letting my hands glide over every inch of bare skin.

She's breathless, watching me with darkened green eyes, her face flushed with arousal. She is laid out on my bed in just her panties, and she is the most beautiful fucking thing I have ever seen.

"I've never done this," she admits, her voice barely a whisper.

I look up at her, meeting her gaze head-on. "I know."

Brushing my fingers along her thigh, letting my thumb skim the edge of her panties. Her breath catches, but I just smile. "Kate, there will never be another for me," I move back up her body, cradling her face between my hands. "I'm yours."

Her eyes flash. And something inside her snaps. She yanks me down, her nails digging into my back as her lips crash into mine. I groan, rolling my hips into her. Let her feel exactly how much I need this.

How much I need her.

Her hands move to my shirt again, pulling it up, pushing it off, fingers exploring every inch of my skin. I'm burning up, every muscle coiled tight, every nerve ending hypersensitive.

I want her so fucking bad. I kiss my way down her chest, my mouth finding the soft skin beneath her collarbone.

She moans, arching into me, her fingers tangling in my hair.

"I want to make love to you all night," I murmur against her skin, pressing a teasing kiss to the valley between her breasts.

I push another pulse of energy, showing her what she's in for. Her body jerks, a strangled moan escapes her lips.

Her eyes snap open, and she stares at me, her cheeks flushed, her lips swollen. Then she laughs, shaking her head. "Bastian," she gives a throaty murmur.

"But first," I smirk, grabbing her wrists, pinning them above her head. Her breath catches. Her legs tighten around my waist, arching into me even more. I nibble at her jaw, dragging my teeth down the curve of her neck.

"First, I need to eat."

She blinks. "What?"

I grin, wicked and teasing, dropping a kiss to her shoulder. "Or I'll probably burn out."

She laughs again, the tension breaking, just for a moment.

I lift her up; her legs wrap around me instantly. I carry her to the kitchen, pressing my mouth to hers every step of the way. Her fingers graze my jaw, her nails dragging through my hair. Her body melts against mine.

I lean her against the counter, not quite releasing her, as I nuzzle into her neck. Kate shifts slightly against me, her hands resting on my shoulders, her legs still wrapped loosely around my waist as I hold her in place.

Her lips quirk into a mischievous little smirk I've seen a million times, the one that drives me insane. But now it just makes me want to devour her.

"Shouldn't I get dressed?" she teases. I grin, tightening my grip on her ass, keeping her exactly where she is. "I wouldn't want to distract you."

I chuckle, brushing my lips against her jaw, inhaling the faintest trace of her perfume, the scent of her. "Kate, you've been a distraction my whole damn life. I can wait twenty minutes." I set her on the counter, reluctantly stepping back just long enough to grab my dinner and quickly return.

Kate watches me, her green eyes flickering with amusement as I take a bite of my sandwich. She steals a chip right off my plate, popping it into her mouth.

"How did you know this is what I wanted?" I ask, eyeing her as she steals another.

"Sebastian," she drawls, rolling her eyes, "I'm an excellent student. And unlike you, an observer. Not all action."

I arch a brow, half amused, half intrigued. "Oh, yeah?"

She leans back, resting her elbows on the counter, smirking. "I've made a study of you."

I grin, setting my plate down, stepping back between her legs. "Do you have a file for me to read?"

Kate just laughs, running her hands slowly up my arms, fingers lingering along my biceps. "No, but I have to say..." she murmurs, squeezing my arm, her touch sending heat straight through me. "...your workouts with my dad are very impressive."

She pinches my biceps playfully, her smirk widening.

I grab a piece of roast beef, offering her a bite. She takes it without hesitation, lips brushing against my fingers as she does.

My brain short-circuits.

Fucking hell.

She grips my arm, reaching for another bite, but I shift effortlessly between her legs, effectively trapping her against me.

Her breath catches. I place the rest of my food down because, fuck food.

There's only one thing I want to devour right now.

"You're right," I murmur, voice rougher now, heat curling low in my gut. "You are a distraction."

She smiles, but it falters slightly when I lean in, pressing my lips softly, deliberately against hers. Slow, controlled.

"I needed the energy to keep from hurting you," I whisper against her mouth. Her hands tighten on my arms, but she doesn't pull away.

"I've had years to dream about being with you, Kate. Now that I have you..." I break off, taking a breath, trying to rein myself in. "I have to hold back. I'll be gentle with you."

She laughs, pushing against my chest, but I don't move.

"Who says I want gentle?" she challenges. My pulse spikes. "Bastian, I want you," she grips my shirt, pulling me even closer, her breath hot against my lips. "I want all of you." Swallowing hard, my hands tighten on her thighs. "I know you won't be gentle," she murmurs. Her confidence in that statement is my undoing. "I want it all the way," she presses her lips to my throat, then moves to my jaw. "Every way."

Fucking hell. This woman.

I slide my hands over her thighs, her waist, up her sides, memorizing every inch of her. I kiss her again, deeper this time, letting her feel exactly what she's asking for.

Gentle? Not a fucking chance.

"Kate," I rasp, voice full of promise, full of need, "I hope you know exactly what you're getting into."

She grins, wicked and wild, running her fingers through my hair. "Oh, I do," she purrs.

And then I lift her off the counter.

She wraps her legs around me; her nails dig into my shoulders as I take her back to my bed.

THIRTY-TWO

Kate

I don't know where I end and where he begins. My heart is pounding, breath ragged. And my body? It's on fire.

I knew it would be like this. But knowing and experiencing, those are two vastly different things.

Bastian moves with purpose, with intent. His hands are everywhere, his mouth claiming every part of me like I belong to him. And it's because I do.

I arch into him as his lips trace a path down my throat, heat coiling low in my stomach as he presses me deeper into the mattress.

I should be nervous, scared. But I am none of those things.

"Kate," he groans, dragging his teeth along my collarbone, his voice thick with need. My nails dig into his back as he grinds against me, the friction almost too much, and simultaneously not enough.

"I need you," I whisper. It's a plea and a demand.

He hisses as if my words physically affect him. "You have me," he murmurs against my skin, his hands sliding lower.

There is no hesitation, no doubt, no second-guessing. Just us. The tension that has built for years finally snaps, and there's no going back.

He claims me with his mouth, with his hands, with every brush of his lips, every slide of his fingers. I am lost in him.

Bastian

She is everything.

Every fight. Every argument. Every moment I pushed her away, every time I let her believe she was anything less than what she is—mine.

She's laid bare beneath me, her body flushes with heat, her shields down completely, her emotions a storm of need and trust and love so overwhelming I can barely breathe.

She's giving me everything.

And fuck if I don't want to drown in it.

I touch her like I've wanted to for years; slow, deliberate, taking my time to memorize every sound, every reaction, every fucking thing about her.

She's gasping, writhing, her body arching into my hands, into my mouth as I learn her, as I worship her. Her pulse flutters under my lips as I trace a path down her throat, along her collarbone, lower. I can feel her need spiking, her anticipation coiling tight—so damn tight—and I smirk against her skin.

I want to tease her, drive her to the edge of madness, make her feel so much she forgets how to breathe. I want to make up for every second I wasted.

I brush my power along hers, coaxing her shields to drop even more, wrapping us in a cocoon of energy that keeps everything and everyone out.

I slide my hands down her bare skin, soft and warm beneath my touch, and she shudders, her breath catching as I move lower. "Bastian," she gasps, her voice barely a whisper, her fingers gripping my shoulders, pulling me closer.

"Shhh," I press a kiss to the center of her chest, right over her heart. I can feel it pounding, a wild rhythm that matches my own.

I move lower, pressing my mouth to the curve of her waist, dragging my teeth along her hip just to hear her moan my name again. Her fingers tighten in my hair, her body trembling beneath me, beneath my hands, my mouth, my power.

I let it slip past my control, sending slow pulses of energy through her skin, down her spine, between her thighs, until she's shaking, gasping, begging.

She's never felt this before. No one has ever touched her like this. And, fuck, I love that.

She is wild beneath me, uninhibited, her body bowing, desperate for more. Her head falls back as she gasps my name, and I grin against her stomach, loving how responsive she is, how much she's trusting me with this. With her.

I slide back up, kissing her slowly, deeply, my hands never stopping, never relent-ing, never letting her catch her breath.

"You're so perfect," I murmur against her lips.

She exhales softly, her hands skimming over my back, my shoulders, up into my hair. She's exploring, learning, and memorizing me the way I'm memorizing her.

She doesn't have to say it, but I feel it. I feel everything. I brace my weight on my forearms, our bodies flush, our breath mingling.

Her green eyes are blown wide, her lips swollen from my kisses, and I swear, she's never looked more beautiful. "Are you sure?" I ask, giving her one last chance to stop this.

But she just wraps her legs around me tighter, pulling me closer, her voice nothing but raw need. "Yes."

There is no more waiting. No more pushing her away. No more denying what has always been inevitable.

I sink into her slowly, carefully, feeling her body adjust, take me in, welcome me.

She gasps, her nails biting into my shoulders, her shields snapping back up for a second before I press a kiss to her jaw, her throat, her heart.

"Drop them, queenie," I murmur against her skin. "Let me in."

And she does. She lets me in completely, our minds and bodies syncing in a way I never thought possible. I feel everything, her pleasure, her need, her love, her trust.

And, fuck, it undoes me.

I start slowly, savoring every second, every movement, every sound she makes. But she's desperate, her hips rolling to meet mine, her body pleading for more, faster, deeper. She doesn't just want soft and slow.

She wants all of me; I give it to her.

Our rhythm turns frantic, primal, our bodies moving in sync, matching each other, demanding more. She is fire beneath me, untamed and burning, and God, I could get lost in this forever.

"Bastian," she gasps, her voice breaking, pleading.

I murmur in her ear, against her throat, pressing every ounce of my devotion into my touch, my movements, my power. "I've got you," I whisper. "I've always got you."

And when she finally falls apart beneath me, because of me, with me, it's not just her body that shatters. It's everything.

Her shields, my control, our past, our fears—all of it combusts. And we are nothing but fire and heat and pure, unrelenting need. I follow right after her, burying myself deep, holding her so close I don't know where she ends, and I begin.

And when we finally collapse, our bodies spent, our hearts racing, our souls tangled.

I know I will never be the same.

I press a kiss to her damp forehead, brushing a stray lock of hair from her face. Her breathing is still uneven, her body still trembling from the aftershocks of what we just did. What we just became.

She looks wrecked in the best way possible; lips swollen, skin flushed, her body still tangled with mine. Completely undone. She settles against me, her fingers lazily tracing circles on my chest, her body finally relaxed, completely at peace.

For a moment, I just hold her. No arguing. No fighting. No tension.

Just her—bare, warm, and mine. I don't say it.

Not because I don't feel it, fuck, I feel it more than I've ever felt anything in my life, but because there's no need to.

It's in every touch. Every kiss. Every time our bodies move together, perfectly in sync.

I let her rest, let her sink into the moment, but it doesn't last.

Kate

The first time is fast, intense, desperate.

He moves like he's been starving for me, aching for me, and I feel it in every touch, every thrust, every whispered curse against my lips. I cling to him, my body arching, surrendering, unable to do anything but feel. And when we both shatter, it's not just physical.

It's everything. Every argument, every fight, every moment of longing we tried to bury — all of it exploded between us.

For a moment, neither of us speaks. We just breathe, tangled together, our bodies still trembling. But he's not done. Not even close.

He kisses me slowly, deeply, his hands roaming, soothing, igniting.

This time, he takes his time. Exploring and learning me. He teases me with slow, deliberate strokes, driving me insane until I'm begging him to take me again. He laughs, but it's rough, strained.

Like he's barely holding on. As if this is affecting him as much as it is me. He needs this just as much.

"Tell me what you need," he rasps, his fingers pressing into my hips. His dominance is effortless; his control is absolute. Until I break it.

"You," I breathe, dragging my nails down his back, a small amount of pain. But his groan is raw, his body tensing above me. Then, he loses himself in this, in us. And gives me everything he has to give and more.

We lie there, our bodies still tangled, our breaths slowly evening out. With my head resting against his chest, I brush my fingers over his jaw, his lips, still trying to convince myself that this is real.

His eyes flicker open, finding mine. He looks sated, exhausted. But there is something else there too. Something that tells me that maybe this is my fairy tale ending after all.

Bastian

Her fingers are still against my chest, her breathing evens out, but she doesn't fall asleep. She's waiting. She's feeling the same thing as I am.

This isn't enough. It'll never be enough. I skim my hand down her spine, slow, teasing, and she shivers, arching just slightly. Before she can blink, I roll her beneath me again, bracing my weight on my forearms, trapping her in place. She gasps, but it's not from surprise.

It's from anticipation. Her legs tighten around my waist, and she tilts her chin up in challenge, her green eyes burning into mine.

God, she's fucking perfect. I run my nose along her jaw, my lips brushing the shell of her ear. "You're not tired, are you?"

Her breath hitches, her hands sliding down my back, nails grazing lightly. I grin against her skin. Those are all the answers I need.

This time, there's no hesitation. I no longer need to hold back.

She needs this just as much. Matching me in every way, pushing me like only she can. And fuck, I've been missing out.

All this time, fighting her, pushing her away, convincing myself we could never work. I was a goddamn idiot. This is everything.

Thirty-Three

Kate

The next morning, I feel different. Not just because my body is pleasantly sore, or because I barely got a few hours of sleep.

But because something inside me feels... settled.

Like something that has been waiting, aching, needing—is finally complete.

Bastian is still asleep, sprawled out in his bed, his sheets tangled around his waist, his bare chest rising and falling.

It's the first time in weeks I've seen him completely at peace. Like he doesn't have to fight the world for once, doesn't have to fight me.

And damn, he looks good. My insatiable X-Two.

I grin to myself, knowing Bastian's completely burned out from last night. Well, physically exhausted anyway. But his power, which I can feel from here, is on another level.

We were probably too loud. I'll have to apologize to his floormates.

Or not.

I slip out of bed, grab his shirt from the floor, and head into the kitchen. I need food, but more importantly, he needs food.

By the time I am almost done cooking, I hear him moving around.

Then, the door opens. And I swear, my heart skips. He steps out of his room, rubbing the back of his neck, stretching slightly, his body all lean muscle, golden skin, and barely there restraint.

The sweatpants hang low, teasing, and his dark hair is an absolute mess, more tousled than usual. I swallow hard.

Then he looks at me. His purple-rimmed chocolate eyes sweep over my body, taking in his shirt on my body, the way it barely covers anything. And the way I am just standing here waiting for him.

Something flashes in his eyes—dark, possessive, and primal.

The same hunger as last night—it's still there. But somehow... more.

And just like that, I feel it too. The pull, like two magnets that can't avoid each other. He steps forward. I don't even realize I've mirrored him until we're standing inches apart, the air between us thick, charged.

My pulse kicks up, my breath catches. And I know if I let him touch me, if I let him pull me back into that room, I'll never make it out today.

So instead, I smirk, gather up my resolve and step back. "I figure I owe you some fuel." His eyes don't leave me. Not for one second. I can feel his hormones spike, feel the way his body tenses, coiling like a spring. I grin back at him. "And you said I was a nympho."

"I wasn't complaining," his voice is rough, low. A shiver crawls down my spine.

I swallow, focusing on the food. "We're going to my parents' in an hour."

He arches a brow; I know he's debating whether he can get me naked before then.

"We don't have time," I add quickly, grabbing his plate and handing it to him. "Later though."

We enjoy breakfast and talk about what comes next, including combat missions. And of course, it soon turns into an argument.

Bastian

"I will not take myself out of rotation," Kate snaps. She's standing in my kitchen, still wearing my damn shirt, looking all soft and so fucking gorgeous—and she chooses now to start a fight.

I refuse, grabbing my towel and heading straight for the shower, letting her yell at my back.

I do not want to have this conversation. Not now, not when I know exactly how it's going to go.

The water beats down on me, hot as hell. But it doesn't help. I am still on edge. Because over my dead body is she going out there without me. Especially now, after last night.

The shower curtain yanks open, and I sigh. "Are we going to talk about this?"

"Nope."

"Nope?" she snaps, arms crossed, power crackling off her. "Damn it, Bastian! Just because we're sleeping together does not give you the right to dictate my life."

I turn then, because now she is pissing me off. "Sleeping together?" I scoff. Her eyes narrow. I step closer, the steam from the shower swirling between us. "I sure as hell didn't sleep last night, Kate."

Her throat bobs, good. "I'm not just sleeping with you. I am mate-bonded to you."

She inhales sharply. And fuck—watching that reaction? Watching her absorb what I just said, watching it settle in her chest... I take another step, but my voice drops, smooth, calm, final.

"I don't dictate your life. I won't." I watch her, watch her reactions. "But you can bet your ass I have the power to ensure you won't go on any missions without me."

I turn back to the water, letting it run over my face. I should've known better.

"Without you?" She laughs, but it's sharp, bitter. "That's rich, coming from you. You're an X-Two, Bastian. Not a One. Not a Three." I tense. "You are not frontline," she presses, stepping forward. "I am. I'm your shield, you moron, not the other way around."

I turn slowly, water dripping down my face, my chest. And she's right there, fury in her eyes. And, fuck me, if it doesn't turn me on.

"You're wrong," I breathe. I remember last night, how she moved to protect me, stepping in front, how she dared to shield me when it should've been the other way around. It makes me snap.

"Speaking of that," I say, stepping toward her. "If you ever put yourself in front of me again, I will fucking lock a mental block around your head so fast, you won't be able to move for a week."

She gasps, "Don't threaten me."

"Then don't test me."

"You wouldn't dare," I smirk. And that pisses her off even more. Her power flares, spiking like a live wire through the air. I try to wrap shields around her, to contain her before she does something reckless. But she pushes them off. I reach out for her, an attempt to calm her. She grabs my wrist instead, and pivots fast.

I forget sometimes just how fast and strong she is. And suddenly, I'm the one backed against the tile. Water runs down her back. And my woman, my other half, is facing off against me, breathing hard, eyes lit with challenge.

I should be pissed, should shove her back. But I don't. Because this, it's just another form of battle for us. And I love every second.

Her breathing is shallow; her pupils are blown wide. She is so worked up, so defiant. My blood roars in response.

"Are you done?" I ask smoothly.

She grits her teeth. "Not even close."

I smirk. Oh yeah, this woman is going to be the death of me.

But, fuck, what a way to go.

"Good," I murmur, dragging my gaze over her soaking-wet form. "Because you just pissed me off enough to ruin my shower."

Her mouth parts, indignant. But before she can speak, I grab her wrist, flip her against the tile.

She gasps, then laughs. All sharp and wicked.

"This is not an argument you're going to win," I murmur in her ear.

"We'll see," her power spikes.

If this is what our fights are going to look like now...then we're going to have some great makeup sex. Daily.

Watching her being angry does something to me. It hits my hormones and power like a lightning strike. The surge is instant, uncontrollable. It crackles through me, igniting every nerve.

She feels it. I see the exact moment she registers it. Her gaze drops, taking in the evidence.

She knows exactly what this is doing to me. And I believe it's doing the same thing to her.

The passion between us flares to life, a deep pull. Then I push, just a little. A tiny spike of power, testing, tasting.

She moans, and her knees buckle. I catch her pulling her to me.

My hands grip her waist, fingers pressing into soft, wet skin. I lean her up, her back against the slick tile, and I crowd her space, caging her in.

Her chest heaves, flushed and damp, skin shimmering under the steam. I reach for my soaked shirt, peeling it off in slow motion. Her gaze tracks my movements; her tongue flicks out, wetting her lips.

But I play dirty, and I push her mentally again. Harder this time.

Flooding her with images, sensations, replays of last night. All the things I did to her; all the erotic, naughty things I still want to do to her.

She arches, gasps, her body reacts to the overload. She can't stop it; her fingers bite into my forearm, her body writhing, unable to control her reaction, and it's the hottest fucking thing I have ever seen.

I pull back just enough, letting her catch her breath.

Her eyes snap to mine. They are dark, dilated, starving.

She doesn't give me a chance to do anything, doesn't hesitate. She lunges, grabs me by my hair, dragging my mouth to hers. Her lips crash into mine like she's about to consume me whole.

"You better make me come right now," she growls, voice breathless, desperate, "Or I will hurt you."

I laugh, low and wicked. There is no way in hell I'm turning that down. I flip the script immediately, going from playing dirty to completely wrecking her. I drag my hands over her body, mapping every slick curve. Memorizing, branding her body.

I push her power higher, mentally adjusting shield cover. I work her over until she is moaning, thrashing, completely unraveling. Until she is clawing at my back, my shoulders, anything she can reach. Until she begs and pleads for more.

By the time she finally shatters, I can feel it. Her power flares so high, it sears through my shields. My own shields barely contained it.

She gasps, clinging to me. Boneless, spent and completely wrecked.

We take a moment just to breathe. To steady ourselves and our racing hearts. I press a slow kiss to her forehead. She sighs, nuzzling into me, soft, sated. We're both physically drained. But power-wise? Unstoppable.

I pull her under the hot spray, letting the water run over us. We are both tired, but focus on getting clean, and then we step out. Dry off. It's quiet but not awkward; we are both calm, in our own heads, but the connection between us keeps growing.

Kate

I move to leave, but his hand shoots out. Before I can react, his lips crash into mine. I don't fight it; I will never fight this. He lifts me effortlessly, my legs wrapping around his waist as he presses me against the wall of his bathroom, his tongue tangles with mine, demanding, teasing, consuming.

My nails dig into his shoulders; the growl that rumbles in his chest sends heat straight through me. I could stay like this forever.

But then my eyes flick to the phone on the counter, and with what time it is, reality crashes back in. I pull away, panting.

"Kate, you're never late for anything," he murmurs, pressing his forehead to mine. His lips trail down my neck, slow and intentional. My body shudders before I can stop it.

"And I am not about to start now. I need to change," I say, though my voice betrays me.

"Do you?" he challenges, his hands still roaming, still coaxing me back in.

I bite my lip, my resolve faltering, but I won't let him win. Not this time. "Bastian," I warn, pushing against his chest. He smirks but lets me go as I throw on my clothes from last night.

Well—most of them, because my underwear is a lost cause. His smirk deepens; he looks like he is going to test my resolve. "No, I need to change," I repeat, then grab his hand and pull him toward the stairs.

I don't even think about it; I just move. Straight to the top floor, to my room, to my space. It's not until we're halfway there that I feel it. The weight of it. I'm not just taking him to neutral ground.

I'm not keeping him at a distance but bringing him into my world. My life. And for once I don't hesitate.

The thought twists something deep inside me. I've spent my life building control, setting expectations, creating structure. But Bastian? He is wild, unpredictable, and dangerous. I should be scared. But I'm not. I want this, him.

His hand tightens in mine and pulls me to a stop just before I reach my door. I glance at him, confused. But then he just cups my face, pressing a kiss to my temple. The gesture is soft, almost reverent.

Out of character, or the character he used to portray. But I am beginning to believe that when it comes to him and me, there are many more layers that I have yet to see. And so far, I love every one of them.

Bastian

While Kate changes, I look around. I don't think I have ever actually been here. Her room is so... Kate.

Organized, polished, controlled. Color coordinated. A warm, soft aesthetic.

The bed is perfectly made, everything in its place, not a thing out of order, like she runs her entire life. Like she tries to run me.

A smirk pulls at my lips. She can pretend all she wants, but she enjoys losing control with me.

On her desk, something catches my eye: a photo. I recognize it; it's a photo of us.

I pick it up, my grip tightening. I remember this; it was just after a mission, nearly four years ago. One of the first ones she ran. She had been so determined, so ready to prove herself, but she had been scared too, not that she would ever admit it.

But I knew; I had felt it. Just like I feel everything with her.

That night had been a disaster; PPG had set us up. It had been a trap. With enough heavy hitters, when Alexi took aim at her... I had reacted. Leveled Alexi so hard he was out cold before he hit the ground. The Bishops had fled after that.

And Kate? She had just stared at me. Like she was seeing me for the first time that night.

When we had gotten back, I had tried to flirt with her. She had brushed it off, as she always did. But there is this picture, this memory. She kept it.

Someone must have snapped it when we were on the balcony. Kate had been wearing a tank top and a skirt. Legs for days. Even back then, she had killed me. I had known then, known she was the one.

Even though I didn't want to admit it. I was too fucking stubborn to let any predetermined cosmic situation define anything for me.

I hear the click of her heels against the floor, and I turn. She's standing there, looking at me. Her eyes soften when she sees what I am holding.

"I didn't know you kept this photo," I say, watching her reaction. She walks over to me, peering at it.

A small smile curves her lips. "It was one of the few times you actually let someone take your picture," she glances up at me, her voice softer now. "It's my favorite."

I pull her close, taking her in. Her outfit is pristine. Another damn skirt suit. I run my hands over the crisp fabric, down her waist, gripping her hips.

"God, these suits," I murmur. She arches a brow. "I swear I'm going to strip this off you later. It's like your fucking armor."

She laughs, a sound that makes my chest tighten. "If you like the armor," she teases, tilting her chin up, pressing her lips to mine, "you'll love the under armor."

THIRTY-FOUR

Bastian

We head out to the parking lot, the crisp morning air hitting us as we step outside. Plenty of people are lingering near the dorms, but most of our combat crew is out somewhere.

I remember I still need to give Mason her present, but right now, my focus is on Kate.

I feel the weight of the eyes on us; everyone is watching. I glance at her, waiting for the usual sharp remark. But she doesn't seem bothered, not even a little. She walks beside me, perfectly composed, her heels clicking softly against the sidewalk.

We're complete opposites. Most people probably think we're insane, that we'll never work. We spend ninety percent of our time arguing, but that's what makes us tick.

The fire. The push and pull. It's not about breaking each other down; it's about challenging each other. And neither of us ever backs down.

I bypass her sleek Mercedes and head toward my ride. The matte black Hemi Challenger sits there like a beast waiting to be unleashed.

Loud. Fast. Powerful. I love this thing; Kate gives me the side-eye. I know what she's thinking; not surprised that I drive something like this.

I smirk as I open her door, gesturing for her to get in. Her brows lift slightly, like she's shocked I have manners. "What? I can act like a gentleman," I tease, shutting the door behind her before she can fire back.

Sliding into the driver's seat, I catch her appraising the car.

Then her eyes flick to me. That flare of desire? She tries to hide it, but I catch it. When I push in the clutch and start the engine, the car purrs.

So does she. Just a little. I bite back a grin.

With a quick reverse, I pull out smoothly and take us toward her parents' house.

The drive isn't long, but my mind is all over the place. Her retort this morning about me being a Two? It stung. Not because she is incorrect, but because she was right.

I can hold my own; I'm offensive when I need to be. But if I were facing an army? Multiple high-level combatants. I wouldn't last.

And that gnaws at me. Not for my sake, but for hers.

Because now more than ever, I feel the need to protect her at all costs.

Driving over, it's not far — ten minutes to the far west side of campus where the Elitus Council live. I try to settle my mind.

This is big. I'm meeting the parents as Kate's mate? Boyfriend? We haven't spoken at length about it, but all indications are that this is forever for us.

I don't mind it one bit. Which is a total 180 from where I was yesterday. I try not to dwell on that. I need to focus on the now.

Dr. Ames is brilliant; she's always been friendly to me. Probably because she sees my intelligence and knows I'm not just a hothead. I challenge Elitus, McGuire, just about everyone, and she respects that.

But Coach Ames? This is going to be interesting.

He's a magnificent coach, a solid mentor. He helped me master my physical routine, my conditioning, especially lately when I was spending more time in the gym. Trying to work out my frustrations.

But he's also Kate's father, her first protector. And I'm sure he knows, maybe not everything, but he knows enough. The heartache, the history, what I put her through.

When we pull up in front of the house, I try to get my bearings. Kate doesn't let me dwell on it; she just lets me settle. Her hand is on mine, resting on the gearshift. I look over at her.

She takes my breath away. Picture-perfect, so far out of my league, I don't deserve her. But I am not about to let her go. I lift her hand to my lips, pressing a kiss there before stepping out.

Rounding the car, I open her door, helping her out, not because she needs it, but because I want to. Her heels bring her almost to my height.

Almost. And I enjoy seeing her eye to eye. Because we are equal.

Different, but equal.

And now, we're in this together.

Kate

Walking into my parents' house, my fingers are lightly tangled with Bastian's, but the moment we step over the threshold, their eyes are on us.

They heard, or saw, or had it reported to them from someone at the ball, maybe all of the above.

I steel myself, but Bastian. He's calm, collected, like he didn't just flip my entire world upside down in less than 24 hours.

Like he didn't just claim me on a balcony in front of half of Elitus.

Like he hasn't been avoiding me for months only to turn around and decide I belong to him. Infuriating bastard. But when his thumb strokes the inside of my wrist, grounding me, calming me, I exhale.

Mom is the first to approach, moving gracefully through the living room. She's a powerhouse, and though she keeps her expression neutral, her green eyes, so much like mine, miss nothing.

Dad, on the other hand? Arms crossed, expression unreadable.

I squeeze Bastian's hand once before letting go and stepping toward them.

"Mom, Dad." They wait. I clear my throat. "You remember Bastian."

Dad's brows lift just slightly. Mom's lips twitch like she's fighting a smirk.

They remember; they also remember everything before last night. The arguments, tension, and heartbreak. But none of that matters anymore.

Bastian steps forward, extending his hand. "Dr. Ames, Coach." Dad hesitates just a beat before gripping Bastian's hand, their shake firm. Measured.

He's testing him. Bastian, cocky shit that he is, doesn't back down.

Instead, he meets my dad's unyielding stare with calm, unwavering confidence.

"Sebastian," Mom says, taking the moment to break the tension. "We're so glad you could come. Would you like some coffee?"

He flashes her a grin—one of those devastating, panty-melting grins that has gotten him out of trouble more times than I can count.

"That would be great, thank you."

Dad's eyes narrow. Mom definitely noticed the grin. I roll my eyes and take a seat at the dining table as Mom leads Bastian toward the kitchen. Dad follows them. I resist the urge to groan.

I don't even have time to settle in before Ryker and Lissa arrive. My brother is casually dressed, his usual confidence radiating off him, but there's something in his stance—some unease. Lissa looks effortless. Radiant. Mated pairs glow, and she glows for him.

I smile at her, offering a soft, "Morning."

She smiles back, warm and genuine. Ryker eyes Bastian, who has just reemerged from the kitchen with coffee for both of us. The tension in the room shifts.

It's not hostile, but it's charged. Bastian says nothing; he just watches, because that's what he always does. He reads, assesses.

Jasper sits down, but he doesn't have Hannah with him today. They have been dating, but they are not mates. Jasper's usual easygoing nature is intact, but there's something off.

Something Bastian picks up on immediately, a slight unease.

The silence stretches, and I clear my throat. "So." I lean back, sipping my coffee. "Are we just going to sit here staring at each other, or is someone going to start brunch?"

Mom laughs lightly. "Of course, let's eat."

Bastian smirks, shaking his head slightly, and just like that the tension lifts.

Bastian

Brunch at the Ames house is casual but structured, just like Kate.

She probably helped plan it, making sure everything was perfect. And damn if I don't appreciate the hell out of her for it. She's been running on adrenaline and willpower for days, and yet she's still hosting, still managing, still carrying half the damn world on her shoulders.

It's one of the things I love about her, and one of the things that scares the shit out of me.

The conversation starts out light. Kate and Lissa talk about the ball. Jasper and Ryker discuss some of the newer combatants moving into the dorms.

Her mom shares some stories about the Elitus medical wing, and her dad... well, her dad watches.

Me.

He hasn't stopped assessing me since I walked through the door, and I get it. He's a father, a protector, a man who's trained countless Wights, shaped the future of our entire combat unit. And now, his daughter's with me.

After brunch, Kate helps her mom in the kitchen, leaving me alone with Coach. The room empties slowly. Jasper and Ryker step outside. Lissa joins Kate.

And suddenly, it's just me and him. I sip my coffee. He sips his.

And we sit in silence for a minute.

"You're taking on a lot," he finally says.

I nod. "Comes with the territory."

"The Power Council," he muses, leaning back. "Big move."

I smile. "McGuire needed a reality check."

He chuckles. "That he did."

We agree on that. Coach hates McGuire's bullshit as much as I do. And knowing that, it gives me a little more confidence that we'll get along. "Kate will not stop fighting," he says, watching me.

"I know."

"She won't back down either."

"Wouldn't love her if she did."

He raises a brow at my bold declaration, but I hold his gaze. This isn't a test I'm going to fail.

"Let's be honest, Bastian." He sets his coffee down. "I know how this ends."

I tilt my head. "How does it end?"

He pauses, face stoic. Long enough for a small amount of unease to creep up my spine. Then he smirks, "With you and Kate butting heads for the next forty years."

I grin. "Sounds about right."

"But here's the thing," he says, his expression shifting back to serious. "I don't want her in combat."

I stiffen. I expected this. Hell, I agree with him. But I also know better than to make that decision for her.

"I won't pull her out," I say. "That's her call."

He nods, observing me. "But I'll protect her," I add, my voice steady.

His jaw tightens slightly. Then, after a beat, he exhales and nods. "I can live with that," he mutters.

Kate walks in a few seconds later, drying her hands on a towel.

Her eyes bounce between us. "Everything good?" she asks.

Coach grunts. I smirk. "Yeah. We're good."

Kate narrows her eyes; she doesn't believe me.

But she doesn't push. Instead, she slides into the chair next to me, stealing my coffee.

Coach chuckles, and just like that?

I think I passed the test.

Thirty-Five

Bastian

Leaving Kate is harder than I expect. She's still tangled in my warm sheets when I slip out, her golden hair spread across my pillow, the soft rise and fall of her breathing tempting me to crawl back in.

But I promised Mason I'd bring her gift by. And if I don't, she'll bitch about it for weeks.

I press a kiss to Kate's bare shoulder, watching her stir slightly but not wake, and quietly pull on my clothes; she needs sleep.

I knock twice before pushing Mason's door open; the first thing I hear is a soft mew. Then I see it—a ball of fur perched on Riddick's shoulder, tiny paws kneading at his collar, purring like a motor. A tiny little fluff ball, with brown fur and bright blue eyes.

I stop, grinning like a jackass. "Well, look at that." I cross my arms. "Big, bad Riddick Moore—brought to his knees by a damn kitten."

Mason smirks from the couch. "She's spoiled already."

"No shit," I reply.

The tiny, obnoxiously fluffy kitten stretches out lazily, rubbing her face against Riddick's jaw. "Her name is Cocoa," Mason tells me.

I raise an eyebrow. "Cocoa, huh?"

Riddick glares at me like he knows I'm about to run my mouth.

I toss Mason a small box. "Happy birthday. It's not a kitten, but it won't keep you up at night, either."

She catches it effortlessly, eyes narrowing in suspicion.

"What is it?"

I shrug. "Open it and find out."

She does, and when she sees the sleek combat knife inside: black matte, weighted and balanced for her small hand, engraved with her initials, her expression softens.

"You shouldn't have," she says.

"Bullshit." I smirk. "Now, you can stab people with a personal touch."

Riddick snorts. Mason looks touched. For a whole two seconds, then her smirk turns sharp. "You really know how to woo a girl, Monroe."

I wink. "You're not my type, babe."

Riddick rolls his eyes. "Jesus Christ."

Mason offers me coffee, which I accept. I don't take a seat. I don't plan on staying too long, but I need to see what's been happening.

Mason's lost in thought. Now that I think about it, Riddick's off too. The air is tense, charged with something unspoken.

Mason sits on the couch, sipping her coffee, Cocoa now sprawled between her and Riddick.

I scan the room, putting the pieces together, my mind working faster than I want it to. Then it clicks.

Mya. Roarke. The fight that was interrupted.

"What happened?"

Mason takes a long sip, composing herself before she answers. "A couple of months ago," she says, voice flat, emotionless, "Mya made an unwise decision. And it's only escalated since then." She leans forward, resting her elbows on her knees, cup clasped between both hands. Riddick puts his hand on her back, soothing it up and down her spine. Riddick and I exchange a glance, and I know it's going to be bad.

"She went to a party," she continues. "Not at the dorms—on campus but still within reach. It was supposed to be Gen 3 and 4, a mix. She thought it would be fun; thought she'd get a chance to be something other than 'the animal' or my shadow. Maybe just... Mya."

The corner of Riddick's mouth ticks down. He hates that nickname, that label. We all do. "She was drinking. Not enough to lose control—not at first. But she trusted the wrong people."

I exhale sharply, already knowing where this is going. "The bad apples," I say, more statement than question. Mason nods.

"Yeah. Them. They drugged her," Mason continues, tone clipped. "She doesn't know with what. Something strong enough to lower her shielding, enough to make her defenses slip just enough. She doesn't remember—just gaps."

A blackout. I grip the back of the chair in front of me, feeling something dark and ugly crawling up my spine. "She didn't tell anyone," Mason says. "Not me. Not you. Not Roarke." She exhales, staring down at the coffee like it holds answers. "I found out later. Much later. And I promised her I wouldn't say anything."

A flicker of guilt crosses her face.

"So why now?" I ask, voice tight.

Mason's lips press into a thin line. "Because Roarke finally knows," she says. "And because Mya's done pretending, she's fine."

I close my eyes, trying to piece it all together.

The fights. The distance. The anger.

Roarke—who has done nothing but watch over her like a goddamn hawk since the day she could walk

"He thought it was consensual," she says. "Until last night." The words hit harder than they should. Roarke thought she had wanted another, had gone to someone else. My stomach churns. I think of all the times he's been a live wire, lashing out at anyone who looked at her wrong, even when he was ignoring her. Mason finally looks up at me, eyes sharp. "The assholes are gone," she says, tone eerily steady. "But they're not getting off."

Kate

I sit cross-legged on his bed, phone in hand, absently scrolling through emails, committee notes, and training schedules. Trying to focus. Trying to do something productive.

But my mind is elsewhere.

The moment Bastian spiked, I felt it—his anger, a sharp flare of power and raw emotion rolling through me before I could shield against it. It was brief, controlled, but it hit hard. Then, almost immediately, he sent a pulse. A tether, a reassurance, that he's fine, and he'll be back soon.

Still, my gut twists with unease. I shift my attention back to my tablet, scrolling through committee updates, Power Council notes, anything to distract myself.

The door opens harder than necessary. Bastian walks in like a live wire, his jaw tight, shoulders coiled with tension. His eyes find me immediately, still heated, still storming, still on edge.

This isn't just anger; this is something deeper. I set everything aside. "What happened?"

He exhales sharply, running a hand through his hair. He's been doing that a lot lately — a tell, a giveaway that he's barely holding his shit together.

I shift on the bed, ready to listen. Bastian doesn't do pointless venting. If he's about to unload, it means he needs to. That worries me.

"They drugged her." The words hit like a gut punch.

I sit up straighter. "Who? When?"

Bastian's hands clench into fists. "The bad apples. Dean. McGuire's spawn. The others." His voice is sharp, clipped, brimming with restrained fury. "They spiked Mya's drink. Took advantage of her."

My stomach lurches. I knew something was wrong—I saw it in her eyes; in the way she carried herself. But I didn't know this. Bastian keeps going, pacing now, too wired to sit still. "She didn't tell anyone, Kate. Not until recently. Mason knew, but only after the fact. Roarke didn't know until last night."

That lands hard. Roarke. Everything makes sense now. His anger, his violence, the way he's been spiraling. But then Bastian stops pacing, turning to me, something darker in his expression. "I should have known," he says, voice tight. "I should have seen it."

My heart clenches. Bastian doesn't do guilt, not like this. I move to stand, but he shakes his head, running a frustrated hand down his face. "I should've done something, Kate.

Years ago." His tone shifts—lower, rawer. "Dean. The others. I should've handled them back then. I should've made Roarke see he was an idiot for believing she wanted anyone else. I should've—"

I cut him off. "Bastian, stop."

His jaw tightens, but I reach for him anyway, sliding my fingers over him. "You didn't know." My voice is firm, even though my insides feel like they're twisting into knots. "None of us did."

His fingers curl around mine, but his guilt is a weight in the air between us.

I feel it myself, the guilt. It crashes into me. I should have helped her. Instead, I made everything worse. Last night, on the balcony. I pushed Roarke, played games, and used him. And Mya saw it.

"I have to talk to her," I say, straightening my shoulders.

Bastian studies me, reading me like he always does. "You think that'll help?"

"I don't know," I admit. "But I have to try."

Bastian doesn't argue. Instead, he lifts my hand, pressing a brief kiss on my knuckles. "Go," he says, soft but firm.

I hesitate before knocking lightly on Mya's door. I know she's in there. I can feel her presence—not just physically, but her energy, her power. It's always been strong, but after everything I just found out. I don't know how she's still standing.

She shouldn't have had to deal with this alone.

A second later, I hear a muffled, "Yeah?"

I open the door and step inside. She's sitting on the edge of her bed, still dressed in workout clothes, like she just got back from training. Her hair is damp from a shower, loose around her shoulders. She looks tired.

Not physically, Mya is built like a damn soldier. But there's an exhaustion in her eyes that has nothing to do with combat.

"Can I come in?" I ask instead, but my voice is softer than usual.

She nods. "Yeah."

There's no hostility in her tone. No anger, but there's something. I sit down next to her, clasping my hands together, searching for the right words.

For once, I don't know where to start. "Mya... I want to apologize for last night."

Her gaze shifts slightly, observing me. "I want you to know that Roarke and I—we never..." I trail off, hating how weak my voice sounds.

"I know, Kate. It's fine." She says it easily, like she's already processed it. Like it doesn't matter. But it does.

"It isn't fine," I press, shaking my head. "I shouldn't have used him."

Mya snorts, a dry, humorless sound. "It got you where you are with Bastian. And rumor has it, that's an exceptionally good spot."

She smirks sarcastically, and despite the heaviness of the moment, I laugh.

"Yeah," I admit, shaking my head. "It is."

Her smirk softens slightly. "It's okay, Kate. Really," she says, exhaling. "It will be okay."

I want to believe her, but I know better. "You don't have to be," I whisper.

"What?"

"Okay," I clarify. "You don't have to be okay, Mya." Something flickers in her expression. "I won't tell you how to feel. I just... I just want you to know that I'm here. We're all here. Many people care about you. We want you to be okay."

She stares at me for a long moment. Then, hesitantly, she reaches for my hand. It surprises me. We work together. Train together, but we're not close.

But this is a moment. And maybe she needs it. And so do I.

Mya inhales deeply before speaking, "Kate... I'm kinda glad it worked out the way it did. Not just for you and Bastian. But for me. I don't know," she continues. "But it's out now. And honestly?" She lets out a small, broken laugh. "It's a fucking relief."

Tears slip down my face before I even realize it. Mya shakes her head at me, exasperated but fond. "So... is a Two really as good as they say?" She teases, raising an eyebrow.

I laugh, wiping at my face. "Better." We chat for a little bit, and she gives me a big hug before I leave her. I feel better, but I think maybe she does too. I let her know Bastian and I will support her in whatever she needs.

THIRTY-SIX

Kate

My mornings start and end with Bastian. I wake up to warm hands, soft kisses, and the touch that leaves me breathless before I'm fully awake.

Bastian doesn't ease into anything, not love, not life, not battle. And especially not me.

He's insatiable, but then again, so am I. It often starts slow, sleepy and languid. A hand running up my thigh, fingers brushing against bare skin, ignited that ever-present need. Then it builds—faster, harder, deeper. We don't have for this. But we take it anyway. It's impossible not to.

With Bastian, it's not just sex—it's connection. It's something I never knew I needed until now.

Eventually, every morning we drag ourselves out of bed. We shower together, which is just another excuse to go at it again. He pins me to the cool tile, whispers dirty promises against my ear, and makes me forget about time, about anything outside of us.

By the time we make it downstairs, I'm already thinking about the next time. And from the way he grins at me over breakfast, he is too.

"We could skip," Bastian suggests as I finish my coffee.

"We can't skip; we skipped yesterday," I tell him, referencing when he dragged me back upstairs and missed out on a morning committee meeting. Well, maybe not dragged. Who am I kidding? I went willingly. I feel him nudge me mentally, a slight emotional pull, which gets my attention and makes me seriously consider his proposition. But I hold firm.

"We can't," I tell him. He frowns but doesn't push. He knows my resolve is weak. Instead, he clears our plates and walks me to my meeting.

A week in, and we already have a routine. Each day after breakfast, we go our separate ways. Bastian walks me to Elitus, our hands intertwined, casual, easy. It's still new—this thing between us—but it doesn't feel fragile. It feels like it's always been this way.

For me, the mornings are filled with meetings, assessments, and new policies being thrown at us.

I work on strategy with Elitus, while Bastian trains the masses. He has a way with people, especially the younger Gens. Even the ones who used to be cocky little assholes—they respect him.

We meet for lunch. After lunch, we sneak away. The chemistry between us has only gotten worse—or better, depending on how you look at it. Bastian doesn't even try to resist anymore. "Five minutes," he murmurs against my skin.

We both know that's a lie.

The afternoon is training for me. I keep my combat sharp, push myself, prove my worth among the others. Bastian, meanwhile, is in Power Council meetings, fighting McGuire at every turn.

When he's not in meetings, he's training others, running strategy, leading.

We thrive in it. Together. Separate. But always gravitating back to each other.

Dinner rotates. Some nights, it's at my parents' house, where my dad gives Bastian grief but secretly likes him. On other nights, his parents are the ones fussing over us.

Sometimes, we grab food in the cafeteria, surrounded by friends.

And then there are the nights when it's just us; in his room, or mine.

With food that neither of us remembers eating, because we're too busy with each other. We end every night the same way we start it.

With hands tangled, lips exploring, bodies pressing closer.

We still argue. But now it's different.

Now, it ends in laughter, in teasing, in the arguments that lead to breathless kisses and tangled sheets.

Bastian is mine. And I am his.

And finally, everything feels right.

Bastian

It's amazing to me how easily Kate and I slip into a routine. Then again, according to Mason, since Kate and I do not keep any shields between us, it helps us sync up.

She is using us as a case study, since she says the rest of the mated couples still leave some type of shields between them, not completely down all the time.

I'm fortunate I haven't been on a high-risk mission yet, nor has Kate. We will see what happens when we come to that hurdle.

Kate and I talked at length last night about Vanguard. I should've asked her the first night if she was on birth control. I assumed she was, but wanted to be sure. The thought of her being unable to control her power or being at risk. It makes my agitation rise.

I have been training and getting Gen Three ready to do their last trials. I have also been preparing for my sister to join us in the dorms.

That plus packing up my room. I should just throw most of it out. I already expect Kate to lose her damn mind. She likes her control. Likes her space, and she wants me to move into it? I was surprised when she asked. I mean, we spend every night in one of our beds, but that's a big step. She just gave me a look, one that told me I was stupid. Which I will admit I was.

We are together; there is no doubt. We still argue; that will never go away, but now, we can eventually come to some type of compromise on most things.

Headed to a Power Council meeting, I grab Mya on the way. Checking in on her.

"Are you doing okay?"

She rolls her eyes. "Yes."

"Mya," I stop; she faces me. "I won't pry. But if you need me to do anything, to take it away. I will."

"I'm fine, Bastian, really. I talked with my mom, Sarah, and Shannen. That plus Dr. Ames has gotten a counselor on campus, who has reached out. Right now, I just need to wrap my head around it. I have ignored it for so long, I want to face it. Then, if I need it gone, I will reach out to you. Trust me. I appreciate you and Kate checking in." I squeeze her hand. "But what I really need is for you to help me with Roarke."

"Is he still giving you a hard time?" I'll kick his ass.

"No, the exact opposite. He's like a wounded puppy. And he freaking isn't blocking the bond at all. He's overcompensating, and it's like another freaking shadow. He has made sure I am good at training, mentally. Checking in, not overbearing, but it's like a freaking 180. Ignoring me to hovering." I laugh at that.

"So, he's back to the way he was before." She looks at me. Then, she smacks herself on the forehead. Guess she didn't realize he's just being the way he was before. Her shadow, her trainer, looking out for her, advocating for her.

"Mya, give the guy a break. You both were suffering, and trust me. Alex and Andy being together was probably tough for him. Imagine how he has felt, especially about keeping it from Alex. You are four years younger than he is. You are not even eighteen yet. You're a big no-no, even if that other stuff didn't happen. Prior to the last couple of months, he was the most controlled individual here. Able to separate drama. Why do you think he is with Mason and Riddick? He balances them out. He cuts through the bullshit and makes smart decisions. Leads with his head, not his heart. But you made him lose his shit, made him realize he wasn't as calm and collected as he thought. And now he blames himself for not believing you, for not seeing it. For not killing them."

"Way to make me feel like shit," she mutters. I laugh. "I guess I can try. Have him chill out a little, please. I am still dealing with my shit before I can focus on the shit between him and me."

"You want me to actually talk to him?"

"No," she sighs. "I just want someone more objective involved in this. Mason is too involved; she still feels guilty for not making me deal with it as soon as she found out. And Riddick is a sucker for whatever Mason wants lately. Charley is always on Mason's side. So, in the Council, I need someone who can advocate for me."

"You're talking missions?"

"Yes. He doesn't want me out there. Not because I am not good enough, but he wants me in a freaking bubble. He knows I'm capable. He is the one who made sure I was. But now, I don't know; I feel like he doesn't trust me. Not with combat. And I am afraid he is going to block me. Or demand to enable with me. Which also isn't an option."

"Teams are set. You are with Kyle and me. We will keep you in check, but I will help with Roarke. Maybe you should talk to him about it; you might be surprised."

"If I have to, I will; hopefully, it's a moot issue, and he doesn't block me again."

Heading into Mason's, Mya leans down to grab Cocoa off the floor and nuzzles her. The living area is set up for our usual meeting.

This is where we do business. Then we take our briefings and line-ups to Elitus later. Give them their marching orders. McGuire looks pissed every time. And that is the highlight of my day.

THIRTY-SEVEN

Bastian

Moving my baby sister into the combat dorms feels like walking a knife's edge.

Ariel is strong. Stronger than she should be at her age, but still not ready.

Not for what's coming, not for the shit that will inevitably come her way. And neither is Rina. Riddick's little sister is a damn firecracker, completely different from Ariel but just as stubborn.

Now they're here, under our watch.

And the weight of that responsibility feels like a goddamn boulder on my shoulders.

When I walk into their new room, I immediately regret every life choice that led me here. It's like a pink-and-black gothic explosion with organized chaos. Ariel is painstakingly placing glow-in-the-dark stars on the ceiling, while Rina is throwing shit around like a tornado.

Mason? Sitting back, sipping her coffee, completely amused. I shoot her a look. She planned this.

Riddick is helping Rina try to get some organization going. They turned a single into a double for them to be together, Mya on the other side of their common area. They are also wall buddies with Mason. That should be interesting. I hope they can shield.

"Where's Siobhan going?" I ask, eyeing the layout.

"Downstairs," Mason answers easily. "Roarke's taking your single, and Siobhan is moving to the main floor, next to Aimee and De."

"Which means Hope is now there as well whenever she can be," I comment. Siobhan is overly protective of her baby sister, never mind their dad Flynn. I pause. "Roarke and Mya, any better?"

Mason sighs and gives me a look.

Which means Mya isn't punching him in the face anymore, but she's still shut down and not really talking to him.

Roarke is miserable as hell, but too damn proud to say anything. He is her shadow, back in training with her. But they are both not completely over their shit and walk on eggshells.

I shake my head. They're both idiots, but they'll figure it out. Or, more likely, Mason will force them to.

I drop onto their bed, watching Ariel fuss over every detail.

Rina doesn't give a shit. But Ariel, she's a neat freak. This is going to be an experience. Both are the youngest sisters in a family full of brothers. Both are used to being the princesses in their houses, so now they have to share. They have the same power, but not rooming habits.

With a knock, the room gets even more crowded. Finley, Siobhan's little brother, steps in. He's a Tier Two combatant, but not at their level. Still, he's their sidekick, and at least he won't be causing trouble.

Once they seem mostly settled, Mason, Riddick, and I head out to a Power Council meeting, i.e. Mason's living room.

We need to get back to planning, strategizing, and making sure everyone, including our idiot siblings, doesn't get themselves killed.

Charley orders pizza for lunch, and by the time Roarke brings it up, the living room is already a war zone of files, laptops, and caffeine.

Mason tosses the mission slate onto the coffee table. "Mostly legitimate, relatively simple," she says. "My father asked for some added patrols, not really missions, at the offsite labs once they get going on Y at the beginning of February. I agree it wouldn't hurt to be cautious." She eyes Riddick, something unspoken passing between them.

"You think Dmitri will move to acquisition?" Roarke asks.

"I put nothing past him," Mya comments, finally speaking up after inhaling half a pizza. She's getting her appetite back. Now that she's not focused on avoiding Roarke like the plague.

"Between what he tried to gather, his visits, his innuendos... he's looking for something," she continues. "I really wish we could get someone on the inside."

"McGuire's working on it," Charley points out, "but as usual, his ego is in the way. If he were smart, he would've figured out his own kid was working against him."

She's not wrong. It's been quiet out of the PPG camp lately, too quiet. Dmitri's new soldiers have been absent, but it won't be long until the shit hits the fan. Especially given the report we got on the Latent Soldier, and the info Mason shared at the last council meeting. Namely, whatever Dmitri used allows them to reanimate. Zombie soldiers is what Roarke referred to them as. The good news is that when you kill them a second time, they don't rise up.

"Elitus is seeking Tier Two support for offsite monitoring and training," Riddick mentions. My gaze snaps toward him. He isn't suggesting Mason or I go there, is he? I mean, I can go, but leaving Kate...

"He approached me first. I mentioned Twos are the focus. I can do it, but he got a volunteer." Everyone is looking at him, then at Mason. I wasn't approached, so I can only guess.

Mason shakes her head. "Reese," she tells me.

"Off site?" I ask. Reese is a very strong mental, a healer by nature, she could clear X level if she wanted to. She just doesn't have the backbone to do harm. She is defensive only.

"Yes," Riddick confirms. "With Max as her bodyguard." That gets a smirk from many of us.

Reese and Max are both quiet, timid, but also both strong powers. Max, like Jared, has Dmitri's shield cover. Riddick has worked with them both in the last two weeks since the Ball to unlock it. Strengthening them into weapons and pushing their powers up. For Max, already a Spectrum, it has opened his Ones and Twos. For Jared, it increased his Two abilities, and much like Reese, if he wanted to, he could probably push and master all the Tier One powers. But they both are getting powerful for one reason only.

Protection, for their other half.

Jared, dumbass that he is, suspected Kym was his, but she blocked him out and told him no way.

The problem though, Jared knew what she was and still hooked up with Charley. At the ball, while Kate and I were getting over our shit, he and Kym dealt with theirs. And they have been together ever since.

You would think it would be awkward for the three of them. Especially since Charley and Jared are combat-enabled together often, Fire & Water make a hell of a combination. But no, I saw them at lunch yesterday. Kym and Charley just gang up on Jared instead. But that's Charley for you. Nothing gets her down; she just goes with the flow and moves on.

"Did Dad ask him?" Mya asks.

"Nope," Riddick smirks. "Rumor has it, Max found out in Elitus' chambers and lost his shit."

"Wow," Charley says, laughing. "In front of everyone?"

"Yes," Mason says. "And for once instead of being calm, Reese just looked at him and told him too bad. And it was like an episode of the Hunger Games; he volunteered to go instead. So now they are both going," we all laugh at that.

"Karma has a way," Mya says, smiling. With a light knock, the door opens, and Kate enters.

She kisses me over the top of the couch like she's been doing it forever and drops some files in front of us. She takes in the room and the obvious calm atmosphere.

"Mason was telling us secondhand about Max and Reese." Kate smiles at them and comes around to take a seat next to me. I throw my arm behind her.

Kate puts down the bottle of wine she brought, and some glasses. I pop the top on it and immediately pour for her and Mya. Mason shakes her head, and I know Charley hates wine. The other two idiots are silently laughing at me. Riddick is one to talk.

What can I say? We might argue about missions and training, but if my girl wants wine. She gets wine.

"Yes, it appears Max and Reese are going off-site for Latent training together," Kate mentions. "It was quite entertaining. I don't think I have ever seen Max so flustered before, nor Reese so difficult. I was proud of her." We chuckle. "Elitus sent over some docs that need to be looked at," Kate says, nodding to the files. "Potential Y candidates for another round. I don't know the science of it, but Ross and Clarke think if you look at it, you might read better patterns. Identify better choices for the next rounds."

Snagging a slice of pizza, she looks around for a plate. I get up, grabbing her a plate, a fork, and a knife. She beams at me. Like I just handed her the keys to the damn world.

The room erupts in laughter. I flip Riddick off.

"Goddamn sap," he mutters. I don't care; Kate's happy. That's all that matters.

"This looks like they're missing some," Mya says, scanning the file. She passes it on to me; not missing, taken.

Mason's expression darkens as she looks it over. I already know what she's thinking. "We'll put it at the top of the list," she tells Kate, then meets my eyes. "Dmitri is gathering them before we can get to them."

My jaw clenches. Motherfucker.

"Well, that's one way to reduce our defense," Roarke mutters, getting up to pace. He's been wound so fucking tight lately. I get it; he's not blocking his mate bond at all with Mya anymore. That makes him one hell of a defender, but also unstable as hell. I tried to talk to him about it, but he's afraid to block it now.

I don't blame him, but I also need him focused. We're going out in a couple of days on a heavy black-ops mission, and he needs to be in control.

"What do we do with them if we gather them?" Charley asks. "We don't have room. Off-site is getting full too. We are expanding too fast."

"Can we enlist some military help? I mean, based on the data, some are better candidates than others," Kate suggests.

Riddick nods. "I'll talk to my dad and Nick."

The conversation shifts to training. Most of the other Twos go today for final testing, so I have to head out with Mason, Riddick, and Charley. Kate tags along.

Well—after a pit stop at Kate's room, that is. Riddick groans, already knowing what's coming.

"You've got twenty minutes, Bastard. Then you're mine for combat trials."

Kate smirks, grabbing my hand. "Fifteen. I don't need twenty."

I hear Mason laughing, and Riddick mutters something about X-Two stamina.

Kate

Bastian is a trooper. He has strangled no one all day. Which, considering his schedule, is a minor miracle.

Move Ariel into the dorms? Check.

Power Council bullshit? Check.

Entertain me? Always.

More training? Obviously.

And now? Now we're at a weird dinner thing. Nala asked us to join, and since she's been trying to get closer to me—probably because she thinks she and Kyle are "together"—I agreed.

Luckily, Reese and Max are here, because if I had to endure this alone, I'd need way more wine.

After the conflict at Elitus, out of character for both, it seems they're better. Max has apologized, but he isn't backing down. She isn't going without him. And since this will happen after graduation, it's almost a done deal. They're scheduled to start off-site next week. But for now, they seem good. Closer even.

I watch Reese and Nala talk, but I am half paying attention. They may be identical twins, but that's where the similarities end. Reese is quiet. Steady. Friendly and polite, but never in a way that makes you feel like she's trying too hard. She's a strong Two, but she never brags about it. She's just... there. A solid presence. Someone you don't realize is a force until you actually pay attention.

Then there's Nala, the princess. Entitled as hell. Neither Reese nor her brother Bailey is like that.

Nala is spoiled, self-centered, and constantly needs to be the center of attention. I barely know the non-combat girls she hangs out with—and that's by design.

The dinner itself is interesting. And by interesting, I mean I don't know why the hell I'm here. She ordered in, which was a relief, because I didn't want to fake enthusiasm for whatever disaster she might've tried to cook. Bastian, Kyle, and Max seem to enjoy themselves.

I am struggling to keep up. Mostly because Nala doesn't shut up, I glance at my wineglass.

It's empty; that's a problem.

Then, the conversation shifts. Gen Three graduation is in two days.

Max lights up when Reese's name comes up, and they talk about her power. It seems the tension from earlier has thawed. He has always cared, been her champion; proud, supportive, the Quiet, gentle giant. But now something is different.

Bastian even comments that he will be sad without her helping him. She is his teacher's assistant and takes care of all the paperwork and stuff he hates. He will have to con someone else into doing it.

But the most interesting thing I watch tonight: Kyle.

I've never paid that close attention to him and Nala. We mostly deal with each other for Elitus business, and whenever he comes around Bastian and me, Nala is never with him.

But here, watching them; they don't fit.

Nala is enamored. Kyle is not. He's calm and seems relaxed. And that's the problem. Kyle is never calm.

"Are you ready to graduate?" I ask Reese and Nala.

"Yes," Reese says quietly. I watch as Max squeezes her hand lightly.

Nala beams, "Of course! I just can't wait to see everyone. It's too bad the big dinner was canceled," she laments. Kyle smiles at her. "I'm sure we will have our own celebration," she finishes with a sly smile at Kyle, while she leans into him. He wraps his arm around her, securing her in place.

"What do you plan to do after you graduate?" Max asks Nala, who looks thrown by the question.

"Besides work in the infirmary?" Nala asks. "I haven't really thought about it."

"You could always work in the labs, or teach," I throw out there. I watch as Kyle and Bastian try to hide their smiles. "Either that or I'm sure you can assist on a committee." I know Nala hasn't assisted or even attended a single meeting. Her clique of drama queens are more than happy to reap the benefits of Elitus and the events, but don't take part, nor are they in combat. And most don't even take an active role in labs or training. It is aggravating, but there isn't much to be done about it.

"I know Andy has taken on more than one," Reese comments. "It's a good way to assist and give back when you don't want to be in the labs nor teaching."

"Yes," Bastian comments. "She has been a big help."

"Yes, because you two clowns don't ever actually submit anything formal as required by Elitus," I comment. Bastian smiles at me as he leans over and kisses my cheek. He is still a pain in my ass, and I refuse to take over doing his work for the committee, so I roped Andy in to help me. She basically plays secretary and keeps them in line. Delilah and Hope have joined too, which helps.

"With you going off-base, who's going to take over the defense alignment?" Kyle asks Max.

"I can still keep up with it, but I spoke with Zack and Bailey, and both will pick up some of the slack. But I will still coordinate. We won't be offsite all the time; it's more daytime job, at least to start."

Reese sports a frown on her face. Whether or not she meant to, she has to know that by volunteering, Max would insist on being her shield. Maybe she feels guilty. Max notices and, pulling another out of character move, hauls her chair closer to him and brushes a strand of hair behind her ear. "You good?" I hear him ask quietly. She gives him a shy smile, and a solid nod. He throws his arm over the back of her chair, and she leans into him.

I know I am sporting my smile as I watch them, as are Kyle and Bastian; it's long overdue. But Nala isn't even paying attention. She's scrolling on her phone, and I get angry on Reese's behalf. I have always watched my brothers; they are very close, and they aren't even identical. They are each other's best friends, although they argue, but they are happy for each other, and have their backs.

Bastian drapes his arm over the back of my chair, fingers idly tracing over my shoulder. I know he feels my tension. The conversation pivots to training changes, plans and more business. Since Nala is checked out anyway, we talk Elitus business. The only Wight missing is Alex.

When talk pivots to sports and other social topics, Nala joins in and starts taking over the conversation. Mostly a monologue, so I spend my time observing Kyle and Nala.

And the longer I watch, the more I realize...

This isn't dinner. It's a show. A performance. A way for Nala to prove something. I don't know to whom.

And if that's the case, I can't help but wonder; What the hell is Kyle thinking?

THIRTY-EIGHT

Bastian

After hearing about the nightmare dinner with Nala and Kyle, Mason felt bad enough to convince Riddick to go out with us the next night.

It wasn't just to make up for that disaster, though. She knows I won't take Kate off base without a solid squad. Call me paranoid; I don't care.

We take the quick port out, somewhere warm, and the scent of salt and ocean hits me the second we land. The soft waves beyond the patio of the restaurant, allow all of us to take a deep breath, and relax.

It's perfect. Serving seafood, which is one of Mason's favorites, Riddick must have picked it, since she gives him a kilowatt smile and kisses his cheek. Kate and I both watch them outside of Elitus, outside the drama of the dorms or missions, the two of them; they work. They are both more at ease with each other. Mason has always had a soft side, but it's been missing for the last year. Riddick—he's never soft, always alert, on edge, but with her, like this—he seems happy. Watching them like this, puts me a little more at ease about their relationship.

I look at Kate as she squeezes my hand, and we head inside. The ambiance of the room is open air, with the sea breeze coming in, so we decide to be on the patio, putting us near the ocean.

Kate is my anchor, and although we still verbally spar, she calms me more than any drink ever could. It makes me stable and makes all the bullshit worthwhile.

Even in the short time we have been together, it's a total shift. The interaction between us is easy; the banter, flirting, arguing, all of it. And every time we spar or disagree, we may spat back and forth, but at the end, we listen, and work to compromise, the best we can.

Taking our seats, Riddick and I positioned ourselves with a clear view of the overall restaurant. No need for any repeats. I know the ladies will relax, but he and I already plan on staying sober and alert. Even when we're relaxed, we're watching.

The conversation flows easily throughout dinner—not just work bullshit, but the stupid, random stuff that reminds me why these are my people. I don't say it, but I enjoy watching Kate and Mason interact.

Mason is my biggest ally, my partner. We've always been on the same wavelength. And her being friends with Kate; that's important. Between them there is no tension, no ego. Just ease.

"Any thought about doing something for Valentine's Day?" Mason asks Kate in between bites of her salad.

"Like an event? We never have, but we could," Kate hedges.

"I figure with all these couples; it might be nice. Nothing crazy formal. But maybe even something that is more laid back for Gen Fours and Fives," Riddick and I both react to that one. Our sisters are already in the dorms, and even though it's only been a couple of days, we are both on edge.

But with our reactions, it's like a coordinated effort; both of our ladies reach across and grab our hands. Trying to reassure us, calm us, even if it's a simple gesture. I grab Kate's hand and kiss it, and she gives me a soft smile.

"Maybe low-key," Riddick points out. "But supervised."

"It's not a horrible idea; we may want to incorporate more for the non-combats. Even if its simple things. When they were at Mason's Independence Day party, they seemed to have a good time. I forget sometimes how much they miss. My brothers included," I tell them. Refilling wine for both.

"Maybe your social committee can put out a questionnaire or something," Mason points out. "Aimee is waiting for the next party. She's mad. I think she thought it was party central every night in the dorms. She was complaining last night." We all laugh at that. Aimee has been trying to get into the dorm for years. Back before last year, yes, it was a constant party. But now, not so much.

"She should've gone into combat when Mya did," I point out.

"She shouldn't be in combat now," Mason says with a glower on her face. "She may have passed from a power perspective, but she does not know what it means. And honestly, unlike with me, Robert is going easy on her."

"It doesn't hurt for her to master her offensive abilities," Riddick points out. "All of you treat her like a baby; you forget she is a High Three. She's often forgotten when we talk about the Clarke power structure. She may surprise you."

"This from you?" Mason asks as she laughs. "Your sister can kick your ass in Twos, and you still act like she needs saving." Riddick just grins at her, doesn't get offended.

"It's not like you didn't dedicate countless hours to those two to make sure they could kick our asses," I point out.

"Hell yeah, I am shooting for an all-female squad," she says with that signature smirk that tells me she is trying to start shit.

"Really?" Kate asks. Now she is going to push too. These two. "Can I join?"

"Absolutely." Riddick and I ignore them, since they are clearly trying to bait us. They chatter on, mostly just talking about how outstanding our sisters are. Riddick and I end up joining in discussing how Ariel and Rina are absolute chaos, stirring up some drama in training and the dorms.

Not on purpose, it's just... They're stronger than most, which means more attention, more pressure. I've been focusing on their Twos, making sure they're solid on defense.

Riddick has been working with them on pathing and weapons. "You really let them train with weapons?" I ask, not even bothering to hide my apprehension.

"Yeah," he says smoothly, cutting into his steak. "It's not like we can stop them. Might as well teach them to do it right."

That's fair but also terrifying. "They're still kids," I mutter, though I know that's not exactly true.

Mason snorts. "Says the guy who entered the dorms at ten."

I glare at her, but she's not wrong. Still, that doesn't mean I like it. We may have spent most of our younger years there, but it was different. Ariel wasn't even born when I went into the dorms. And we were only a year behind the Gen Ones, including Kate. Even when Mason and the rest of Gen Three joined, we were close in age. Now there are six years separating Gen Five and Four, never mind the eleven-year gap between Five and One.

Dessert arrives, because Mason never skips it. I watch as she and Kate split another bottle of wine, laughing and chatting about plans, upcoming missions, and the general shitstorm brewing with PPG. Kate gives more detail on Reese and Max's confrontation, and their interaction last night, as well as the plans for their off-campus work.

I don't drink, and neither does Riddick, so we sit back, letting them carry on with the conversation.

But when Mason's graduation comes up, Mason gets quiet. Her fingers tighten around the stem of her glass. She won't meet my eyes, nor anyone else's.

Kate notices first, setting down her glass. Riddick sees it too, eyes narrowing as he watches her.

I already know; she graduates tomorrow, and she's thinking about what comes next. What she can't say. What's been weighing on her for months.

Now, with the actual declaration, the bullseye on her is amplified. Never mind, it's already apparent that Dmitri hopes to get both Mason and Riddick. Giving him the ultimate power couple, along with breaking Elitus in ways no one can comprehend.

Riddick reaches across the table, drawing her attention. She gives him a sad smile.

Kate and I exchange a look. We are an open book to each other. When things quiet down between us, in bed or over dinner, we talk. Really talk, not argue. In two weeks, she knows almost all of my secrets, and I know hers. I have kept little out of the inner workings of my combat teams, including the complicated relationships that Mason has. Not only with Riddick, but in the turmoil with Kyle, that flares up from time to time.

But what worries Kate most are the premonitions and the visions. Riddick, Kyle, Mason, Aimee and Wyatt's younger brother Dante, are the strongest on campus. But that doesn't mean they see the same things, nor can they predict anything with exact certainty.

That's the thing about fate; there are always choices involved. Your destined path can shift. Mason believes in Karma as much as she does Fate.

Therefore, making changes, adjustments, choices, because of visions or predictions, creates other reactions to a path. Whether a multiverse or simulation, as Dante refers to it, it's a thought process that is out there.

Kyle and Riddick both use theirs to help make choices. Kyle is more strategic in his usage. Riddick's are more mission based. Aimee is a happy dreamer, or that's what Mason calls her. Hers are dream-oriented, which are future events that are positive. She can't predict anything with exact certainty, but she gets a lot of déjà vu.

Dante can predict things in public, not specific to Elitus. Major crises in the world, stock market crashes, accidents. But with us, he can't see anything. He can channel it to a specific situation if he really pushes his power, but it drains him.

But Mason, she avoids hers. Hers aren't just small snapshots, or impressions like Kyle. Hers are full-on crystal ball shit. And she hates it. She tries to block them and disconnects from them.

Part of that is because for so long, Elitus didn't listen to her. She predicted several major incidents, including Conrad Taylor coming on base, killing his ex-wife, and taking his daughter, Sage, one of Mason's best friends, and also Matt Dean's sister Serena. They were killed several days later in a failed Elitus rescue attempt.

Mason had predicted it. Sage and Serena were part of her and Charley's crew. All headed to combat. Sage was a superior Two, borderline X-level. And Serena, a spectrum with High One and Three abilities. Mason had begged her father, told him about it. But at the time, Elitus thought they were secure, and that they had enough protection to prevent anything like that from happening. They were wrong.

That wasn't the only time, but one of many. After a while, Mason just started keeping them to herself. It was about the same time; she stopped allowing anyone to call her given name, Mia, and instead went by her middle name, which is also her mother's maiden name, and Maria's nickname before she married Robert.

Although I understand the never-ending pressure because of her power, I also hate how it took so long for anyone to acknowledge it. I knew, her brothers, Riddick, Kyle, even Roarke knew; we could sense it from her at a young age. But convincing Elitus of that wasn't easy. Pepe supported her the most, with Calvin and Dr. Miller right behind him. Robert thought that fighting her on it would make her stay home and go back to being Mia.

But she never gave up. She still did her research, using me as her soapbox. If I brought about ideas, it was good to go. She submitted her dockets, hoping Riddick or Kyle would work to implement as much as they could. It was the only way she could help.

Now in the last couple of months, she's gone from fighting them to revamping and leading the whole combat and training program. Working side by side with both Wyatt and Kyle to make changes. Helping the Power Council and Elitus work together to eliminate threats. Even assisting her father with Latents. It's a big shift.

Her primary goal is developing new plans and training for the younger ones, as well as adult trainings for Latents. Especially Kennedy's age group. Kennedy, much like Mason, isn't in an official Gen, but she is close in age to Gen Six. Maria also started X once pregnant, much like she did with Mason. So far, any powers Kennedy has are latent. Or at least that's what her charts say.

"You deserve it more than anyone," Kate says quietly to Mason, drawing me out of my thoughts. Mason looks at her. "I know it's overwhelming, but you have worked so hard for it. Whether you have a medallion saying it, it's been apparent. And maybe you feel like it's the end or the beginning; either way, we will celebrate it, and everything will be okay. If not, we will make it okay." With a nod, Mason empties her glass.

"Do you want to walk the pier before we leave?" Riddick asks us to lighten the mood. Kate smiles, and Mason laughs.

"Rocco needs a new friend," she tells him. Now I know why she was so happy when we got here.

This place isn't far from a pier with a Ferris wheel and some games. Since I'm only a gossip with her and the girls, I am aware, this place was a turning point for Riddick and Mason. In a rare moment, he gave her a break from the drama at the dorms and made her happy. She needs more moments like that.

Kate

Dinner was wonderful. It was nice to see Bastian relax, outside of our bedroom, that is. He keeps a wall up. Although he has always been the class clown, in the brief time we have been a couple, I have figured out that it's a mask he wears. He appears lighthearted, a sarcastic pain in the butt; but he cares deeply about so many things, and his friends, this family we have made with each of our Wight friends.

That's what truly matters to him. Keeping everyone happy and level. That's his goal most days. He is never at ease with others around. But away from the dorms, away from the drama, he is more himself.

Now, don't get me wrong. Riddick and he both were constantly scanning, allowing Mason and me to just be. But it was still calmer and more social than I have seen him in a while. Now as we walk hand in hand down the pier, Riddick and Mason beside us, it's natural. A true double date, like we are normal college-age kids out.

Sometimes the stress, the missions, the constant planning and defense we are on, makes me feel like I'm ancient. I have been in heavy-duty training, and under awareness of the never-ending threat since I was ten years old. We never had a childhood. We were weapons in training.

The first true mission launch was when I was sixteen. It was Mason, Kyle, Riddick and Bastian. From then on, it was preparing for combat, contracts, and missions. What we were created for.

Our parents tried to control as much as they could, but all the funding, everything about the Wight program was about creating soldiers, combat operatives. There was no avoiding it.

Mason grabs Riddick's hand and drags him over to a game. I see the prize collection and look at Bastian, who smirks at me. "Which one?" he whispers in my ear, his breath on my skin making my whole-body heat.

"Doesn't matter," I murmur. He pokes at me, but I've never been to a carnival, or anything like this. "Aren't the games rigged?" I ask.

"Of course," Mason says. "But that won't stop us." Riddick pays the guy for both him and Bastian to give it a shot. It's a ball-throwing game where they have to knock over some old-fashioned milk cans. The first two Riddick throws miss. The last, knocks all of them down. He smiles down at Mason, who points to a huge stuffed neon purple dinosaur. I can't help but laugh at her excitement. I could've sworn I saw Riddick scowl at the thing.

"You're up," Mason says with a nod to Bastian.

Bastian doesn't even pretend to care as he knocks them all down with his first ball. Everyone looks at me, including the guy running the game. I don't know which one to get; they all would clash horribly with my room. Nothing white or pastel in the bunch. "You pick," I tell Bastian. He shakes his head at me, which means I have to decide. Frustrated, I decide on the most muted colored thing they have, a black and white panda, with blue eyes. Grabbing it down, I smile at the thing. Bastian just laughs and carries it. Before we leave, we take a spin on the Ferris wheel, chatting and enjoying each other's company.

Mason doesn't leave until she has some fried dough, which is an experience. "Bastian, you need to take her out more."

"Well, not all of us can just port anywhere in the world whenever we feel like it," he points out to her. She smiles and nods, but I am sure she's already planning another date. It's nice to be out, to do things. We don't get the chance too often, mostly because of Bastian's never-ending protective streak he has going. I haven't been on any missions, nor has he since we got together.

"We will have to make plans to do something," Riddick comments. "Besides, you can always ask Kyle and Nala to join you."

"Hard pass," Bastian comments. Mason is quiet, but the look she gives Bastian makes me pause. Maybe she questions it too. Kyle and Nala do not appear to have any type of mate bond, although Nala swears she feels it. Mason and Riddick don't have a bond, but they work well together—the connection, their devotion, it's real—you can feel the togetherness between them.

Nala and Kyle, it's a show. A highly over-produced show that merely highlights the lack of a bond between them. I still haven't figured out what Kyle is doing with her. Nala, I vaguely understand. Kyle was always the ultimate catch, and her being so focused on being popular and the center of attention, I'm sure in her crowd of friends, this is a big win. But even she must realize that he isn't in love with her. "Do you think they'll last?" I ask Mason. Her eyes shoot to mine.

Jasper is already faltering with Hannah. They are together, but it's not how it once was when they started out. Mason is aware of it, and I know she and Bastian have discussed non-mated pairs.

"I think as long as Kyle pretends he is happy with her, it will," Riddick comments. "Nala is so focused on what she looks like with him; she doesn't care if he is actually into her."

"She acts like he's a status symbol," Mason says quietly. "I'm not even sure when it started, if Kyle even wanted her then." The way she says it makes the hair on my arms rise.

"Are you saying she manipulated him?" I ask. Nala is a relatively high mental player, with persuasion and manipulation in her wheelhouse of tricks.

"I don't know. I just know Kyle. She is all wrong for him, yet he pretends he is into it." Bastian is quiet, but his hand on my thigh tightens just slightly. Highlighting his own concerns.

"I'm sure his pretending to be into her has nothing to do with us," Riddick comments. Mason frowns at that. "Whether she did to start, he knows what he is doing now. Is he leading her on? That's what I would be concerned about more than anything. She won't react well when he breaks it off."

"That's an understatement," Bastian comments. "Mason, don't worry about Kyle. He has chosen to be with her. I have talked to him many times. He won't deviate, and from the outside, they look happy. But he's not miserable. He makes his own choices, you know that."

Riddick puts his arm around her back, pulling her into him. He kisses her forehead as she rests it on his chest. Getting up to toss our plates, we depart down the pier and into a back alcove, departing to campus. Landing on the quad, in front of the dorms, we all just take a moment to take in the scenery.

"It's changed a lot in a few short months," Mason comments. We hear some music inside, not crazy loud, but enough to know people are hanging out. It's a warm night for January, so there are a few hanging out around the back porch area.

"Much needed change," I tell her with a smile. Bastian has me tucked up against him, his arms protectively around my body. I lean into him instinctively as we head towards the entrance. Riddick and Mason are similar, close together. "Thanks for tonight," I tell them.

"No thanks needed; we will try to make it a regular thing. We need this, this normal, whatever that may be," Mason says, reaching out to give me a quick hug, and punches Bastian in the arm. Riddick nods his head at us as they depart through toward the back, where I can clearly hear Charley's voice. Bastian looks at the common area. His sister is sitting on the couch with Rina, Siobhan and Finley watching a movie.

"You want to join them?" I ask him.

"No," he says. He turns to face me, with one arm still around me. With his free hand, he cups my face, brushing his thumb across my cheek. I can't help the sigh that escapes my mouth, and the way I relax with that small simple move. I lean into his touch, and he finishes my sentiment of longing with a heated kiss.

"Get a room!" Ariel yells from the couch. Bastian flips his little sister off. And then smirks at me. Shifting faster than I can react to, he uses the momentum to throw me and my panda over his shoulder.

"What the fuck, Bastian!" He smacks my ass as he strides up the stairs with me. What a neanderthal. "You'll pay for that," I tell him.

"Promise?"

Thirty-Nine

Kate

I take my seat next to Bastian, smoothing the front of my dress as I glance around the auditorium.

Everything is exactly how I envisioned it—draped in deep purples and blacks, elegant but commanding, a perfect reflection of Gen Three's strength.

This night was always going to be important. But now, it feels like something more. Bastian leans in, brushing a soft kiss against my temple. His outward calm is deceptive. I feel the tension in him, in all of them. The combatants shouldn't be nervous, but they are.

Because tonight isn't just a graduation.

It's a declaration.

And the entire room knows it.

This class is the strongest we've ever seen - more High Ones, stronger Twos, a few reaching truly dangerous levels. And then, of course, there's Mason.

She wasn't supposed to exist. For years, they didn't know what to do with her. The whispers, the resistance, the constant underestimation.

But now, she's at the top. They can't ignore her anymore; even those who resented her rise have been forced to accept it. Mason has proven herself.

Time and time again; she is the best of us. Tonight, she officially takes her place.

Still, there's a shadow hanging over tonight. The five that aren't here; Connor, Adrian, Matt, Everett, and Jaden. Their absence is loud; they chose their side. But that doesn't mean they won't show up, eventually. And when they do, it won't be for celebration.

I don't miss them. No one does. And knowing what they did to Mya, along with the other bullshit they pulled. They belong anywhere but here.

I shove the thought away as Mason moves past Riddick, air throwing him a playful kiss. He smirks, shaking his head, but there's warmth there. They've settled into each other in a way that makes sense. That's what tonight is; the culmination of years of work.

Victory. Validation. But also a warning, because from this moment forward, everything changes.

Bastian

Mason is the last one to step onto the stage; every eye in the room locks onto her.

This is it. The official designation. The title cements what we've all known for years. She finally will have it, and I won't let anything—or anyone—ruin this moment for her.

Before she even reaches the podium, I throw out shields, layering them tight. I feel Riddick's energy snap into place beside mine, Kyle and others joining almost instinctively.

Tonight is more than a ceremony. It's a statement, a line in the sand.

Mason has earned this. She has fought tooth and nail, clawed her way through every roadblock, every doubt, every goddamn person who underestimated her. She's been the one all along; I've known that longer than most.

When Robert calls her name, both her father and Pepe are there to give her the title she has earned.

X One. X Two. X Three. Spectrum.

The leader we all knew she was. Now, without a doubt, she is the most powerful Wight on the planet. Placed over her head, she hugs both her father and grandfather. Everyone is on his or her feet for this. Which only adds to her nerves, but I tighten the shield cover.

A gentle squeeze pulls me from my thoughts. Kate, she's watching me, her green eyes warm and knowing, and I lean over, pressing a light kiss to her cheek.

She did this, planned it, designed it, organized every detail, and did it flawlessly, like she always does.

I don't say it often enough, but damn, I'm proud of her. All the events she's pulled off over the years—coordinating, planning, ensuring everything runs like a well-oiled machine. Mason descends the stairs and joins the rest of us. A deep breath for all of us, as the weight of what her designation means is on our minds, and all that comes with it.

The night has been a whirlwind; mingling, congratulating, celebrating. The weight of what just happened: the official designation, the shift in power, the reality of what Mason now represents—it lingers in the air.

But here, at this moment, with Kate's hand in mine, leading me toward her office; everything else fades.

Her space is impeccably organized, much like her. Neat stacks of documents, pristine surfaces, everything in its place.

And yet, in the middle of it all—the orchids. The ones I sent her just a couple of days ago, a smirk tugs at my lips. I sink into her chair, watching as she rifles through some files.

She's focused, moving with precision, completely unaware of the effect she has on me. Or maybe she's not. That dress was made to be taken off.

And those damn heels? I shift slightly, adjusting myself, already anticipating the torment of what's underneath. Because I know. Stockings. Garters. Some crazy expensive lace that I fully intend to destroy. She glances over her shoulder; our eyes lock.

And just like that, the air changes; the room charges.

The second Kate steps toward me, the air shifts; the tension coils between us, electric, alive. She knows exactly what she's doing, how to move, how to look at me just so; how to unhinge my entire fucking world without saying a word.

And I let her take control, just for a moment. Long enough for her to think she's got the upper hand.

She climbs onto my lap, legs on either side of me, dress hiking up inch by agonizing inch.

I groan, dragging my hands up her thighs, brushing over the soft lace and silk straps connecting her stockings to her garters.

"You did this on purpose, didn't you?" I murmur; my voice is rough.

She tilts her head, feigning innocence. "What gave it away?"

I tighten my grip on her hips, pulling her flush against me.

She gasps—exactly the reaction I want. Her hands fist my shirt, nails scraping against my chest, and I feel the bond between us crackle. I can feel her desire, her need, and it's just as sharp as mine.

I trail my hands up her back, spreading my fingers wide, feeling the warmth of her skin beneath the thin fabric of her dress.

She shivers when I reach the zipper, when I tug it down, slow, deliberate.

Her breath hitches. "Every time I sit in this chair, I'm going to think about this," she murmurs.

That single sentence sets something off in a dark, possessive part of me I don't bother restraining anymore. I groan, standing, taking her with me, and place her on the desktop. Before she even has time to react, I press her back onto the desk, caging her beneath me.

Her legs wrap around my waist instinctively, her heels digging into my lower back, urging me closer.

She needs me just as much as I need her. As if she can't stand the thought of me pulling away.

Good. I have no intention of stopping.

"Yeah?" I murmur against her throat, trailing my lips over her pulse point, feeling it hammer beneath my mouth. "Then I'd better make sure you never forget it."

Her fingers tangle in my hair, pulling me down as she tilts her head back, surrendering completely.

I nip at her jaw, my hands sliding up her thighs, pushing her dress up.

She's hot against me, flushed, needy, already squirming beneath my touch. And I feel her need, her desire, the pull between us crackling like a live wire. Our bond is a fire now, burning, consuming, endless.

I pull back slightly, just enough to look at her. She's breathless, eyes dark, lips swollen from my kisses.

She shudders when my hands skim higher, my thumb running along the garters, and up. She's still mostly dressed, but I don't care.

Her like this—wanton, lust drunk. The need in her eyes, the demand across the bonds we have, it makes it impossible not to take her like this. To show her she is my entire world.

I make a slow circle with my thumb over her clit, and she arches her back on the desk. Lost in the sensations.

I lean into her, pressing her into the desk, as my fingers work their magic. I take her mouth in a searing kiss, pouring all my lust and need into it. The moan she elicits is like electricity across our bond.

I can feel her power rising as her orgasm approaches fast. I wrap shields around us knowing when she peaks it'll be powerful, like it always is.

She sends me a small signal across our bond, what she wants, what she needs. I smirk against her lips, and do as she asks. Taking the lace between her thighs in my hand, yanking hard, it tears easily, exposing her to me.

She pushes herself up off the desk as I pull her hips to the edge of the desk. She works fast, undoing my belt. She is just as eager and needy as I am.

When she takes me into her hand, and pumps, I swear I see stars. Fuck, she is so goddamn perfect. She stands and pushes me back into her chair.

With the look she has on her face, I can't help but smile at her. She is a Queen, and I am just her peasant.

She gives me just enough time to adjust myself before she is straddling me, and sliding down on my cock.

She is exquisite, powerful, and mesmerizing as she takes control. My hands on her hips, helping her move over me. Our tongues tangle.

She's close, but Fuck, so am I. I take her mouth again as I rise to meet her downward thrusts. It's wild, and perfect.

I feel her, both mentally and physically, as she hits the peak. A guttural moan rips from my throat; I can't hold back.

She collapses on top of me, still connected, but with her head on my shoulder.

"Wow," she murmurs as she nuzzles my neck.

I run my hands up and down her back, letting some of the adrenaline recede. "You're going to regret having no panties at the party."

"No," she murmurs. "But it will drive you insane." Fucking hell, this woman.

I love her more than I ever thought I could. Her fairy tale is mine now too. Our connection or bonds, they keep growing.

Every touch, every time I take her apart and put her back together again, it's like another piece of me sinking into her. Another part of her brands itself into me. I can feel her, even when I'm not touching her.

Even when we're not together, I know exactly where she is, how she's feeling.

Like the bond between us is threading tighter, weaving into every part of who we are. Until we aren't separate anymore.

Until we're just... us.

She sits back, my hands on her hips, hers resting on my shoulders. I hear the buzz of my phone again. I've been ignoring it. But we can't stay here forever.

"Enough memories for you?" I ask with a cocky smile. I know she secretly loves.

"It'll do," she says with a smile as she stands. Still in heels, and her dress. I've made a mess of her, but she looks thoroughly sexed. It's one of my favorite looks.

We both clean up. I help put her desk in somewhat of an order since I tossed most of her papers on the floor. I know the anxiety of it is on her mind, but I push a small pulse of power to lighten it.

"Thank you," she murmurs, as we walk out of her office, hand in hand.

"For what?" I ask, brushing a kiss across her knuckles.

"For choosing to be mine." I stop and turn to face her.

"Kate," although we have no shields, I can feel her vulnerability in that statement, and in her entire demeanor. I don't know if it's afterglow, or what, but this moment. I won't let it pass. "Queenie," I murmur, tilting her head up to meet my eyes. "What I chose was to be a fucking idiot for years. To be a coward, afraid to make myself vulnerable to another. That's what I choose to do. And I will spend the rest of our lives making up for all the time I wasted not being with you. That choice, that was a stupid one. It not only kept us apart, but what's worse is how my behavior, my inaction regarding what I knew was freaking fate, caused you to hurt. I will never forgive myself for that mistake, but know, regarding being yours. I have been yours, I swear, since birth. I was just an idiot for a while." I brush aside her tears that are streaking down her face.

"I love you Kate, this, us, you never have to thank me. I should be thanking you. For putting up with me, for forgiving me for being a complete idiot. For not giving up on the thought of us. I don't deserve you, but just like I'm yours, you're mine, and I'm never letting you go."

She wraps her arms around me tight, her breathing hitched, her tears wetting my shirt, but the bond pulls even tighter, weaving a little more between us. She pulls back a little, giving me a soft kiss.

"I love you," She smiles as she kisses me again. "But regardless, I don't want thanks either. Fate has a way. We just took the long way here," she smiles softly again, and rests her head on my shoulder.

My phone buzzes again, and we both laugh. "Our friends are waiting for us."

"They should know better by now; giving us alone time could mean 10 minutes or 10 hours," I mutter, but she just smiles and gives me another brush of her lips, as we head out and off to the afterparty.

Kate

The night air is crisp as we head back. Bastian's words still linger in my mind, rolling around. I know he loves me, I never doubt that. But his confession, it made my heart skip a beat. He truly meant what he said, and just like that, I know that nothing will be able to break our bond. We are both committed to this, to us.

However, when he finally looked at his phone he had a dozen missed calls and texts from Charley, asking where the hell we were. It appears we have to retrieve Mason and forcibly drag her to her own damn party.

Charley and Mason are the same in so many ways, unless it comes to celebrating themselves. Mason would rather train than attend a party in her honor, but Charley won't let that happen.

We scoop up Wyatt on the way; he takes one look at me, his lips twitching, his head shaking slightly, as if he already knows. Bastian grins, completely unapologetic, throws an arm around my waist and pulls me in.

Wyatt sighs, looking between us. "I really should've placed a bet on you two. Could've made a fortune."

Bastian snorts. "Please. We all knew it was happening, eventually."

Wyatt levels him with a look. "Some of us had our doubts."

Bastian arches a brow, smirking. "Oh, yeah?"

I elbow Wyatt before he can dig deeper. "Don't encourage him. He'll be smug about it for weeks."

Bastian leans down, whispering in my ear. "Try forever."

The back-and-forth between them feels so natural now. There was a time when I wasn't sure how this would go—if Bastian and Wyatt could ever be friends.

Now there's an ease between them, a friendship forming that I hadn't even realized I wanted until I saw it happening.

Wyatt has been my rock, my equal, my supporter. For years, he was the person I relied on the most.

And now, here he is, laughing with the man I love, giving me shit like nothing has changed. It's a relief in a way I can't quite put into words.

Dragging Mason out of the Clarke's was no easy feat, but we managed. She grumbled, cursed, and threatened to port herself back home, but we held firm.

The dorms are already overflowing when we arrive. Combat units, Elitus, Power Council—almost every Wight on base is here. Someone has commandeered the speakers, music blasting through the halls, the energy buzzing in the air. It's the first real celebration in weeks.

And Mason, despite herself, doesn't look miserable.

She does her first round, playing hostess despite her protests. Congratulating Gen Three, dodging well-wishers, accepting drinks she won't drink. The usual. But I don't miss her gaze darting to the stairs, like she can't wait to escape. Riddick is patiently waiting for her to give the sign.

Bastian smirks beside me, arms crossed. "How long before she bails?"

I tilt my head, pretending to think. "Five minutes? Maybe less."

Wyatt laughs, stealing my drink. "Two tops."

Sure enough, before long, Mason makes a quiet retreat, Riddick in tow.

I nudge Bastian. "You taking notes?"

He shoots a look at me. "What? You want me to sneak you upstairs?"

I just smile. He smirks, dragging me to his side. "Later," he murmurs.

Mason is gone just long enough that most people don't notice. Bastian and I are making our way through the crowd, dodging Kyle and Nala's showboating, when the room shifts again.

Bastian stiffens, then exhales sharply. I turn just in time to see Mason re-enter—only she isn't alone.

Ariel and Rina are with her.

This just got interesting. I don't even have to look at Bastian to know.

He's already bracing himself, already adjusting. It's one thing for his little sister to be in the dorms.

It's another for her to be here—in his space, among the combat units, among the energy of it all.

I press a hand to his chest, grounding him. He exhales again, this time slower, readying himself. But I see it in his eyes; he's not ready for this.

Riddick looks like he's about to start flipping tables. It's not that he's blind. He knows this was inevitable.

But knowing it and seeing it are two different things. Because right now, he sees it. Riddick sees his and Bastian's little sisters stepping into the world he's spent years trying to keep them out of.

Mason looks unbothered. She's fully aware of the chaos she just unleashed. In fact, I think she's enjoying it.

I suppress my laugh, but Bastian just mutters, "You've got to be fucking kidding me." But then Riddick falls in step behind them, like he already knows he's going to be the one who has to deal with this.

The party is tame, something I am thankful for.

Ariel and Rina—or "Ri and Re" as Charley and Mya have dubbed them—sit off to the side, sipping on water bottles while getting hustled in a card game.

I have a glass of wine, letting the warmth of it settle over me. Bastian sits back, arm draped over my chair, throwing in his usual commentary. Just giving everyone a hard time. Roarke and Riddick supervise from the bar.

It's nice, really nice. It feels like a moment of normalcy, something I have had little of lately. A group of friends, now a family, unwinding, laughing, no stress, no threats lingering over us.

But the moment is short-lived, because the second we step into my room, my chest tightens. Bastian had been moving his stuff little by little over the last few weeks, and while I had asked him to, the sight of the clutter is too much.

Piles of clothes, his things mixed with mine, my carefully curated order completely disrupted.

I shuddered a breath, trying to suppress the anxiety rising in my chest. He feels it immediately. "I can keep what I need and move the rest into Kyle's," he offers, voice calm.

I exhale. "No, it's okay." He gives me a look. The one that says, *Babe, I know you.* "I have to adjust," I say, almost to myself.

Bastian nods slowly, stepping closer, his presence anchoring me. "And this is minor, babe. Seriously. I need little—half this shit I should've just tossed. It's fine." He leans in, kissing my nose softly. "Give me tomorrow to square it away," he reassures, his voice a gentle promise. I nod, still processing, still adjusting, but his words ease the tension.

Then he moves to grab a drink—water. I tilt my head. "You aren't drinking?" I ask, even though I had already noticed.

"Nah, just a couple of shots." He shrugs. "I owe Riddick a favor, so I'm a babysitter now." I raise an eyebrow. "He's taking Mason to the Palace tonight."

I guess they're finally taking the last step. Mason and I have grown closer these past couple of weeks. She confided in me she's nervous to take the last step, sex. Without the mate bond, she's leery.

Especially since she's been watching Bastian and me like a case study. Apparently, the way we keep zero shields between us is odd for couples. I don't really care, honestly; it makes life easier.

I have nothing to hide from him.

And until I go on my first combat mission, I haven't needed to shield.

But he has; I feel it when he's out. He's only been on small-scale ones, nothing full combat. But the moment his shields go up, a dull ache settles in my chest. It's an adjustment, one I'm still trying to get used to.

I know when he goes full combat, it will be even worse. I don't know if his current load is by design or a coincidence, but I know it won't last.

Eventually, I'll have to manage that. I'll have to manage us.

"Well, that's a very special graduation present," I murmur. He seems agitated. I glance at him, catching the flicker of irritation in his eyes. But it's not jealousy. It's a concern; for Mason, for Riddick, for what this could mean.

"They're not mates," he says, his voice gruff, firm. Not a question, but a statement.

It lingers in the air between us, heavy with unspoken consequences.

I hesitate. "Do you think she has a mate?"

He exhales slowly, shaking his head. "Honestly, I don't know." His jaw tightens. "If she does, I hope we find him for her."

That stops me cold. Find him for her? My stomach twists. What about Riddick? He wouldn't start something with her if he had a mate.

A ripple of unease spreads through me. "Bastian," I press carefully, my voice sharpening. "Does he have a mate?"

If he does, if Riddick has someone else out there, waiting, tied to him by fate, then Mason is the one who's going to bleed for it.

Bastian exhales, dragging a hand through his hair. "I don't know." His answer doesn't satisfy me. "Riddick's shield cover has always been different," he explains. "I can never fully read him. Mason can't either, nor does she want to."

I frown. That's not like her. She's one of the strongest telepaths on base; if she wanted to find an answer, she would. "I don't think his mate is here," Bastian continues. "Whether there's a tether somewhere else... I don't know." There's a pause. Then, quieter, "I won't lie, it worries me."

I study him, seeing the war raging inside him. This isn't just about Mason. Or Riddick. This is about all of us.

"I get it," he admits. "But Riddick is a stubborn son of a bitch who's been half in love with her since she was a kid." He shakes his head, rubbing a hand over his jaw. "He won't hurt her—not purposely. And I think he really wants this with her."

I want to believe that. But what if we're mistaken?

"Did you see the ring he gave her for Christmas, Kate?" Bastian asks suddenly. His tone shifts—something deeper. More weighted. I think back to Mason's hand, the delicate band wrapped around her finger. Ruby and Onyx, with black platinum. A simple but heavy gesture. She doesn't wear it to train, but for tonight's ceremony, dinner last night, and the ball, I've seen it.

"That's his mother's," Bastian tells me. I inhale sharply. "This... it's not just some game," he continues, observing me. "He's not doing this to win her over. He's not trying to convince her." His voice softens, something flickering behind his eyes. "He's fully committed to her."

I step forward, closing the space between us, wrapping my arms around him and pressing my head against his shoulder. "You've thought about it," I murmur.

I can feel the conflict within him. The push and pull of being one of Mason's best friends, wanting her to be happy but wanting to protect her.

And knowing that Riddick—mate or not—is a risk.

"She shouldn't be alone and miserable because her mate isn't here," I whisper. He stills. I pull back slightly, lifting my gaze to his. "And we can't worry about 'what ifs.'" I exhale. "We have to take all we can now and live our lives."

I see it click. Not just for Mason. For us.

Bastian cups my jaw, tilting my chin up. There's something unreadable in his gaze, something that makes my chest ache. He nods once, unshakable. "Yeah," he murmurs, brushing his lips against mine—a silent promise. "We do."

His lips crash into mine, a hungry, demanding force, pulling me under so completely that I forget where I am for a moment. The taste, heat and power wrapped in something purely Bastian, makes my body hum in anticipation.

He doesn't hold back. He never does.

His hands slide down my back, gripping my ass firmly as he pulls me flush against him. Hard. Needy. Desperate. I smirk against his lips, my hands threading into his hair as I push closer, reveling in the way his body tenses beneath my touch.

"Besides," he murmurs against my mouth, teasing, breathless, already drowning in him. "Just because I'm on shields doesn't mean I forgot the way you teased me all goddamn night at that table—" I nip his bottom lip, "—with my sister sitting right there."

I smile at him, and Bastian lets out a dark chuckle, his breath warm against my skin. His voice is low, rough, and dangerous. He shoves me back against the wall, his body pressing into mine, caging me in.

"But see, I battled back." He runs his lips along my jaw, his hands slipping under my dress, fingers brushing over bare, heated skin. "And now? I get to collect."

I shiver, my legs tightening around him as he lifts me easily, as if I weigh nothing.

"You're so damn cocky," I whisper, biting back a moan as he grinds against me, the fabric between us doing nothing to ease the ache between my thighs.

He grins against my neck. Smug. Knowing. Mine.

"Maybe." He presses a kiss below my ear, sending a rush of pleasure straight through me. "But you like it."

Bastian shreds through my last remaining restraint—mental and physical—our connection blazing open, raw and uninhibited. I gasp as pleasure rushes through me, amplifying everything.

It's not just his hands on me anymore—it's his power, his essence, sinking into my bones, curling inside me, twisting with mine.

It's overwhelming. Exhilarating. There are no barriers, no walls, no shields.

His hands tremble slightly as he drags my dress up and over my head, leaving me in nothing but the lingerie I wore for him. His breath hitches. "Fuck, Kate," he murmurs, taking me in. Dark, reverent, hungry.

I smile, trailing my nails down his chest. "I wore it for you."

A growl rumbles deep in his chest. "And I'm going to fucking ruin the rest of it." I barely have time to react before he tears through the lace, his mouth crashing back to mine.

His hands roam, the touch igniting fire across my skin. Each caress sends waves of pleasure curling through my core. It's more than just physical. Every time he strokes me, kisses me, moves against me, I feel it deep inside, through the bond growing between us.

I reach for him, dragging his shirt over his head, raking my nails down his toned abs, memorizing every muscle, every ridge, every inch of him.

"Impatient," he teases, his voice thick with amusement and desire.

I grin wickedly, pushing him toward the bed, reversing our positions. "You love it."

He lets me push him down, settle on top of him, take control. But his hands are still on me—guiding, demanding, never yielding.

And then, with one swift move, he flips us, pinning me beneath him, devouring me with his mouth, his hands, his power. I moan, arching into him, begging without words.

More. Deeper. Harder.

And he gives it to me repeatedly.

Until we are one.

Until there is no him, no me; just us.

Until he buries himself so deep inside of me, I swear I will never be whole again without him.

And by the time we finally collapse, tangled together, breathless and spent, I know I don't want to be.

FORTY

Bastian

Heading into the war room, I gear up, adjusting the weight of my holsters, checking ammo and my blades. Roarke and I are heading out on this one, with Mason and Riddick. It's on McGuire's "must-do" list—a PPG target, which means there's always a risk. It should be relatively clean, but nothing is ever clean when PPG is involved.

I scan the room, taking in the usual pre-mission routine. Everyone is checking gear, running last-minute paths, ensuring their shields are tight. The tension is there, simmering under the surface, but it's not fear—it's focus.

Mason stands to the side, letting Riddick run last checks with the others, but my attention is already locked elsewhere.

Kate. She's here to see me off, as she always is, standing with me, chatting with the Twos and the lab team, arms folded, her suit pristine as ever. God, she makes it hard to leave.

Checking her over, I note her stance. I know I already talked to Kyle. He is on protection detail here, but he promised it's all good. I am seriously considering approaching Wyatt about what I need from him when I am out. Wyatt hates combat and refuses, but he is a weapon, and when it comes to Kate. I know he will protect her with his life.

Kate rolls her eyes at me, catching my silent assessment, but instead of arguing, she leans in and presses a soft kiss to my jaw.

I exhale, rolling my shoulders back.

This is the first actual high-threat mission out with all the new couples and connections, and while we aren't all at the same level, there's an unspoken understanding between us now.

Reese is here as our lead healer, with Rina and Ariel backing her up. Max is here too, standing close to Reese in that slow, steady way they've been moving toward something more. He's quiet, but he doesn't have to say anything to know that she is his priority.

Mason steps forward, shifting gears into leader mode.

She has us locked in, reviewing last-minute details while Riddick stands next to her, his entire posture radiating tension. I don't have to guess why; I can feel it.

Their connection is stronger than ever, but with it comes an extra layer of protective instincts. Riddick's always been wired for it, but now, he's wound so damn tight I half expect him to snap.

And he's not the only one.

Kate is here, and that means I'm leaving her behind.

I hate it. I don't let it show—not the way Riddick does—but it's there, crawling under my skin, making my shields feel too tight.

Mason's voice cuts through the room. "Are we ready?"

She looks at McGuire, waiting for confirmation.

She'll take the lead, as she always does. I'll provide cover and scout for any outside threats. Riddick is the power, and Roarke handles transport and is auxiliary.

We've run dozens of missions together. We know each other's moves, strengths, weaknesses.

This should be routine. But it's not. This isn't just about retrieving data or securing intel.

This is McGuire sending a message. And with PPG on the other side of that line in the sand, I already know nothing about tonight will be clean.

But if I had a dollar for every time a mission didn't go as planned...

This one was supposed to be a quiet in-and-out. Information gathering. Proof of the testing, data collection, and a clean port-out. High risk, but a low probability of conflict.

Mason and Roarke went over entry points and plans while Riddick powered up. Meanwhile, I was already cloaking, doing my best to keep us off their scanners. But seeing as PPG isn't made up of complete idiots, we knew they'd catch something. Roarke would have to provide protection coverage for me while Mason and Riddick ported in.

We knew the drill. Mason would move discreetly, blending into the environment while Riddick secured evidence. She'd scan their systems, capturing images and downloading key files directly to her memory. Once done, she'd signal him to move to the next phase, gathering additional intel before Roarke pulled us out.

Simple. Right?

Wrong.

Roarke goes to take us out, but he stops mid-stream. Every one of our internal alarms flares to life. Mason reacts instantly, throwing a shield over us.

Roarke tries again—nothing. A hard bounce back. "How?" he growls.

Mason's voice is flat. "Nikolai."

And right on cue, they step into the outer marker. Nikolai. Alexi. The Bishop twins.

No Coral or Tara again. But this isn't good.

Riddick pages base immediately, but Mason already knows—if we can't port out, Kyle can't port in.

We're on our own.

Nikolai's eyes rake over Mason, and I feel Riddick's power spiking before she even has time to send a warning path for him to stand down.

Too late. Nikolai catches it, and the bastard laughs.

"Oh, Riddick, don't play with fire," he taunts, "you will get burned."

Riddick grits his teeth, his power still rolling under the surface, but he doesn't take the bait.

Alexi tilts his head. "You were told not to re-activate. Guess McGuire thinks you're all expendable."

Mason powers up. I already know our play. I drop shields and cloaking—stealth doesn't matter anymore. We've been made. Now, the only focus is on reserving enough power in case we need to heal.

But I also get ready to go on the offensive.

I might be X-Two, but with my mental blasts, I can drop someone into a coma with a flick of my fingers.

Roarke is searching. He's a master of gravity. If he can pinpoint what Nikolai is doing to block our port, he can break it.

A volley of power blasts out toward us, meant to knock us back or down, but Riddick swats it away like a gnat. Mason's shields holding steady.

"You better bring more power than two Mids and the Weather Channel if you want to play with us, Nikolai," Riddick mocks.

The Bishop twins falter as he pushes back, sending his own power back, but I note he's going easy on them.

Good. We need energy reserves. Roarke paths Mason—he found it. She shifts immediately, throwing a cover shield while Roarke disrupts the blockage.

The second Nikolai's grip is gone; Mason doesn't hesitate.

A burst of power—a hand grab—we port.

Landing hard on the lawn outside the labs back at base, I don't even have a second to reorient before Riddick rounds on her.

"What the hell are you thinking?"

He's pissed, irrational. Mason ignores him completely.

"Get the docs inside." Her voice is sharp as she speaks to Roarke. He hesitates but nods, knowing she won't engage with Riddick while she's running hot.

I don't leave her side. Riddick is crackling with power, his shields flickering, unsteady. Mason is in control, but the weight of leadership is hitting her.

I knew this would happen, but not this soon. Not on their first combat mission together after being official. Mason did everything right. She made the right calls. But Riddick is shaken. Not from the mission, but from her being in danger.

And I get it. I really do. But if he can't figure out how to control his shit in the field.

I'll separate them. Even if it kills me, even if it destroys them.

This cannot happen again. Mason meets my eyes, and I see the truth there. She knows it too.

"You made the right decision," I tell her firmly. "Nice to see you're learning how to lead—not just fight."

Then I turn to Riddick. "And you—" I don't sugarcoat it. "You need to control your goddamn signals. If you want to play with her, then you better figure out how to separate that shit in the field. Or you won't be out there when she needs you."

His eyes flash dangerously, but I don't wait for a response.

I path Mason, *let me know if you need me.*

I also path Kyle. Not as gossip—but as a warning.

If Riddick can't get his head on straight, she'll need a full-time replacement as her backup.

Because the next time she steps into a war zone, I won't risk her life for his feelings.

Kate

Bastian arrives back late.

I felt the spike in his power hours ago; a burst of anger and adrenaline that made my chest tighten. But almost immediately after, he sent a pulse back to me, something soft, something meant to tell me he was fine and that he'd be back soon.

Still, it didn't stop my worrying. I'm sitting on the couch in our room, scrolling through reports on my tablet when he walks in. He looks worn, his usual cocky demeanor muted under something heavier, something I don't like.

"You're late," I comment, setting my tablet aside as I take him in. His stance is rigid, like he's holding onto something, and it makes my stomach churn.

"Yeah," he sighs, rubbing his face before he moves toward me. "Shit hit the fan."

I raise an eyebrow. "Bad?"

He lets out a short laugh, but there's no humor in it.

"Would've been worse if Mason wasn't fast as hell," he mutters, dropping onto the couch beside me. His body is warm, still thrumming with energy. His arm drapes over the back of the couch, fingertips grazing my shoulder.

I turn to face him. "What happened?"

Bastian rolls his shoulders like he's working out the tension, then launches into the breakdown.

The mission was supposed to be clean—a standard information-gathering op at a PPG site. In and out.

But of course, PPG is never that easy.

Nikolai. Alexi. The Bishop twins. All were waiting for them.

"They knew we were coming," Bastian says, jaw clenching. "Or, at the very least, they knew someone would be coming. And Nikolai? He locked Roarke out of porting."

"Mason got us out, but Riddick—" He stops, shaking his head. "He lost his shit."

My stomach twists. "What do you mean?"

"I mean, he barely kept his power in check, and it almost cost us." His voice is gruff, laced with something more than just frustration. Concern.

I knew Riddick was struggling with his protective instincts, but for it to jeopardize the mission. Bastian leans back, staring at the ceiling. "He can't separate his personal shit from the field. And Mason knows it. She won't admit it, but she knows it. And if he doesn't figure it out..."

I nod, finishing his thought. "He won't be on her missions anymore."

Bastian looks at me; his expression is grim but firm. "I told him as much," he admits. "If he can't control himself, he will not be out there to protect her at all."

I exhale slowly, feeling the weight of what that means. Mason and Riddick's connection is strong, but if this is where they are heading, I don't know how they come back from it.

Bastian shifts beside me, his fingers tracing circles along my arm. He does that when he's thinking.

"There's more," I breathe. His gaze flicks to mine, and his walls drop slightly.

"Yeah," he mutters. "McGuire's pushing more black ops missions. Ones that the Power Council is going to have to approve or reject."

I sit up straighter. That's not good. Bastian nods, reading my reaction. "It means we're going to be handpicking who goes where and deciding which missions are worth the risk." His jaw clenches again. "Which means when shit goes wrong, it's on us."

I reach for his hand, intertwining my fingers with his. "You're not responsible for every mission, Bastian."

He huffs out a laugh, shaking his head. "Feels like it."

I squeeze his hand. "We'll handle it. All of us."

He looks at me then, and something in his expression softens. His free hand lifts, brushing my cheek, tucking a loose strand of hair behind my ear. "Yeah," he murmurs. "We will."

Kate

One week.

That's how long it took before Mason decided she needed guinea pigs for testing bonds and relationships in combat couples.

Bastian isn't thrilled about it. Not in the slightest. But when Mason's mind is set on something, there's no stopping her. And in truth? We need to figure this out.

Combat is what we do. It's who we are. If relationships are going to function in the field, we need to understand how to separate emotions from instincts and still work as a team.

So here we are. Bastian, Mason, Riddick and I—running a low-level mission designed to push our limits but not completely overwhelm them. At least, that's the idea. Nothing is ever truly without risk.

The mission itself is straightforward—a reconnaissance job.

We track movement, retrieve some surveillance data, and assess whether this PPG location poses an immediate threat or if we leave it alone for now. It's about as low-risk as we can get while still gaining field experience.

But despite that, Bastian is on edge. I feel it in the way he moves. The way his shields shift almost subconsciously, layering around me, even when I don't need them.

He's trying not to, trying to prioritize the mission over me.

But instinct is a challenging thing to fight. And for Bastian, his instinct to protect me is woven into the very fabric of who he is. Our bond only magnifies his natural protective instincts.

Mason and Riddick take point, sweeping through the compound while Bastian and I hang back, covering the exits and monitoring for any movement outside the perimeter.

We're synced. We work well together. But I feel his power—not quite smothering, but heavy enough that I know it's there.

He doesn't even realize it. But I do. And so does Mason.

She paths me, *"We need to figure this out, or you two will never work together out here."*

She's right. And that's the entire point of this mission.

So, I test it. I take a calculated step forward, breaking Bastian's shield cover.

The reaction is instantaneous. Bastian moves, gripping my arm before I've even taken another breath. His shields snap tighter, locking me in place.

"What the hell was that?" He snaps sharply; his voice edged with frustration.

"Testing a theory."

His grip tightens. He's not amused. *"Kate."*

I exhale, turning toward him. His eyes glow faintly in the darkness.

"You're shielding me too much."

"You're my priority."

"No." I shake my head. *"The mission is your priority. You're my partner, Bastian. Not my babysitter."*

His jaw clenches, but I see the flicker of understanding behind his frustration.

Ahead of us, Mason and Riddick are doing exactly what we need to learn how to do.

They move together, but separate when necessary. They're synced, but not so interwoven that one can't function without the other. Riddick isn't overcompensating with shields or stepping in front of Mason when she doesn't need it. And Mason isn't hesitant to step up and lead, even with him watching her back.

They've figured something out over the last week, and we need to do the same.

I glance back at Bastian. *"We need to trust each other to handle ourselves."*

He knows I'm right.

"You know I trust you." His voice is quieter, but firm.

"Then show me."

He doesn't argue; instead; he lets me go. I feel his shields retract slightly, not completely, but enough.

When we port back to base, Mason is grinning. She saw it. The shift. It's not perfect, but it's something.

"I'd call that progress," she says, nudging Riddick's side.

Bastian exhales, running a hand through his hair. "Yeah. Sure. Let's go with that." He doesn't sound thrilled, but he'll get there.

Bastian

Back in the dorms, I throw myself into breaking down the mission—analyzing every decision, every misstep, every success. It wasn't a disaster, but it wasn't smooth either.

Mason and Riddick made it work, balancing their connection without losing focus. They weren't perfect, but they adapted, which is more than I can say for myself.

Kate and I, we're still figuring it out.

I pull up the footage, replaying the key moments on my tablet. The instant I felt her step out of my shields; a gut-wrenching panic surged through me. I reacted blindly—without hesitation. I gripped her, shielded her, prioritized her above everything. It was instinct, uncontrollable.

That can't happen again.

Neither of us can afford to let emotions override decisions in the field. We knew this wouldn't be easy, but the mission just proved how much more we need to work through. Mason and Riddick are already paving the way, willing to be the first test subjects on how bonded pairs function in combat. Even if they aren't bonded. Riddick's protective instincts override his logic.

But it's not just about them. It's not just about us.

More combat pairings are forming. Roarke and Mya, although not bonded, will be eventually, I am sure.

Max and Reese. Off-base, working. Max's protection detail still needs to leave room for decisions that affect more than just Reese. Never mind if there is an attack on base.

If we don't figure out a way to work in combat without breaking our focus, our strategies—our fucking ability to lead—we're screwed.

I rub a hand over my face and start mapping out theories. Shielding techniques that allow us to sense each other without distraction. Combat scenarios where the goal isn't just winning, but staying connected without becoming a liability. We need more live trials, more adaptability in the field.

I need to run this by Mason and Kyle.

We need to move fast.

Dmitri isn't waiting for us to get our act together. PPG is only getting stronger, and if they target our connections—our emotions? We'll be dead before we even realize we were compromised.

And then there's Kate.

I shut my eyes, picturing her out there in the field. I trust her, trust her mind, her skills, her control. She's smart, precise, and capable of holding her own. But every instinct in me screams to get her away from it.

Not because she isn't ready.

Because she is. And that's the problem.

I know what happens to strong women in the middle of a war. Mason is already a primary target. Kate has been lucky that her role has kept her behind the scenes, in strategy, in leadership. But if she keeps pushing into combat, she won't stay in the shadows.

They'll come for her.

Just like they came for Mason.

Just like they came for Mya.

Just like they came for Sarah and Maria.

I won't block her, won't force her hand. I won't be the reason she resents me.

But in my fucking heart? I want her out. Somehow, I need to make this work. For both of us. For all of us.

I'll do everything I can to ensure this war doesn't take her from me. But deep down I know. War doesn't care about what I want; it only cares about what it can take.

S.H. Reynolds is an indie author, who writes emotionally charged, character-driven stories that blend romance, suspense, found family, with fierce heroines, and morally grey heroes.

Her books blend sarcasm, banter, and found family vibes to make you want to immerse yourself in their world.

An avid reader all her life, she recently got back into writing after a hiatus to raise a family. Her debut series, The Elitus Saga, explores the dark side of genetic engineering, military control, and what it means to fight for your own future.

When she's not writing, S.H. Reynolds can be found working a 9-5, lost in a good book, spending time with her family, or being a dedicated crazy cat lady.

Follow S.H. Reynolds on her Social Media
Goodreads: SHReynolds_author
TikTok:@SHreynoldsauthor
FB :@S.H. Reynolds Author
Pinterest: @SHReynoldsauthor
Amazon Author: S.H. Reynolds

www.ingramcontent.com/pod-product-compliance
Lightning Source LLC
Chambersburg PA
CBHW050015120726
47903CB00006B/1785